THE BLACK SHEEP'S INHERITANCE

BY
MAUREEN CHILD

MILLS & BOON

Published in Great Britain 2014
by Mills & Boon, an imprint of Harlequin (UK) Limited,
Eton House, 18-24 Paradise Road, Richmond, Surrey, TW9 1SR

© 2014 Harlequin Books S.A.

Special thanks and acknowledgement to Maureen Child for her contribution to the Dynasties: The Lassiters series.

ISBN: 978 0 263 91463 4

51-0414

Harlequin (UK) Limited's policy is to use papers that are natural, renewable and recyclable products and made from wood grown in sustainable forests. The logging and manufacturing processes conform to the legal environmental regulations of the country of origin.

Printed ar
by Blackp

Maureen Child writes for the Mills & Boon® Desire™ line and can't imagine a better job. Being able to indulge your love for romance, as well as being able to spin stories just the way you want them told is, in a word, perfect.

A seven-time finalist for the prestigious Romance Writers of America RITA® Award, Maureen is the author of more than one hundred romance novels. Her books regularly appear on the bestseller lists and have won several awards, including a Prism, a National Readers' Choice Award, a Colorado Romance Writers Award of Excellence and a Golden Quill.

One of her books, *The Soul Collector,* was made into a CBS TV movie starring Melissa Gilbert, Bruce Greenwood and Ossie Davis. If you look closely, in the last five minutes of the movie, you'll spot Maureen, who was an extra in the last scene.

Maureen believes that laughter goes hand in hand with love, so her stories are always filled with humor. The many letters she receives assures her that her readers love to laugh as much as she does.

Maureen Child is a native Californian, but has recently moved to the mountains of Utah. She loves a new adventure, though the thought of having to deal with snow for the first time is a little intimidating.

To Stacy Boyd and Charles Griemsman,
two editors who make writing Desires
such a terrific experience

One

The lawyer's office at the firm of Drake, Alcott and Whittaker was too crowded for Sage Lassiter's tastes. He much preferred being out on his ranch, in the cold, crisp air of a Wyoming spring. Still, he had no choice but to attend the reading of his adoptive father's will.

J.D. Lassiter had been dead only a couple of weeks and Sage was having a hard time coming to grips with it. Hell, he would have bet money that J.D. was far too stubborn to actually *die*. And now that he had, Sage was forced to live with the knowledge that now he would never have the chance to straighten things out between himself and the man who had raised him. Just like J.D. to go ahead and do something whether anyone else was ready for it or not. The old man had, once again, gotten the last word.

Sage couldn't have said when the tension between

him and J.D. had taken root, but he remembered it as an always-there kind of feeling. Nothing tangible. Nothing that he could point to and say: *There. That was it. The beginning of the end.* Instead, it was a slow disintegration of whatever might have been between them and it was beyond too late to think about it now. Old hurts, old resentments had no place in this room and nowhere to go even if he had let them take the forefront in his mind.

"You look like you want to hit something." His younger brother Dylan's voice came in a whisper.

Shooting him a hard look, Sage shook his head. "No, just can't really take in that we're here."

"I know." Dylan pushed his brown hair off his forehead and gave a quick look around the room before turning back to Sage. "Still can't quite believe J.D.'s gone."

"I was just thinking the same thing." He shifted, folded his arms across his chest and said, "I'm worried about Marlene."

Dylan followed his gaze.

Marlene Lassiter had stepped in as surrogate mother to Sage, Dylan and Angelica after Ellie Lassiter died during childbirth with Angie. She'd been married to J.D.'s brother Charles, and when she was widowed, she'd come home to Wyoming to live on Big Blue, the Lassiter ranch. She'd been nurturer, friend and trusted confidante for too many years to count.

"She'll be okay, eventually," Dylan said, then winced as they watched Marlene hold a sodden tissue to her mouth as if trying to stifle a wail of agony.

"Hope you're right," Sage muttered, uncomfortable seeing Marlene in pain and knowing there wasn't a damn thing he could do about it.

Marlene's son, Chance Lassiter, sat to one side of her,

his arm thrown protectively around her shoulders. He wore a leather jacket tossed on over a long-sleeved white shirt. Dark blue jeans and boots completed the outfit, and the gray Stetson he was never without was balanced on one knee. He was a cowboy down to his bones and the manager of J.D.'s thirty-thousand-acre ranch, Big Blue.

"You have any idea what the bequests are?" Dylan asked. "Couldn't get a thing out of Walter."

"Not surprising," Sage remarked with a sardonic twist of his lips. Walter Drake was not only J.D.'s lawyer, but practically his clone. Two more stubborn, secretive men he'd never met. Walter had made calls to all of them, simply telling them when and where to show up and not once hinting at what was in J.D.'s will. Logan Whittaker, another partner in the firm, was also working on J.D.'s will but he hadn't been any more forthcoming than Walter.

Sage wasn't expecting a damn thing for himself. And it wasn't as if he needed money. He'd built his own fortune, starting off in college by investing in one of his friends' brilliant ideas. When that paid off, he invested in other dreamers, and along the way he'd amassed millions. More than enough to make him completely independent of the Lassiter legacy. In fact, he was surprised he had been asked to be here at all. Long ago, he'd distanced himself from the Lassiters to make his own way, and he and J.D. hadn't exactly been close.

"Have you talked to Angelica since this all happened?" Dylan frowned and glanced to where their sister sat beside her fiancé, Evan McCain, her head on his shoulder.

"Not for long." Sage frowned, too, and thought about the sister he and Dylan loved so much. Her much-anticipated wedding had been postponed because of their father's death and who knew when it would happen now. Angelica's big brown eyes were red rimmed from crying and there were lavender shadows beneath those eyes that told Sage she wasn't sleeping much. "I went to see her a couple of days ago, hoping I could talk to her, but all she did was bawl." His scowl deepened. "Hate seeing her like that, but I don't know what the hell we can do for her."

"Not much really," Dylan agreed. "I saw her yesterday, but she didn't want to talk about what happened. Evan told me she's not sleeping, hardly eating. She's taking this really hard, Sage."

Nodding, he told his brother, "She and the old man were so close, of course she's taking it hard. Not to mention, J.D. collapsing at her rehearsal dinner adds a whole new level of misery. We've just got to make sure she gets past this. We'll tag team her. One of us going to see her at least every other day…"

"Oh," Dylan said, chuckling, "Evan will love having us around all the time."

"He's the one so hell-bent on marrying into the Lassiter family," Sage pointed out wryly. "If he takes one of us, he gets all of us. Best he figures that out now anyway."

"True." Dylan nodded then sat back in his chair. "Okay, then. We'll keep an eye on Angelica."

Dylan kept talking, now about his plans for the restaurant he was opening, but Sage had stopped listening. Instead, he watched Colleen Falkner, J.D.'s private nurse, slip quietly into the room, then make her way to the front, where she took a seat beside Marlene. The older woman gave her a watery smile of welcome and took her hand in a firm grip.

Sage narrowed his gaze on Colleen and felt a hard jolt of awareness leap to life inside him—just as it had the night of the rehearsal dinner. The same night J.D. died.

That night, he'd really *noticed* her for the first time. They'd met in passing of course, but on that particular night, there had been something different about her. Something that tugged at him. Maybe it had been seeing her long, amazing hair loose, cascading down her back in beautiful shimmering waves. Maybe it had been the short red dress and the black heels and the way they'd made her legs look a mile long. All he knew for sure was when he'd caught her eye from across the room, he'd felt a connection snap into place between them. He had started toward her, determined to talk to her—then J.D.'s heart attack had changed everything.

She wasn't wearing party clothes today, though. Instead, she wore baggy slacks, a sapphire-blue pullover sweater and her long, dark blond hair was pulled back into a braid that hung down between her shoulder blades. She had wide blue eyes that were bright with unshed tears and a full, rich mouth that tempted a man to taste it.

If he hadn't seen her in a figure-skimming red dress at the party—a dress that remained etched into his memory—Sage never would have guessed at the curves she kept so well hidden beneath her armor of wool and cotton.

He hadn't had much interaction with Colleen, since he and J.D. hadn't exactly been on the best of terms, so Sage didn't spend much time on Big Blue. But that night at the party, she'd intrigued him. Not only was she beautiful, but when J.D. collapsed, she had sprung into action, shouting orders like a general and taking charge until the paramedics showed up.

She had been devoted to J.D., had earned the family's affections—as evidenced by the way Marlene reached out to take the woman's hand—yet through it all had remained a bit of a mystery. Where was she from? Why had she taken a job working for a grumpy old man on a remote, if luxurious, ranch? And why the hell did he care?

"Colleen do something to you?"

He glanced at Dylan. "What?"

"Well, you're staring at her hard enough to set her hair on fire. What's up?"

Irritated to have been caught out, Sage muttered, "Shut up."

"Ah. Good answer." Dylan just smiled, shook his head and leaned forward to ask Chance something.

Sage let his gaze slide carefully back to Colleen. She bent her head to whisper something to Marlene, and he watched that long, silky braid slide across her shoulder, baring the nape of her neck. Soft blond curls brushed against her skin and he suddenly had the urge to touch her. To stroke that skin, to slide his fingers through her hair, to— He cut that thought off as fast as he could and scowled to himself.

The only possible reason she had for being here was if she was mentioned in J.D.'s will. Sure, J.D. had needed a nurse over his last few months, with his health failing, but such a beautiful one? Was that why she'd taken the job of caring for the old man? Had she been hoping for a nice payoff someday? Maybe he should spend a little time looking into Colleen Falkner, he thought. Do some checking. Make sure—

"You're looking at her again," Dylan pointed out.

Glaring at his brother and ignoring the smile on the man's face, Sage grumbled, "Don't you have something else to do?"

"Not at the moment."

"Lucky me."

"I just think it's interesting how fascinated you seem to be by Colleen."

"I'm not fascinated." *Much.* He shifted uncomfortably in his chair and told himself to stop thinking about her. How could the woman have gotten to him so easily? Hell, he hadn't even really *talked* to her.

"Not what it looks like from where I'm sitting."

"Then maybe you should sit somewhere else." He wasn't fascinated. He was…interested. Attracted. There was a difference.

Dylan laughed shortly. True to form, Sage's younger brother was almost impossible to insult. He was easygoing, charming and sometimes Sage thought his younger brother had gotten all the patience in the family. But he was also stubborn and once he got his teeth into something, he rarely let it go.

Like now, for example.

"She's single," Dylan said.

"Great."

"I'm just sayin'," his brother continued, "maybe you could leave your ranch once in a while. Have an actual date. Maybe with Colleen."

Sage drew his head back and stared at his brother. "Are you running a dating service I don't know about?"

"Fine," Dylan muttered, sitting back in his chair. "Have it your way. Be a hermit. End up becoming the weird old guy who lives alone on an isolated ranch."

"I'm not a hermit."

"Yeah? When's the last time you had a woman?"

Frowning, Sage said, "Not that it's any of your business, but I get plenty of women."

"One-night stands? Nice."

Sage preferred one-night stands. He didn't do commitment, and spending time with women who felt the same way avoided a lot of unnecessary hassle. If his brother wanted to look for more in his life, he was welcome to. As for Sage, he liked his life just the way it was. He came and went as he pleased. When he wanted a woman, he went and found one. When he wanted to be left the hell alone, he had that, too.

"Now that you mention it," he said quietly, "I haven't noticed you busy developing any serious relationships, either."

Dylan shrugged, folded his arms across his chest and said, "We're not talking about *me*."

"Yeah, well, we're done talking about *me*, too."

Then the office door opened, and lawyer Walter Drake stepped inside and announced, "All here?" He swept the room with a sharp-eyed gaze and nodded to himself. "Good. Then we can get started."

"I don't know if I'm ready for this," Dylan grumbled.

Sage was more than ready. He wanted this day done and finished so he could get back to his ranch.

After settling himself behind a wide oak desk, Walter, an older man who looked like the stereotypical image of an "old family retainer"—handsome, gray haired and impeccably dressed—picked up a stack of papers and straightened them unnecessarily. That shuffle of paper and the rattle of the window panes as a cold wind gusted against it were the only sounds in the room. It was as if everyone had taken a breath and held it.

Walter was clearly enjoying his moment in the spotlight. Every eye in the room was on him. Once again, his gaze moved over the people gathered there and when he finally came to Angelica, he gave her a sad, sympathetic smile before speaking to the room. "I know how hard this is on all of you, so I'll be as brief as possible."

Sage would be grateful.

"As you all know, J.D. and I knew each other for more than thirty years." Walter paused, smiled to himself and added, "He was a stubborn man, but a proud one, and I want you all to know that he took great care with his will. He remade it just a few months ago because he wanted to be sure to do the right thing by all of you."

Scraping one hand across his face, Sage shifted in the uncomfortable chair. He flicked a quick glance out the window and saw dark clouds rushing across the sky. *April in Wyoming,* he mused. It could be sunny in the morning and snowing by afternoon. And right now, it looked as though a storm was headed their way. Which only fed the urge to get back to his ranch before the bad weather hit.

"There are a lot of smaller provisions made to people J.D. thought well of over the years," Walter was saying. "I won't be reading them aloud today. Nor will I make mention of other estate business that will be handled separately."

Sage frowned thoughtfully and shifted his gaze to Walter. Handled separately? Why? What was the lawyer trying to hide? For that matter, what had *J.D.* been trying to hide? He braced his elbows on his thighs and leaned forward, keeping his gaze fixed on Walter as if the man was about to saw a woman in half. Or pull a dove from a magic hat.

"That part of the will is, at this time, not to be shared with the family."

"Why not?" Sage's question shattered the stillness left in the wake of Walter's startling statement.

The older man met Sage's gaze squarely. "Those were J.D.'s wishes."

"How do we know that?" An insulting question and he knew it, but Sage didn't stop himself. He didn't like secrets.

Dylan jammed his elbow into Sage's side, but he didn't so much as flinch. Just kept staring at the lawyer waiting for an answer.

"Because I tell you so," Walter said, stiffening in insult.

"C'mon, Sage," Dylan muttered. "Let it go for now."

He didn't want to, but he would. Only because Marlene had turned in her seat to give him a worried frown. Damned if he'd do anything to upset her any further than she already was. Nodding to the woman he thought of as a mother, he promised himself that he'd keep his silence for now, but that didn't mean this was the end of it.

"Now," Walter said firmly, "if that's settled, I'd like to continue. After all, the heart and soul of the will is what we're here to discuss today." He paused only long enough to smooth one hand across his neatly trimmed silver beard. "I appreciate you all coming in on such short notice, and I promise to get through this as quickly as possible."

Sage didn't know if the man was deliberately trying to pump up the suspense in the room or if he was just a naturally dramatic lawyer. But either way, it was working. Everyone there shifted uncomfortably in their seats as Walter read aloud the strange, coma-inducing legal phrases leading up to the actual bequests. One or two of those phrases resonated with Sage.

Sound in mind and body. Well, in mind, anyway, Sage told himself. J.D. had been sick for a while, but the old man's brain was as sharp the day he died as it was when he was nothing but a kid starting out. Which meant J.D. had had a reason for keeping these so-called secrets from the family even after his death. A flicker of anger bristled inside him, and Sage admitted silently that it sucked to be angry at a dead man, because you had no way of confronting him. J.D. was probably loving this, he thought. Even after he was gone, he was still running the show.

But as soon as he had the chance, Sage promised himself a long talk with J.D.'s lawyer.

"To my dear sister-in-law, Marlene…" Walter paused to smile at the woman in question. "I leave a ten-percent share in the Big Blue ranch along with ownership of the main ranch house for as long as she lives. I also leave her enough cash to maintain her lifestyle—" Walter broke off and added, "J.D. got tired of all the 'legal speak,' as he called it, and had me write the rest down just as he spoke it." He took a breath and continued, "Marlene, I want you to have some fun. Get on out there and enjoy your life. You're a good-looking woman and too damn young to fold up and die alone."

Marlene sniffed, then laughed shortly and mopped at her tears. The rest of the room chuckled with her, and even Sage had to smile. He could hear the old man's gruff voice as if he were there with them. J.D. and Marlene had been an unofficial couple for years. More than that though, Marlene had been a rock to three motherless young kids and to a man who had lost the love of his life.

"To Chance Lassiter, my nephew, I leave a sixty-percent share in Big Blue and enough cash to take some time and enjoy yourself a little." Walter paused and added, "The cash amounts mentioned in the will are specific and will be discussed privately with each of you at a later date."

Chance looked stunned and Sage was glad for him. The man loved that ranch and cared for it every bit as meticulously as J.D. had himself.

"You take care of Blue, Chance," Walter kept reading, "and she'll do the same for you."

"To Colleen Falkner," he went on and Sage shifted his gaze to the blonde. "I leave the sum of three million dollars."

Colleen gasped and rocked back in her chair. Blue eyes wide, mouth open, she stared at Walter as if he had two heads. If she was acting then send her an Oscar fast, Sage thought dryly. She looked as genuinely surprised as he was. J.D. had left three million dollars to his *nurse?*

Walter kept reading. "Colleen, you're a good girl and with this money, I want you to go on and chase your dream down. Don't wait until it's too late."

"Oh, my—" She shook her head in disbelief, but Walter was moving on already and Sage braced himself for whatever came next.

"To my son Dylan Lassiter, I leave controlling interest in Lassiter Grill Group, and enough cash to tide you over while you take it to the top. Oh, and I'm giving you ten-percent share of the Big Blue, too. It's your home, never forget that."

Beside Sage, Dylan looked shell-shocked and he

couldn't blame him. Hell, the man was now the owner of one of the fastest-growing restaurant groups in the country. If that didn't stop your heart a little, you weren't human.

"My son Sage Lassiter—"

Sage tensed for whatever was coming. He wouldn't have put it past J.D. to take one last swipe at him from the grave. To remind him publicly of the distance that had grown between them over the years. Like oil and water, Sage thought, he and J.D. had just never managed to mix well together.

"Sage," Walter read with a shake of his head, "you're my son and I love you. We butted heads too many times to count, but make no mistake, you're a Lassiter through and through. I'm leaving you twenty-five-percent interest in Lassiter Media, a ten-percent share in Big Blue— to remind you that's always your home—and lastly some cash that you won't want and don't need."

Surprised and touched, Sage snorted.

Walter continued word for word, "You're building your ranch your own damn way, just like I did. I admire that. So take this cash and buy something for that ranch. Something that will always remind you that your father loved you. Whether we could get along together or not."

Damn. The old man had surprised him one last time, was all Sage could think. His throat felt like a fist was squeezing, closing off his air. If he didn't get out of here soon, he was going to make a damn fool of himself. How the hell did J.D. know how to touch him, even from beyond the grave? How had he scripted words in a will months ago that could reach out long after he was gone to do what he hadn't been able to do in life?

"And lastly," Walter was saying, "I come to my beloved daughter, Angelica Lassiter. You are my heart and soul and the light of my life."

Sage glanced at his sister and saw her beautiful face crumple into tears again.

"And so," Walter read, "I leave you, Angelica, a ten-percent share of Big Blue, just like your brothers, the Lassiter estate in Beverly Hills, California, enough cash for you to spoil yourself some and finally, a ten-percent share in Lassiter Media."

"What?" Sage jumped to his feet, outraged, and Dylan was just a breath behind him. All of the warm feelings for his adoptive father vanished in a blink. How could he do that to Angelica? He'd groomed his daughter for years to take over the day-to-day operations of Lassiter Media, a conglomerate of radio, TV, newspapers and internet news outlets. Hell, she'd practically been running the damn thing on her own since J.D. got sick. And now he cut her out of the thing she loved?

"You can't be serious," Sage argued hotly, with a quick look at his sister's shocked, ashen features. "She's been running Lassiter Media for J.D. He left *me* more interest than Angie? That's insane!"

"We'll challenge the damn will," Dylan was saying, moving toward his sister to lay one hand on her shoulder in a show of solidarity.

"Damn straight," Sage agreed, glaring at the lawyer as if it were all his fault.

"There's more," Walter said, clearing his throat uncomfortably. "And I warn you, try to challenge this will and you might all be sorry—but more about that later. For now, voting control with forty-one-percent share of Lassiter Media, chairmanship and title of CEO, I leave to Evan McCain."

"Evan?" Angelica pulled away from her fiancé even as he was rising to his feet, stunned speechless.

"What the hell is going on here, Walter?" Sage demanded, coming around the corner of the man's desk to snatch up the will and read the terms himself.

"J.D. knew what he wanted to do and he did it," the lawyer argued.

"Well, it won't stand," Marlene said.

"Damn right it won't," Dylan piped up, charging the desk and snatching the will from his brother's grasp.

"It's not right." Chance came to his feet slowly, his calm, quiet voice nearly lost in the confusion.

"I can't believe it," Angelica murmured, looking at her fiancé as if she'd never seen him before.

"I swear I don't know anything about this," Evan said, taking a step toward her only to stop when she backed away from him.

"Well, somebody does, and I'm going to find out what's going on," Sage promised, then snapped his gaze to the door. Colleen Falkner was slipping out of the office like a damn ghost.

She'd gotten what she wanted, he told himself. He only wondered what she'd had to do for three million dollars. And he also had to ask himself if she'd known about J.D.'s plans. Had she been involved in his decision to rob Angelica of the very thing she cared most about?

Damned if he wouldn't find out.

Colleen leaned back against the door briefly, closing her eyes and forcing herself to drag a deep breath into her lungs. Her heart was pounding so hard and so fast she felt dizzy.

She hadn't expected anything like this.

Three million dollars?

Tears burned her eyes, but she frantically blinked them back. Now wasn't the time to indulge in tears for the loss of her friend—or for thinking about the future he had just made possible.

Behind her, she heard muffled shouts through the closed door. Sage Lassiter's voice was the most unmistakable. Though he didn't have to shout to be heard. The cold steel in his deep voice was enough to get the attention of anyone in the room.

God knew, he'd had *her* attention.

She'd felt him watching her earlier. Had sneaked a peek or two over her shoulder at him in return. He made her nervous. Always had. Which was why any time he'd come to the Big Blue ranch to visit his father—which wasn't often—Colleen had made herself scarce.

He was so…*male*.

Sage Lassiter was a force of nature. The kind of man women drooled over. And she was the kind of woman men like him never noticed. Well, not usually. He'd certainly noticed her today, though. And he hadn't looked very happy about it.

Tossing a quick look at the closed door behind her, Colleen hurried down the long beige hallway toward the elevators. She wanted to be long gone before Sage left that room.

Two

She made it as far as the parking lot.

"Colleen!"

Standing beside her car, Colleen took a breath and braced herself. That deep voice was unmistakable.

Goose bumps broke out on her arms and it wasn't because of the icy wind buffeting her. Blast Wyoming weather anyway. One day it was spring and the next, it was winter again. But the cold was the least of her worries.

It was him. Colleen had only been close to Sage Lassiter one time before today. The night of Angelica's rehearsal dinner. From across that crowded restaurant, she'd felt him watching her. The heat of his gaze had swamped her, sending ribbons of expectation unfurling throughout her body. He smiled and her stomach churned with swarms of butterflies. He headed toward her, and she told herself to be calm. Cool. But it hadn't worked. Nerves fired, knees weakened.

And just as he was close enough to her that she could see the gleam in his eyes, J.D. had his heart attack and everything had changed forever.

Looking back on that night, she told herself she was being silly even thinking that Sage might have been interested in her. He'd probably only wanted to ask her questions about his father's care. Or where the restrooms were.

In her own mind, she'd built up the memory of that night into something magical. But it was time to remember that she simply wasn't the kind of woman a man like him would ever notice. Sadly, that didn't stop *her* from noticing *him* and she hadn't been able to stop thinking about him since that night.

Now he was here, and she had to battle down a flurry of nerves. She turned and brushed a few stray, wind-blown hairs out of her face as she watched him approach.

Her heartbeat sped up at the picture he made. Sage Lassiter *stalked* across the parking lot toward her. It was the only word that could describe that long, determined stride. He was like a man on a mission. He wore dark jeans, boots and an expensively cut black sports jacket over a long-sleeved white shirt. His brown hair flew across his forehead and his blue eyes were narrowed against the wind. His long legs closed the distance between them in a few short seconds and then he was there. Right in front of her.

She had to tip her head back to meet his gaze and when she did, nerves skated down along her spine. For three months, she'd listened to J.D. Lassiter as he talked about his family. Thanks to those chats, she knew that

Sage was ruthless in business, quiet, hardheaded and determined to make his own way rather than capitalize on the Lassiter name. And though that last part had irritated J.D., she knew that he'd also admired Sage for it. How could he not? The older man had done the same thing when he was starting out.

Still, being face-to-face with the man who had filled her mind for weeks was a little unnerving. Maybe if she hadn't spent so much time daydreaming about him, she wouldn't feel so awkward right now. Colleen took another deep breath and held it for a moment, hoping to calm herself. But there was a flash of something she couldn't quite read in his eyes and the nerves won.

Wind slid down off the mountain, wrapped itself around them briefly then rushed on, delivering chills to the rest of Cheyenne. Ridiculously, Colleen was grateful for the cold wind. It was like a slap of common sense and though it wasn't enough to completely dampen her hormones, her next thought absolutely was.

The only reason she and Sage were here, about to talk, was because they had both attended the reading of his father's will. Remembering that helped her keep her voice steady as she gave him a smile and blurted, "I'm so sorry about your father."

A slight frown crossed his face briefly. "Thanks. Look, I wanted to talk to you—"

"You did?" There went her silly heart again, jumping into a gallop. He really was impossibly handsome, she thought absently—tall, dark and glower-y. There was an aura of undeniable strength that emanated from him. He was the kind of man other men envied and women wanted. Herself included. A brand-new flock of butterflies took off and flew in formation in the pit of her stomach. "You want to talk to me?"

"Yes," he said, his voice a deep rumble that seemed to roll across every one of her nerve endings. "I've got a couple questions…"

Fascination dissolved into truth. Instantly, Colleen gave herself a mental kick. Here she was, daydreaming about a gorgeous man suddenly paying attention to her when the reality was, he'd just lost his father. She knew all too well that the families left behind after a loss often had questions. Wanted to know how their loved one had been feeling. What they'd been thinking. And as J.D.'s private nurse, she had been with him the most during those final days.

And now that reality had jumped up to slap her, she was forced to acknowledge that Sage Lassiter had probably planned to talk to her the night of the party for the same reason. What had she been thinking? She'd half convinced herself that the rich, gorgeous Sage Lassiter was interested in *her*. God, what an idiot. Embarrassment tangled with a wash of disappointment before she fought past both sensations, allowing her natural empathy to come rushing to the surface.

"Of course you do." Instinctively, she reached out, laid her hand on his and felt a swift jolt of electricity jump from his body to hers. Totally unexpected, she felt the heat from that brief contact sizzle inside her. It was so strong, so real, she wouldn't have been surprised to actually *see* the arc of light shimmering between them. Quickly, she drew her hand back, then curled her fingers into her palm, determined to ignore the startling sensation.

His eyes narrowed further and she knew he'd felt it,

too. Frowning a little, he pushed one hand through his hair, fixed his gaze on hers and let her know immediately that whatever he might have felt, he was as determined as she to ignore it.

Shaking his head, he said, "No. I don't have any questions about J.D. Actually, *you're* the mystery here."

"Me?" Surprised, Colleen stared up at him, practically mesmerized by those cool blue eyes of his. "You think I'm a mystery? I'm really not."

"Oh, I don't know," he mused. "You went from nurse to millionaire in a few short months."

"What?" Confused now, she shook her head as if that might help clear things up a little. It didn't.

His lips curved but the smile didn't reach his eyes. "Sure, it's a big step, isn't it? I just wanted to say congratulations."

"Con—what? Oh. What?" Colleen's mind was slowly working its way past the hormonal surge she'd first felt when Sage had walked up to her. And now that she was able to think almost clearly again, it finally dawned on her what he was talking about. The bequest. The money J.D. had left her. He was making it sound…ugly.

Stung, she said quietly, "I don't know if *congratulations* is the right word."

"Why not?" He set one hand on the roof of her old, but completely reliable, Jeep and leaned in closer. "From private nurse to millionaire in one easy step. Not many people could have pulled that off."

Cold slithered through her and it was an icier feeling than anything the weather could provide. She glanced around the nearly empty parking lot. Only a half dozen or so cars were sprinkled around the area. The law office adjoining the lot seemed to loom over her, so for a second or two, she let her gaze drift past the city to the mountains in the distance. Sunlight glanced off the snow still covering the peaks. Gray clouds scudded across the deep blue sky and the ever-present wind tugged at her hair.

Just like always, the view of the mountains soothed her. She and her mother had moved to Cheyenne several years ago, and from the moment they arrived, Colleen had felt at home. She hadn't missed California and the beaches. It was the mountains that called to her. The wide-open spaces, the trees, the bite of cold in the air. In a moment, she was ready to face the man glaring at her. "I don't know what you mean."

But she did. She really did. His eyes were icy, detached and a muscle in his jaw ticked as if he were biting back all kinds of words he really wanted to say. J.D. had told her so much about Sage, and for the first time, she was seeing the less than pleasant aspects. *Ruthless. Hard.*

He was more different now from the man who had flirted with her from across a crowded room not two weeks ago than she would have thought possible. Did he really believe she had somehow engineered this bequest? That she'd tricked J.D. into leaving her money?

"I think you know exactly what I mean." His head tilted to one side as he studied her. "I just find it interesting that J.D. would bequeath three million dollars to a woman he didn't even know three months ago."

While she stood there, pinned in place by the sheer power of his gaze, Colleen felt like a bug on a glass slide under a microscope. The cold inside her began to melt beneath the steam of insult. She was still feeling a little shaky over J.D.'s death and the fact that he'd remembered her in his will. Now, staring up into Sage's eyes, seeing the flash of accusation gleaming there, she had to wonder if others would be thinking the same thing. What about the rest of the Lassiter family? Did they feel the same way? Would they also be looking at her with suspicion? Suddenly, she had a vision of not just the Lassiters but the whole town of Cheyenne whispering about her, gossiping.

That thought was chilling. She'd made Cheyenne her home and she didn't want her life destroyed by loose tongues spreading lies. Anger jumped to life inside her. She'd done nothing wrong. She'd helped an old man through his last days and she'd enjoyed his company, too. Since when was that a crime?

Gorgeous or not, Sage Lassiter had no right to imply that she'd somehow tricked J.D. into leaving her money in his will. Lifting her chin, she glared at him. "I didn't know he was going to do that."

"And you would have stopped him if you *had* known?"

The sarcasm in his tone only made the sense of insult deeper. She met his gaze squarely. On this, she could be completely honest. And she would keep being honest until people believed her. "I would have tried."

"Is that right?"

"Yes, it is," she snapped, and had the satisfaction of seeing surprise flicker in his eyes. "Whatever you might think of me, I'm very good at my job. And I don't ordinarily receive gifts from my patients."

"Really?" He snorted. "You consider three million dollars a *gift?*"

"What it represents was the gift," she countered, then

stopped herself. She didn't owe him an explanation and if she tried, he probably wouldn't accept it.

His features looked as if they'd been carved from marble. There was no emotion there, nothing to soften the harsh gaze that seemed to bore right through her as if he were trying to read everything she was.

Colleen fought past the temper still bubbling into a froth in the pit of her stomach and tried to remember that people grieved in different ways. He'd lost a father he'd been estranged from. There had to be conflicting emotions roiling inside him and maybe it was easier for Sage to lash out at a stranger than to deal with what he must be feeling at the moment. Though she knew from her many long talks with J.D. that he and his oldest son weren't close, Sage was clearly still dealing with a loss he hadn't been prepared for. That was bound to hit him hard and it was scarcely surprising that he wasn't acting rationally at the moment.

With that thought in mind, the tension inside her drained away. "You don't know me, so I can understand how you might feel that way. But what J.D. did was as big a shock to me as it was to you."

A long second or two ticked past as he watched her through those deep blue eyes of his. She couldn't help wondering what he was thinking, but his features gave her no clue at all. Seconds ticked past as the wind blew, the sky grew darker and the silence between them stretched taut. Finally, he straightened up and away from the car, shoved both hands into his pockets and allowed, "Maybe I was a little harsh."

She gave him a tentative smile that wasn't returned. Despite his words, he wasn't really bending. Sighing, she said, "A little. But it's understandable, considering what you're going through. I mean…I understand."

"Do you?" Still watching her, though the ice in his eyes had melted a bit.

"When my father died," she said, sliding back into her own memories, "it was horrible, despite the fact that we knew for months that it was coming. Even when death is expected, it's somehow a surprise when it actually happens. It's as if the universe has played a dirty trick on you. I was so angry, so sorry to lose him—I needed someone to blame." She paused and met his gaze. "We all do."

He snorted. "A nurse *and* a psychologist?"

She flushed. "No, I just meant…"

"I know what you meant," he said shortly, effectively shutting her down before she could offer more sympathy he clearly didn't want.

And just like that, the ice was back in his eyes. Then he glanced over his shoulder, noted that his family was walking out of the office building behind them and turned back to her. "I have to go."

She looked to where Marlene and Angelica were holding onto each other while Chance, Dylan and Evan squared off, obviously arguing. "Of course."

"But I'd like to talk to you again," he said, catching her by surprise.

"Sure, I—"

"About J.D.," he added.

A tiny flicker of something lovely disappeared in a wash of sympathy. Of course he wanted to talk to her about his father. He wanted to hear from the woman who had spent the most time with him in his last several months. Ridiculous to have ever thought that he

might be interested in *her*. Sage Lassiter dated women
who were socialites or celebrities. Why on earth would
he ever be attracted to a private nurse who didn't even
own a bottle of nail polish?

"Sure," she said, giving him another smile that went
unreturned. "Anytime."

He nodded, then turned and strode across the parking lot toward his family.

Alone in the quickening wind, Colleen threw one
look up at the sky and realized that a storm was coming.

"What was he *thinking?*" Dylan took a sip of his beer
and set the bottle back onto the table. "Cutting Angie
out like that? Dad had been grooming her for years to
take over Lassiter Media."

They were at a small bar on the edge of the city. Marlene had taken Angelica off for a spa day, hoping to relax
her. Evan had gone back to the office and Chance was
at the ranch. Left to their own devices, Sage and Dylan
had opted for drinks, and the chance to talk things over,
just the two of them.

The customers here were locals, mostly cowboys,
ranch hands and a few cops and firemen. It was a comfortable place that didn't bother trying to be trendy.
The owner didn't care about attracting tourists. He just
wanted to keep his regulars happy.

So the music was loud and country, blasting from a
jukebox that was older than Sage. The floorboards were
scarred from wooden chairs scraping across them for
the past fifty years. The bar top gleamed and the rows
of bottles behind the bar were reflected in a mirror that
also displayed the image of the TV playing on the opposite wall. People came here to have a quiet drink. They

weren't looking to pose for pictures or listen to tourists talking excitedly about "the Old West." This was modern-day Cheyenne, yet Sage had the feeling quite a few people rode into town half expecting stagecoaches and more than just the staged gunfights in the streets.

"I don't know," Sage muttered, unnecessarily answering his brother's rhetorical question.

Dylan kept talking, but Sage wasn't really listening. Instead he was remembering the look in Colleen's eyes when he'd confronted her in the parking lot. He'd wanted to talk to her. To see what she knew. To find out if she'd had any idea what J.D. had been up to.

Instead, he'd put her on the defensive right from the jump. He hadn't meant to just launch into an attack. But with the memory of his sister's tears still fresh in his mind, he'd snapped at Colleen.

Scrubbing one hand across his face, he realized that he was going to have to use a completely different tactic the next time he talked to her. And there *would* be a next time. Not only did she intrigue him on a personal level but there were too many questions left unanswered. Had she swayed J.D. into leaving her the money? Did she know why Angelica had lost everything? Did she maybe know something that might help him invalidate the will? His brain was racing.

"Angie was looking at Evan like he was the enemy instead of the man she loves."

"Hard not to," Sage said, mentally dragging himself back to the conversation at hand. "In one swipe, Evan took everything Angie thought was hers."

"Well, it's not like he stole it or anything," Dylan told him. "J.D. *left* it to him."

"Yeah," he grumbled. "J.D. was just full of surprises,

wasn't he? Still, doesn't matter how it happened. Bottom line's the same. Angie's out and Evan's in. Not surprising that she's angry at him."

"True." Dylan picked up his beer for another sip, then held the bottle, rubbing his thumb over the label.

"It was always tricky, the two of them engaged and working for the same company. But now that Angie's not even the boss anymore?" Sage shook his head grimly. "I just hope this will doesn't cause a breakup."

"Worst part is, I don't know what we can do about it. From the little Walter said, I don't think we'll be able to contest the will without everyone losing."

"That's Walter's opinion. We need to check into that with an impartial lawyer."

"If there is such a beast," Dylan muttered.

"I know." Sage lifted his glass and took a slow sip of very old scotch. The heat swarmed through his system, yet did nothing to ease the tight knot in the pit of his stomach.

His sister had been crushed by their father's will. His aunt Marlene was happy with her bequest but naturally worried for Angie. Chance was good, of course. Big Blue ranch was his heart and soul. Evan had looked as though he'd been hit in the head with a two-by-four, but once the shock eased, Sage couldn't imagine the man complaining about the inheritance. Except for how it was affecting Angie.

There was going to be tension between Evan and her. But Sage hoped to hell they could work it out and find their way past all of this. But for now, their wedding was still postponed and after the will reading, Sage had no idea how long that postponement was going to last.

As for himself, Sage was still staggered by his bequest from J.D. Hell, he'd gotten a bigger share of Lassiter Media than Angie had—and that just wasn't right. Every time he thought about this, he came back to one question: What the hell had J.D. been thinking? And the only way he had even the slightest chance of figuring that out was by getting close to Colleen.

She was the one who had spent the most time with J.D. in the past few months. Sage had heard enough about the young, upbeat, efficient nurse from Marlene and Angie to know that she had become J.D.'s sounding board. He'd talked to her more than he had to anyone else in the last months of his life. And maybe that was because it was easier to talk about your problems to a stranger than it was to family.

But then, J.D. had always been so damned self-sufficient, he'd never seemed to need anyone around him. Until he got sick. That was the one thing he and Sage had always shared in common—the need to go it alone. Maybe that was why they'd never really gotten close. Both of them were too closed off. Too wrapped up in their own worlds to bother checking in with others.

He scowled at the thought. Funny, he'd never before considered just how much he and his adoptive father were alike. Went against the grain admitting it now, because Sage had spent so much of his life rebelling against J.D.

Yes, he knew that Colleen was the one person who might help him make sense of all this. But he hadn't been prepared for that spark of something hot and undeniable that had leaped up between them when she touched him. Sure, he had been interested in her the night of the rehearsal dinner—a beautiful woman, alone, looking uncomfortable in the crowd. But he hadn't had a chance to talk to her, let alone touch her, before everything had changed in an instant. Now he thought again of that flash of heat, the surprise in her eyes, during their confrontation a little while ago, and had to force himself to shove the memory aside. It was clear just by looking at her that she wasn't a one-night-stand kind of woman—but that could change, he assured himself. He couldn't get the image of her out of his mind. Her wide blue eyes. The sweep of dark blond hair. A soft smile curving a full mouth that tempted a man. His body tightened in response to his thoughts. The attraction between them was hot and strong enough that he couldn't simply ignore it.

"So what were you talking to Colleen about?"

"What?" He snapped his gaze up to meet Dylan's, shoving unsettling thoughts aside. "I...uh..." Uncomfortable with the memory of his botched attempt at getting close to the woman, Sage scrubbed one hand across the back of his neck.

"I know that look," his brother said. "What did you do?"

"Might have gotten off on the wrong foot," he admitted, remembering the look of shock on Colleen's face when he'd practically accused her of stealing from J.D. Was she innocent? Or a good actress?

"Why'd you hunt her down in the first place?"

"Damn it, Dylan," he said, leaning across the table and lowering his voice just to be sure no one could overhear them. "She's got to know something. She spent the most time with J.D. Hell, he left her three million dollars."

"And?"

"And," he admitted, "I want to know what she knows. Maybe there's something there. Maybe J.D. bounced ideas off of her and she knew about the changes to the will."

"And maybe it'll snow in this bar." Dylan shook his head. "You know as well as I do that J.D. was never influenced by anyone in his life. Hell," he added with a short laugh, "you're so much like him in that it's ridiculous. J.D. made up his own mind, right or wrong. No way did his *nurse* have any information that we don't."

He had to admit, at least to himself, that Dylan had a point. But that wasn't taking into consideration that the old man had known he was getting up there in years and he hadn't been feeling well. Maybe he started thinking about the pearly gates and what he should do before he went. That had to change things. If it did, who better to share things with than your nurse?

No, Sage told himself, he couldn't risk thinking Dylan was right. He had to know for sure if Colleen Falkner knew more than she was saying. "I'm not letting this go, Dylan. But it's going to be harder to talk to her now, though, since I probably offended the hell out of her when I suggested that maybe she'd tricked J.D. into leaving her that much money."

"You *what?*" Dylan just stared at him, then shook his head. "Have you ever known our father to be tricked into *anything?*"

"No."

Still shaking his head, Dylan demanded, "Does Colleen seem like the deadly femme fatale type to you?"

"No," he admitted grudgingly. At least she hadn't today, bundled up in baggy slacks and a pullover sweater. But he remembered what she'd looked like the night of the party. When her amazing curves had been on display in a red dress that practically screamed *look at me!*

"You've been out on your ranch too long," Dylan was saying. "That's the only explanation."

"What's that got to do with anything?"

"You used to know how to charm people. Especially *women*. Hell, you were the king of schmooze back in the day."

"I think you're thinking of yourself. Not me," Sage said with a half smile. "I don't like people, remember?"

"You used to," Dylan pointed out. "Before you bought that ranch and turned yourself into a yeti."

"Now I'm Sasquatch?" Sage laughed shortly and sipped at his scotch.

"Exactly right," Dylan told him. "You're practically a legend to your own family. You're never around. You spend more time with your horses than you do people. You're a damn hermit, Sage. You never come off the mountain if you don't have to, and the only people you talk to are the ones who work for you."

"I'm here now."

"Yeah, and it took Dad's *death* to get you here."

He didn't like admitting, even to himself, that his brother was right. But being in the city wasn't something he enjoyed. Oh, he'd come in occasionally to meet a woman, take her to dinner, then finish the evening at her place. But the ranch was where he lived. Where he most wanted to be.

He shifted in his chair, glanced uneasily around the room, then slid his gaze back to his brother's. "I'm not a hermit. I just like being on the ranch. I never was much for the city life that you love so much."

"Well, maybe if you spent more time with people instead of those horses you're so nuts about, you'd have done a better job of talking to Colleen."

"Yeah, all right. You have a point." Shaking his head, he idly spun the tumbler of scotch on the tabletop. He studied the flash of the overhead lights in the amber liquid as if he could find the answers he needed. Finally, he lifted his gaze to his brother's and said, "Swear to God, don't know why I started in on her like that."

Dylan snorted, picked up his beer and took a drink. "Let's hear it."

So he told his brother everything he'd said and how Colleen had reacted. Reliving it didn't make him feel any better.

When he was finished, a couple of seconds ticked past before Dylan whistled and took another sip of his beer. "Man, anybody else probably would have punched you for all of that. I know I would have. Lucky for you Colleen's so damn nice."

"Is she?"

"Marlene loves her," Dylan pointed out. "Angie thinks she's great. Heck, even Chance has had nothing but good things to say about her, and you know he doesn't hand out compliments easy."

"All true," Sage agreed.

And yet…Sage's instincts told him she was exactly what she appeared to be. A private nurse with a tantalizing smile and blue eyes the color of a lake in summer. But he couldn't overlook what had happened. What J.D. had done in his will. And the only person around who might have influenced the old man was the one woman who had spent the most time with him. He had to know. Had to find out what, if anything, she knew about the changes to J.D.'s will.

And if she had had something to do with any of this, he would find a way to make her pay.

Three

The Big Blue ranch seemed empty without the larger-than-life presence of J.D. Lassiter. Colleen glanced out the window of the bedroom that had been hers for the past several weeks and smiled sadly. She was going to miss this place almost as much as she would miss J.D. himself.

But it was always like this for her, she thought sadly. As a private nurse, she slipped into the fabric of families—sometimes at their darkest hours. And when her job was done, she left, moving on to the next client. The next family.

She tugged on the zipper of her suitcase, flipped the lid open and then sighed. Colleen hated this part of her assignments. The packing up of all her things, the saying goodbye to another chapter in her life. Positioning these memories onto a high shelf at the back of her mind, where they could be looked at later but would be out of the way, making room for the next patient.

Only this time…maybe there wouldn't be another family.

She shook her head and realized that the silence of the big house was pressing down on her. The only other people at Big Blue right now were the housekeeper and the cook, and it was as if the big house was…lonely. It wouldn't be for long, though. Soon, Marlene, Angelica and Chance would be returning, and she wanted to be gone before they got home. They didn't need her here anymore. By rights, she should have left two weeks ago after J.D.'s death, but she'd stayed on at Marlene's request, to help them all through this hard time.

Colleen walked to the closet and gathered an armful of clothes, carrying them back to the bed. On autopilot, she folded and then stacked her clothing neatly in the suitcase and then went back for more. It wouldn't take long to empty the closet and the dresser she had been using. She'd only brought a few things with her when she moved into the guest room.

Normally, she didn't live in when she took a private client. But J.D. had wanted her close by and had been willing to pay for the extra care, to spare his family having to meet all of his needs. In the past couple of months, Colleen had grown to love this place. The ranch house was big, elegant and yet still so cozy that it wasn't hard to remember that it was, at its heart, a family home.

At that thought, Sage crept back into her mind. He, his brother and sister had all grown up here on this ranch, and if she listened hard enough, she was willing to bet she would be able to hear the long-silent echoes of children playing.

And strange, wasn't it, how her mind continually drifted back to thoughts of Sage? To be honest, he had been on her mind since the rehearsal dinner. He starred nightly in her dreams and even his coldly furious outburst that morning hadn't changed anything. In fact, it had only made her like him more. That outburst had shown her just how much he had cared for his father, despite their estrangement. And the sympathy she felt for the loss he'd suffered was enough to color his accusations in a softer light.

Her brief conversation with Sage Lassiter had left Colleen more shaken than the news that she was now a millionaire. Maybe because the thought of so much money was so foreign to her that her brain simply couldn't process it. But having the man of her dreams actually speak to her was so startling, she couldn't seem to think of anything but him. Even though he'd insulted her.

"Not his fault," she assured herself again as she folded her clothes and stuffed them into the suitcase. "Of course he'd be suspicious. He doesn't know me. He just lost his father. Why should he trust me?"

All very logical.

And yet the sting of his words still resonated with her. Because she couldn't get past the thought that everyone else would believe what he'd blurted out. That somehow she had tricked a sick old man into leaving her money. Maybe she *should* turn it down. Go back to the lawyer, tell him to donate the money to charity or something.

Releasing a breath, she stopped packing and lifted her gaze to the window of the room that had been home for the past three months. The view outside was mesmerizing, as always.

There were no curtains on the windows at Big Blue.

In the many talks Colleen and J.D. had had, she'd learned that was a decree from J.D.'s late wife, Ellie. She'd wanted nothing to stand between her and the amazing sweep of sky. There were trees, too—all kinds of trees. Pines, oaks, maples, aspen. There was a silence in the forest that was almost breathtaking. She loved being here in the mountains and wasn't looking forward to going back to her small condo in a suburb of Cheyenne.

But, a tantalizing voice in her mind whispered, *with your inheritance, you could buy a small place somewhere out here. Away from crowds. Where you could have a garden and trees of your own and even a dog.* A dog. She'd wanted one for years. But she hadn't gotten one because first, her father had been sick, and then when she and her mother moved to Cheyenne, they'd lived in apartments or condos. It hadn't seemed fair to her to leave an animal cooped up all day while she and her mom were at work.

Now, though…her mind tempted her with the possibilities that had opened up to her because of J.D. She could quit her job, focus on getting her nurse practitioner's license and start living the dream that had been fueling her for years. More than that, she could help her mom, make her life easier for a change. That thought simmered in her mind, conjuring up images that made her smile in spite of everything.

The winters in Cheyenne were beginning to get to Colleen's mother. Laura Falkner was always talking about moving to Florida to live with her widowed sister and maybe the two of them taking cruises together. Seeing the world before she was too old to enjoy it all.

With this inheritance, Colleen could make not only her own dreams come true, but her mother's, as well.

Her hands fisted on the blue cotton T-shirt she held. Should she take the money as the gift it had been meant to be? Or should she reject it because she was afraid what small-minded people might say?

"Wouldn't that be like a slap in the face to J.D.?" she asked aloud, not really expecting an answer.

"Lots of people wanted to slap J.D. over the years."

She whirled around to face Sage, who stood in the open doorway, one shoulder braced against the door-jamb. He leaned there casually, looking taller and stronger and somehow more intimidating than he had in the parking lot. And that was saying something. His cool blue gaze was locked on hers and Colleen felt the slam of that stare from all the way across the room.

Her heartbeat jumped into a gallop, her mind went blessedly blank for a second or two and her mouth dried up completely. There was a buzzing sensation going on inside her, too, and it was tingling long-comatose parts of her body back into life. What was it about this man that could turn her into such a hormonal wreck just by showing up?

"What? I mean," she muttered, irritated that once again she felt tongue-tied around him. She'd always thought of herself as a simple, forthright kind of woman. Before now, she had never had trouble talking to anyone. But all Sage had to do was show up and her mouth was so busy thinking of doing other more interesting things that it couldn't seem to talk. "I didn't know you were there."

"Yeah," he said, pushing away from the wall and strolling confidently into the room. "You seemed a little…distracted." He glanced around the sumptuous room, taking in the pale blue quilt, the dozen or more pillows stacked against a gleaming brass headboard and the brightly colored throw rugs covering the polished wood floor. "This place has changed some."

"It's a lovely room," she said, again feeling a pang about leaving.

He glanced at her and shrugged. "When I was a kid, this was my room."

His room. Oh, my. A rush of heat swept through her system so completely, she felt as if she'd gotten a sudden fever. She'd been living in Sage's room for the past few months. If she'd known that before, she might not have been able to sleep at all.

She smiled hesitantly. "I'm guessing it looks a lot different to you, then."

"It does." He walked to the window, looked out, and then turned back to her with a quick grin. "The trellis is still there, though. You ever climb down it in the middle of the night?"

"No, but you did?"

"As often as possible," he admitted. "Especially when I was a teenager. J.D. and I…" His voice trailed off. Then he cleared his throat and said, "Sometimes I just needed to get out of the house for a while."

Colleen tried to imagine Sage as an unhappy boy, escaping out a window to claim some independence. But with the image of the strong, dynamic man he was now, standing right in front of her, it wasn't easy.

"So," he said abruptly, "what do you want to slap J.D. for?"

The sudden shift in conversation threw her for a second until she remembered that he'd been listening when she was talking to herself.

"I don't. I mean…" She blew out a breath and said, "It's nothing."

"Didn't sound like nothing to me," he mused, turning his back on the window and the view beyond to look at her again.

Backlit against the window, he looked more broad shouldered, more powerful…just, *more.* The bedroom suddenly seemed way smaller than it had just a few minutes ago, too. Sage Lassiter was the kind of man who overtook a room once he was in it, making everyone and everything somehow diminished just with his presence. A little intimidating. And if she was going to be honest with herself, a *lot* exciting.

Which wasn't helping her breathing any. "I was thinking out loud, that's all."

"About?"

She met his gaze. "If you must know, about whether or not I should accept the money J.D. left me."

Surprise shone briefly in his eyes. "And the decision is?"

"I haven't made one yet," she admitted, dropping the T-shirt onto her half-packed suitcase. "To be honest, I don't know what I should do."

"Most people would just take the three million and run."

Colleen shrugged helplessly. "I'm not most people."

"I'm beginning to get that," he said, stuffing both hands into his jeans pockets as he walked toward her. "Look, I came on a little strong earlier—"

"Really?" She smiled and shook her head. She remembered everything he'd said that morning. Every word. Every tone. Every glittering accusation he'd shot at her from his eyes. She also remembered that electrical jolt she'd gotten when she touched him.

He nodded. "You're right. And I was wrong. J.D. wanted you to have the money. You should take it."

"Just like that?" She studied him, hoping to see some tangible sign of why he'd changed his mind, but she couldn't read a darn thing on his face. The man was inscrutable. As a businessman, the ability to blank out all expression had probably helped him amass his fortune. But in a one-on-one situation, it was extremely annoying.

"Why not?" He moved even closer and Colleen could have sworn she felt actual *heat* radiating from his body to enclose her in a cocoon of warmth. Warmth that spread to every corner of her body. She swallowed hard, lifted her chin and met his eyes when he continued. "Colleen, if you're thinking about turning down your inheritance because of what I said, then don't."

A cold breeze slipped beneath the partially open window and dissipated the warmth stealing through her. That was probably a good thing. "I admit, what you said has a lot to do with my decision. But mostly, I'm worried that other people might think the same thing."

He pulled one hand from his pocket and slapped it down on the brass foot rail. "And that would bother you?"

Stunned, she said, "Of course it would bother me. It's not *true*."

"Then what do you care what anyone else thinks?"

Did he really not see what it would be like? Were the rich really so different from everyone else? "You probably don't understand because you're used to people talking about you. I mean, the Lassiters are always in the papers for something or other."

"True," he acknowledged.

"And as for you, the press loves following you around. They're always printing stories about the black sheep billionaire." She stopped abruptly when she caught his sudden frown. "I'm sorry, it's just—"

"You seem to keep up with reports about me," he said softly.

"It's hard not to," she lied, not wanting him to know that she really did look for stories about him in the paper and magazines—not to mention online. God, she was practically a stalker! "The Lassiter family is big news in Cheyenne." She covered for herself nicely. "The local papers are always reporting about you and your family."

He snorted. "Yeah, and I'm guessing the will is going to be front-page news as soon as someone leaks the details."

Surprised, she asked, "Who would do that?"

"Any number of clerks in the law offices, I should think," he said. "The right amount of money and people will do or say anything."

"Wow…that's cynical."

"Just a dose of reality," he said, his hand tightening around the brass rail until his knuckles whitened. "I used to think most people were loyal, with a sense of integrity. Then I found out differently."

"What happened?" she asked, caught up in the glimmer of old pain and distant memories glittering in his eyes. The house was quiet, sunlight drifting in through the bedroom window, and it felt as though they were the only two people on the planet. Maybe that's why she overstepped. Maybe that's why she allowed herself to wonder about him aloud rather than just in her mind.

He almost looked as though he would tell her, then in an instant, the moment was gone. His features were once again schooled in pokerlike stillness and his eyes were shuttered. "Doesn't matter. The point is, you shouldn't let gossips rule your decisions."

Colleen was sorry their all-too-brief closeness was gone, but it was just as well. "It sounds so simple when you say it like that, but I don't like being gossiped about."

"Neither do I," he said, glancing down at her suitcase, then lifting his gaze to hers again. "Doesn't mean I can stop it."

He was right and she knew it. Still, he was a Lassiter and rumors and prying questions came with the territory. She was a nobody and she preferred it that way. "Maybe if I don't accept the inheritance, they won't bother because there would be nothing to talk about."

He smiled, but it wasn't a comforting expression. "Colleen, people are going to gossip. Whether you take the money or not, people will talk. Besides, trust me, a beautiful woman like you taking care of J.D. all these months…there's gossip already."

Beautiful? He thought she was *beautiful?* Then what he said struck home. A flush of embarrassment washed over her as she realized he was probably right. There was no doubt talk already, and with her living here at the ranch, she had fed the flames of the gossip.

"That's just awful. I was his *nurse.*"

"A young, pretty nurse with a sick old man. Doesn't take much more than that to get tongues wagging."

She argued that because she had to. For her own peace of mind. Colleen hated to think that people were making ugly accusations about a sweet old man. And oh, God, had her *mother* heard the talk? No. If she had, she would have said something, wouldn't she?

Shaking her head, Colleen said, "But J.D. wasn't my first patient. This has never happened to me before."

He shrugged the argument aside. "You'd never worked for a Lassiter before, either. I'm only surprised you haven't already heard the speculation."

She plopped down onto the edge of her mattress, her mind racing as images from the past few months flashed across her brain. She hadn't really paid attention before, but now that she was looking at things in a new light, she realized he was right. The gossip had already started. She remembered knowing winks, slow smiles and whispered conversations cut short when she entered any of the local shops.

"Oh, my God. They really think that I—that J.D.— oh, this is humiliating."

"Only if you let them win," he said quietly and she looked up at him, waiting for him to continue. "Small minds are always looking for something to occupy them. If you live your life worried about what they're saying, you won't do anything. Then they win."

"I really hate this," she murmured. He did have a point, but this was the first time in her life that she was the subject of gossip. She'd led a fairly quiet existence until she'd taken the job with J.D.

Sage was looking at this from an entirely different angle. The truth was, as a Lassiter, he was insulated from the nastiest rumors and innuendos. He didn't have to worry about what people were saying about him, because his career was already made, and he had a powerful family name behind him. Besides, how bad was it to have people discussing how incredibly gorgeous you were?

No, this was different. If people were talking about her, it could affect her work. Her life. If the nursing agency she worked for got wind of any of this, they might be reluctant to send her out on other assignments—and that made her cringe. On the other hand, if she simply accepted J.D.'s generosity, she could make her own way. Though she would still, as a nurse practitioner, have to work through local doctors and hospitals.

"My head hurts," she muttered.

He laughed and it was such a rich, surprising sound, it startled her. Looking up at him, she saw that his eyes were shining and the wide smile on his face displayed a dimple she was fairly certain didn't show up very often.

"You're thinking about this too much."

"It's very hard not to," she told him, shaking her head. "I've never been in this position before and I'm not really sure what to do about it."

"Do what you want to do," he advised.

Want was a big word. She *wanted* a lot of things. World peace. Calorie-free chocolate. Smaller feet. Her gaze drifted to Sage's mouth and locked there. And she *really* wanted to kiss him.

As that thought settled into the forefront of her mind, Colleen cleared her throat and tried for heaven's sake to get a grip. Honestly, she'd been alone so long, was it really so surprising that a man like Sage Lassiter would tangle her up into knots without even trying?

"Everything okay?" He was frowning now.

"Fine. Fine." She breathed deeply and repeated, "What I want. Do what I want."

"Not so hard, is it?"

"You wouldn't think so..." But she'd been raised to consider more than her wants. There was doing the right thing, and in this case, she just didn't know what that was.

"You know," he murmured, "once you show people you don't care what they think, they usually stop talking about you."

Wryly, she asked, "And if you *do* care what they're saying?"

His lips quirked into a quick half smile that tugged at something inside her. "Well, that's a different story, isn't it? But why would you care?"

"Because I have to work here. Live here. If people think—" She swallowed hard. Everything she'd worked toward, everything she'd built in the past five years. Her reputation...her hopes and dreams. It could all disappear.

Suddenly, the windfall from J.D. looked like more of a curse than a blessing.

"You're giving other people all the power here," Sage said, drawing her attention away from her thoughts.

"I don't want to, but..." Shaking her head, she folded her hands together on her lap. "Ever since this morning, my mind's been filled with questions. And now I don't know what to do about this."

"Not much you can do about it." Sage walked around her, pushed the open suitcase out of his way and took a seat beside her on the bed. "The will's a done deal."

"But I could donate the money."

He shrugged. "People would still talk. The only difference would be you wouldn't have the money."

She sighed heavily and turned to look at him. He was so close to her, his muscular thigh was just a bare inch from brushing against hers. Heat rushed through her and

Colleen forced a deep breath as she met his gaze. His eyes weren't as frosty as they had been earlier, yet they were still unreadable. As if he'd drawn shutters down, to keep others from sensing his emotions. He was so closed off—much like J.D. had been when she'd first come to take care of him. But, she reminded herself, it hadn't taken her long to bypass the older man's defenses and get him to really talk to her.

The difference was, Sage wasn't her patient. He was a strong, completely masculine male who made her feel things she hadn't felt in far too long. Which was, of course, not only ridiculous, but inappropriate. He was the son of her patient. A family member who'd just gone through a devastating loss. He wasn't interested in her and she would only do herself a favor if she found a way to tamp down the rush of attraction she felt every time he came close. Of course, *way* easier said than done.

"Look," he said, his voice quiet, "why don't we have dinner tonight? Give us a chance to talk some more."

She blinked at him, so stunned she could hardly manage to croak, "You're asking me out?"

One corner of his mouth lifted. "I'm asking you to have dinner with me."

Not a date. Of course it wasn't a date. Idiot.

"Why?" *And why are you questioning it,* her mind demanded.

"Well, I still want to talk to you about J.D.," he said. "And it's been a long day. For both of us."

Of course. That explained it, Colleen told herself firmly. He wanted to talk about his father and all she'd managed to do was talk his ear off about *her* problems.

"Okay," she said after a long moment. "That would be nice."

"Great." He stood up and looked down at her. "I'll pick you up at seven."

"I'll give you my address."

"I know where you live," he told her. "I'll see you tonight."

He knew where she lived. What was she supposed to make of that?

"Can I carry your suitcase down to the car?"

"What? Oh. No, thank you." She glanced around the room. "I've still got a few things to pack up."

"All right then, I'll leave you to it," he said, heading for the doorway. When he got there, he paused, turned around and speared her with an unfathomable look. "See you tonight."

When he left, Colleen stared after him for a long minute. Her heartbeat was racing and her knees felt a little wobbly. Her reaction to Sage was so staggering, she wasn't really sure how to deal with it. However, as the sound of his footsteps faded away, Colleen told herself that she couldn't really be blamed for her response to his presence. He was like a force of nature. Sage Lassiter was a gorgeous steamroller, flattening everything in his path.

And Colleen realized that now, for whatever reason, *she* was in his path.

Four

"So how's the rest of dealing with the will going, Walter?" Sage drove straight from Big Blue to the lawyer's office. He wanted a chance to talk to J.D.'s lawyer without the explosive release of emotion that had happened when the family was gathered together. Not that he'd been able to dismiss the anger churning inside him. The plan had been to arrive, calm and cool, and outstare the older man. That didn't happen though, because he was far from feeling cool and detached.

Tension played in every one of his muscles and tugged at the last threads of his patience. Being with Colleen had ramped his body up to the point where he'd practically had to limp his way out of the ranch house. Just sitting beside her on the bed in her room had tested his self-control, because what he'd really wanted to do was lay her back on the mattress and explore those amazing curves she kept so carefully hidden.

Instead, he'd talked to her. And talking to Colleen hadn't solved a damn thing—it had only muddied waters that were already so damn thick it might as well have been concrete. He couldn't make her out. Was she the innocent she seemed to be? Or was she working him as she had worked J.D.? He had to find out…but that was for later. Right now, he had a couple of questions for his late father's lawyer.

"It's coming along but I'm not discussing it with you, Sage, and you damn well know it." Walter Drake steepled his fingers, leaned back in his leather chair and looked at Sage with the barely hidden impatience he would have shown a five-year-old. "J.D.'s will is a private matter. I've already read publicly the parts that affect the family. As for the rest…"

Sage jumped out of his chair and stalked to the far window. Yeah, he was too on edge to be facing down a lawyer. He should have known better than to come here today, but damn it, there were just too many questions about the will.

Looking down on the street below, he focused for a second on the traffic, the pedestrians wandering along the sidewalks and even the mountains jutting into the sky in the distance. He looked anywhere but into the smug features of J.D.'s lawyer.

Going in, Sage had guessed that Walter wouldn't talk. Hell, he wouldn't have even if he *could*. The man liked holding all the power here. Liked having information that no one else did. And getting anything out of him would probably require dynamite—or someone with far more patience than Sage possessed. Fine, then. He'd back off the topic of the rest of the will for the moment and try a different tack. Half turning, he faced the man watching him through hooded eyes.

"All right," Sage said, "never mind."

Walter nodded magnanimously.

"But there's still the matter of J.D. leaving control of Lassiter Media to Evan instead of Angelica."

Walter frowned at him, sat up and braced both elbows on his desktop. "J.D. had reasons for everything he ever did, Sage. You know that."

J.D. had sure thought so. But Sage had given up trying to figure out the old man years ago. The whole time he was growing up, the two of them hadn't even been able to be in the same room together without snarling and growling like a couple of alpha dogs fighting for territory.

But Angelica was different. Right from the start, she had been J.D.'s shining star. So how he could have cut her out of her rightful inheritance was beyond Sage. "Yeah, but what reason could he have for cheating his daughter out of what should have been hers?"

"I can't tell you that."

"Can't?" Sage demanded, walking back to stand opposite the man's desk. "Or won't?"

"Won't." Walter stood up, since staying in his chair required him to look up at Sage, and he clearly didn't enjoy that. "J.D.'s my client, Sage, dead or alive. Not you. Not the Lassiter family."

"And you'll protect him from his damn *family* even after his death?"

"If I have to," Walter said softly.

Frustration clawed at him. "None of this makes sense. You know as well as I do that J.D. had been grooming Angie for years, getting her ready to run Lassiter Media."

"True…"

"So does it seem rational to you that he would leave the company to Angie's fiancé?" There went his grasp on the last slippery thread of temper.

The lawyer only stared at him for a long minute or two. "If you're trying to insinuate that J.D. wasn't competent to make this will, you're wrong. And that allegation would never stand in a court."

"I'm not talking about court." *Yet.* "I'm talking about your knowledge of J.D."

"As I've already said, J.D. had reasons for everything he did, and this is no different."

Sage had no idea why J.D. would have done this. It made no sense at all.

The lawyer's deliberate refusal to give anything away just increased the sense of outrage snarling inside him.

"This isn't getting either of us anywhere, Sage. So if you'll excuse me, I've got business to take care of and—"

"I'm not done with this, Walter," Sage promised. "We all want answers."

For the first time, a flicker of something that might have been sympathy shone in the other man's eyes. "And I wish I could give them to you," he said. "But it's out of my hands."

Frustrated, Sage conceded defeat. At least for now. "Fine. I'll go. But once the family gets over the shock of all of this, I won't be the only one showing up here demanding answers. I hope you're ready for that."

At any other time, Sage might have laughed at the beleaguered expression on the man's face. But right now he just wasn't in the mood to be amused.

Once out in the parking lot, Sage hunched deeper into his black coat as a cold mountain wind pushed at him. Even nature was giving him a hard time today. He crossed to his black Porsche and climbed in. During the winter, this car spent most of its time locked away in a temperature-controlled garage on his ranch. Right now, he was glad he had the sports car. He had a driving need to push the car to its limits, wanting the speed, needing the rush of the moment.

He peeled out of the lot, drove through Cheyenne, and once he was free of the city, cut the powerful engine loose. He backtracked, headed to the Big Blue ranch. By now, Colleen would be gone, but Marlene and Angie would be there. And he had to see his sister. Find out for himself if she was okay. But how could she be? She'd been betrayed by someone she trusted. And Sage knew just how that felt.

The growl of the engine seemed to underscore the rage pumping just below the surface of his mind. Speeding along the road to the ranch forced him to focus, to concentrate on his driving, which gave him a respite from everything else tearing through his brain. He steered the car through the wide ranch gates, kicked up gravel along the winding drive and then parked outside the front doors.

From the stable area came the shouts of men hard at work. He caught a glimpse of a horse in a paddock, running through the dirt, and realized that J.D. being gone hadn't stopped *life* from going on. This ranch would go on, too. The old man had seen to that. But what the hell had he been thinking about the rest of it?

Sage climbed out of the car and paused long enough to take a quick look around the familiar landscape. Much like Sage's own ranch, there were plenty of outbuildings, barns, cabins for the wranglers who lived and worked on the ranch, guest cabins, and even a saltwater pool surrounded by grass, not cement, so that it looked like a natural pond. His gaze fixed on the ancient oak that shaded the pond and a reluctant smile curved his mouth. He, Dylan and Angelica had spent hours out here when they were kids, swinging from a rope attached to one of the oaks' heavy limbs to drop into the cold, clear water.

So much of his life had been spent here on this ranch, and in spite of his estrangement from J.D., there were a lot of *good* memories here, too. He shifted his gaze to the house. Built from hand-cut logs, iron and glass, it was two stories high and boasted wraparound porches with hand-hewn wood railings on both levels. Those porches provided Adirondack chairs with colorful cushions and views of the mountains from almost everywhere.

Sage took a breath. He'd left here only a couple hours ago, but it felt like longer. After mentally dueling with a crafty lawyer, he wanted nothing more than a drink and some quiet. The minute he entered the ranch house, though, he knew the quiet was something that would elude him.

"Why would he do this to me?" Angelica demanded, her voice carrying through the cavernous house.

Three or four people answered her at once and Sage followed the voices to the great room. The heart of the house, the main room was enormous, with honey-toned wood floors, log walls and what seemed like acres of glass windows affording views of the ranch and the wide blue sky that had given the ranch its name above. He'd heard the story often enough to know it by heart.

J.D. and his wife, Ellie, had bought this ranch, then

only two hundred acres, and Ellie had so loved the expanse of deep blue sky that J.D. had decreed the ranch would be named Big Blue, after the sky overhead. Here they'd begun the Lassiter dynasty. Over the years J.D. had added to the property, expanding the ranch into the state's largest cattle herd and building the land holdings up to more than thirty thousand acres. They'd put their stamp on Wyoming and in Cheyenne, the Lassiter name was damn near legend.

Maybe that was part of what Sage had rebelled against all these years. The Lassiter name and what it had meant to J.D. What it had been like to not be born a Lassiter, but *made* into one. With that thought simmering in his brain, he took another step into the chaos.

"Thank heaven," Marlene muttered. "Sage, help me convince your sister that her father wasn't angry at her about anything."

He glanced quickly around the familiar room. The massive stone fireplace, the wide French doors that led to a flagstone patio, the oversize leather couches and chairs dotting the shining wood floor. And the family members scattered across the room, all looking at him.

"What other reason could there be?" Angie asked, throwing both hands high only to let them fall to her sides again. Flipping her dark hair back out of her face, she looked at her oldest brother and said, "I thought he was proud of me. I thought he *believed* in me."

"He did, Angie," Chance put in and she turned on her cousin.

"This is an odd way to show it, don't you think?"

Chance sighed and scrubbed one hand over his face impatiently. Sage could sympathize. The poor guy had probably been trying to cheer Angie up for hours with no success.

"Angie." Evan McCain spoke up then and all eyes turned to him. "You're overreacting."

"Am I?" Shaking her head, Angie looked at the man she had been poised to marry only two weeks ago and it was as if she'd never seen him before. The wedding had been postponed after J.D.'s death, but the two of them had remained close. Until today. Until Evan had been given the company Angie loved. "He gave the company—*my* company—to you, Evan." She slapped one hand to her heart. "I was his daughter and he left it to *you*."

Evan shoved one hand through his hair and looked to Sage for help. But hell, Sage didn't know what he could do. He didn't believe that Evan had tried to undermine Angie. But who the hell knew anymore? Mysterious benefactors. Nurses who inherited three million dollars. A daughter who got cheated out of what should have been hers. None of this made a damn bit of sense.

Still, if they went to war with each other over it, that wouldn't solve a thing either—it would just splinter them when they needed each other most.

"Angie, taking it out on Evan isn't going to help," Sage finally said and he caught a brief look of relief on Evan's face. "We just have to try to figure out what was in J.D.'s mind and then do what we can to change things."

"Can we change anything?" Marlene looked worried, her gaze darting from Angelica to Evan and back again. "The will is done. And even though J.D. was sick, he was mentally competent right up until his last day."

"I know." Sage walked to the woman who had been a mother in all but name to him since he was a kid and wrapped one arm around her shoulders. The scent of her perfume drifted up to him and colored his mind with memories. Marlene had been the one stabilizing influence in his life. Through all of his rebellion with J.D., his aunt was there, talking him down, trying to build a bridge between Sage and his adoptive father. That bridge had never really materialized, but it hadn't been for lack of trying on her part.

Sage dropped a kiss on the top of her head, then looked across the room to Dylan, sprawled in one of the oversize leather chairs.

"You don't have anything to say?"

"I've said plenty," his brother countered, then shifted a glare to their sister. "I was shouted down."

"I didn't shout," Angie argued.

"Like a fishwife," Dylan told her, then glanced at Evan. "If you still want to marry her, you're either brave or brain-dead."

"You're not helping," Sage said.

"Yeah, I heard that from our darling sister an hour ago," Dylan told him tiredly.

"You don't understand how this feels, Dylan," Angelica said, giving him a look that should have set fire to his hair. "Dad didn't take away the business you love, did he?"

"No, he didn't," he admitted.

"Angie," Evan said, stepping toward his fiancée and laying both hands on her shoulders. "I love you. We're getting *married*. Nothing's changed."

She slipped out from under his grip and shook her head. "Everything's changed, Evan. Don't you see that?"

"I don't want to run your company, Angie. You'll

still be doing the day-to-day," he argued. "You're still in charge."

"I don't have the title. I don't have the power. The only reason I would still be in charge is because you *allow* it." She shook her head and bit down hard on her bottom lip before saying, "It's not the same, Evan."

"We'll figure this out," he countered, but Angelica didn't look convinced.

Sage wondered suddenly if maybe J.D. hadn't done all this just so he could hang around as a damn ghost and watch his family jump through the hoops he'd left behind.

"I think we've all had enough for one day," Marlene announced, interrupting what looked as though it could turn into a battle. She walked over to give Angelica a hug, then smoothed a stray lock of her dark brown hair back with gentle fingers. Giving the younger woman a smile, she spoke to the room at large.

"Why don't we all go into the kitchen? We'll have some coffee. Something to eat. It's been a hard day but I think we all have to remember—" she paused, letting her gaze slide around the room "—that we're *family*. We're the *Lassiters*. And we will come through this. Together."

"There's no reason to be so nervous." Jenna Cooper took a sip of her white wine and smiled as Colleen changed clothes for the third time in a half hour.

"I'm not nervous," she replied, "I'm just hyperalert."

Jenna chuckled and curled up into a corner of her chair. Colleen met her friend's amused gaze in the mirror and released a sigh. "Fine. Maybe I'm a little nervous, but there's no reason to be. This is not a date. It's just dinner with a family member of a patient I've lost."

"Uh-huh."

"You might sound a little more convincing when you're placating me."

"I'll work on it," her friend said, still laughing.

Jenna Cooper lived next door, with her husband and adorable three-year-old twin boys, Carter and Cade. At five foot two, Jenna looked like a pixie with very short black hair that curled around her elfin features. Her green eyes were always shining and she and Colleen had been good friends since the second week Colleen had lived in the condo complex two years before.

Knowing Colleen was a nurse, Jenna had come to her door in a panic late one night because one of the boys had had a fever seizure. Colleen had recognized it for what it was immediately and helped them lower Carter's temperature, then she had stayed at the house with a sleeping Cade while Jenna and her husband took Carter to the E.R. to be checked out, just to be on the safe side.

Jenna took a sip of her wine and murmured, "I still can't get over Mr. Lassiter leaving you so much money."

Colleen's stomach churned uneasily and she slapped one hand to her abdomen in a futile attempt to stop it. "Neither can I."

She'd had several hours to think about it, yet it still didn't seem real. Though everything Sage had said to her earlier kept replaying in her mind. The thought of gossip gave her cold chills, but…

"So, have you told your mother yet?"

"About the money?" She shook her head and then frowned at her reflection. Tugging at the scooped bodice, she tried to pull it a little higher, but no matter what she did, you could see cleavage. A *lot* of cleavage. "I never really noticed just how big my boobs are."

"That's because you've usually got them covered up under a layer of cotton and wool." Jenna stood up, smacked Colleen's hand away from the fabric and smiled. "You look gorgeous. Stop fussing. God, that's an amazing dress."

"It is." And ordinarily, she never would have bought anything like it. But Angelica had insisted on taking Colleen shopping for the perfect dress to wear to the rehearsal dinner. Sage's sister had picked this dress out for Colleen and she'd worn it the night Sage had first noticed her. The night...her eyes widened suddenly. "Oh, God. I can't wear this dress tonight. I was wearing it the night Sage's father collapsed and *died*. What was I thinking?"

She turned to head for her bedroom and the pitiful offerings she might find in her closet, but Jenna stopped her with one hand on her arm. "You can't retire the dress, Colleen. For one thing, it didn't kill Mr. Lassiter, and it's just too amazing to be tossed into the dark abyss that is your closet."

"Thank you."

"And for another thing, trust me when I say that when Sage gets a look at you in this dress—" Jenna took a step back, swept her gaze up and down Colleen and whistled "—it won't be funerals that'll spring to mind."

A tiny thrill dazzled Colleen before she remembered that Jenna was her *friend*. Of course she was going to compliment her. *But,* she told herself firmly, *let's be realistic.* Sage Lassiter was *not* interested in her. Going to dinner with him meant absolutely nothing.

"This is crazy," she said aloud. "I'm acting like this is a date and it's not." Colleen wrung her hands together until she realized what she was doing, then she stopped that pitiful action. "Honestly. Slacks and a sweater. That's what I should wear."

"If you change one more time, I'm going to tie you to a chair," Jenna warned. "You look great, you've got a date—"

"Not a date—"

"—you're going to dinner with the most gorgeous man in Wyoming, possibly the United States—"

"I wonder what Tom would say if he heard that."

Jenna grinned. "He's not worried. My Tom's not gorgeous, but he has other…compensations."

"You're impossible." Colleen could admit silently that she felt more than a little envy of her friend's relationship with her very cute husband.

"Tom thinks so…" She grinned again and wiggled her eyebrows for emphasis.

If Colleen had half the confidence that Jenna had, she wouldn't be the slightest bit nervous about her nondate. As it was though…the bats in her stomach—too big for butterflies—were flying in tighter and tighter circles. It was as if they were winding an invisible spring inside her and Colleen was terrified that it was going to snap at just the wrong moment.

Maybe the red dress would help. It was beautiful and wearing it, she couldn't help but feel more confident. Besides, she told herself, Sage might not even remember that she was wearing this dress at the rehearsal dinner.

"Have some wine." Jenna offered her own glass and Colleen snatched at it, taking a big gulp, hoping to drown the bats. Apparently though, they knew how to swim.

"This is a mistake," she muttered and handed the glass back to her friend.

"No, it's not. You're a terrific person, Colleen. It's about time you let some man figure that out for himself."

"It's not a—"

"Yes, yes." Jenna walked back to the love seat, dropped onto the slipcovered cushions and stared up at her. "Now, tell me how my best friend becomes a millionaire and gets a date with *the* Sage Lassiter."

"Weren't you listening? It's *not* a date."

"Whatever." She patted the cushion beside her. "So how're you doing, really, with this crazy, world-shifting, life-altering day?"

Good question. "Actually, I think I'm feeling better about the money."

"Yay!"

Smiling, Colleen thought about sitting down, but she didn't want to wrinkle her dress. How did the beautiful people do this all the time? "Really, I've had all day to think about it, and you know, Sage was right. Even if I give up the money to charity, people will still talk. I'll just be poor while they're talking about me."

"He's obviously brilliant as well as gorgeous. I like him already."

Colleen did, too. Which was worrying on a whole different level. Still, first things first. Now that she'd decided to accept J.D.'s amazing gift, her life was going to change. Big-time. Laughing to herself, she said, "You know this means I can quit my job."

Jenna lifted her glass. "Excellent. Soon-to-be nurse practitioner Colleen Falkner."

Colleen put one hand to her abdomen to ease those bats that were still flying in formation in the pit of her stomach. But it was a futile gesture. Her body had been through so many ups and downs today, there was no calming it. Oddly enough, it wasn't even the money or the knowledge that she could make her dreams come true that was really affecting her. Nope, that was all Sage Lassiter. His eyes. His mouth. The deep rumble of his voice, the impossibly broad shoulders.

Oh, God.

She shouldn't be going to dinner with him. Colleen turned and glanced into the mirror again and what she saw didn't make her feel any better. Her eyes were too wide, her boobs were too big, her hair was a mass of waves on her shoulders because no matter what she'd tried, she hadn't been able to clip it up and keep it from looking like a rat's nest.

Why was she putting herself through this? What if she couldn't talk? What if staring at him across a table turned her into a mute? Or worse, her mind taunted, what if she babbled incoherently?

"Stop."

"What?" Colleen came up out of her nerve-racking thoughts like a drowning woman breaching the surface of a lake. She was practically gasping for air.

Shaking her head, Jenna said, "You're making yourself nuts. It's just dinner, Colleen. You eat dinner every day. You can do this."

Could she? She didn't think so. Heck, her last date had been…oh, God, she couldn't even *remember* when she'd dated last. All she could recall was that the guy in question had bored her to tears and then tried to grope her on her front porch. Good times. "I'm being crazy, aren't I?"

"Just a little."

"Right." Sage certainly wouldn't be boring, she told herself. And if he tried to grope her, she might just let him. Oh, boy. *Get a grip,* she told herself silently. She was making too much of this. Sage wanted to talk about his late father. All she had to do was keep remembering that and she'd be fine. By talking to him, spending time with him, she could help him get the closure he no doubt needed.

This wasn't about *her* and her fantasies. This was about a man, who in spite of his wealth and remarkable good looks, had lost a link to his past. With that thought firmly in mind, she let her sympathy for his loss rise up to drown her silly hormonal meltdown.

"You're right," she said, and reached out to take another sip of Jenna's wine. Colleen hadn't poured herself any because she hadn't wanted to risk alcohol on a nearly empty stomach. But the crisp, sharp taste of the Sauvignon Blanc felt like bliss sliding down her too-tight throat. Then the cold, wheat-colored liquid hit her stomach and immediately soothed those pesky bats.

She took a breath, handed the glass back and checked her reflection one last time. "It's just a meal with a grieving man."

"Yep. Just dinner with the gorgeous, incredibly sexy, unattainable black sheep billionaire," Jenna said with a grin. "No pressure."

Oh, God.

Five

The condo was small, even for a condo.

Sage gave it a quick once-over as he approached the front door. It was tidy, with its cream-colored paint and postage stamp–sized front garden, where spring bulbs were pushing up through the earth. There was a wreath of silk flowers hanging on her front door and when he pushed the doorbell, he wasn't even surprised to hear a series of melodic chimes sounding out from somewhere inside.

What *did* surprise him was Colleen.

She opened the door and every scrap of air escaped from his lungs. She was wearing that red dress again. The one she'd worn the night of the rehearsal dinner. The night he'd really *seen* her for the first time. That damn dress was designed to bring a man to his knees. It molded her figure, defined her luscious breasts and skimmed across rounded hips that made a man think of long, dark nights and hot, steamy sex. Her dark blond hair tumbled over her shoulders and looked like raw honey. He caught the wink of gold earrings when she tossed her hair back and then his gaze dropped lower— to the expanse of smooth, pale flesh that ended in a spectacular display of the tops of her breasts. It was all he could do to lift his gaze to meet her eyes.

"You look beautiful," he said before he could think better of it. Hell, he was always in control of any given situation, and at the moment, he felt like a teenager on his first date. Hard body and vacant mind.

She beamed at him as if he'd handed her flowers, and immediately he told himself he should have done just that. If he was trying to sway her into spilling her secrets, then he should use all the weapons he could bring to bear.

"Thank you," she said, her voice just a little breathless. "Let me get my coat."

She reached into a hall closet, pulled out a heavy black coat and slipped into it, covering herself up so thoroughly, Sage's brain was able to kick back into gear.

She stepped onto the porch, locked her front door, then joined him with another smile. "Shall we go?"

And he knew at that moment, when her blue eyes were staring into his, that this night was not going to go according to plan.

At the restaurant, Sage was grateful for the clink of fine crystal and the murmured conversations that reminded him they were in a public place. Otherwise he might have been in trouble. She was damned distracting, sitting across from him.

"This is lovely," she said, turning her head to look

around the interior of Moscone's Italian restaurant. It was filled with small round tables, covered in white linen and each boasting a single candle in the center. A sleek black-and-chrome bar stood along one wall and Italian arias played softly over the loudspeaker. The floors were tile, the waiters were all in white aprons and the scents filling the air were amazing. "I've never been here before."

"Food's good," Sage mused. "But they're going to have some serious competition when the Lassiter Grill opens up." Damn. He could hardly get words past the knot of need in his throat. Sage took a sip of the wine the waiter had poured just moments before.

"It was really nice of you to bring me here," she said, "but it wasn't necessary. We could have talked at my house."

But then she wouldn't have worn *the dress*. Sage shifted uncomfortably on the black leather bench seat. He hadn't expected to spend the night in agony, but apparently he was going to. And just by looking at her, he knew she had absolutely no idea what she was doing to him. He had to take back control of this situation or he was going to achieve nothing.

"What can you tell me?" he asked, blurting the question out to divert himself from the thoughts plaguing him.

"Anything you want to know."

Like if you talked an old man into leaving you money? Did you steer him away from giving Angelica the company she loves? Did you wear that damn dress on purpose, knowing what it would do to me?

Couldn't start with those questions, though...could

he? His brain scrambled, coming up with a different way to begin.

"First tell me about you. How long have you been a nurse?" Good. Get her talking. Then later, once she'd relaxed her guard, he'd be able to slide the more important questions in.

She took a sip of wine and he watched, hypnotized by the movement in her throat as she swallowed. Not good.

"Eleven years," she said, setting the goblet back onto the table and sliding her fingertips up and down the long, elegant stem.

Sage's gaze fixed on to that motion, and his brain fogged over even as his body went rock hard. He had to force himself to pay attention when she continued to speak quietly.

"When my father got sick, it was such a blessing to be able to help my mom take care of him." Old pain etched itself into her eyes briefly. "After he died, I realized that I was more interested in taking care of people one-on-one than in a hospital setting. I decided to become a private nurse. So I could make a real difference in the lives of families who were going through what we went through."

Was she really as selfless and kind as she appeared? He wanted to spot deception, gamesmanship in her eyes, but those soft blue depths remained as clear and guileless as ever. Was she really that good an actress, he wondered. Or was she really an innocent?

No, he mentally assured himself. There were no innocents anymore. And a woman this staggeringly beautiful had no doubt learned before she was five just how to work a man.

Pleased that he'd managed to wrest control of his

own urges, he asked, "How long ago did you lose your father?"

"Six years," she said softly and her features once again twisted with sorrow.

"Then," she added, "Mom and I both decided we needed a change, a chance to get away from the memories, so we left California and came here."

"Why Cheyenne?"

She laughed a little and her blue eyes sparkled with it. Instantly, his control drowned in a sea of pulsing desire that grabbed hold of him and wouldn't let go.

"You won't believe it."

"Try me."

"Okay." She leaned in a little closer, as if telling a funny story. Unfortunately, this increased his view of the delectable cleavage that dress displayed.

"We laid a map of the U.S. out on the dining room table and Mom closed her eyes and poked her finger down. She hit Cheyenne and here we are."

Surprise and a bit of admiration rose up inside him, however reluctantly. "Just like that. You packed up and moved to somewhere you'd never been before."

"It was an adventure," she told him with a smile. "And we both needed one. Watching someone you love die by inches is horrible. At least you were spared that. I know it's not much comfort though."

He didn't speak because, frankly, what the hell could he say? She'd obviously had a much better relationship with her father than he'd had with his.

"Although," she added, "the snow was hard to get used to. We're California girls through and through, so we needed a whole new wardrobe when we got here."

"I can imagine." His mind brought up the image of

her seeing her first snowfall, and he almost wished he'd been there to witness it.

"When your winter coat is a sweatshirt and you can wear flip-flops year-round…" Another bright smile. "Let's just say it was even more of an adventure than we'd thought it would be."

"But you enjoy it?"

"I love it," she said simply. "I'd never had a change of season before. I love the fall. And the snow is so beautiful. Then the spring when everything comes alive again. Mostly though, I love the mountains."

"Me, too." Funny, he hadn't thought they'd find common ground, but here it was. Unless, his mind chided, she was saying what she thought he wanted to hear. After all, if J.D. had talked about him as she said, then she knew Sage owned a ranch in the high country, and why else would he do that if he didn't love the mountains?

"I know… J.D. told me about your ranch."

Ha! Proof then. But he played along. "If I can help it, I rarely come down off the mountain into the city."

"I know that, too," she said, her hand stilling on the wineglass. "J.D. talked about you a lot. How you preferred your ranch to anywhere else in the world. He missed seeing you, but said that you almost never left the ranch."

A flare of something hot slashed through him. Guilt? He didn't *do* guilt. "J.D. didn't have much room to talk. You could hardly blast him off the Big Blue with a stick of dynamite."

"True," she said, agreeing with him. "He told me. Truth is, he used to worry that you were too much like him. Too ready to cut yourself off from everything."

"I'm not cut off." Hadn't Dylan said the same thing

to him just hours ago? Why did everyone assume that because a man was happy where he was that he was missing out on other things?

"Aren't you?" It was softly asked, but no less invasive.

He stiffened and the desire pumping through him edged back just a little. Sage hadn't brought her there to talk about *him*.

"No," he assured her, and even he heard the coolness in his tone. "Just because I didn't visit J.D. doesn't mean I'm a damn hermit."

Hermits had a hell of a lot more peace and quiet than he ever got. It wasn't that Sage didn't love his family, he did. He only preferred the solitude of his ranch because nothing good ever came of mixing with people—

He cut that thought off and buried it amid the rubble of his memories.

"He missed you."

Three words that hurt more than he would have thought possible. Sage and J.D. had been at odds for so many years, it was hard to remember a time when things were different. He didn't want to feel another sting of guilt, but how the hell could he avoid it? J.D. had been old and sick and still Sage hadn't been able to get past their differences. Would that haunt him for the rest of his life? Would he have yet another regret to add to the multitude he already carried?

Shaking his head, he told her, "Our arguments were legendary. J.D. and I mixed about as well as oil and water. There's just no way he missed me, so you don't have to worry about telling pretty lies and trying to make me feel better. I know the truth."

About that, anyway.

"It's not a lie," she said, pausing for another sip of her wine.

What was it about the woman's throat and the slim elegance of it that fascinated him?

"He did miss you." She smiled at him again and the warmth in her eyes washed over him. "He told me about your arguments. And really, I think he missed them. He had no one to butt heads with, and that must have been frustrating for a man as strong and powerful as he once was."

Frowning now, Sage saw that she might just have a point. Even though his relationship with J.D. had never been a close one, he knew that his adoptive father had gone through life like a charging bull. Putting his head down and rushing at problems, determined to knock them out of his way through sheer force of will.

J.D. Lassiter had been the kind of man who let nothing stand between him and his goals. He'd bent the world to his whim and pushed those around him into line—or in Sage's case, had *tried* to. For him to be reduced to a sick bed because his heart had turned on him must have been wildly frustrating. Surprisingly, Sage felt a twinge of sympathy for the old man rattle around inside him before he could stop it.

"He told me that he and his wife adopted you and Dylan when you were boys."

Seemed J.D. had talked her damn ears off. Which gave him hope that somewhere in there, he might have confessed the reasons behind his will.

"They did," he said and reluctantly was tossed into the past.

He had been six and Dylan four when they went to live on Big Blue. Their parents had just been killed in a traffic accident and they'd clung to each other in an unfamiliar world. Then J.D. and Ellie had swooped in and suddenly, everything was different. Their lives. Their home. Their parents. All new. All so damned hard to accept. At least for Sage. Dylan, maybe because he was younger, had accepted the change in their lives with much more ease.

Sage had refused to let go of his memories...of the life he'd been forced to surrender. He'd bucked against the rules, had fought with his new parents and in general been a pain in the ass, now that he thought about it. He'd grumbled about everything, comparing their new life to the old and the new always came up short.

Ellie had tried relentlessly, through patience and love, to get through to Sage and eventually she'd succeeded. But J.D. hadn't had the patience to carefully win Sage over. Instead, he'd simply demanded respect and affection and Sage had refused to give either.

The two of them had fought over everything, he remembered now. From doing chores as a kid to driving as a teenager. Sage had instinctively gone in the opposite direction of anything J.D. recommended. There'd been plenty of battles between them, with Ellie stepping in as peacemaker—until she died after giving birth to Angelica.

And the love they shared for Sage's sister was the one thing he and J.D. had ever agreed on. She had been the glue in their shattered family. Without Ellie there, they would have all floundered, but caring for Angelica kept them all afloat. Then Marlene had moved in and because she hadn't expected their love, she'd won their hearts.

Shaking his head now, Sage reached for his wine and gulped it down as if it were water. The waiter appeared, delivering their meals, and for a moment or two, there was silence. Then they were alone again and Colleen finally spoke.

"I'm sorry. I didn't mean to bring back unpleasant memories."

"You didn't," he lied, smoothing his voice out as easily as he mentally paved over memory lane.

"Okay." She took a small bite of her ravioli, then chewed and swallowed. "Well, I've been talking forever. Why don't you tell me about your ranch?"

Sage stared at her for a long minute as he tried to figure out what she was up to. But damned if he could see signs of manipulation on her features.

So he started talking, grateful to be in comfortable territory. He watched her face as she listened to him, and enjoyed the shift and play of emotions she made no attempt to hide. But as he told her about his place, Sage realized something. He wasn't going to be getting the information he needed tonight. She was either really skillful at turning the conversation away from her—or she was as sweet and innocent as she appeared to be. But either way, it was going to take longer than he'd thought to find out exactly what she knew.

Oddly enough, that thought didn't bother him at all.

"You can't be serious." Laura Falkner dropped into her favorite chair and stared up at her daughter as if she'd just sprouted another head. "Three million dollars?"

Colleen drew a deep breath and realized that over the past few days, she had actually gotten *used* to the idea of having three million dollars. Okay, it was still a little weird to know that she wasn't going to have to worry about paying her cable bill—or anything else. But she'd finally come to grips with the idea that J.D. had meant for her to have this. That he'd wanted to help her reach her dreams, and she only wished that she could look him in the eye and say *thank you*.

Now, seeing her mother's reaction to her news made Colleen excited all over again. She was so glad she'd waited a few days to tell her mom. Colleen had wanted to get everything in order, have her plan set in stone so her mom couldn't argue with her over any of it. It hadn't been easy to wait. The past three days had been a whirl-wind of activity. She'd hardly had a chance to really sit down and appreciate just how much her life had changed.

And thanks to J.D.'s generosity, her mother's life was about to change, too.

Looking around the apartment she and her mom had shared when they first moved to Cheyenne, Colleen smiled. There were good memories here, but soon her mother would be making new memories. Enjoying the dreams she'd always tucked aside. And that pleased her, even though she knew she would miss her mom being so close by.

"I'm completely serious," Colleen replied, sitting in the chair opposite her mother. She reached out and took her mom's hands in hers. "It's all true. I'm going to get my nurse practitioner's license and buy myself a cabin in the mountains as soon as possible."

"Honey, that's wonderful." Laura pulled her hands free of her daughter's grasp, then cupped Colleen's face between her palms. "It's been your dream for so long, having a rural practice." Leaning back in her chair, she smiled even more broadly. "I'm delighted for you. Of course I was so sad to hear that Mr. Lassiter had died, but it was so good of him to remember you."

"It really was." She could see that now and accept J.D.'s bequest for the gift it was. She didn't care anymore if people talked. As Sage had pointed out, either way, she couldn't stop them, so why shouldn't she be grateful to J.D. and enjoy what he'd tried to give her?

Sage.

Just the thought of his name sent ripples of anticipation racing through her. It had been three days since their dinner together, and the one-time-only night to talk about J.D. had turned into something more. Sage had taken her to a movie two nights ago, and last night to a country-western club for dancing. She still didn't understand why he wanted to spend so much time with her, but she was enjoying herself more than she would have thought possible.

Dragging herself away from thoughts of Sage, Colleen focused on what she'd come to tell her mother. "There's more, Mom."

"More?" Laura just blinked at her. "You have financial security. You're about to make your dream job a reality. What's left?"

"Your dreams."

"What?" Her mother had the wary look in her eyes that she used to get when Colleen was a child and up to something.

"You know how you're always talking about moving to Florida to live with Aunt Donna?"

The two sisters were both widows now, and they'd discussed for years how much fun it would be if they could live together. But neither of them had been able to afford the move, so it just hadn't been possible. Until now.

"Yessss…"

"Well, you're going to."

"I'm—" Her mother's mouth snapped shut. "Don't be silly."

"It's not silly." Colleen had it all worked out in her mind. In fact, since the reading of the will three days before, she'd spent a lot of time on the phone, talking to lawyers, bankers, real estate agents and travel agencies. She had wanted every detail clear in her mind before broaching the subject to her mother. It had all been worth it, too, because as she started laying out her plans, Laura was dumbstruck.

"I've found a perfect house for you and Aunt Donna. It's gorgeous and it's in this lovely retirement community outside Orlando."

"You can't do that, you don't have the money yet and—"

Colleen cut her off quickly. "It's amazing how willing banks are to give you a line of credit based on a lawyer's sworn affidavit that a will's bequest is coming."

"You didn't."

"Oh, yes, I did." Walter Drake wasn't the easiest lawyer to talk to, but he had assured Colleen that she would be able to draw on her bequest almost immediately. And he'd gone out of his way to set up the line of credit with a local bank.

Laura pushed out of the chair and walked the few steps to the narrow, galley-style kitchen. Busily, she filled a teakettle with water and set it on the stove, all the while shaking her head and muttering.

"Mom—"

"You shouldn't have done that, Colleen," her mother said, not even looking at her. She turned the fire on under the kettle, then grabbed two mugs from a cupboard and dropped a tea bag into each of them. "I don't want you spending money on me. I want you to have that money to keep you safe."

Colleen's heart turned over. Her mom was the most unselfish person she'd ever known in her life. She always gave and never once had she done anything purely for herself. Well, that was about to change, whether she liked it or not.

Joining her mother in the kitchen, Colleen gave her a hard hug, then said, "I couldn't spend all of that money if I tried and you know it."

"Just the same—"

"Mom." Colleen tried another tack. "Getting a house for you and Donna, so you can live without the snow making your arthritis worse, that makes me feel *great*. And, I only put a down payment on it. I would never buy you a house you haven't even seen."

"I don't like this…"

"You will," Colleen said, hugging her again. "And anyway, if you don't like the house, we'll find something else. I just thought it would be a good idea because this community has people to take care of your yard and watch over your house while you're traveling—"

"Traveling?"

This was so much fun, it was like Christmas morning. Colleen grinned. "Yes. You're going to travel. Just like you always wanted to."

"Honey, enough. You know I can't let you do this. Any of it." Laura finally found her voice and naturally she was using it to try to turn down her daughter's generosity.

"Too late, it's already done." Colleen hurried back into the living room, grabbed her purse and carried it back to the kitchen. She set it onto the small round table, slid one hand inside and came back up with a batch of cruise brochures. Handing them over to her mother, she tapped her index finger on the top one.

"A world cruise?" Laura dropped into one of the kitchen chairs as if she'd suddenly gone boneless.

"Yes." Colleen really did feel like Santa. A tall, busty Santa with big feet. "It doesn't leave for another three months, though, so you and Aunt Donna have plenty of time to get your passports and shopping done, and I thought we could talk about your moving to Florida as soon as you get back. Of course, if you'd rather move right away, I understand, but I don't know that I'm ready to have you leave just yet and…"

She stopped talking when she saw the tears spill from her mother's eyes and run down her cheeks. "Don't cry. You're supposed to be happy! Did I mention that you and Aunt Donna are going to be sharing the presidential suite on your cruise? There are pictures in the brochure. You have a full balcony. And butler service and twenty-four-hour room service and—"

Laura choked out a laugh, then lifted one hand to her mouth, shaking her head in disbelief.

"Mom, are you okay?"

"I don't think so," she murmured, staring down at the brightly colored brochures displaying pictures of England, Scotland, Switzerland and more. "I can't let you do this, honey…"

"Mom." Colleen hugged her mother tightly, then leaned back and looked into watery blue eyes much like her own. "You've given me everything for so long. I want to do this. I *can* do this now and if you fight me on it—"

Laura laughed a little again. "You'll what?"

"I'll hold my breath." She smiled, hoping to coax an answering smile from her mother. Holding her breath had been her threat of choice when she was a little girl and using it now was a deliberate choice.

"You never could stop talking long enough to hold your breath for long," her mother finally said, and Colleen knew she'd won.

"Well, I had very important things to say. Just like now." She plucked one of the brochures from her mother's hands and spread it open, showing the sumptuous cabin her mother and aunt would be sharing on their twelve-week cruise. "Just look at this, Mom. Can you imagine?"

"No," she said, sliding one hand across the high-gloss paper, "I really can't."

"I'm going to want lots of pictures cluttering up my in-box."

"I'll email every day." She frowned. "They do have computers on board, right?"

"Absolutely. Complete with Skype. We can talk face-to-face whenever you have time." As she thought about it, she said, "Maybe we'll get you a computer tablet, too, so you can video chat with me from Stonehenge!"

"Donna's not going to believe this," her mother whispered, unable to tear her gaze away from the pictures of a dream of a lifetime coming true.

<u>Six</u>

A few hours later, Colleen sat across from Sage in a local coffee shop. "You should have seen my mother's face," she said, grinning at the memory.

"She must have been shocked." He could imagine. Hearing her talk about what she'd done for her mother had stunned Sage into silence himself.

Far from the grasping, manipulative woman he'd assumed her to be, she'd arranged for her mother and aunt to have the trip they'd always dreamed instead of spending her money on herself. Admiration flowed through him, along with the desire that had become as familiar to him as breathing over the past few days.

Since that first dinner hadn't brought him any information, Sage had made it his business to spend as much time with Colleen as possible. Though they hadn't been able to speak at the movies, watching her reaction to the drama playing out on the screen had fascinated him. Tears, laughter, a jolt of surprise at the happy ending—she was so easy to read and at the same time, so damn complicated he didn't know what to make of her.

Long ago, he had decided that women weren't to be trusted. That they turned their emotions on and off at whim, the better to acquire whatever they happened to be after at the time. Tears were a woman's best weapon, as he'd discovered early on. But on the surface, at least, Colleen seemed...different.

And that both intrigued and worried him.

"Oh, she really was." Shaking her head, she picked up her burger and took a bite, still smiling. "Mom and Aunt Donna have been planning fantasy trips for years. They go back and forth, deciding what hotels they'll stay in, what countries they'll see. They go online and look up cruise packages, just to torture themselves." She took a breath and sighed happily. "Knowing that they're going to actually get to go and *experience* everything they've always talked about is just...amazing."

"*You're* amazing," he murmured, thinking his voice was so soft it would be lost in the clatter and noise from the rest of the patrons surrounding them.

He should have known she'd hear him.

"Why?"

Sage shrugged, sat back in the booth and draped one arm along the back. "Most people, receiving a windfall like you did? They'd go out and buy themselves fast cars, a house that's too big and too expensive, all kinds of things. But you didn't. You bought your mother's dreams."

She smiled. "What a nice way to put it."

Her eyes were shining and that smile lit her face up

like a damn beacon. Something inside him turned over and he was pretty sure it was his heart. That was unsettling. Sage had spent most of his life carefully building a wall around his heart, keeping out anything that might touch him too deeply. His family was one thing. His brother and sister were a part of him, and he accepted the risk of loving them because there was no way he could live without them.

But to love a woman? To trust love? No. He'd nearly made that mistake years ago, and he'd steered clear of it ever since. He'd had a narrow escape and hadn't come away unscathed even at that. So the women he allowed into his life now were nothing like Colleen. They were temporary distractions…just blips on a radar that was finely tuned for self-protection. Colleen was something different. If she was who he now believed her to be, then he had no business being around her. But for the life of him, he couldn't stay away.

Frowning now, he said, "What about your plans? Your dreams?"

She picked up her iced tea and took a long drink. "Well, I already told you my main goal. I'm going to get my nurse practitioner's license."

"Because?"

"Because what I'd really like to do is have a rural practice," she said, leaning toward him over the table.

He caught himself wishing she was wearing that red dress again so he could get another peek at her luscious breasts. Instead though, she wore an emerald-green sweater over a white T-shirt with a slightly V-shaped neckline. Her jeans were soft and faded and hugged her curves like a lover's hands. And even the casual clothing couldn't dispel the desire that pumped through him just sitting across from her.

For a man who prided himself on his rational thinking and ability to concentrate on the task at hand, it grated that while she talked, all he could think about was laying her down atop the table and burying himself deep inside her.

"There are a lot of people in the high country who live so remotely it's hard to get into town to see a doctor," she was saying and he could read the excitement on her face with every word she spoke. "Or if they can, they can't afford it."

She kept surprising him.

Wanting to devote herself to a rural practice would be a hard, even dangerous way to build a career. Why wasn't she like other women? Why wasn't she making plans for spa trips and exclusive shopping excursions? Hell, she'd bought her mother and aunt an around-the-world cruise. But for herself, she wanted to live and work in the wilderness areas?

That thought settled in his mind and his brain drew up a series of uncomfortable images. Colleen trying to dig her way out of a blizzard. Colleen's little Jeep careening off a mountain road and sailing down into a rock-strewn canyon. Colleen freezing to death in her car because she'd gotten lost.

His stomach twisted into knots and he told himself that it was none of his business if she wanted to risk her life by working somewhere she had no knowledge of. He was only with her to find out what she knew. There was no real relationship between them. She wasn't his to protect.

But damn it, *someone* had to set her straight.

"Driving up into the mountains from Cheyenne is going to make for a hell of a commute. Especially in winter," he pointed out, with a warning note in his tone that he hoped would get past the spirit of adventure he saw so clearly in her eyes.

Colleen flashed him a smile that shone from those cornflower-blue eyes and hit him like a sledgehammer.

"That's part two of my plan," she said, clearly pleased with herself. "I'm not going to be commuting every day. That would be silly and time-consuming. Instead, I'm selling my condo and I'm going to buy a cabin or a small house higher up in the mountains."

Those mental images rose up again, only this time, he saw Colleen in a remote cabin, no help for miles around. An icicle dropped down his spine.

"And live there by yourself?" He didn't like the sound of that. Not that there were a million crazies running around the mountains or anything, but hell, you didn't need a human enemy to worry about. Nature could kill you just for the hell of it. And nature in the wilderness had attitude.

"I'm a big girl," she countered, airily brushing aside his concerns. "I can take care of myself."

"No doubt," he said, though he doubted it very much. "In the city. Where there are police to call if you need help. Neighbors right next door. Grocery stores. Not to mention that you grew up in California. What do you know about digging yourself out of ten-foot snowdrifts or how to stockpile firewood for winter? What do you know about driving on roads that haven't been cleared by the county after a storm?"

She frowned a little, then took a breath and admitted,

"Okay, there's a learning curve. But I can adapt. I'll figure it out as I go. It'll be another adventure."

"Learning as you go can turn it into a *final* adventure."

Sighing, Colleen pushed her lunch plate to one side, apparently losing her appetite as they talked. She took another sip of her iced tea, then set the glass down. "Why are you raining on my parade, Sage? You live up on the mountain and you love it."

"This isn't about shooting down your dreams, Colleen," he said tightly. "This is about being realistic. Thinking things through."

"I have thought it through. I've *been* thinking about this for years." She leaned even closer and Sage was caught in her eyes. "I could make a real difference in people's lives."

"Or end your own," he told her, hating that the shine in her eyes dimmed a little at his words. But better she be disappointed than in danger. "I was raised up there, Colleen. I know how to survive bad weather. More than that, I know not to turn my back on the mountain. I don't take anything for granted."

"You weren't born knowing all of that, though," she said, determination clear in her voice. "You learned. So can I."

Sage tore his gaze from hers and glanced around the coffee shop. He needed a minute to get ahold of himself. To keep from *ordering* her to stay off the damn mountain. Conversations rose and fell from the dozens of customers gathered in the sunlit restaurant. An occasional burst of laughter rang out, and the scent of coffee and hamburgers hung in the air. Coming here to the coffee shop had seemed like a good idea at the time. With the amount of tension he'd been living with the past few days, he'd figured that taking Colleen to a crowded place in the middle of the day was one way to help him keep a tight grip on his control. Naturally, that wasn't working out as he'd planned. Pretty much nothing had since he'd first met Colleen.

Shaking his head grimly, Sage noticed the number of strange faces among the crowd. Tourists were streaming into Cheyenne already, clogging up the streets and making the restaurants even more crowded than usual. Soon, the summer crowds would be arriving. By the end of July, thousands would be here for Cheyenne Frontier Days, reliving the Old West and enjoying the world's largest outdoor rodeo. There would be ten days of parades, carnivals and food fairs. For a second, he thought about the rodeo itself and remembered what it had been like to ride in front of thousands of cheering people.

Of course, it wasn't just the rodeo that drew people to Cheyenne. Summer was filled with tourist attractions from the eight-foot-tall painted fiberglass cowboy boots situated all over the city to the carefully staged, G-rated "gunfights" acted out daily by the Cheyenne Gunslingers. There were tours, art festivals and so many other activities, people came to Cheyenne and poured hundreds of thousands of dollars into the local economy.

As for Sage, he tried to stay on the mountain to avoid all of those people. He spent summers working with the horses and trying to forget that there was a world outside his ranch. Right now, though, summer was still months away and Sage's mind was preoccupied by the thought of Colleen, midwinter, all alone on the mountain. Cold dropped into the pit of his stomach and stayed there.

He shifted his gaze back to hers and barked, "You can't do it."

"Excuse me?" Her face went blank for an instant, and then her cheeks flushed with color and her eyes started firing sparks at him.

"Maybe I put that the wrong way," he allowed, since he hadn't been thinking at all when the words shot from his throat.

"You think?"

Colleen felt a quick spurt of irritation, then squashed it again quickly. Yes, Sage was being a little authoritarian, but he had backed off quickly, too, hadn't he? It was in his nature to take command. She could tell that by the way he stood, so tall and alert, his gaze constantly darting around his surroundings, as if checking for any problem that might arise. He was the kind of man who would always do what he could to keep people safe— whether they appreciated it or not.

And now, he was trying to protect *her*. Which made her feel good enough that she was willing to overlook the fact that he was also trying to keep her from doing what she'd always dreamed of doing. Actually, she could hardly believe she was out with him. Again. And the past few times she'd been with him had absolutely been dates.

Even Jenna agreed that this had moved way beyond him wanting closure after his father's death. There was something else going on here. They rarely talked about J.D. anymore, instead sharing stories about their lives and talking about everyday things. So if it wasn't about his dad, what else could it be? She wasn't sure, but she had decided to simply enjoy this time with Sage for as long as it lasted. Because she knew, at the heart of it, she just wasn't the kind of woman to capture and hold the interest of a man like him.

"I didn't mean that you *can't*," he was saying and Colleen came up out of her thoughts to focus her attention on him. "What I meant was that you can't just decide to live in what could be dangerous terrain while knowing nothing about survival." Colleen couldn't help it—she laughed. He looked so serious. So…growly. A small, tiny part of her thrilled to hear him trying protect her. But the reality was, she took care of herself very well.

"You make it sound as though I'm talking about moving to the middle of nowhere. This isn't the frontier, Sage. I'll be perfectly safe."

"Probably," he agreed, "but the country—especially the *high* country—can be dangerous."

She shook her head, then pushed her hair back from her face and gave him a patient smile. "How dangerous can it be, really?"

"Bears?" he fired back.

Before she could react to that disturbing thought, he continued.

"Mountain lions? Snakes? Blizzards?" He picked up his coffee and took a drink. "You're not in any way prepared for that kind of life, Colleen. You're asking for trouble if you do this."

He was right. She hadn't really considered any of that, and she could admit, at least to herself, that the thought of facing any *one* of those dangers on her own was… intimidating. All right, terrifying. But there had to be a way to make this work. "Fine, I admit you have a point."

He nodded.

"*But* if I knew how to handle myself in those situations, I'd be okay, right?"

"Sure," he said, one corner of his mouth curving up. "*If.* And that's a big *if.*"

"You could teach me."

"What?" He paused, coffee cup halfway to his mouth.

The idea had just leaped into her mind, but now that it was there, she ran with it. J.D. had told her so much about Sage—there was no one she would trust more to show her what she needed to know. "I promise, I'm a quick study. And you said yourself that you grew up in the mountains. No one knows them better than you do, right?"

"I suppose…" He set his still-steaming mug of coffee down onto the table and stared at her. And that penetrating stare was so…disconcerting, it was hard to draw an easy breath. His eyes were just hypnotic. At least to Colleen. Honestly, she was proud of herself just for being able to speak coherently while looking into those deep blue eyes of his. His jaw was tight, his dark brown brows drawn into a scowl, and still she thought he was the most gorgeous man she'd ever seen.

Every time he looked at her, she felt that swirl of batwings in the pit of her stomach—not to mention heat that burned just a bit lower. She'd never been so aware of herself as a woman as she was when she was with Sage Lassiter. He made her feel things she'd never experienced before and *want* things she knew she shouldn't.

Being with him was a kind of pleasurable torture, which had to be an oxymoron or something, but she really couldn't think of another way to put it. She enjoyed his company, but her body was constantly buzzing out of control around him, too. Which left her breathless, on edge and in a constant state of excitement. It was the most alive she'd felt in years.

"What do you think, Sage?" She kept her gaze fixed on his. "Will you show me what I need to know?"

His features froze and she watched a muscle in his jaw twitch spasmodically. His fingers drummed against the tabletop and he shifted in his seat. He was thinking about it, and Colleen anxiously waited to see what he would say.

Finally, her patience was rewarded.

"You want to learn to survive on the mountain."

"Yes." She bit her bottom lip.

"Fine," he said. "I'll teach you."

A wash of relief and something that felt like eager anticipation swept through her. "That's *great,* thank you."

He laughed shortly. "Save your thanks. By the time we're finished, you'll probably be cursing me."

"No, I won't." She shook her head and reached across the table to cover one of his hands with hers. "J.D. always told me how kind you were and I've really seen that for myself in the past few days."

He just stared at her through eyes that had been carefully shuttered. "J.D. was wrong. I'm not kind, Colleen."

His features were hard, his body language cold. He was pulling back from her even while he was within reach. She didn't know why. "If it's not kindness," she asked quietly, "what is it?"

He just looked at her for a long moment and she had the feeling he was trying to decide whether to answer her or not. Then she got her answer.

"You said you don't have a job to go to anymore, right?"

"No, I don't. I turned in my resignation at the agency." And hadn't that felt incredible? She had liked her job well enough, but now that her dream was within her reach, she didn't mind at all saying goodbye to the private agency. "Until I get my practitioner's license, I'm officially unemployed."

"All right then," he said, coming to some internal decision. "We'll start day after tomorrow. You come up to my ranch and stay for a few days. We'll go up the mountain from there."

"Stay? At your ranch?" Heat sizzled through her veins, and even while a delicious tingle settled deep inside her, Colleen felt a tiny niggle of worry.

He was going to teach her to survive in the mountains. But who could teach her how to survive a broken heart when this time with him was over?

Logan Whittaker was handsome, friendly and professional. Late thirties, he was tall, with nearly black hair, warm brown eyes and when he smiled, a disarming pair of dimples appeared in his cheeks. He wore a sports coat over a pair of black jeans and a long-sleeved white shirt, black cowboy boots betraying his Texas heritage.

As a partner at Drake, Alcott and Whittaker, he was able to meet with Colleen the next morning, when Walter Drake was busy elsewhere.

She walked into his office and took a quick, admiring look around. The room was huge, befitting a partner. Neutral colors, with navy blue accents, including a navy blue sofa and matching visitor chairs situated on one side of his massive desk. There was a blue-and-white-tiled fireplace on one wall with an empty mantel over it. No family pictures to clutter up his office.

The windows along the hallway boasted electric shades that were in a halfway-down position. It was all very businesslike but hospitable, much like Logan himself seemed to be.

"I really appreciate you seeing me on such short notice."

"Not a problem," Logan said, stepping forward to take her hand in a firm shake before steering her toward one of the visitor's chairs. "Walter and I are sort of working a tag team on the Lassiter will. We're each dealing with different angles, and sometimes the lines cross."

She had to smile. The slight hint of a Texas accent flavored his speech, but couldn't hide the fact that he seemed agitated and a little harried. "Having some trouble with J.D.'s will?"

He blew out a breath, took a seat in his chair behind the wide desk and then shot her a heart-stopping grin. "Is it that obvious?" A short laugh rumbled from his throat as he shook his head. "Let's just say there are some issues with the estate that I'm not at liberty to discuss and leave it at that."

"Well, that sounds frustrating."

"Oh, it is." He pushed one hand through his hair and said, "But I'll get it done."

The look in his eyes was sheer determination, and Colleen didn't doubt for a minute that he would succeed.

"Now, how can I help you, Ms. Falkner?"

"Colleen, please." She scooted forward to the edge of the leather chair and leaned her forearm on his desk. "Walter helped me set up a line of credit at a local bank, but—"

"What is it?" He gave her his full attention, and Colleen thought at any other time, she might have been mesmerized by his eyes. The man was exceptionally good-looking and when he looked at a woman with his complete concentration, she could only assume that most women melted into a puddle at his feet. As it stood now, though, Logan Whittaker, as handsome and compelling as he was, couldn't hold a candle to Sage Lassiter.

Letting go of that train of thought, she brought herself back to the business at hand. The reason she'd come here.

"I really just wanted to make sure everything is going through without any trouble." Shrugging, she added, "I'm about to sell my condo so I can buy something closer to where I will be working, and—"

He gave her a knowing smile. "And you're worried that something might go wrong with the dispersal of the will."

"Exactly." It was nice that he understood her concerns and didn't make her feel silly for having them.

"You have nothing to worry about," Logan told her. "J.D. set this will up in such a way that it would be almost impossible to contest it."

"Almost?"

He grinned. "Caught that, did you?"

"I did, and it's a little scary to think about. If someone contested the will, all of the bequests might be nullified, right?"

"It's possible, yes," he admitted, then leaned back in his oversize leather swivel chair. "But highly unlikely. J.D. was competent when he made his will. And it was his estate to divide how he saw fit. I know some of the family are upset with what that will said, but there's not much they can do about it. So to answer your question, I don't see any problems looming. Go ahead and sell your place. Buy the one you want."

Colleen released a breath she really hadn't been aware she was holding. Somehow she felt even more reassured than she had when talking to Walter. Maybe it was because the older lawyer tended to speak more in legal terms, and Logan made the process seem less confusing. "Thanks. I feel better."

"Happy to help," Logan said, rising to come around his desk. "I know this must be strange, suddenly coming into so much money. But it's all real, Colleen. You can trust it."

She stood up and offered her hand. This was what she'd needed to hear: the confirmation that her new life was about to begin. For some reason, she'd been half expecting someone to pull the rug out from under her and leave her sprawled, broken and bruised, on the floor. Metaphorically speaking, of course.

Now though, she would reach out and grab hold—with both hands—of the changes headed her way.

Logan walked her to his door and smiled. "Try to relax and enjoy all of this, Colleen. J.D. clearly wanted that for you."

"I think he did," Colleen agreed as she shook Logan's hand one last time. "I really appreciate your time."

"If you have any more worries, feel free to come back."

But she wouldn't be worried now. At least not about the bequest. Instead, she would worry about Sage Lassiter and how important he was becoming to her. When just the thought of his name sent an electrical charge buzzing through her, she knew she had *plenty* to worry about.

Seven

"Wow," Jenna chirped later that day. "According to Google, Sage Lassiter is worth about ten *billion* dollars." She glanced up from the laptop and fanned herself with one hand. "I mean I knew he was rich…but that is *seriously* rich."

The two of them were in Colleen's bedroom at her condo. The room was small but neat, with cream-colored walls, a bright quilt on the bed and dozens of jewel-toned pillows stacked against the headboard. Colleen looked at her friend, sitting cross-legged on her bed. "You're supposed to be checking real estate on the mountain for me."

"I am, on another webpage," Jenna said with a shrug. "But I can multitask. Besides, I had to look him up. You're going to stay at his ranch for a few days and I want to see what my friend's getting into. You know, I bet there are rich serial killers, too."

Laughing, Colleen said, "He's not a serial killer."

"No harm in checking," Jenna told her. "So, according to this website that is all gossip all the time, Sage made his first million by investing in some thingamajig for computers that his college roommate invented."

"Well, that tells me he believed in his friend, so that's nice."

"And made a boatload off that investment," Jenna continued, scrolling down the page, "which he then invested in several other inventors with great ideas."

"That's a good thing. He helped a lot of people get started and they all became successes." Colleen folded another T-shirt and dropped it into her suitcase. She would drive up to Sage's ranch in the morning and nerves were beginning to settle in. Three days at his house. God, she could hardly sit across from him in a restaurant without her body erupting in dangerous wants and needs. The next few days were going to be agonizing.

Unless, she thought wildly, something happened between them to release all this tension she felt building inside her. But if they did sleep together, then what? From everything she'd learned from J.D., she knew that Sage wasn't interested in a real relationship. And even if he were, he wouldn't want her, she knew that already.

So what would she gain by going to bed with him?

Lovely memories, her brain shrieked. *Orgasms galore,* her body chimed in.

She shivered again.

This had seemed like such a good idea, having Sage show her the mountains and how to avoid danger.

Which was really funny if you thought about it, because Sage himself was dangerous to her. He was becoming too important to her. While she planned her new life, looking forward to all the exciting things stretching out in front of her, Sage was in those mental images, too. He had become a part of the dream she'd nurtured for so long and she didn't know how to separate them now.

The only thing she *could* do was try to protect her heart from the inevitable crash that was headed her way.

"Hello?" Jenna demanded her attention. "Did you know he was that rich?"

In spite of everything, Colleen laughed. "It never crossed my mind to ask J.D. what Sage's bank account looked like."

"Well, it just doesn't seem fair, does it?" Jenna turned the laptop so that Colleen could see the screen, where an image of Sage stared out at her. "A man should not be allowed to be *that* amazing-looking *and* rich to boot. Just seems selfish somehow."

Colleen would have laughed, but she was staring at the image of Sage, drawn from some tabloid site. He looked impossibly handsome in a tux and was glaring at the camera even as the woman on his arm, last year's Oscar winner, beamed at the photographer as she draped herself against Sage's broad chest.

There it was, she told herself silently. Proof that whatever was between her and Sage wasn't permanent. Wasn't anything more than a temporary fantasy on her part, just a lot of chemistry that sizzled and flashed between them.

So, knowing it was all fleeting, what was she supposed to do? Stay home? Avoid Sage? Or should she accept the fact that this was all transitory and simply enjoy it for what it was? A swirl of expectation swam in her veins, side by side with a few slim threads of reality. It would be interesting to see which sensation finally won out.

"Anyway," Jenna was saying as she slapped the laptop lid down, shattering the spell Colleen had been under. "I found a couple of cabins for sale. One has a lot of land with it—like thirty acres—the other's close to a county road."

"Sounds great." She smiled appreciatively as Jenna handed over a piece of paper with the addresses. "I'll see if Sage can take me to look at them."

"We're depending on Sage a lot lately, aren't we?"

Colleen quirked a smile. "Is that the royal *we?*"

"It's the *you* we," Jenna said, leaning back against the headboard of Colleen's bed and stretching out her legs to cross them at the ankle. "You've really been seeing a lot of him and now you're off to stay with him at his place."

"Not *with* him," Colleen corrected, though her body hummed at the idea. "Just at his house."

"Uh-huh." Jenna just looked at her for a second or two, then she huffed out a breath. "It's crazy, I know, but I'm worried he's going to break your heart."

"What?" Surprised, Colleen stared at her friend.

"Okay, sure, I was caught up in the whole billionaire-suddenly-wanting-to-date-my-friend thing, too. But honestly, now that he's stuck around for a while, I'm just… uneasy."

"Why?" Colleen knew why Jenna was uneasy, of course. Because she still couldn't quite bring herself to believe that Sage was actually interested in her. But she'd like to hear her friend's reasons.

"Because he's too damn solitary," Jenna blurted. "Anybody who's alone *that* much? There's probably a reason and I don't want to see you get caught up in whatever his issues are."

Colleen laughed shortly.

"What's so funny?" Jenna demanded.

"Nothing." Waving one hand, she said, "It's just, I thought you were going to say what I've been telling myself. That I'm not the kind of woman he usually goes for. Not sophisticated enough or beautiful enough or rich enough for him."

"Please." Clearly offended, Jenna sat straight up. "He'd be lucky to have you. You're plenty beautiful and way better than sophisticated or rich, you're *real*. You have a warm and generous heart. Maybe sometimes too generous."

Colleen reached over and hugged Jenna tight. When she let her go again, she said, "Thanks for that. But don't worry, okay? I'm pretty sure that whatever this is, it's short-lived. I'm not going to let my too-generous heart get all gooey and involved. Honestly."

"You know the too generous thing was a compliment, right?"

"Absolutely."

"Good." Jenna nodded. "So…back to mystery mountain man."

"He's not a mystery," Colleen insisted. "And this isn't some romantic getaway. Sage is going to show me around the mountain and probably try to scare me out of the idea of living alone up there."

"If only he could."

"Thank you for your support," Colleen said wryly.

"Oh, I support you, sweetie." Jenna sat up, grabbed a T-shirt and folded it as she continued, "But you forget, I've lived in Wyoming all my life. I know how dangerous the mountains can be. Beautiful, yes, but also deadly if you're not careful."

Colleen started to talk, but her friend cut her off.

"I don't like the idea of you living in the high country all on your own." She waved one hand as if to dismiss the argument she didn't give Colleen a chance to make. "Yeah, yeah, feminists, hear us roar, but just because you *can* do a thing doesn't mean you *should* do it, you know?"

Colleen dropped onto the edge of the bed, pushed the suitcase out of the way and faced her friend. "Fine. I'm a little anxious about being alone up there, I admit it, but I'll get used to it. And Jenna, I'm not helpless or stupid. I'll take care and I'll make sure to get help if I need it."

"I know." Jenna nodded and shrugged helplessly. "Maybe I just don't want you to move away."

Colleen leaned in and gave her friend another hug. "I'll miss you, too. But we'll still see each other."

"Oh, you bet we will. You're not going to get rid of me *that* easy." Jenna handed her the folded shirt. "But do me a favor. When you see the cabins, even if you fall in love…don't make a hasty decision. I don't want you to rush into something that you won't be able to get out of easily."

That was good advice. And not just about the cabins. She was about to head off to stay at the home of a man who turned her knees to mush. Was she already in way too deep for her own good? Would she get out now if she could?

No.

Colleen thought about it while she finished packing and realized that if it would be smart to stay far, far away from Sage Lassiter…she'd rather be stupid.

* * *

It had only been a week.

But in that week, Sage had spent a lot of time with Colleen and when he wasn't with her, she was filling his mind. He still wasn't sure how she'd managed it, but whenever they were together, she actually got him to talk. He'd opened up to her about his ranch, his plans, his life—something he hadn't done with anyone else. Not even Dylan or Angelica.

Colleen had slipped up on him. He hadn't expected to actually *like* her. Hadn't thought that he'd want her so badly that every night was a torture and every day was a lesson in self-control. Plus, he was no closer to finding out what he needed to know than he had been before this started.

Was this a deliberate maneuver on her part? Suck him in, distract him with her big blue eyes and then set the sexual tension bar so damn high that he couldn't think straight?

If that was her plan, it was a damn good one.

Hell, he hadn't even *kissed* her. How could he be this torn up and feel so out of control over a woman he hadn't even *kissed?*

"And why haven't you kissed her?" he asked himself in disgust. Because he knew that the moment he tasted her, took that luscious, amazing mouth with his, that there would be no stopping. He'd have to have *all* of her. And that had not been the plan. But then, he'd expected that he would have answers by now. Since this was going to take longer than he'd thought, the plan had to change.

As that thought settled into his mind, Sage took his first easy breath in a week. Talking to her wasn't working, so he would seduce any secrets she held out of her.

He'd use sex—crazed, hot, sweaty, incredible sex—to find out if she was withholding any information he might need to contest the will.

Then when he had what he needed, he would walk away.

She wasn't the kind of woman to go for a one-night stand, and once she discovered that was all he was willing to offer her, she'd *let* him walk.

But first, he would have her. Under him. Over him. And then he'd finally be able to get her out of his mind.

He scrubbed both hands over his face, then adjusted the fit of his jeans, hoping to ease the ache that had locked around his groin for the past week. It didn't help. Nothing would. The only way to ease that pain was to bury himself inside Colleen and thankfully, that was about to happen. He'd felt the chemistry between them. Knew that she was strung as tightly as he was. Seducing her wouldn't be difficult.

She was going to be here. Every day. Every night. He could hear her voice in his mind again: *Will you show me what I need to know?* Oh, there was plenty that he wanted to show her and very little of it had to do with survival.

What the hell had he been thinking, asking her to stay here? "Must be a closet masochist," he muttered darkly.

Or he *had* been, before he'd altered his plan. But things were different now. When Colleen finally showed up here at the house today, he was going to do what he should have done days ago: kiss the hell out of her. And then he'd get her into his bed as quickly as possible and scramble her mind so completely, she'd tell him whatever he needed to know.

Gritting his teeth against yet another wave of desire

thrumming inside him, he turned into the stable and headed down the long center aisle. The familiar scents of horses, straw and leather combined to welcome him and he sighed in gratitude. One thing he could count on was that being with the horses he bred and raised eased his mind. Here, he could push thoughts of Colleen aside—however briefly.

He paused long enough to greet one of the mares who poked her head through the half door to her stall.

"Belle, you're a beauty," he whispered. The chestnut mare butted his shoulder with her head as he stroked her jaw and neck, murmuring soft words that had the animal whickering in delight. It was this he lived for. Being around these animals that he loved. Caring for them, training them. Horses didn't lie. Didn't betray you. They were who they were and you accepted them at face value. You always knew where you stood with an animal.

It was people who let you down.

"Hey, boss!"

Frowning at the interruption, Sage gave the horse one last pat and turned to look back at one of the cowboys who lived on his ranch. "What is it, Pete?"

"Thought you'd like to know your sister just drove up."

Of course she did. Grimacing tightly, Sage muttered, "Okay, thanks."

So much for looking in on the newest foal born on the ranch. Instead, he gave the mare another long stroke over her neck, then headed back out of the stable. Pushing one hand through his hair, he told himself that it seemed women were destined to plague him lately. Wouldn't you know his sister would show up on the very day he was at last going to taste Colleen Falkner?

Sage couldn't even remember the last time Angie had come up the mountain to see him. Hell, usually she was living in L.A., but when she did come home, she stayed at Big Blue and visited her friends in Cheyenne.

But this visit was different, wasn't it? She'd lost her father, and then lost faith in him. She was upset about the will and having lost control of Lassiter Media, he knew. What he didn't know was what he could do about it. He and Dylan had talked this through several times and neither of them had come up with a way to challenge J.D.'s will.

So far, it had been made plain to them all that J.D. had definitely been in his right mind when he had the will drafted, and fighting his last wishes might very well invalidate the whole document. Until they could be sure of their next moves, he and Dylan at least had agreed to take this slowly.

Since J.D. was gone now, that made Sage the head of the family—and he had to consider everyone's inheritances, not just Angie's. He didn't want to risk Chance losing the ranch, or their aunt Marlene losing her bequest.

As much as it pained him, Sage couldn't make this any easier on the sister he loved. All he could really do was listen. A damned helpless feeling for a man more accustomed to having the answers than scrambling unsuccessfully for them. Scrubbing his hands over his face, he pushed those unsettling thoughts from his mind and headed for the main house.

The ranch yard was laid out a lot like Big Blue, he thought as he walked across it. But that wasn't a homage to J.D., he assured himself. It just made sense. The main house was set back at the end of a curving drive.

A landscaped sweep of greenery and flowers spread out in front of it in barely tamed splendor. The barn, stables and cabins for the cowhands who worked and lived on the ranch were set farther back and there was a pool that curved around a rock waterfall, with a stone patio surrounding it.

And from every spot on his property, the views were tremendous. He'd had his architect build the house to accommodate the beauty and become a part of the mountains itself. Acres of wood and glass and stone made the house look as though it had always been there, as if it had grown from the rocks and the forest. Trees were everywhere, and the scent of pine flavored every breath.

In Wyoming, winter held on, sometimes even into summer, especially this high up the mountain. An icy wind tore at Sage's hair as he walked toward his sister. Angelica was just climbing out of her car when he approached, and one look at her told Sage that she wasn't in much better shape than she had been when he'd seen her a couple nights ago.

True to their plan, he and Dylan had dropped in on their sister at Big Blue. It still wasn't easy walking into that house, cluttered with memories, but for his sister, he was willing to bite the bullet.

Evan had been there too, of course, but the tension between the formerly happy couple was unmistakable. Evan was doing his best to make this work, but Angie was so hurt and angry at her father that there wasn't a lot of give in her at the moment. How they were managing to work together through this was a mystery to Sage. Judging by the tight expression on Angie's face now, that tension hadn't eased up any either.

"Sorry to just drop in," she blurted, shrugging into

a navy blue sweater that dropped to midthigh. "I had to get out of the house."

"You're welcome here anytime," Sage told her, mentally letting go of his plans for Colleen—at least until his sister was on her way again. "What's going on now?"

"What *isn't?*" she snapped, then stopped, gave him a sheepish look and said, "I'm sorry, Sage. Seriously, I'm acting like queen bitch of the universe and I can't seem to stop myself."

"Hey," he said, dropping one arm around her shoulder and pulling her in for a hug, "that's my baby sister you're talking about."

Angie wrapped both arms around his waist and held on. Tenderness swamped Sage as he simply stood there holding her, knowing there was nothing he could say to make things better. Since she was a little girl, Sage had done everything he could to protect her. To take care of her. He hated not being able to help her now.

After a long minute or two, she pulled back and looked up at him. "You always steady me. How do you do that?"

"It's a gift," he quipped and gave her another squeeze. "Now, you want to fill me in on what's happening?"

She leaned into him. "It's just a rumor."

"Plenty of them to go around," Sage said, giving her a squeeze. "Tell me what you heard."

Tipping her head back, she looked up at him and bit her lip. Then she finally blurted, "The word is, Jack Reed is interested in Lassiter Media."

Jack Reed. Sage wasn't really surprised...how could he be? Jack Reed had the reputation of a great white shark. He bought up companies in trouble, then broke them down to the bare bones and sold off the pieces.

If Reed was interested, then it wouldn't be long before more sharks started circling the Lassiter family. They couldn't afford to be divided right now. They had to stand together against all comers. Which was just what he told Angie.

"We *are* together," she argued.

"What we are is pissed," he said flatly. "We all are. And we're spending too damn much time trying to figure out what was running through J.D.'s mind when he made that will."

"I know, I know." She stepped away from him, pulled the edges of her sweater tighter and wrapped her arms around her middle. "My first instinct, you know, was to contest the will."

"Yeah, I felt the same way," he said, "so did Dylan." He didn't add that he and their brother hadn't been able to come to a decision.

She took a deep breath and tossed her hair back from her face. "I don't know what the right thing to do is anymore, Sage. I want that company, but now I don't know how to get it. Do I fight my father's dying wishes? Do I try to accept this? How?"

"The whole situation's screwed up, that's for damn sure. But we'll figure something out," Sage said. He knew what J.D. had done had eaten away at her confidence, her self-assurance—hell, even her own image of herself. Their dad had spent a lifetime building her up and then with one stroke of the pen, he'd torn her down.

Why?

She laughed shortly and threw both hands into the air. "I'm a mess, sorry. I shouldn't have just driven up here and thrown myself on you. But I really needed someone to talk to. Someone who would understand."

"You can drop in on me any damn time you want and you know that, Angie," he told her. "But just out of curiosity, where's Marlene?"

"Oh, she's at the ranch," she said, and started walking toward the wraparound porch on the main house. Sage matched his strides to her shorter ones. "And yes, she's always willing to listen, but she can't be objective about Dad...and I really wish Colleen were still at Big Blue. She was super easy to talk to."

Yeah, he thought. Colleen was easy to talk to. Easy to look at. She also made it easy for him to forget why he'd started all of this.

As if just thinking about her could make her appear, an old red Jeep pulled up the drive and everything in Sage quickened. Like a damn kid waiting for a date with the girl of his dreams, he felt his heartbeat thundering in his chest, and an all-too-familiar ache settled low in his gut and grabbed hold.

"Well," Angie said thoughtfully, with a pointed glance at him. "This is interesting."

Instantly, Sage tamped down the internal fires raging through him. He didn't need his sister making more of this than there was. "It's not what you're thinking, so dial it down."

"Really?" she asked as the car engine cut off and the driver's side door opened. "Because that looks like a suitcase she's pulling out of her car...."

His insides tightened even further. "Don't even start, Angie...."

Colleen wrangled her overnight bag out of the car and set it at her feet. She looked at the ranch house and quickly swept it in one thorough gaze. It was smaller than Big Blue, but not by much. Its windows gleamed in the afternoon sun and the long wraparound porch boasted plenty of chairs for sitting out and enjoying the view. The honey-colored logs looked warm and inviting, the scent of pine was pervasive, and the two people on the porch were both watching her.

She hadn't expected to find Sage's sister here, too, but maybe that was a good thing. All morning, Colleen's stomach had been twisting and turning in anticipation of her arrival here at Sage's ranch. For longer than she cared to think about she had been fascinated by him. And now that they'd actually been spending time together, that fascination had escalated into something that was as scary as it was thrilling. Having Angie as a buffer might make these first few minutes easier.

"Angie, hi." Though she spoke to his sister, Colleen's gaze went first to Sage, and even that one brief connection with his intense blue eyes sent goose bumps racing along her spine.

"Hi, yourself." Angelica walked out to meet her and gave Colleen a hug. "I've missed you since you moved out of Big Blue."

"I missed you, too." Focusing on his sister gave Colleen the chance to tear her gaze from Sage's. "How is everyone doing? Marlene?"

"She really misses Dad. A lot. We all do, of course, but…" Angie shrugged. "It's hard. And since the reading of the will, it's even harder." Taking a deep breath, she looked up at Sage. "Why don't you get Colleen's suitcase and I'll walk her in."

"Oh, that's okay, I can—"

Sage nudged her hand off the handle, and a now-familiar buzz of sensation hummed from her fingers, up her arm, to rocket around in the center of her chest.

He looked at her, and in his eyes, she saw the realization that he'd felt it, too. That electric spark that happened whenever they touched. As if a match had been held to a slow burning fuse that was about to reach the explosives it was attached to.

Then he picked up her suitcase as if it weighed nothing—and Colleen knew she hadn't packed light. For another long second, he looked at her and Colleen's heart beat began to race. Her mouth went dry, her knees went weak and if Angie hadn't been there, watching the two of them, she might have just thrown herself at Sage.

"Come on," Angie said then, splintering that happy little fantasy. Colleen followed her into the house and once she was there, she buried those feelings in the curiosity she had for Sage's ranch. She'd heard J.D. describe it, of course, but the reality was so much more.

Outside, it was set up much like the Big Blue. Outbuildings, barns, stables, though from what she'd seen at a quick glance, there was a much bigger corral for working horses than J.D.'s ranch provided. Obviously, that made sense, because she knew that Sage bred and raised racehorses. But it was the *inside* of the main house that had her captivated.

It, too, was constructed of hand-hewn logs, but there the similarity with Big Blue ended. Instead of the ironwork that made up much of the Lassiter home ranch, Sage's place was all wood and glass. Wood banisters on the wide staircase, intricately carved to look like vines climbing up posts. Bookcases that looked as though they'd been sculpted into the walls, boasted hundreds of leather-bound and paperback books.

The wide front windows afforded a view that was so spectacular it took her breath away. Despite the number of trees on the property, the view was wide-open and provided a glimpse of the valley and the city of Cheyenne that at night must be staggering. A stone fireplace dominated one wall and the hand-carved mantel displayed pictures of his brother and sister and a young couple who must have been his biological parents.

While Sage and Angie talked, their conversation veering from muted tones to half shouts, Colleen wandered around the great room. Oak floorboards shone in the sunlight slanting through the windows. Brightly colored rugs dotted the floor, adding more warmth to a room that rang with comfort. Overstuffed brown leather chairs and sofas were gathered in conversational knots and heavy oak tables were laden with yet more stacks of books. She loved it.

The house was perfect and she couldn't wait to explore the rest of it. It was just as she would like her own home to be—on a smaller scale, of course. A comfortable refuge.

"You don't understand," Angie was saying and had Colleen turning around to face the siblings. "Evan is acting as if this is nothing. He keeps offering to let me run the company. But he doesn't get that him *giving* me control isn't the same as *having* control. He's trying to take a step back for me at the office, but I don't want him doing that, so it's a vicious circle. He thinks I should have control, and I want it, but if Dad *didn't* want me to have it, how can I try to claim it? We're arguing all the time now, and I can't help wondering why Dad did this. Did he want Evan and I to break up? Or was he really that disappointed in me?"

Colleen saw the torment on Sage's face and when he reached for his sister, pulling her in tight and wrapping his arms around her, Colleen felt a pang in her tender heart. He was so kind. So loving. Yet when she'd told him just that, he'd denied it. Why couldn't he see it?

"Dad loved you," he said simply. "Something else is going on here, Angie, and we will find out what it is."

His gaze speared into Colleen's and she felt a quick bolt of ice that snaked along her spine and made her shiver. There was nothing tender in that look. But before she could really wonder what he was thinking, the expression dissolved once again into concern for his sister.

Angie pulled away, spun around and looked at Colleen. "You're the one who spent the most time with him toward the end. Did he tell you why he was doing this? Why he cut me out as if I were nothing?"

With both Lassiters staring at her, Colleen felt completely ill at ease. She didn't have answers for them, though she wished she had.

Shaking her head, she could only say, "No, Angie. He didn't talk about his will with me. I had no idea what he was going to bequeath to everyone."

"That's really not an answer though, is it?" Sage muttered and her gaze locked on his. The shutters were in place, but even with him closing her out, she felt the cold emanating from him. Only minutes ago, he'd given her a look filled with heat, and now it was as if he'd shut that part of himself down.

"He talked to you, Colleen," he prodded. "If not about his will, then about how he was feeling. What he was thinking. And you know what he said. So tell us."

She blinked at him. "What can I tell you that you don't already know? He loved you all. He talked about you with such warmth. So much pride…"

"Then why would he do this?" Angie demanded. *"Why?"*

"I just don't know." Colleen sighed heavily. "I wish I did."

Sage's features went very still, as if he were considering what she said and wondering if she was holding something back. Finally he muttered, "Angie, she doesn't know. No one does. *Yet.* We'll find out, though, I swear."

"For all the good it'll do," she said and forced a smile. "I'm really sorry. I don't mean to dump on you guys. I'm just so torn up about this and so…*confused.*"

"Your father loved you, Angie," Colleen said softly. "He was proud of you."

Her eyes glistened with tears, but she blinked them back and lifted her chin. "I want to believe you, Colleen. I really do."

"You can."

"I hope so." Nodding, she turned to her brother. "I'm gonna go. I promised Marlene I'd take her into town for a nice dinner, and if I'm going to make it, I've got to start back now."

"Okay," Sage said, dropping a kiss on her forehead. "Try not to worry. We'll work this out."

"Sure." She flashed a smile at Colleen. "And now, I can leave you two alone to do…whatever you were planning before I showed up."

Colleen flushed. "Oh, please don't get the wrong idea. I'm just here so Sage can show me what life in the mountains is like. I want to move up here and—"

"You're going to move here?" Angie interrupted.

"Not *here,* here," Colleen corrected with a fast glance at Sage to see what his reaction was to his sister's teasing. But it was as if he wasn't listening to Angie at all.

His gaze was locked with hers and the heat in his eyes warmed her all the way to her toes. Still, she added for Angie's benefit, "Just here in the mountains, here."

She was babbling and now felt like an idiot. Of course Angie hadn't meant anything by what she'd said. She knew that there was nothing between Colleen and Sage. Nothing but a lot of chemistry that neither of them had acted on.

"Right, so you have a place in mind?"

"I have the addresses of a couple of cabins that are for sale. I was hoping Sage could show me where they are."

"Oh, my big brother is so *helpful,* I'm sure he won't mind at all." She smiled at him. "Will you, Sage?"

"Don't you have somewhere to be?" he asked pointedly.

Brother and sister stared at each other for a long minute or two, then finally Angie said, "Yeah. I guess I do. After dinner with Marlene, I'm meeting Evan in town tonight. We both thought it would be better to talk away from the office. It's just too…hard when we're there. But we do have to talk about plans for the company."

"That's good, Angie."

"In theory," she said. "We'll have to see, now that he's my *boss.*"

Colleen winced and wished she knew why J.D. had done this to his daughter. She would love to be able to give Angie a reason. An explanation. Something. But she simply had no idea why he would turn his family on its head like he had. And she couldn't help but feel guilty every time she thought about what Angelica was going through. She'd been hurt by her father's will while Colleen had been given a gift for which she was immensely grateful.

"Anyway," Angie said, crossing the room to hug Colleen. "You guys have fun or whatever. Don't let him turn you into Dan'l Boone or something, okay?"

Colleen laughed. "I don't think that's going to be an issue."

"You never know when the hermit of the mountain's involved."

"'Bye, Angie," Sage said firmly.

"Uh-huh." Angie shifted a sly look between the two of them then flashed a knowing smile at Colleen. "I'm sure Sage will show you *everything* you'll ever need to know."

And with that loaded insinuation, she left, Sage walking her out. Alone in the great room, Colleen found herself suddenly wondering if the lessons she came to learn weren't going to be very different than what she'd expected.

Eight

Once his sister was gone, Sage went back into the house and stopped in the doorway of the great room. Colleen had her back to him as she stared out the windows at the wide, uninterrupted view of trees and sky. His gaze raked her up and down and his body roared into life in response.

Hell, he'd been with beautiful, glamorous women who spent hours in front of mirrors, and had their own fashion stylists, hair people, makeup artists, and he'd never felt the pulse-pounding desire for them that he did for Colleen. Her hair was loose, hanging over her shoulders in a windblown tousle of waves and curls. She wore jeans, sneakers and a red sweater over a white shirt. And she looked amazing.

As if sensing his presence, she turned to face him and their eyes locked.

"I feel really bad about all of this will business," she said, her soft voice barely discernible in the cavernous room.

A brief spark of suspicion rose up inside him. Was she going to confess to conspiring with J.D. to cheat Angie out of what was rightfully hers? Hell, he almost hoped not, because he *really* wanted to seduce it out of her. "Why should you?"

"I know how upset she is over the will…and yet for me, it was life changing."

"For her, too," Sage said wryly.

She winced. "I know. I wish I could help."

With the afternoon sunlight streaming in through the window behind her, Colleen looked as though the tips of her hair were dusted with gold. She seemed to shimmer in that soft light and damned if he didn't feel that lurch of something that was more than attraction. More than simple desire.

Shaking his head, he asked, "You actually mean that, don't you?"

"Of course I mean it," she said, clearly confused by the question. "Why wouldn't I?"

Why indeed. If she was hiding something, she was damn good at it. And if she was innocent—that didn't change anything. He still wanted her and he would still *have* her.

"Never mind," he said, walking toward her in long, easy strides. "Let me see the addresses of those cabins."

She dug the paper out of her pocket and handed it over. He knew both places. One wasn't far. The other was much higher up the mountain. "Okay, let's go take a look."

* * *

"This is Ed Jackson's place," Sage said as he steered Colleen down the rocky path toward the small one-bedroom cabin. The first address she'd given him was about two miles higher up the mountain from Sage's ranch. The roads were in good repair, but the sharp curves and the straight-down drop off the edge were enough to give even the best drivers nightmares.

And he hadn't missed the fact that Colleen had had a death grip on the armrest every time he maneuvered around one of those curves that had been carved out of the mountain. But now that they'd arrived, the look on her face told him that she was so entranced by the setting she'd already forgotten the treacherous ride to get there. He held on to her hand as they took the narrow path to the front door, relishing the buzz of sensation that simply touching her caused.

The flower beds had long ago gone to seed and now there were only monstrous weeds fighting each other for space. The cabin itself was well built, but the white paint on the wood-plank walls was cracked and peeling. The front porch still boasted two chairs, and he remembered coming up here as a kid to find Ed and his wife sitting side by side, talking and laughing together. But then Helen had died five years ago and Ed lived here alone, refusing to move to the city. Finally, though, age had conquered his stubbornness, forcing him to put the home he loved up for sale and move to an assisted-living apartment in Cheyenne.

"It's pretty," she said, stopping to take it all in. "I love all the trees standing like guarding sentries around it."

"Nice spot," he agreed, trying to keep his mind off the

fact that she was close enough to touch. Close enough to— "Come on. I'll show you the inside."

"We can get in?"

"Ed always left a key above the doorframe." He found it, unlocked the front door and stepped into the past. The furnishings were at least forty years old and the air smelled of neglect and loneliness.

He watched as Colleen walked through the small house, checking out the tiny bedroom, the single bath and then the functional but narrow kitchen. Every window sported a view of the surrounding forest and the deep ravine that tracked off to one side of the house. "Why's the owner selling?"

He told her Ed's story and watched as sympathy filled her eyes. She was intriguing. Always. He liked that she cared why a house was for sale and that she felt pity for the man forced by time to give up the house he loved. He felt a swift stab of something beyond the pulsing desire still throbbing inside him, but he ignored it and looked at the cabin through objective eyes.

"You'd have to get a generator," he said, scanning the interior. "Ed didn't care about losing power, but I'm thinking you would."

She smiled and his heart rate jumped into a gallop. "You're right."

"You've got a wood-burning stove, so that's good," he continued, slapping one hand down on the dusty cast-iron fireplace in one corner of the living room. "But those pines along the side of the house will have to be cut way back or down altogether. Too dangerous. A heavy snowfall or a high wind could bring them crashing down on your roof. Not to mention, you should have a clearing around the house in case of forest fires."

"But those trees have been there for *years*."

"Yeah, Ed wasn't worried about the *what-ifs,* because he could patch a roof or get out there and hack out a clearing fast if he needed to." He paused meaningfully. "You couldn't."

She frowned slightly, walking through the room, running her fingertips across the backs of the chairs, straightening framed photographs on the walls.

"Structure's sound enough, I guess," he mused, looking around in an effort to keep from staring at her. "But you'd have to have an inspection to be sure. County road's at the end of the drive, so the snow would get cleared fairly quickly out there."

She glanced at him. "What about the drive itself?"

He looked at her then and shook his head. "The county's not going to clear your drive. You'd have to get a snowblower or hire someone to come in after a storm."

Colleen nodded and huffed out a breath as she considered everything he was saying. She was getting a hard lesson in what it meant to live so far from the city, and he almost felt sorry for her. Almost, but not quite, because he still didn't like the idea of her being up here on her own. There were women on this mountain capable of taking care of any kind of emergency, and he knew that. But Colleen was city through and through, and she had no idea of what she might be letting herself in for.

"You'll want the roof checked out, too," he added. "We had heavy snows last winter and Ed wasn't in shape to take care of things like that himself."

"Right. Another inspection," she murmured, looking around the room wistfully.

"This lot's on high ground, so you don't have to worry too much about spring runoff, but you should have the gullies cleared so melting snow won't get backed up and flood the house."

She laughed a little. "So I have to worry about the snowfall and then about when the snow melts."

"Pretty much." He leaned against one wall and watched as she peered through the kitchen window at the surrounding trees.

"How long did Ed and his wife live here?"

"About forty years," he said with a shrug. "After Helen died, Ed didn't visit much with anyone. They never had kids—it was always just the two of them. And without her, he kept to himself. Didn't really keep up with the cabin, either."

"He missed her." She turned to look at him.

Gaze locked with hers, he nodded. "Yeah, he did."

Which was yet another reason to keep to yourself. If you never let anyone in, you didn't miss them when they were gone. He'd learned that lesson as a kid—and then again later on, when he should have known better, but took a risk, only to be slammed for it.

"I want to look around outside," she said and he wondered if she could read minds. She was staring at him oddly and she'd suddenly gone quiet, and that just wasn't like Colleen.

But he followed her out, locked the door after them and returned the key to its resting place. She walked to the end of the porch, leaned on the railing and gazed out over the rocky ravine that dropped from the edge of the porch and ran down the side of the mountain. Her hair trailed over her shoulders and as she leaned out farther, her jeans tightened over her behind, making Sage's breathing a hell of a lot harder to control.

Then everything changed.

He heard a snap, then a squeak of alarm, and he was moving before he even realized it. In a blink, he reached out and caught her arm as the railing gave way. He heard the crash and rattle as the heavy wood barrier, rotted by time and weather, clattered and rolled down into the rocks below.

Pulling Colleen tight against him, he wrapped both arms around her and held on. He felt her trembling and knew that he was doing the same damn thing. "I told you he hadn't kept the place up." His voice came out in a harsh rasp of tension and what felt a lot like fear. "Never lean on a railing you're not sure about. Hell. Never lean on a railing no matter what."

"Good advice," she murmured, her voice muffled against his chest. When she lifted her head and looked up at him, Sage felt the last of his control snap as completely as that rotted-out railing had.

Her mouth was *right there.* Her breathing was fast and the pulse point in her throat throbbed. He knew she was shaken. So was he. If he hadn't grabbed her so quickly, she might now be at the bottom of that damned ravine. Broken. Bleeding. Hell, she'd have been lucky to survive the fall.

But she hadn't fallen. And now she was pressed close to him and when his control snapped, all he could think was *thank God.* He bent his head, covered her mouth with his and tasted her for the first time.

Heat slammed into him and Sage surrendered to it. His kiss was hard and fierce and desperate. No time for subtle seduction. This was need. Hot and thick and running through his body like lava. He ground his mouth over hers and felt her surrender when she lifted her arms to wrap them around his neck.

He groaned in response and flipped them around until her back was braced against the cabin wall. His tongue parted her lips and he delved deep, determined to taste all of her after waiting so long. Longer than he'd ever waited before to claim a woman he desired. And he'd never wanted a woman as he wanted Colleen.

Fire roared through his veins, blurring his mind, leaving only his body in charge, and the aching throb in his groin let him know he couldn't wait much longer. Need pounded inside him, feeding the flames threatening to consume him. Her breasts pressed to his chest, her fingers sliding up into his hair and all he could think was *too many clothes*.

The icy-cold wind sliding off the top of the mountain didn't deter him as he reached down and tugged the hem of her shirt up. She shivered, but continued kissing him, giving him everything she had, pouring her own need and desire into the melding of their mouths.

His hands cupped her breasts and she gasped, tearing her mouth from his to lean her head back against the cabin wall and arch her body into his touch. Even through the fragile lace of her bra, he thumbed her nipples until she was groaning, leaning into him, offering herself.

And he took. Lifting the bra up and out of his way, Sage looked his fill of the full, luscious breasts that he hadn't been able to stop thinking about since the first night he'd seen her in that red dress. Her dusky-rose nipples were hard and erect and he couldn't help himself. He dipped low and took first one, then the other into his mouth, rolling that sensitive tip between his lips and tongue, scraping the edges of his teeth across the pebbly surface until she was sobbing his name. She held his head to her tightly and when he suckled her she actually shrieked. That unfettered sound went straight to his groin and pushed him to take more. To give more.

To have it all.

He straightened up, dropped his hands to the waistband of her jeans and quickly undid the snap and zipper. Their eyes were locked on each other as he dipped one hand down, sliding across her abdomen, beneath the sliver of elastic of the panties she wore, and then delved deeper, cupping her hot, wet core. At his first touch, her so-expressive eyes glazed over and she rocked her hips into his hand, silently asking for more. But he held still, not moving, not stroking, torturing them both. He luxuriated in the feel of her hot, slick flesh beneath his hand and gritted his teeth as he fought for control. Then he slid the pad of his thumb across one particularly sensitive spot and her body jerked in response.

Her breath hissed in and out of her lungs, her eyes grew wide, her lips parted and her tongue swept out to lick them. He bent his head and kissed her briefly as he continued to tease her, stroking that bud of sensation, enjoying the tremors that continued to rack her body as she twisted and writhed in his grasp.

"Sage, please…" She tore her mouth from his to beg him for the release he continued to keep just out of her reach. "You have to," she murmured, her gaze imploring him, pleading with him to ease the coiled tension inside her. "Touch me. Take me."

He lost himself in her eyes and gave her what she needed. What they *both* needed. Sage dipped his fingers into her depths, stroking, caressing. Her movements quickened, her breath was strangled, and still she whispered his name as the cold air wrapped itself around them in an icy embrace. He felt the magic of her tight heat as she groaned and writhed wildly against him. She clung to his shoulders, widened her stance to give him more access and moved with him at every stroke of his hand.

He watched her. Couldn't take his eyes off of her. He'd never seen anything more beautiful than Colleen in the grip of passion. Small, breathless sounds escaped her throat. She chewed at her bottom lip and locked her gaze with his until all he could see of the world were her amazing, deep blue eyes.

Everything she felt shone clearly on her face, so he knew when her climax was hurtling toward her. Knew when she reached the precipice and fused his mouth to hers when she finally bolted over the edge, trembling and quaking in his arms with the force of her release.

And when it was done, he wanted more. He was hungrier for her now than he had been before he had touched her, and damned if he was going to wait any longer.

"Come with me," he blurted, hoping she could hear him through the sexual haze clouding her mind and her eyes.

He didn't bother doing up her jeans again. He'd only have to undo them in a second or two. Taking hold of her hand, he marched back to the front door, grabbed the key and unlocked it. Pulling her inside after him, he threw the bolt on the door, then grabbed her and held her tightly enough to him that she couldn't help but feel the hard thickness of his own arousal pushing into her. Still, she was a little nervous about going into someone else's home like this.

"Can we do this? In a stranger's house?"

"Ed's not a stranger to me," Sage whispered. "Trust me, he'd approve. So? What do you think?"

Colleen hoped he was right about what Ed would think because she really didn't want to waste this moment. He was staring down into her eyes and her sense of caution was washed away in a rising tide of desire.

"Yes," she whispered in answer to his unspoken question. "Yes, Sage. Now."

She licked her lips and then went up on her toes to kiss him as hungrily as he had kissed her the first time. He met that passion with all of his own. Tearing her sweater off, he then pulled up her shirt and whipped it over her head before tossing it to the nearest chair. She was pulling at his jacket, too, then ripping at his shirt. He heard a couple of buttons sail across the room and he didn't give a damn. Anything to have her skin against his. Now. This minute.

No more waiting.

He was blind to everything but her. Sage had never known such all-consuming desire before. Sex had always been fast and hot and no deeper than a puddle. This was more because *she* was more. But he didn't want to think about that now. Didn't want to consider just *why* he was so desperate to have her. It was enough that he needed. Wanted.

She pulled free of the kiss, reached for his belt buckle and undid it, her gaze on his, never shifting. *Nothing sexier than a woman who can look you in the eye while getting naked.* She unbuttoned his jeans and then reached inside to cup her hand around his aching, rock-hard erection.

At the first touch of her fingers, he damn near lost it and that was humiliating to admit, even to himself. But he was wound so tight, hurting so bad, it wasn't surprising. Her grip was strong and gentle, firm and soft, and the touch of her fingers on his sensitized skin was like putting a match to dry kindling.

"Don't." Gritting his teeth, he took hold of her hand and pulled it free as he gave her a half smile to take the sting out of his sharp warning. "You keep that up, and it's over before we get started."

"Okay then. Can't have that." She toed off her sneakers before taking hold of her jeans to drag them off.

"I'll do that," he said, stroking his hands across her breasts, cupping them in his palms, thumbing her nipples, until she swayed unsteadily on her feet. "I've been thinking of nothing but stripping you out of your jeans for the past few days. I want to enjoy the moment."

"Hope it's okay if I enjoy it, too," she whispered.

"Absolutely." Smiling, he dropped his hands to the waist of her jeans and slowly pushed them down over her generous, gorgeous hips. He took that tiny swatch of lace panties with him as he went, and going down on his knees, he left a trail of kisses along her flesh as it was exposed to his gaze. "You have an amazing body," he murmured.

She squirmed in his grasp and reached down to slide her fingers through his hair, dragging her nails across his scalp. "My boobs are too big," she argued in a quiet voice. "And so are my feet and my butt."

"You're wrong," he whispered and as if to prove a point, he slid his hands around to cup her behind, his fingers kneading her tender flesh until she whimpered and swayed unsteadily. "You have a great butt and your breasts…beautiful."

She held on to his shoulders to keep herself steady

and then stepped out of her jeans when he wanted her to. Then she was naked, standing there in a splash of watery sunlight, as glorious as he'd known she would be. He ran his hands over the line of her hips and all the way down her long, shapely legs to her narrow feet. "I love your curves. A man could get lost in your body and happily stay that way."

She cupped her hand under his chin and tipped his head back so she could look into his eyes. "You mean that," she asked after a long second or two, "don't you?"

"Babe," he assured her, "your body is a wonderland."

She had curves and he liked them. She had long legs and he wanted them wrapped around his hips, pulling him deeper into her body. And the dark blond curls at her center were at just the right height for him to do something he'd been dreaming of doing for far too long.

Still looking up at her, Sage reached out to brush those curls aside, clearing a path for his mouth, his tongue. She knew what he was about to do. Her eyes went wide and she sucked in a deep breath and held it. "Sage…"

"I want to taste all of you," he said and leaned in, covering her heat with his mouth.

She gasped and arched into him, her fingers digging into his shoulders, her short, neat nails scraping his skin. She wobbled unsteadily, but his hands on her butt kept her still, held her in place.

He licked and kissed and stroked and fed the frenzy leaping inside him. He sensed the tension in her body and tightened it with every slide of his tongue. His hands ran up and down her thighs, over her hips, and then dipped down so that he could invade her heat even while he tasted her.

The world shrank down until there was only Colleen. Her taste, her scent—she was all. She was everything. Every soft moan and gasp that escaped from her throat made him more frantic to feel her body bucking under his. He sensed she was close to another climax, and this time, he was going to be buried deep inside her when she came.

And suddenly he couldn't wait another second to bring them together in the only way that mattered. He pulled away, stripped off his jeans and laid her down on the threadbare rug with its pattern of faded pastel flowers. He levered himself over her as she reached for him, parting her legs, so ready, so eager, so—

"Damn it."

"What?" She shook her head, blindly blinking to bring him into focus. "What is it? Why'd you stop? Please, don't stop."

He dropped his forehead to hers and if he'd been strong enough, he would have jumped to his feet and kicked himself. But hell, he hadn't carried protection around with him in the hopes of getting lucky since he was a kid. "Have to stop. No condom."

"No problem."

He lifted his head, stared down into her eyes and asked, "You're covered?"

She licked her lips again, driving him further along the road of no return. "I am. I went on the pill a couple of months ago to regulate my period. As long as you're healthy, we're covered."

Relief flooded him along with a renewed pulse of desire that damn near strangled him. "I'm so healthy I should be two people."

She choked out a laugh. "I only need one of you at the moment."

He grinned. Hell, he'd never talked with a woman once he had her naked. He'd never joked with one, either. Colleen was different on so many levels from every other woman he'd ever known. There was another hard lurch in his chest as his heart thudded like a jackhammer. He wasn't going to examine anything here. Now wasn't the time for thinking—it was just about feeling.

"That's what you're gonna get, babe," he promised and moved to cover her body with his.

Finally, skin to skin. The soft smoothness of her flesh sang against his. Her breasts rose and fell with the quickness of her breath and she lifted one leg to stroke her foot along his calf. Sensations coursed through him, too fast and too many to count. And he didn't need to. Didn't need to worry about a damn thing but getting where he needed to be.

He eased back on his haunches, looked down at her and spread her wide. Stroking her core with his fingertips, he smiled as she twitched and writhed before him, as frantic, as desperate as he.

"Sage, don't make me wait anymore." She lifted her hips in invitation and offered a weak smile. "If you're not inside me soon, I may explode."

"Can't have that," he said, and leaned over her, pushing his body into hers in one swift, sure stroke.

"Sage!" She arched up off the floor at his invasion and he held perfectly still, though it cost him, until she began to adjust to the size of him. Once she had, she moved, lifting her hips, taking him deeper. That provocation was all he needed. He moved against her, his hips rocking, settling into a fast, hard rhythm that she matched. Breaths mingled, kisses lingered, as bodies raced along the line of tension stretched so tautly between them. Hands explored, whispered words lifted into the silence, and the sighs and groans of two bodies merging became a kind of music.

Sage felt surrounded by her, engulfed by her, and he'd never known anything quite like it. Her slick heat held him, her body welcomed him and her hands left trails of fire along his skin wherever she touched him.

Again and again, they parted and came together, each of them eager for the climax just out of reach. Each of them trying to draw out the moment. His mind raced, his heartbeat thrummed in his ears. She locked her incredible legs around his hips and called his name out as the first wave of tremors crashed down on her. He felt every one of them and took her mouth in a hard, deep kiss, swallowing her cries, her breath, everything he could, drawing her into him in every way possible.

And then he let himself follow. Finally surrendering his slippery grip on control, he tumbled off the edge of the world and felt her arms come around him to cushion his fall.

Colleen didn't want to move. Ever. She'd be happy here, forever, just like this, on the hard floor with Sage's muscular body covering hers. She felt alive in a way she never had before. It was as if her entire body had suddenly awakened from a deep sleep. Her heartbeat slowly returned to normal even as she still shook with the force of the release she'd found with Sage.

And already, one pesky corner of her mind was springing into life trying to quantify what had just happened. Trying to explain the unexplainable.

She wasn't a virgin. She'd had sex exactly twice before this time, and looking back, she had to admit that neither of those times had come even *close* to what she'd just experienced.

In fact, it wasn't very long ago that Colleen had decided she simply wasn't a very sexual person. That maybe she was one of those people who would *never* see fireworks or feel the earth move during sex.

Well, she told herself with a self-satisfied grin, so much for *that* theory.

Sage eased up onto one elbow, and instantly, she missed the feeling of him lying atop her. "You okay?"

"Oh, yeah," she said on a sigh. "I'm terrific. You?"

He laughed shortly. "I think so. Come on, that floor can't be too comfortable."

"I'd rather stay here until my legs work again, thanks."

He shook his head and gave her an all-too-brief smile. "I think that's the nicest thing any woman's ever said to me."

And there had no doubt been plenty of them, Colleen thought sadly. The sophisticates. The skinny women with tiny feet in designer shoes. Ah, yes. Well, that thought was enough to put a damper on the lovely residual heat spreading inside, and have her moving to sit up and grab for her clothes.

"So," Sage asked as he, too, got dressed, "what do you think of the cabin?"

She looked up at him and found his eyes unshuttered, filled with a warmth she hadn't seen before. "I like it. Well, everything except the railing." She grimaced. "I didn't even thank you for saving me from that drop."

"I think," he said, "we pretty much thanked each other."

How funny. He'd saved her but couldn't accept her gratitude. As if by keeping an emotional distance, he could compartmentalize what had just happened between them. Which was enough to have Colleen drawing her romantic notions to a quick close.

"Actually, I'm feeling pretty fond of that railing myself," he said, and stood up to tug on his jeans. "If it hadn't snapped…"

She shivered at the thought, remembering the view of the steep drop. Of that moment of sheer terror when she'd thought she was going to fall. Of feeling Sage grab her, pull her in tight and then…

"Hey, Colleen," he said softly. "You okay?"

"Oh, I'm better than okay," she assured him and hoped he didn't hear the tremor in her voice. She was so not okay. She was in turmoil. Because she had just realized that tumbling down a rocky ravine might have bruised and broken her body—but sex with Sage Lassiter just might break her heart.

Nine

He scowled a little. "You surprise me all the damn time."

"That's a bad thing?"

"I don't know yet," he said. He looked down at her as if trying to read her mind, see into her heart. And Colleen really hoped he couldn't. Because right now, he'd see too much. Know too much.

Frowning slightly, he turned his head, glanced out the window and abruptly said, "We have to go. It's snowing."

"Snowing?"

"A spring snow is nothing new, you know that." Sage turned to her and there was a grim expression on his face. "This high up, it's even more likely to happen."

Colleen looked, too, watching as huge white flakes drifted from a cloud-studded sky. An hour ago, it had been cold and clear. But weather in Wyoming was unpredictable at the best of times, as she already knew. When she and her mother had first moved here from California, the first thing they'd learned was, if you don't like the weather, wait five minutes. These few flakes could wink out of existence in minutes—or they could be the herald of a heavy storm. There was just no way to tell.

In a few minutes, they were dressed and leaving the cabin behind. They walked to the car in silence, and on the way down the wickedly winding road, that silence stretched on. Colleen's mind whirled with too many thoughts to sort through. Besides, the silence was deafening and she had to wonder if Sage was regretting what had happened. If he planned to just pretend it *hadn't* happened at all. Maybe it would be better if she pretended the same thing. Heck, if her body wasn't still alive with sensation, Colleen might have been able to believe it.

How could he shut down so completely? Moments ago, there had been heat and wonder and something... *more* between them. And now it was as if he'd already moved on. There was no closeness between them. No sense of extended intimacy.

There was only the softly falling snow.

And the quiet.

By the next morning, Sage had convinced himself that he had overreacted to what had happened the day before.

That long ride from the cabin back to his home ranch had been a tension-filled misery. He'd felt her waiting for him to say something, but what the hell could he say? He'd just thrown her down onto a dirty cabin floor and taken her so fast and so hard she'd probably have bruises. It had been damned humiliating to know how completely he'd lost control. To know that she'd taken him to the edge and then pushed him over. So what the hell could they possibly have talked about?

The storm had faded away soon after they returned to his ranch, leaving just a chill in the air and a few patchy spots of quickly melting snow. He'd needed some space. Some time to get his head together, so he'd ordered up an early dinner, showed Colleen to a room just down the hall from his and said good-night.

He'd seen the flash of surprise in her eyes when he walked away, but he'd had to. If he'd stayed another minute he'd have found a way to tip her back onto the guest-room bed and have her again. And he refused to lose control twice in the same damn day.

The hell of it was, rather than being satisfied by their encounter, he had been wound even tighter than he was before. It was as if the tension, once released, had instantly coiled inside him again. There was no relief. Only more hunger. That one climax with Colleen had taken him to a place he hadn't even guessed existed—and his instincts wanted to go back.

Always before, bedding a woman who'd gotten under his skin had eased that itch. That nagging pulse of desire.

But with Colleen, it was just the opposite. He wanted her even more, now that he knew what having her was like.

Of course, after practically dumping her in her room and leaving her to fend for herself last night, there wasn't much chance of having more of her. He'd seen that look of surprise on her face when he'd walked away. Surprise, mixed with something else. Hurt? Maybe. Hell, didn't she understand he'd left her alone for her own good? Probably not.

Everything about Colleen was different. Her openness. The innocent pleasure always shining in her eyes. Her smile. Her laugh. The way she consistently looked for the good in people—and didn't stop until she found it. He liked her, damn it, and that had *not* been a part of the plan.

Racked with guilt over that tense, awkward goodbye, he'd devoted several mind-numbing hours to paperwork and emails and going over new contracts his lawyers had sent on. He'd also looked into Jack Reed to see if there was any more information to be gathered—there hadn't been. There was bound to be trouble if Reed was interested in Lassiter Media and Sage just added that complication to the growing list in his mind.

He'd buried himself so completely in the mundane tasks of maintaining the empire he was creating, it was long after midnight before he finally closed his books and trudged upstairs to his bedroom suite. Not that it had done him any good. How the hell could he sleep, knowing she was just down the hall?

No, instead of sleeping, he'd spent all night long reliving those moments with her in the cabin. When he did close his eyes, even briefly, her face was there. In front of him. And even if he *had* been able to sleep, she would have been in his dreams. The scent of her, the warmth of her. The slick slide of her legs around his hips.

By dawn, he'd given up on any pretense of rest and gone to work. God knew there was enough to do on a working ranch to exhaust him enough that even thoughts of sex with Colleen wouldn't be able to keep him awake.

"Pitiful. Seriously pitiful." Disgusted with himself, Sage tossed the hammer and nails into the bucket at his side, then sat back on his heels and stared up at the late-morning sky. The view from the roof of the main stable was pretty damn impressive, yet all he could think about was her.

He could see her, lying beneath him, staring up at him from the floor in a dusty cabin. *Nice seduction moves, Sage.* Pull out all the romantic stops to get her to spill her secrets. Way to go. Of course, his mind argued, he hadn't been thinking of seduction. Only the need to claim her. To be a part of her.

And now he wanted to do it all again.

He shifted his gaze from the sky to the ranch yard. He saw the place he'd built, the men who worked for him, his dog—a big golden retriever—taking a nap in the shade. The sky was that deep, startling blue you only found in the mountains. Thick white clouds sailed in the wind that shook the trees and rattled their leaves. In the corral, two of the cowboys were working with a yearling mare, putting her through her paces.

Sage smiled, grateful for the distraction from his own thoughts. That mare was going to be a star one day. She was already faster than most of the horses in his stable and she was proud enough that she liked winning.

Still smiling, he started down the ladder propped against the side of the stable, thankful that he hadn't fallen off the roof and broken his neck due to lack of concentration. Colleen had affected him so much that she'd ruined his focus, and yet he couldn't seem to mind.

Shaking his head, he neared the bottom of the ladder and dropped the bucket holding shingles, a hammer and nails to the ground.

"What were you doing up there?"

He went completely still, amazed at the sensation of heat that snaked through him just at the sound of her voice. He could hardly believe she'd stayed after what had happened yesterday. But he was glad she had. What the hell was wrong with him? A few weeks ago at the rehearsal dinner, he'd been intrigued enough by the look of her that he'd wanted to talk. Maybe take a quick roll in the hay if she was interested.

Now he knew her. He understood that there wasn't a dishonest bone in her body. Hell, there was just no way Colleen would even think of tricking or deceiving a sick old man. She hadn't slicked her way into a fortune. Hadn't cheated the Lassiter family. He knew that now. Knew her mind, her sense of humor, her generosity, and he knew what touching her did to him. She was paving right over all the roadblocks he'd had set up around his mind and heart for years…and it was damned disconcerting.

Colleen stood not a foot from the ladder, watching him, and he wondered why he hadn't heard her walk up. Too busy thinking of her, he told himself wryly. Yeah, this seduction plan was working out nicely.

"Loose shingles on the stable roof," he said, hitting the ground, then bending over to snatch up the bucket before straightening to look into her eyes. Instantly, he felt that punch of something raw and elemental—and it was getting harder to ignore.

He'd missed her at breakfast, too. Deliberately. He'd grabbed a cup of coffee and one of his housekeeper's famous muffins and headed outside—where he'd stayed, keeping as busy as he could. "The wind kicked up last night, and after last winter a few of the shingles were ready to go."

She looked up, squinting into the late-morning sunlight, as if she could see where he'd been working. "You do the repairs yourself?"

"Sometimes," he admitted, and hefted the ladder across one shoulder. When he started walking toward the equipment shed where tools were stored, she followed him. "Why sound so surprised? It is my ranch."

The golden retriever rose lazily from his spot by the barn and stretched before trotting to Colleen's side. She stopped, dropped to one knee and smoothed both hands across the top of the lucky dog's head. A hell of a thing, Sage thought, when a man envied his dog.

"He's so sweet," she said, throwing a quick look up at Sage. "But I don't understand his name."

In spite of what he was feeling, Sage choked out a laugh. "You mean Beback?"

She scrubbed the dog's ears, then stood up, tucking her hands into the pockets of her jeans. "Yes. What kind of name is that?"

Shrugging, Sage said, "When he was a pup, he kept running off into the forest, but he was always running right back. One of the guys said it reminded him of a famous line in a movie...*I'll be back*."

Colleen laughed and, God, he loved the sound of it. And as soon as that thought slid through his mind, he pushed it back out again. *Love?* What the hell?

"Beback. I like it," she said with a grin as she watched the dog race off after one of the cowboys. "I always wanted a dog. In fact, I'm going to get one as soon as I find my place."

"Not the Jackson cabin?"

She threw him a quick look and her eyes flared as if she were remembering their encounter. "I don't know yet. Maybe."

Nodding, Sage continued on to the shed and sensed rather than heard her follow him. And naturally, she was still talking.

"Going back to me being surprised at you doing the repairs to one of the buildings...I don't know, I guess I thought you would have one of the men who work for you do the minor repairs." She waved one hand to encompass the whole of the yard and the half dozen or so ranch hands working at different tasks.

His long strides never slowed, though he knew she had to be hurrying to keep up with him. "J.D. always said, 'Don't be afraid to do your own work. Men will respect you for it.'"

Frowning, he wondered where that had come from. He wasn't really in the habit of quoting his father. Yet it seemed that since J.D. died, Sage had thought more about him than he had in years. And the situation wasn't helped by Colleen's presence. After all, the only reason they were together at all was because of the old man.

"So you do have some good memories of J.D."

"Didn't say they were good ones," he muttered, leading the way into the shed. "Just memories."

Inside it was cool and dark. The walls were covered with hooks from which clean, cared-for tools hung neatly. One wall contained a long workbench with drawers beneath it and the rest of the place held everything from shovels to snowplows.

With her standing so close to him, it was hard to keep hold of his own self-control. Desire pulsed heavily inside him even while his brain kept shouting for caution. If he had any hope of keeping his mind clear, he needed some distance between them. Releasing a breath, Colleen glanced around the shed. "I won't need anywhere near this much equipment," she said as if to herself.

"You'll need plenty of it, though," he warned, taking the opportunity to spread a little more doubt in her mind. "Snowblower or plow. Shovels, pickaxes, and by the way, that old Jeep of yours isn't going to cut it up here, either."

"What?" She flashed him a stunned look. "Why not?"

"For one thing, it's too small. You'll need a truck."

At that, she laughed a little. "Why would I need a truck? My Jeep has been fine for me in the snow."

"The wheelbase is too short," he told her, and shook his head when he saw the blank confusion in her eyes. "Too easily tipped over. And in a high wind on the mountain road…"

She shivered as he'd meant her to—because the thought of her navigating those switchback curves alone in a storm gave him a damn heart attack.

"For another thing," he added, "you'll need the truck bed, because there's no trash collection here. You'll have to make trips to the dump yourself."

She chewed at her bottom lip and Sage felt a confusing mix of satisfaction and guilt. He didn't necessarily want to be the one to ruin her dream. But hell if he wanted her alone in a situation she wasn't prepared for either.

"Where's the dump?"

"I can show you." And that would serve as a negative, too. Once she got a whiff of the dump, she'd be less inclined to have to go there regularly.

"Okay…"

"There's no mail delivery up here either," he said

while he still held her attention. "You'll have to get a P.O. box in town."

She sighed. "I hadn't thought it would be so complicated." Turning in a slow circle, she let her gaze wander over the walls of tools as if she were trying to figure out how to use them. "All I want to do is live on the mountain, closer to where my patients will be."

"Most things generally are complicated," he said, emptying the work bucket he'd brought in with him. He opened drawers, returning the hammer, nails and leftover shingles to their proper places and when he was finished, he turned to find Colleen staring at him, a smile as bright as sunlight on her face. "And when you live up here—especially alone—you have to expect to take care of a lot of things most people don't worry about... what are you smiling at?"

"You." She shrugged. "It's funny, but I don't think I ever pictured you as being a fix-it kind of guy."

"Yeah, well." He closed the drawer and walked to set the bucket down in a corner of the shed. "J.D. had Dylan and I working all over Big Blue when we were kids. The two of us had a chores list that would make a grown man weep. We worked with the cattle and the horses, learned how to rebuild engines and shingle roofs when they needed it." He leaned one hip against the workbench, folded his arms across his chest and continued, "J.D. thought we should know the place from the ground up. Be familiar with everything so we were never at the mercy of anyone else. During school, we had plenty of time for homework, but during summer, he worked us both."

She tipped her head to one side and looked up at him. "Sounds like it was hard work."

"It was," he admitted, realizing he hadn't thought about those times in years. When they were kids, he and Dylan had hated all the chores. But they'd learned. Not that Dylan needed most of those lessons today, what with spearheading the Lassiter Grill Group. But Sage could admit, at least to himself, that everything he'd learned on the Big Blue had helped him run his own ranch better than he might have done otherwise. Sourly, he acknowledged that growing up as J.D. Lassiter's son had prepared him for the kind of life he had always wanted to live.

All those hot summers spent training horses, riding the range rounding up stray cattle. The long hours sweeping out the stable and the barn. The backbreaking task of clearing brush away from the main house. He and his younger brother had become part of the crew working Big Blue. The other wranglers and cowboys accepted them as equals, not the boss's adopted kids.

Shaking his head, Sage looked back on it all now and could see that J.D. had been helping them build their own places on Big Blue. To feel a part of the ranch. He'd been giving them a foundation. Roots to replace the ones they'd lost.

"Crafty old goat," he muttered, with just a touch of admiration for the father he had resented for so long.

"He really was, wasn't he?"

Sage caught the indulgent smile on her face and stiffened. But Colleen was unaware of the change in him, because she kept talking.

"He used to make me laugh," she was saying. "He couldn't get out much in his last couple of months, but he managed to steer everyone around him into doing just what he wanted them to do. He ran the ranch from his bed and his recliner. He even convinced me to accompany him to the rehearsal dinner," she added softly, "when I *knew* he wasn't well enough for the stress of the evening."

"That wasn't your fault," he said quickly.

"Wasn't it?" Her gaze locked with his. "I was his nurse. Supposed to guard his failing health, not give in to him when I knew it was dangerous." She reached up and pushed her hair back from her face, and suddenly Sage thought of how it had felt to have his own hands in that thick, silky mass.

Gritting his teeth, he pushed that thought aside and only said, "J.D. had a way of getting just what he wanted from folks. You shouldn't feel guilty about being one of them."

"He was a lovely man," she whispered. "Hard, but fair. Tough, but he loved his family. All of you. He talked about you all so much…"

Sage's ears perked up. "Did he?"

"Oh, yes." She walked closer to him, running her fingertips along the edge of the workbench. "He was so proud of Dylan's work with the grill. And he talked about Angie all the time—"

She broke off, as if remembering that J.D.'s will sort of belied that last statement.

"And you." She moved even closer and he caught her scent on the still, cool air. The scent that had haunted him all night long. Her eyes shone up at him with innocence and pleasure, as if she was really enjoying being able to share all of this with him. "He took so much pride in what you've built. He used to go on and on about how you made your first million while you were in school, and how he'd had to go to great lengths to convince you to stay at college when all you really wanted to do was build your own ranch—"

Sage's vision went red. And just like that, the seductive, sensual air between him and Colleen sizzled into an inferno that apparently only he could sense. His mind burned and thoughts chased each other through the darkness spreading through him. Years-old fury reawakened as if it had never gone to sleep, and he trembled with the force of the control required to keep from shouting out his rage.

Her voice was just a buzz of sound now, but even through the anger churning within, he could see that Colleen clearly believed that she'd scored a point. That she'd made Sage see his father as the *caring, thoughtful, generous* man she thought he was. That she'd found a way past the old angers and hurts. But instead, all she had done was relight the fuse that had been smoldering for years.

He took a breath and interrupted her stream of conversation. "Yeah. He was proud. Too damn proud. And he wasn't the kindhearted, feeble old gentleman you think you knew."

"What are you talking about?"

He threw a glance at the open shed door and the ranch yard beyond. Golden sunlight washed over his ranch, making the inside of the shed seem even darker in comparison. But damned if he'd have this talk out in public so that anyone could overhear. He strode across the straw-littered floor, slammed the door and threw the lock. Only then did he turn around to face Colleen again, and in the back of his mind, he noted that her eyes were wary.

"You met J.D. when he was old and tired and looking to find the fast track into heaven," Sage finally said and had the small satisfaction of seeing her blink in surprise. "I knew him back in the day and trust me, he wasn't a sweetheart. He was domineering, a know-it-all and damned arrogant with it."

One dark blond eyebrow lifted. "Remind you of anyone?"

He snorted in spite of the anger bubbling into an ugly brew in the pit of his stomach. "Okay, I can accept that maybe I picked up a few of his less pleasant traits along the way. But I never—" Damn. The words were stuck in his throat like bitter bile. He hadn't talked about this in years. And he'd *never* told anyone else about this. Not Dylan. Not Angie. The only person he had ever been open with about it was J.D. Because the old man himself was at the heart of it.

Shaking his head fiercely, as if he could dislodge the blackness wrapped around his memories, he muttered, "You said he wanted me to stay in college. That he told you he *talked* me into it."

"That's what he said, yes."

"Well, then, he had a really selective memory," Sage said flatly. "Because he didn't talk me into anything. He maneuvered me until he got his way. Just like he did everything else in his life."

"What do you mean, maneuvered?"

He hadn't meant to allow old memories to nearly choke him as they rushed up from the black bottom of his heart to spill through his mind like tar. But there they were, and he'd come too far to stop now.

"Unlike J.D., I never figured that I knew best how another man should live his life. I never made it my business to take something from a person just because I could."

"*What* are you talking about?"

"I was in college. My sophomore year. Twenty years old and I figured I had all the answers." He pushed one hand through his hair and tipped his head back to look up through the skylight at the cloud-scudded sky. Even with his age-old fury pushing his words, they caught in his throat and had to be forced out. But if he was going to say it, he was going to look into those oh-so-innocent eyes that saw only the good in people. That way he could be a witness when she finally had to admit that J.D. was nothing like she'd thought he was.

"What happened?" The concern in her voice was as real as the touch of her hand on his arm. The electrical whip of heat that sliced through him did battle with the anger and lost.

He snorted. "What happened? J.D. happened. I went home one night and told him that I was leaving school."

"Why?"

His gaze speared into hers. "I was in love. Or at least I thought I was. I told J.D. we were going to get married and start up my ranch."

Her voice was soft and uncertain as she asked, "What did he say?"

"Oh," Sage said on a sharp bark of laughter, "J.D. said all the right things. Told me he'd help me get into the inheritance my parents left me. Wasn't much," he added, "but it would've given me a start."

"That's good though, isn't it?" Her eyes were shimmering with hurt and he didn't know if it was for him or herself. "J.D. said he'd help you."

"Yeah, and then the next day, when I got to my girlfriend's place, her roommate told me she was gone and wouldn't be back." Amazing, Sage thought, that it could still hurt after all these years. That the betrayal was as sharp. The fury as thick.

"Why would she leave?"

He looked at her and quirked one eyebrow, inviting her to fill in the blanks. When she didn't, he did it for her. "She left me a note. Told me that it had been fun, but she was moving to Paris to paint. And she wasn't supposed to let me in on it, but apparently she didn't mind turning on J.D., either, because she told me in the note that he'd paid her two hundred thousand bucks to leave."

Colleen looked up at him, and for the first time in her life, didn't have the slightest clue what to say. This J.D. was not the man she had known. How could he have hurt his son so badly? And while her heart hurt for Sage, there was pain for herself, as well.

Sage had been in love. He'd wanted to get married. And though it was years ago, a part of her ached hearing the words.

He scrubbed both hands across his face. "I called him on it right away and he was furious that Megan had told me what he'd done." He shook his head and choked out another laugh. "He didn't see anything wrong with what he'd done, of course, but he was pissed as hell that I'd found out about it. Told me he'd done it for my sake. That Megan wasn't the kind of woman to stand by a man—"

She opened her mouth and he spoke quickly to cut her off.

"—before you can say it, yeah, he was right about Megan. If she had loved me, she never would have taken the money. But he should have let *me* find out the truth about her myself. Instead, he charged in, just like always, and rearranged the world to suit himself."

Megan was a fool. An idiot. She'd had this proud, strong, yes, *arrogant* man's love and she'd sold it. Colleen would never have betrayed him. She would have been proud to have his love, to work with him to build a ranch, a legacy for the family they would build and—

Colleen's throat closed up. All of a sudden she couldn't breathe. Couldn't stop the sting of tears in her eyes. What on earth was wrong with…

Oh, God. *She was in love.*

For the first time in her life, she was madly, completely, passionately in love with a man who probably would never return the feeling. The realization staggered her and if she hadn't had the workbench behind her as a brace, she might have just slumped to the floor. How was she going to get past this feeling? How could she possibly be in love with a man who wanted nothing to do with love and family? Who believed that love meant betrayal?

Sage was still talking and she forced herself to listen. He didn't need to know what she was feeling, that her heart was breaking. What he needed was to get past the old pain still gnawing on him. "Sage…"

"Forget it. You can't say anything, Colleen. J.D. was a bastard. End of story."

Her own feelings didn't matter right now, she told herself. What *did* matter was the pain Sage was still in. She couldn't bear seeing him cling to old injuries that were only hurting him, keeping him from moving on, and understanding that though his father had treated him badly, it wasn't because he hadn't loved him.

Colleen moved in closer, laid one hand on his chest

and said, "What he did was terrible, you're right. But he did it because he loved you."

"Hell of a way to prove it," he muttered. "He betrayed me, bottom line. And so did Megan, though in the long run, she did me a favor."

"Can't you say J.D. did, too?"

He snorted. "Don't know that I'm ready to thank him. But looking back, I can see that I mistook lust for love and I'm guessing J.D. saw that more clearly than I did back then." He blew out a breath and Colleen saw the anger fade from his eyes as he began to let go of the past. "I can say that if he hadn't stuck his nose in, I might not be standing here in front of a woman who turns my blood to fire with a look."

Instantly, Colleen's whole body lit up as if a sudden fever erupted inside her. She loved him. She wanted him. She stared into his eyes and knew that though he might not love her back, his desire was real and every bit as powerful as her own. "Sage..."

"I'm done talking about J.D. right now, Colleen," he murmured, dropping both hands to the workbench on either side of her, pinning her in place. "I've been trying to stay away from you—"

"I know," she said. "Why?"

"Because I want you too much. You're all I think about. All I give a flying damn about. You're in my blood, Colleen."

"You're in mine, too," she whispered, reaching up to cup his face between her palms. Her thumbs traced across his cheekbones and he held perfectly still as she went up on her toes, moved in and kissed him.

That soft brush of her lips against his was a benediction of sorts. A wiping away of the past and a welcome into the present—the future?

He fell into her kiss willingly, eagerly, and wrapped his arms around her. Colleen gave herself up to the moment, letting go of everything but the magic shimmering in the air between them.

But just as the kiss was deepening, spiraling out of control, Sage pulled back, looked down at her and muttered, "Damned if we're going to be together in an old cabin and then in an equipment shed where any one of my cowboys could glance in the window for a peek."

She flushed and laughed, burying her face briefly against his chest. "I forgot entirely where we were."

"Yeah, you have that effect on me, too," he confessed. "But today we're going to try an actual *bed.* Come with me."

He took her hand and led her out of the shed toward the main house and all Colleen could think was, she would go with him anywhere.

Ten

She woke up early in the master bedroom to find that Sage was already up and gone.

Colleen sighed and stretched languorously in the big bed she'd shared with him all night. Her mind filled with images of the night before and bubbles of residual heat slid through her bloodstream like champagne. She'd only managed about two hours' sleep all night, but she'd never felt more awake, more aware.

Who would have guessed that *love* could heighten every sense? Could make you both grateful and miserable with the kind of feelings that were so overwhelming? She couldn't stay, she knew she couldn't. She loved him and he didn't love her and never the twain would meet just like when it happened in those literary, depressing love stories.

But God, she didn't want to go. Her gaze fixed on

the wall of windows and French doors leading to a wood deck, beyond which she saw an amazing sweep of stormy sky that was punctuated by the tips of pine trees. It looked as though they would get another storm, and she knew she should go before that storm hit. Now all she needed was the courage to make the move. She was in love, but he wasn't. In fact, he would probably panic and run if he knew how she felt about him. But when she remembered the tenderness, the amazing heat that spiraled between them when they made love, it was hard not to dream that one day, he might love her back.

"Oh, God," she murmured, pulling her pillow out from under her head to drop it onto her face. "Try not to be a complete idiot, Colleen. Sex isn't love. Just because he's good at it doesn't mean he cares. He's just… thorough."

She threw one arm across that pillow so that her voice was muffled and she wouldn't have to listen to herself. Honestly, this was a serious mess. Falling in love was just—unavoidable, she thought. Now she had to work out what to do about it. Keep her mouth shut, obviously. And get off this mountain as quickly as possible. Because the longer she stayed, the harder it would be to eventually walk away.

Just as that depressing thought took up root in her mind, Colleen's cell phone rang and she rolled out of bed to grab her jeans off the floor. Fumbling through the pockets, she found her phone, saw the caller ID and winced. "Hi, Mom."

"Hi, sweetie, how's it going?"

"Great, really. Um…" She looked around for *something* to slip on. She couldn't just stand there naked and chat with her mother. Finally settling for a sheet, she snaked it off the bed and wrapped it around her.

"So." Laura's voice was bright and happy. "Did you find the house you want to buy?"

Memories of the cabin rose up in her mind and she smiled wistfully. "I think so," she said, "but I'm still looking."

Because she loved that cabin and thought it would be perfect for her. But the question was, would she be able to live with the memories of what she and Sage had done there once they weren't together anymore? Could she really face those memories every day?

"That's wonderful, honey. It's so nice of Sage to take the time to show you around."

"Yep, very nice." And so much more.

"I know it's early to call, but I had to tell you, your aunt Donna is coming for a visit next week."

"That's great." She could hear the excitement in her mother's voice and Colleen sent another silent thank-you to J.D. for making this possible. Even if her own life was teetering on the brink of despair, at least her mother was having fun.

"We're going to plan our trip together and get our passport photos taken together," Laura said in a tangled rush of words. She kept talking, outlining her plans and laughing more than Colleen had heard her laugh in years. Finally, though, her mom slowed down and said, "You're awfully quiet."

"What?" Damn. She should have been paying closer attention. Her mother always had been really good at picking up on Colleen's moods.

"Never mind trying to play it cool, kiddo. Spill it."

Colleen dropped onto the edge of the bed, stared out

at the view and took a deep breath before saying, "I screwed up."

"Impossible."

She laughed and a little of her depression lifted. "Thanks, Mom."

"Tell me what's wrong, sweetie."

"I'm in love with a man who likes me."

"But that's wonderful." Laura practically cheered.

Colleen shook her head and with one hand, pushed her hair back from her face. "I think you missed the most important part in that last sentence, Mom. He *likes* me. He doesn't love me."

"He will, though. How could he not?"

God bless mothers, Colleen thought with a sad smile. Though her mom would always support her, always believe in her, there was no way she could understand how Colleen was feeling right now. Her parents had fallen in love at first sight. They'd only known each other a month before they got married and they'd stayed deeply in love until the day Colleen's father died. So with that kind of background, her mother would never be able to see just how hopeless Colleen's situation was.

"It's not that easy." Not when his past held memories of a woman who had betrayed him.

"Who said it was supposed to be easy?" her mother asked, then added, "Okay, yes, your dad and I had it easy. We found each other and it all fell together. But Sage likes you. That's not so far from love."

Outside, the sky opened up and rain pelted the windows. They'd had sun, snow and now rain in just a few days. Colleen shivered a little and wondered if the storm was an omen. Then she dismissed that thought. No need to get crazy here.

"Have you told him how you feel?"

"Of course not," she said, horrified at the thought. She'd like to hang on to a little bit of dignity if she could. "I can't admit to that. How humiliating."

"Or," her mother said slyly, "how liberating. You risk nothing but a little pride. And honey, love is worth any price you have to pay."

A few minutes later she hung up, but her mother's words were still echoing through Colleen's mind. Was she right? Should she tell Sage what she was feeling? Or should she just pack up her heart before it got bruised and run back to reality?

An hour later, she was dressed and downstairs, looking for a cup of coffee. She was packed and would be leaving as soon as she spoke to Sage. She just still hadn't made up her mind what exactly to say to him and was hoping caffeine would help her think more clearly. When she heard Sage's voice, she followed the sound without even thinking about it. Walking down the long, gloomy hall, her sneakered footsteps were quiet on the wood floor. She tapped gently on his office door, then opened it.

He was sitting at his desk, holding the phone to his ear, which explained her hearing his voice. His back was to her, his gaze fixed on the raging storm beyond the wide glass window. Adrenaline pulsed through her as he started speaking again, as if her body was tuned to the timbre and richness of his voice. But before she could back out of the room and give him privacy for his call, *what* he was saying caught her attention.

"Dylan," he said, sounding bored and impatient as he talked to his brother, "dating Colleen was the only sure way to find out exactly what J.D. was up to before he died."

Her heart stopped and a thin sliver of air worked its way down her lungs. Blindly, she reached out one hand to the doorjamb and held on as if it meant her life.

"She was the closest to the old man and it's entirely possible that she knows something she's not even aware of," Sage continued.

Colleen felt sick. Her heartbeat was slow. Heavy. Like a movie played in extremely slow motion. Ice dropped into the pit of her churning stomach and the cold seemed to spread, snaking out tentacles that reached throughout her body until she shivered with reaction.

She should leave.

She knew she should turn and run. Hit the front door, race to her car and get off the mountain. But she couldn't move. It was as if her feet were nailed to the floor. She wanted to be struck deaf so she wouldn't have to hear any more. She wanted to have never come downstairs. To have never come here to this ranch at all.

Sage shook his head and laughed at whatever his brother was saying. "You're wrong, Dylan. Trust me, I'm not getting too close to Colleen. I don't *do* close. Besides, this isn't about what I *want*—it's about what I want to find out."

Did she make a sound? She might have. A tiny gasp. A small moan. Of course she did. How could her body contain so much pain without letting some of it escape? Whatever that sound was, he heard it, because he slowly swiveled around in his chair, spotted her across the room and said simply, "Colleen."

Funny. It was the look in his eyes that finally freed her enough to run. The shock. The surprise. The *guilt*. By the time he slammed the phone into its cradle, she was gone.

* * *

Panic roared into life in Sage's chest and had him bolting from his office, racing after her, determined to catch her. To explain. To— Hell. He didn't know what he'd do.

"Damn it, Colleen, *wait!*" He caught her at the front door and slammed one hand on the heavy oak panel so she couldn't yank it open no matter how hard she tried.

"Get away," she said and he heard tears choking her voice.

Pain lanced him as he called himself all kinds of vicious but accurate names.

"I mean it, Sage," she muttered thickly. "Let me go."

"It's raining, Colleen. You can't leave in a storm."

"I know how to drive in the rain—and I'm leaving."

"I can't let you do that." That panic was still bubbling up inside him and staring down into her damp eyes, it only got worse. She was trying to leave and he couldn't let her. Not like this.

"What you heard back there? It wasn't true." He hung his head and gave it a shake before finding the strength to meet those tear-filled blue eyes again. "I was just trying to get Dylan off my back, that's all."

"No," she said, her mouth twisting as if she were trying desperately to keep her bottom lip from quivering. "It was true. All of it. I'm only surprised I didn't see it sooner."

Seeing tears clouding her clear, beautiful eyes tore at him. Knowing he had caused it nearly killed him. The worst kind of bastard, he'd hurt a woman who didn't deserve it, all to cover his own ass and save his pride with his brother.

"Why else would you ever go for a woman like me?"

Shaking her head, she lifted her chin and he saw what that defiant, proud move cost her. "So don't tell me that conversation with your brother wasn't true. Recent behavior notwithstanding, I'm not an idiot, Sage. Now open this door and let me leave."

"You don't really want to go and I don't want you to," he said, gaze moving over her lovely features, searing her face into his mind. He drew her scent in deep and felt her permeate every cell in his body.

He should have locked the damn office door. Then this wouldn't be an issue. She never would have overheard him. They could have gone on as they were, and both of them would have been happy. Instead, he had to try to unravel the damage he'd done.

The thing was, he hadn't meant a damn thing he'd said to his brother. He just hadn't wanted to admit to himself, let alone Dylan, that he'd come to…care for Colleen. Oh, it might have started out differently, using her as a means to an end, but somewhere along the line, that had changed. Into what, he couldn't say. All he was sure of was that he hated seeing her in pain. Hated knowing he was the cause.

Bending his head, he kissed her and refused to allow her to turn her face from his. Wouldn't let her ignore the fire between them. And in seconds, in spite of the turmoil churning inside her, she was kissing him back. His heart gave one wild lurch as he realized that maybe, just maybe, he could still salvage what he had with her. He wrapped his arms around her and held her tightly, losing himself, as always, in the heat that engulfed him the moment they came together.

Seconds, minutes, it could have been hours that passed as they stood, wrapped up in each other, mouths fused, hearts beating in tandem. But when he tried to draw back, to lead her toward the stairs and his bedroom, Colleen said, "No."

He stared at her, confused by the refusal. "What?"

"No," she said again, pulling away from him, taking a step back to increase the space between them. "I won't go back upstairs with you, Sage. I can't."

He shoved one hand through his hair. "But you kissed me back just now. You believed me when I told you that I didn't mean any of what you heard."

"Didn't you?" Her eyes were wounded. There was no sign of tears now, but the cool detachment he saw in her expression worried Sage more than a flood of tears might have. "Why did you first come to see me, Sage? Why did you first want to spend time with me?"

Instead of answering, he asked a question of his own. "Why are you doing this?"

She laughed shortly, but the sound was harsh and strained. "I really don't want to, but I have no choice. So tell me why, Sage."

He wouldn't lie to her. Couldn't bring himself to look into those honest, oh-so-innocent eyes and lie just to save his own ass. He'd bring her more pain and it would rip him apart, but she deserved the damned truth.

"You know why." As his gaze locked with hers, he saw her eyes widen slightly and another slash of pain dart across their surfaces.

"So it's true."

"It's not true *now*," he countered and took a step toward her. He stopped when she backed away, maintaining the distance between them. "I didn't know you," he said, forcing himself to keep meeting her eyes, acknowledging the pain he was causing her even as it sliced at him, too. "All I knew was that J.D.'s will had been changed. He'd cheated my sister out of what should have been hers, and J.D.'s private nurse was suddenly a millionaire."

She sucked in a gulp of air and the gasping sound filled the quiet house. "You really believed I had somehow tricked J.D. into leaving me money and cheating your sister?"

"Don't you get it, Colleen? *Nothing* was making sense. J.D. turned on his daughter. Thinking you were somehow behind it all made as much sense as anything else." It sounded so stupid now, knowing her as he did. But in his own defense, hadn't he had his own experience with J.D. paying women off? "Can you blame me? You know what my father did to me once before. He betrayed me then...and now, from the damn *grave,* he's doing the same thing to Angie."

She shook her head sadly. "You've let that one horrible experience color your whole life, haven't you?"

"Why shouldn't I? It was a valuable lesson and I learned it well."

Her luscious mouth twisted into a parody of a smile that was almost harder to see than the single tear escaping her eye to roll along her cheek.

"Oh, Sage," she said, her voice aching with the hurt he'd just dealt her. "What you *didn't* learn was that J.D. didn't do that to hurt you. He did it to protect you. That's what we do for people we love."

"*Protect* me?" He laughed, astonished that she could still take J.D.'s side in this, in spite of everything. "How? By making me doubt myself, my judgment? By ensuring that I wouldn't trust another damn soul? Some help."

Shaking her head again, she looked at him with disappointment. "You chose that path, Sage. Your father didn't put you on it." Her voice was so quiet he had to strain to hear it over the thundering beat of his own heart. "He was trying to save you from more pain later on down the road." She paused, then hurried on before he could speak. "Sure, he made mistakes. But people do. Especially the people who love us."

What the hell was he supposed to do with a woman like her? She continually looked for the good in people—and had found it in J.D. Despite what he'd done to Sage so many years ago, the old man had done the best he could by *all* of his children, and maybe Sage was now willing to accept that. If he did, it just made the will that much more perplexing.

As confusing as the woman standing before him. He didn't want to examine those feelings. Didn't want to explore the wild explosion of thoughts and sensations churning in his mind. All he wanted was *her*.

And he couldn't have her.

A tight fist was squeezing his heart and lungs, making it almost impossible to draw an easy breath. Finally though, he said, "So can't you see that I made a mistake? About you? Can't you forgive that and let it go?"

That sad smile curved her mouth again as she murmured, "I can forgive it, but I'm still leaving."

"Why?" That one word was a demand.

"Because I love you, Sage," she said simply. "And I deserve better."

Staggered, he couldn't think of a single thing to say. She loved him? She *loved* him. And she was leaving anyway? She was opening the front door and the sound and scent of a driving rain sneaked across the threshold. She loved him. Those three words kept echoing in his mind, rattling his soul.

"Before I go, though, there is one thing J.D. told me that you should know."

His eyes narrowed on her as suspicion leaped up to the base of his throat. "What?"

"God. Even now you're still wondering if I betrayed you or not."

"No." He denied it. He knew she wasn't capable of betrayal. Knew that she was too intrinsically honest to be a part of any deception. Just as he knew that when she said she loved him, she meant every word.

"J.D. was proud of you. And he regretted that the two of you weren't close." She blew out a breath. "He was heartsick that his sons believed he didn't care."

He wished he could believe that she was lying about all of this. Because if it was all true, then he and J.D. had both been cheated of the relationship they might have had.

"He also told me," she said softly, "that he left you the Lassiter Media shares so that you would always remember that you're family. So you would realize that family is important and that *love* is all that matters."

Then she was gone.

And he was alone.

Two weeks crawled past.

Sage didn't see her. Didn't speak to her. Didn't do much of anything, really. In that first week, he couldn't give a damn about the ranch that had once been the most important thing in his life. He didn't care about stock prices or the phone calls and emails he kept getting from the various boards of the companies he sat on.

All he could think about was Colleen and the last words she'd said to him. Words that J.D. had often said when Sage was a kid. *Family. Love was everything.*

Love.

Sage hadn't really known what that was until Colleen had loved him and left him. As a younger man, he'd mistaken lust for love and just as Colleen said, he'd allowed that one poor choice to color the rest of his life. He'd cut himself off, in theory to protect himself, but in reality all he'd been doing was hiding.

Well, he was through hiding. That's why he spent the second week setting wheels in motion. There were things to do. Things to be said. A life to be lived.

When Sage walked through the front door of Big Blue, he looked around and for the first time in years, he didn't cringe from the memories rushing toward him. His heart was still heavy, but that had nothing to do with J.D. Not anymore. Sage had finally come to accept that his father was just a man, as capable of making mistakes as anyone. God knew Sage had made plenty. Especially lately.

"Sage! What're you doing here?" Angie came down the stairs, a smile on her face, and rushed toward her oldest brother for a hug. "I'm so glad to see you. And hey, *honored* that you left your ranch."

"Yeah, well," he told her, "a lot of things have changed." And how was she going to take what he had to say to her? He didn't want to hurt his sister. Hell, he'd do anything to avoid that. He just didn't see a way around it.

"No kidding," she said wryly and he knew that she was still thinking about the will and what J.D. had done to her.

It was the perfect opening for what he'd come to say. They had talked about this before, but at the time, he hadn't made the final decision that he now had to share with his sister.

"Angie, we can't fight the will."

"What?" Confused, she said, "Why not?"

He took both of her hands in his, glanced around the entry hall and felt the years of being a Lassiter settle down onto his shoulders. He was J.D.'s son and it was high time he started acting like it.

"Because if we do that and lose, a lot of people could be hurt. Marlene. Chance..." *Colleen,* he thought but didn't say.

"But you said we'd do something about this. That we'd figure it all out. I thought you were on *my* side."

His heart squeezed. "I am on your side, honey. You're my sister and I love you. But you know, too—hell, we *all* know, that J.D. loved you to death." He squeezed her hands. "So he had a reason for what he did no matter how crazy it seems to us. We're going to sit back and trust that our father did the right thing."

"That's easy for you to say." Angie yanked her hands from his and glared at him. "Dad didn't turn on you."

"Yeah, I know. Just like I know that J.D. had a *reason* for everything he ever did. We just have to find out the reason behind this."

"And that'll make it better?" The short laugh that shot from her throat told him how she felt about that.

"Didn't say that." Shaking his head, Sage looked at his sister and tried not to see the unshed tears glittering in her eyes. "We both know J.D. would never do anything to deliberately hurt you, so there's a reason for what he did. We're going to trust it's a good one."

"I can't believe this." There was hurt in her eyes, but mostly she was furious.

Well, he could deal with an angry sister. Anger he understood.

"Angie, I spent a lot of years mad at J.D. I wasted what I could have had." Disgusted with himself and sad that missed chances could never be recaptured, he said, "I'm through wasting time. I'm through holding a grudge against our father. I love you, Angie, but I won't support you if you try to fight the will."

"Sage—"

"You, me, Dylan," he said, cutting off whatever she might have said, "we're family. And love is all that matters."

She choked out a strained laugh. "You sound just like Dad."

Sage grinned. "About time, don't you think?"

Colleen hadn't expected love.

At thirty-one, she'd long ago given up on the whole Prince Charming thing and had made up her mind to enjoy her career and her life, and if love found her, then great. If not, that would be okay, too.

Well, love had found her. When she'd least expected it, love had arrived. "And lucky me, now I know exactly what it's like to try to live without it."

The past two weeks had been awful. Just awful. She was tired of putting on a happy face for her mother—but it was necessary because she didn't want her mom worrying. And it was a strain pretending everything would be great to Jenna—who wanted to drive up the mountain and kick Sage. The worst part of it all was trying to get by on fifteen minutes of sleep every night.

Sage was on her mind all the time. She couldn't sleep, couldn't eat—at least she'd lost six pounds—and just the thought of never being with him again made Colleen want to crawl into a hole and die. How was it possible, she wondered, for your whole world to change completely in just a matter of weeks?

Looking back, she could see how it had all happened. She'd been half in love with Sage from the moment J.D. had told her the first story about his oldest son. She was lost from the moment she'd seen him at the rehearsal dinner. And now she was just lost.

Sitting at the table in her condo kitchen, she looked over the sales papers and signed her name at every highlighted X. The condo was sold and she was now officially homeless. She still had to finish qualifying as a nurse practitioner, but most of that could be done online. And when she had to come to Cheyenne for classes, she was willing to drive down off the mountain to do it. She was ready for change. Ready to start living the rest of her life.

All she needed now was to find a place to live.

"Poor little rich girl," she murmured, flipping through the pages. Three million dollars and no home to call her own. She'd have to start over, looking for a place, because she couldn't buy that cabin. Not now. Not ever. She wouldn't be able to live there, remembering the passion, the incredible sense of rightness that she'd felt with Sage so briefly.

"It's okay," she told herself, signing her name with a flourish. "I'll find something else. There's more than one cabin in the mountains. I'll still—"

God, who was she trying to kid? Who was she being brave for? She was all alone here. No mom. No Jenna.

She could cry and wail and weep if she wanted to—for all the good it would do her. It had already been two weeks. Sage had forgotten all about her and it would really be a good thing if she could do the same.

Nodding, she picked up the sheaf of papers, slid them back into the envelope her real estate agent had dropped off and then sealed it. It was done. Her house was sold. Her new life was about to begin. She only wished she could be happy about that.

When the doorbell rang, she jumped up, eager for any distraction to take her mind off her depressing thoughts. To keep her too busy to think of Sage and everything that might have been.

She pulled the door open and there he was. For a second, his presence didn't really compute. It was as if she'd spent so much time thinking about him that her mind had actually conjured a vision of him just for her. But that silly thought was gone the moment he opened his mouth.

"We have to talk."

"No, we don't." Colleen shook her head and tried to close the door, but his booted foot kept it open. "I'm really not a masochist, Sage, so if you don't mind I'd appreciate you just going away. If you're here to apologize, thanks. You're forgiven. Happy trails and all of that."

God, what it cost her to tell him no. But how could she let him back in, even temporarily? *Salt, meet wound.* No. She just couldn't do it. Already she wasn't sleeping or eating and her eyes were constantly red from all the tears. She had nothing left.

"I'm not here to apologize," he muttered through the gap between her door and the wall.

"You're *not?*" She glared at him through that same gap. "You should be."

"You already forgave me, remember?"

Frowning, she was forced to admit he had a point. "Fine. Then there's no reason for you to be here at all. So go away."

"Beback misses you."

"That's just mean," she snapped. He knew how much she liked his dog. How much she wanted one of her own.

"I miss you."

"You miss the sex," she countered because she simply would not let herself believe anything else. She was through building castles in the air. Just because he was here didn't mean anything between them had changed.

"Sure I do. Don't you?"

She looked into his eyes, those really amazing, wonderful, soulful eyes and couldn't deny it. Naturally she missed the sex. "Yes."

"And you miss me," he said softly.

Oh, she did. She really did.

"I'll get over it," she told him and shoved harder on the door. But the man was just too strong for her.

"I don't want you to get over it. Or me."

"Sage…" She sighed, leaned her forehead against the door and murmured, "*Please* go away?"

He reached through the gap, covered her hand with one of his, and Colleen felt that so familiar zing of heat that whispered inside her, urging her to listen. To let him in. To remember how good they were together. But remembering wouldn't change anything, so why go there?

"Why are you here?" She pulled her hand free of his, though she missed the warmth of his touch.

"I have to show you something," he said softly. "Will you take one more trip with me up the mountain?"

"Why should I?"

"There's no reason in the world you should," he admitted and pulled his foot out of the doorway. "But I'm asking you to anyway."

If he'd tried to smooth talk her into it, she might have refused. Instead, he'd played a new game. Honesty. And frankly, she was tired of fighting him. She knew she'd regret it later, of course, but at the moment, going with him was just easier.

The ride was tense, neither of them talking much. Colleen's mind was whirling with possibilities and questions. Why had he come? Where were they going? Why?

She sneaked glances at him, and he was always the same. Stoic. Eyes focused on the road ahead, which should have relieved her, since this drive could be treacherous. But she wished that he would glance her way. Give her some indication of what was going on. Instead, he drove the narrow, winding road up the mountain in silence, passing his ranch gates, and she turned in her seat to look at them as they drove by. "I thought we were going to your house."

"No," he said, not looking at her, focusing instead on the road stretched out in front of them.

Her stomach swirled uneasily as she realized where they were probably headed. The cabin. Where else would he be taking her on this mountain road? But then, why would he take her to the cabin? It was the first question she asked when he pulled into the drive and parked.

"Like I said at your house," he told her, climbing out of the huge SUV, "there's something I want to show you."

He took her hand, just as he had the first time, as they headed along the path to the cabin. But it was different now. The flower beds were weeded and bursting with newly planted, bright spring blossoms. Their scent rose up into the air and twisted with the ever-present aroma of pines.

The path itself was covered in fresh gravel. The surrounding pines had been trimmed back, still providing shade for the cabin but no longer threatening to tip over in a storm. The walls were painted a crisp white with navy blue trim around the windows. The chairs on the front porch had brand-new, dark blue cushions and there was a sturdy iron railing snaking along the porch, replacing the rotted wooden one that had snapped on their last visit.

It was beautiful. It was perfect. But she still couldn't buy it. "I can't," she said, looking up at him. "I can't buy this cabin, Sage. I appreciate you fixing it up for me but—"

"The cabin's not for sale anymore."

"What?"

"I bought it last week." He closed in on her and Colleen's heartbeat sped up. "Went to see Ed at his new place and paid him for it on the spot."

"Why?" she asked and was lucky she'd managed to squeeze out that single word.

"Let's go inside. There are some things I want to say to you."

She walked the path, ran her fingertips over the heavy black wrought-iron railing. When he noticed, he said, "I had my guys over here every day this week, fixing this place up. But the railing I installed myself." He caught her hand in his. "It's sturdy enough that you could do handstands on it, but I'd take it as a favor if you wouldn't. I don't want to risk losing you again."

Pleasure slid through her heart, leaving a trail of eager

anticipation in its wake. Was he saying what she thought he was? Could she believe? Her logical mind told her emotional half to get a grip, but it wasn't listening.

He smiled at her and tugged her along after him. "Come on."

She followed and the minute she stepped into the cabin, she realized he'd been at work here, too. The wood floors were gleaming under a fresh coat of wax. Bright throw rugs added splashes of color. Bookcases stood on either side of the wood-burning stove and there was a scent of lemon polish still hovering in the air.

"Linda, my housekeeper," Sage was saying as she walked through the little cabin that was now as shiny as new pennies. "She handled most of the inside work, though my guys did the paint job."

"It's beautiful," she told him, walking back to stop just a foot from him. "But I still don't understand. Why did you buy it?"

"For us," he said simply. He stood there opposite her in his black jeans, black leather jacket and white shirt and looked more gorgeous than she remembered. Just looking at the man gave her chills, but what he said next had every sense reeling.

"I bought it for us, Colleen. I wanted us to have this place to come to, just the two of us. I want us to always remember that we started here. That what's between us grew from here."

Oh, God. Her heartbeat was hammering so quickly now she could hardly draw a breath. But she didn't need air, Colleen realized. All she needed was to know that he meant this. Because if he had done all of this for the two of them, that could only mean that he loved her, and that would be everything.

"See," he said, moving toward her, laying both hands on her shoulders so that she could feel the strong, steady warmth of him seeping into her body. "I know now that I wasted what time I had with my father. I don't want to waste another minute of my time with you."

"Sage…"

"You said you loved me," he reminded her and gave her a slow smile. "I hope that hasn't changed, because I love you, too, Colleen."

Her eyes filled with tears and her breath caught in her throat. It was everything she'd hoped for. Only better.

"I love your mind. Your humor. Your kindness. I love everything about you."

"I can't believe this," she murmured, wondering if somehow she had fallen asleep back at the condo and maybe this was all just a very real, very involved dream.

"Believe it," he said, bending low enough to kiss her forehead before drawing back to look at her again. "Remember what J.D. said? Family is important and love is all that matters?"

"I remember." His eyes were shining down on her. The shutters were gone. They were clear and beautiful and glittering with emotions so deep they stole her breath.

"Well, *you're* my family. And my love for you is everything." He pulled her in close to him, lifted both hands and cupped her face between his palms. "I'm asking you to marry me, Colleen. Marry me and make a family of our own. Kids. Dogs. Horses. We'll have it all if you'll just say yes."

She wanted to. More than anything in her life, she wanted what he was offering. But she had to say, "I still want to get my practitioner's license. I want to have that rural practice I told you about."

He grinned and her heart nearly leaped up her throat. Would he always have this effect on her? God, she hoped so.

"Not a problem, honey," he said. "When you have calls to make, I'll watch the kids."

"Kids," she repeated, because she loved the sound of it.

"At least five or six."

She laughed then and felt her whole world come right again.

"So, will you marry me, Colleen?" He kissed the tip of her nose, then brushed her mouth with his. "Trust me, love. I've learned enough to listen. To know that though I could make it through my life alone, I don't want to. I want you—I *need* you—by my side. Always."

"There's really nowhere else I'd rather be," she said as she leaned into him. Her heart was full, and she had everything she'd ever dreamed of, right there offering her his heart. His life. His love. "Sage, I love you so much, of course I'll marry you."

"Thank God," he whispered and kissed her there in the room where they had first begun. Where they would come when they wanted to remember. When they wanted to celebrate the fact that love really was the only thing that mattered.

Epilogue

The wedding was two weeks later.

Colleen was amazed at just how quickly everything could come together. But Sage hadn't wanted to wait, and really, neither had she. Why wait when you had at last found the one person in the world for you?

Sage's ranch was decorated with flowers everywhere. He'd arranged for both a florist and a gardener to come in and turn the yard into a rainbow of color. There was also a hastily constructed dance floor on the wide front yard, lit by miles of tiny white twinkling lights that in the dusk looked like stars being born. Music from a local country band had the dance floor crowded and the scent of barbecue tempted everyone there.

It had been perfect, Colleen thought. Even the weather had cooperated, blessing the ceremony with a cool, clear day and a starry night.

She'd been on her feet for hours now, but she wasn't the least bit tired. Joy filled her, keeping a smile on her face and a thrill in her heart. She took a sip of champagne and looked out across the ranch at the people who had come to celebrate with them. It had been a small ceremony, only friends and family, and somehow that had made the whole thing more special.

Marlene was dancing with Walter Drake, the older woman laughing at something he said. Angie and Evan looked to be involved in a heated discussion, and Colleen frowned slightly. She could only hope that the situation would be cleared up soon, before it destroyed what the couple shared. Dylan was supervising the barbecue station and Chance was talking to Sage's ranch manager. Jenna and her husband were dancing and Colleen's mother and Aunt Donna were huddled at a table, no doubt planning their upcoming cruise.

"You're looking way too thoughtful for a bride," Sage said, coming up behind her. "And did I tell you how beautiful you are?"

She felt beautiful in her floor-length, off-the-shoulder white dress that skimmed her curves and swirled at her feet. But then, Sage was handsome in a black suit that was so elegantly cut he took her breath away.

"You did," she assured him, "but feel free to repeat yourself."

He chuckled, slid his arms around her middle and held her close to him. Colleen laid her hands on his arms and leaned her head back against his broad chest. "It's just such a perfect day."

He bent his head briefly to kiss her neck. "Any day I can get Colleen Falkner to say 'I do' is a good day."

She looked up at him. "That's Colleen Lassiter to you, mister."

He grinned and her heart did a flip. "Sounds good, doesn't it?"

"Sounds wonderful," she agreed, then nodded toward her mother and aunt. "They're so excited about the house you're having built for them on the ranch."

He laughed a little. "I know. Between the two of them, they're about to drive the architect wild enough to jump out a window."

Colleen's gaze slid across to the other side of the wide, manicured lawn, where the foundation of a house had already been laid. Sage had surprised her, and thrilled her mother, with his plans to build a three-bedroom house on the property for Laura and Donna. They would have their own place but be close enough to the main house that they could come and go as they pleased. The two women hadn't stopped talking about it since.

"They've changed the layout of the downstairs three times already," Sage mused, humor evident in his tone.

"You realize that with this beautiful house, they probably won't want to move to Florida after all?" And really, the two women had only decided on Florida because Aunt Donna already lived there and it would have been the easiest solution. Now things were different.

"Why would they, when Wyoming has everything?" he asked, then, smiling gently he added, "They only wanted to live together. Now they don't have to be in Florida to do it. And if your mom gets sick of winter, we'll buy the two of them a condo in Florida and they can go as often as they like."

Her heart did the flippy thing again as she realized

just what an amazing man she'd fallen in love with. "You're incredible."

"Not really," he said wryly, "but I'm glad you think so."

"I really do," she told him, turning in his arms so that she could look at him. Colleen knew that every ounce of love she felt for him had to be shining from her eyes, because she felt lit from within, as if she was absolutely glowing with the happiness she'd found.

"Besides," he said on a low laugh, "once the two of them have their passports in hand, I have a feeling they're going to be taking lots of trips. They can't wait for that cruise you're sending them on. But home will always be here. Waiting for them."

She studied his features, wanting to be absolutely sure he was okay with this and not just doing it because he knew she'd love having her family close by. "Are you really positive, Sage? There aren't many men willing to have their mother-in-law, not to mention her sister, living right on his doorstep."

All trace of amusement left his face as he met her eyes. He lifted one hand to smooth a stray lock of her hair back behind her ear before saying, "J.D.'s not here today—and damned if I don't wish he was. But I know what he'd say and I feel the same way. Family is important. Love is all that matters."

Tears filled her eyes. "Oh, you really know how to touch my heart."

"You are my heart, Colleen." He bent to kiss her gently, briefly. "And your mom. Donna. They're nice women. Why shouldn't they be with their family?" He grinned. "Besides, when our babies start arriving, how great will it be to have two willing babysitters close by?"

They'd already started trying to make their family, and Colleen sighed with the thought. Babies. A husband who loved her. Her vision still blurred with a wash of tears she was too happy to shed, she went up on her toes and kissed him. "I love you, Sage Lassiter."

"Damn straight you do," he said, his half grin taking all of the arrogance out of the statement.

"You're impossible."

"And very lucky," he added.

"Oh, that too," she agreed, sliding her arms around his waist and cuddling in close. He held her tightly enough that she heard the steady thump of his heart beneath her ear. Closing her eyes, she smiled to herself and relished the sensation of having her life be everything she could ever have hoped for.

A beautiful, love-filled wedding on a gorgeous ranch that was now her home. Her family was close and happy. Soon, she would be on her way to getting her practitioner's license and she had the love of her life holding her so gently it was as if she were a fragile, priceless treasure.

"So," he whispered, "how much longer do you figure we have to stay at this party?"

She smiled up at him. They would be spending their wedding night in the cabin where this had all begun. Tomorrow they were off by private jet for a week in Paris. And then home again to start their lives together. She couldn't wait. Colleen was as anxious as Sage to be alone with him.

"I love that we'll be at the cabin tonight," she told him.

"Me, too. And just think," he said, drawing her close for a hard squeeze, "one day, we'll take our grandkids out there, show them the railing and tell 'em about the day Grandma almost fell off the mountain—but how their strong, brave grandpa saved her, carried her inside and—"

Playfully, she slapped his chest. "We can't tell them *that*."

He caught her hand in his and kissed her palm. "How about we just tell them that Grandma saved Grandpa that day, too?"

Her heart melted. How was it possible to love a man as much as she loved Sage? And how had she ever lived without that love?

"How about we give the party one more hour?" she asked.

He groaned. "Deal. One hour, then if I don't have you, you'll be married to a dead man."

Colleen hugged him tight and turned her face up to his. "One hour. You can make it."

"For you," he promised, *"anything."*

Then he drew her onto the dance floor, and as their family and friends cheered, they danced their way into the future.

* * * * *

"I don't want to fall in love with you, Liam."

The shock of her words knocked him back half a step. He ran a hand across the back of his neck. "I don't know how to answer that. And besides, I don't think you're in much danger. According to someone I know, I'm bossy and uptight and judgmental and I have a king complex."

"Don't forget arrogant."

He held out his hands. "See? You have nothing to worry about."

They continued walking, but his mind was not on the magnificent scenery. Had Zoe been expecting some sort of reciprocal response on his part after she made her veiled statement about having feelings for him? Had he hurt her by remaining silent? And did he want her to love him? Did he want to love her?

* * *

A Not-So-Innocent Seduction
is part of The Kavanaghs of Silver Glen series:

In the mountains of North Carolina, one family discovers that wealth means nothing without love

A NOT-SO-INNOCENT SEDUCTION

BY
JANICE MAYNARD

MILLS &
BOON

Published in Great Britain 2014
by Mills & Boon, an imprint of Harlequin (UK) Limited,
Eton House, 18-24 Paradise Road, Richmond, Surrey, TW9 1SR

© 2014 Janice Maynard

ISBN: 978 0 263 91463 4

51-0414

Harlequin (UK) Limited's policy is to use papers that are natural, renewable and recyclable products and made from wood grown in sustainable forests. The logging and manufacturing processes conform to the legal environmental regulations of the country of origin.

Printed and bound in Spain
by Blackprint CPI, Barcelona

Janice Maynard is a *USA TODAY* bestselling author who lives in beautiful east Tennessee with her husband. She holds a BA from Emory and Henry College and an MA from East Tennessee State University. In 2002 Janice left a fifteen-year career as an elementary school teacher to pursue writing full-time. Now her first love is creating sexy, character-driven, contemporary romance stories.

Janice loves to travel and enjoys using those experiences as settings for books. Hearing from readers is one of the best perks of the job! Visit her website, www.janicemaynard.com, and follow her on Facebook and Twitter.

For Charles—my husband, my best friend.
I could dedicate every book to you and never run
out of reasons why. Thanks for being my hero. :)

One

Zoe Chamberlain's vintage Volkswagen van, aqua and white with yellow daisies stenciled on the doors, rolled to a halt in the scenic vista pull-off and gave up the ghost. She wasn't too surprised. The engine had been rebuilt three times. But like knowing an aging pet was living on borrowed time, it was hard to imagine letting go.

More than anything or anyone else, Bessie—Zoe's VW bus—was the constant in a life that rarely stayed the same from one week to the next. Apparently, Bessie had decided that Silver Glen, North Carolina, was Zoe's next stop.

Zoe stepped out of the van, yawning and stretching, enjoying the cool morning air and the April sunshine. At her feet, spread out in a narrow valley between two mountainsides, lay a charming town. From this distance the houses and businesses looked like an alpine postcard. Switzerland in miniature.

Unfortunately, the quaint village did not have taxi service. As she scrolled through the options on her phone's search function, she grimaced. Her only choice for transportation appeared to be the Silver Beeches Lodge, a pricey hotel that offered shuttle service. Presumably, they had in mind trips back and forth to the nearest airport, but Zoe had no doubts about her ability to wrangle a ride.

A nomadic lifestyle meant getting along with all sorts of people in all manner of places. Zoe could blarney with the best of them. And she'd been told that her smile could melt the hardest of curmudgeons.

So here she was again. A new town. A new set of problems to handle. In her heart of hearts she knew this couldn't go on much longer. She was tired of running. And her recent illness had taken more out of her than she first realized. The excitement of seeing new horizons every week—sometimes every morning—was beginning to pall. Though she tried to ignore it, a feeling of yearning grew ever stronger. Yearning to put down roots, to feel a part of something bigger than she was.

She had used a quest for adventure as justification for her cowardice. Yes, she had seen the world. And yes, travel was broadening. But the truth was, her past was going to catch up with her. If not here, then in the next place.

It was time to face her demons and take a stand, but she wasn't ready yet. First, she needed rest and time to recoup. Making such a change would be scary.

The town below seemed incredibly peaceful. At this moment in her life, peace was a commodity to be craved. Maybe Silver Glen could offer her that. First on the agenda would be leisure and complete recovery. Once she was back on her feet, both in mind and body, she'd be ready for whatever happened. Hopefully.

She patted Bessie's fender and sighed. "Well, old girl. I guess this is where I'm hanging my hat for a little while. I'll get you towed as soon as I can. In the meantime, enjoy the view."

Liam Kavanagh spotted the slender blonde the moment she set foot in the lobby. She would be hard to miss under any circumstances, but carrying a guitar case and wearing a multicolored cotton skirt that swished around her ankles, she looked like a 1960s love child returning from an outdoor rock concert. The bounce in her step and the upward curve of her lips gave her a girl-next-door appeal.

The highly trained staff at the Silver Beeches knew to greet guests with warmth and charm. Liam had watched them in action time and again. He rarely took the time to personally interact with visitors unless they were close friends of his.

He didn't know this woman. At all. But some powerful response propelled his feet forward. Before Pierre, the concierge, could offer to help, Liam intercepted the eye-catching female. "Welcome to the Silver Beeches Lodge. May I help you?"

The woman hitched a large raffia tote higher on her shoulder and gave him a winsome smile. Her eyes were the blue of a summer sky. "I'd like to check in, please."

He lifted a mental eyebrow. Rooms in the hotel started at eight hundred a night and went up from there. This beautiful creature hardly seemed the type to avail herself of the upscale amenities, but he'd been surprised before. "Do you have a reservation?" he asked.

"I do. Made it online an hour ago. Is that a problem?"

He deserved her frown. The tone of his voice had come across as suspicious. He shrugged. "Of course not. I thought I had looked at all of today's check-ins, but I must have missed yours since it was recent. Welcome." He motioned for her to accompany him. "Marjorie, there at the desk, will take care of you. Please let me know if you need anything at all. Our wish is to make you as comfortable as possible."

"So gallant," she said, smiling at him in a way that made the back of his neck hot.

Was she mocking him? It wouldn't be the first time someone had accused him of being too serious. "It's what we do," he said, wincing at the stiffness he heard in his response. He didn't intend to be a stuffed shirt, but he'd been the head of a large and rowdy family since his father disappeared over two decades ago. The weight of his responsibility—and a certain bitterness about his father's lack thereof—didn't leave much room for lightheartedness.

He nodded briefly and excused himself as Marjorie took over. Crossing the lobby to where Pierre held court, he kept an eye on the newcomer. "Not our usual clientele."

Pierre pursed his lips. In his sixties now, he had worked for the Kavanagh family since he was a young man. He wore his formal black tuxedo with pride and ruled his realm with a firm hand. "Pretty," he said.

Liam nodded absently. He couldn't place her age. Pale skin so pure and fine it seemed almost translucent made her seem youthful, but in her serene gaze he saw the patina of experience. He wasn't sure why she fascinated him so. Perhaps because she was the antithesis of the expertly made-up women who often checked into the Lodge.

Visitors to the Silver Beeches were either retirees with plenty of disposable income, younger generations whose careers afforded them fame and fortune, or merely those who wanted to hide from the world. Privacy was an unspoken amenity. From rock stars to movie idols, from politicians to European royalty, every guest was pampered.

As a bellman came in from outside with the new guest's single suitcase, Marjorie handed a key card to the young woman and pointed her toward the elevators. When the bellman and his charge disappeared, Marjorie slipped from behind the desk and approached Liam and Pierre.

Liam frowned slightly. "Problem?"

Marjorie, a stout woman in her mid-fifties with salt-and-pepper hair, shook her head. "Not exactly. But I thought you'd want to know. She booked a basic room for six weeks."

Both men stared at her. Liam recovered first, though his gut tightened with unease. "Any problem with authorizing her method of payment?"

The seasoned receptionist shook her head. "Platinum card. No limit. But tell me—who books a reservation like that on the day of arrival? Spontaneity is one thing, but this is weird, don't you think?"

Liam kept his expression neutral with effort. Red flags were popping up all over the place, but he didn't want his staff to see that he was perturbed. "I'm sure she has her reasons."

Pierre straightened his spine, his gaze fierce. "I'll keep an eye on her, sir. If there's any funny business, I'll let you know."

Maeve Kavanagh appeared from the direction of the back stairs, her bun slightly askew and her reading glasses dangling from a chain around her neck. Liam's mother was a vibrant sixty-year-old with dark snapping eyes and a nose for sniffing out trouble. "You all three look like you've eaten a lemon. What's going on?"

Liam kissed her on the cheek. "Not a thing. Marjorie checked in a new guest. We were merely speculating about her background."

Maeve sniffed. "Not your place," she said firmly. "You know I can't abide gossip."

Liam smiled wryly. "Yes, ma'am. I remember." Inwardly, he was far less amused. The irregularities about the new guest's booking set his teeth on edge. He hated mysteries and secrets. His father's hidden life had nearly destroyed their family. And in the end had led to Reggie Kavanagh's premature death.

The one trait Liam couldn't abide in a woman, or a man for that matter, was a predilection to bend the truth. Even if the potential prevaricator came wrapped in a very appealing package.

Before he could give in to the temptation to initiate further contact with the blonde, he managed a smile for his mother and Pierre and Marjorie. "If you three will excuse me, I have some calls to make." Striding down the hall to his office, he told himself he was jumping to conclusions.

The newcomer could have any number of valid reasons for deciding on the spur of the moment to stay alone at a pricey hotel for six weeks.

Trouble was, despite his best efforts, Liam couldn't come up with a single one.

Zoe grilled the bellman on the way upstairs. "So tell me. Who's the yummy guy that looks like a young Harrison Ford?"

The teenage bellhop grinned. "That's Mr. Kavanagh. Mr. Liam Kavanagh. His family owns the Silver Beeches. Well, that and most of the town, as well."

"He works for a living?" She was surprised. In her experience, the überrich kept to themselves as much as possible.

The young man waited politely for her to step out of the elevator when they reached the top floor. "Every one of the Kavanagh men does something. They were brought up to respect a hard day's work, even though the whole family is richer than God. Mr. Liam manages the hotel along with his mother."

Inside the room, Zoe reached in her bag for a generous tip that made the kid's eyes light up. "Thanks for your help," she said.

He bowed awkwardly. "All you have to do is dial the front desk if you need anything. Room service is available 24/7. In the center drawer of the dresser you'll find listings about all the restaurants here and off-site as well. Welcome to Silver Glen."

Alone in her luxurious new quarters, Zoe opened the armoire and smiled as she imagined how little of the space her belongings would fill. Learning to travel light had been a necessary lesson, and one she had mastered long ago. Nevertheless, she carefully unloaded her suitcase and put away everything she had brought with her. Being neat was perhaps a relic of her parents' influence, the one trait she couldn't shake.

There were still a few items in the van, but nothing she

needed urgently. She turned in a slow circle, taking in every detail of her new accommodations. Here in the mountains of North Carolina, one might have expected a more rustic decor, but the Silver Beeches Lodge was elegant in the extreme.

The lobby alone telegraphed that message. Italian marble floors. Sparkling chandeliers. Priceless Oriental rugs of massive size. Enormous urns filled with fresh flowers. It had taken Zoe only moments to decide that Bessie had been correct about her silent suggestion. Zoe needed to rest, and this lovely hotel promised to be peaceful.

Never mind that it cost an arm and a leg. Her usual lifestyle was lean and frugal, so this splurge would not break the bank. Besides, after the winter she had endured, she deserved a little pampering.

Walking barefoot across the plush ivory carpet, she opened her guitar case and removed the instrument. The comfy bay-window seat was covered in crimson velvet. Poor Bessie would never have made it up the incline to the hotel. The Silver Beeches Lodge had literally been built into the side of the mountaintop, and its location gave guests a bird's-eye view of the valley floor far below.

Zoe curled her legs beneath her and bent her head over the instrument that had traveled so many miles with her. Strumming it absently, she hummed a tune that had been dancing in her head. She'd had to resist the urge to coax the bellhop into lingering for a bit to answer her questions about the hotel owner. Just because she was lonely was no reason to get the kid in trouble.

Her reaction to meeting Liam Kavanagh was the equivalent of experiencing a crush on a movie star. His in-your-face masculinity made her feel dainty and feminine. She might even have swooned a little bit. Even now, her throat flushed as she remembered the way he looked at her. The man was a walking fantasy. She glanced out the window and sighed.

Night was falling rapidly, and shadows crept across the

valley. Her stomach rumbled. She remembered that her last meal had been an orange and a Diet Coke at a rest stop on I-40. She wished she could go into town and explore, but until Bessie was fixed, she was stuck here in the hotel. Dialing room service, she ordered a large dinner, including a serving of tiramisu. She was still a good fifteen pounds underweight, so the extra calories wouldn't hurt her.

She'd spent the last week in Asheville playing at a little coffee shop in the downtown district. Asheville was filled with artists and performers and had a character and charm that delighted her. If she'd had her way, she might have bought a place and put down some roots. But one evening she had seen a familiar face on the street, and she had known it was time to move on. The hotel's strict privacy policy would stand her in good stead. No one would know she was here, and if she wore a bit of a disguise in town, she might be able to stay for even longer than the month and a half she had booked.

After finishing her larger-than-normal meal, she felt both satiated and guilty. Changing into yoga pants and a sports bra, she checked the hotel directory and discovered that the workout facility was located on the basement level. She threw a light jacket over her shoulders, more for modesty than anything else, grabbed her room key and a bottle of water, and slipped out the door.

Liam strained with all his might as he lifted the challenging weights in one last rep. Red-faced and sweating, he wiped his forehead and neck with a towel, realizing ruefully that the punishing exercise had not dulled the throbbing arousal that plagued him.

He wasn't sporting an erection, but his body hummed with the need for sex. It had been too long, and the blonde who checked in that afternoon was exactly the type he found irresistible. Her silky hair brushed her shoulder blades. Though she was thin, her curves were all woman.

If she was staying for an entire six weeks, he would have to be on his guard. Just because he felt a visceral interest in Ms. Zoe Chamberlain didn't mean the feelings were reciprocated. And because there was clearly more to Zoe than met the eye, he wouldn't allow himself to pursue the attraction. Most men were vulnerable to a sexy woman. But Liam understood the consequences of becoming entangled with a liar.

If he had to choose between satisfying the burning in his gut and being won over by a con, he would take a lot of cold showers. Zoe's seeming innocence was dangerous. He'd learned the hard way at age sixteen that a pretty face could disguise a multitude of sins. He would cut off his hand before he ever put his mother and siblings through that kind of pain again. As the head of the Kavanaghs, his loyalty to his family superseded any fleeting attraction he might experience.

Besides, for all he knew, Zoe could be married. He couldn't imagine any husband in his right mind letting such a fresh, appealing woman take a solo six-week vacation, but who knows? The Silver Beeches had seen more than its share of odd relationships over the years.

After showering and changing back into his dress shirt and slacks, he wandered out into the gym only to stop dead when he saw his new guest walking briskly on a treadmill. Her slender frame resonated with life and passion. At the moment, she was the only occupant of the facility other than himself, and he didn't want to startle her. She was wearing earbuds attached to an iPod tucked into a hot-pink armband. Her ponytail swung energetically in time to the music only she could hear.

Despite his lofty intentions and self-lecturing, he was drawn to her as inexorably as a green boy seeing his first seminude woman. His heartbeat picked up even as his breathing grew choppy. Telltale signs that his libido was far more powerful than his intellect.

Deciding to take the long way around to the door, Liam

assumed she would see him in her peripheral vision and thus not be alarmed. But even though he stayed far to the other side of the room, as soon as she caught sight of him, she hopped off the treadmill, shut it down and removed her earphones. "Hello, Mr. Kavanagh."

As she walked toward him, he studied the sensual grace in her movements. "You know who I am?" Though he tried to keep his gaze on her face, only a saint could ignore the rest of her body. Her Lycra-covered curves were mesmerizing…. That and the sheen of perspiration on her skin. He imagined she would look just this way after an enthusiastic round of lovemaking.

She nodded, wiping her forehead with her forearm. "I pumped the bellman for details about you. A failing of mine. Curiosity killed the cat, and all that."

Liam liked knowing she was interested enough to ask questions. That was a good sign if he planned on pursuing her. Which he wouldn't. Probably. He ran a hand through his hair, knowing from her expression that she had recognized his sexual interest. "A fairly minor sin, I'd say. Are you satisfied with your room?"

She lifted an eyebrow. "Are you kidding? It's amazing. The view alone is worth the price. Your hotel is beautiful."

"Thank you. My family built it just after World War II. And we've continued to add on and make improvements as the years go by." He'd never had any trouble talking to women, but for some reason he didn't understand, Zoe made his palms sweat. She wasn't the most beautiful woman he'd ever met, nor the most polished. Usually, people were intimidated by *him,* not vice versa. He couldn't say why he was bungling what should have been a casual, polite encounter, but he was sure she didn't want to hear a documentary on the Silver Beeches. "I'd better get back upstairs."

She cocked her head. "Was your offer sincere?"

"I beg your pardon?" Her artless question befuddled him.

"You said you would do anything to make me comfortable. I'm merely asking if that was standard hotel hyperbole, or if you meant it."

He felt his neck get warm. Was she coming on to him, or was she merely eccentric? "Of course, I meant it. Was there something you wanted?"

Zoe supposed it would be poor form to blurt out *You!* Even if his intensity and unsmiling sexiness definitely flipped her switches. She was having a hard time reading Liam Kavanagh. He seemed interested in her the way a man is interested in a woman he wants, but on the other hand, his body language telegraphed a definite wariness. Maybe he felt like she was too bourgeois to stay at his fancy hotel.

If that were the case, she wouldn't disabuse him. She was a pro at keeping secrets. Perhaps Liam might have a few of his own. Could two people with such defenses in place make any kind of connection?

Her walkabout ways the last few years had made it virtually impossible to sustain any kind of deep relationship with a man. Since she wasn't into casual hookups, she ended up alone most of the nights of her life. Ordinarily, she was able to convince herself that solitude was preferable to intimacy with a guy who might turn out to be a jerk.

But now, with Liam Kavanagh in touching distance, she was suddenly and intensely aware of how long it had been since she'd been with a man. She was young and healthy. Liam exuded all sorts of breath-stealing pheromones. She had a gut feeling that his experience was exponentially ahead of hers…and that he was the kind of man a woman never forgot.

What frightened her was the knowledge that he was unlike any man she had ever wanted before. Was her whole life about to change? She'd been prepared to face her mistakes. But Liam was a bend in the road she hadn't anticipated. Could she deal with the complicated past and the intriguing present all at once? He didn't appear to be a man who would be easily *handled*.

Clearing her throat, she summoned a cheeky smile. Liam's wary courtesy made her want to ruffle his feathers. "I've never been to Silver Glen before," she said. "How about buying me a drink in the bar and giving me a quick rundown of the *must-sees*." She knew how to flirt. It came naturally to her upbeat personality despite the fact that she lived like a nun most of the time.

He appeared taken aback by her request. But he recovered rapidly, his gaze scanning her from head to toe with an assessment that was as personal as her deliberate come-on. "I could do that."

A nasty thought occurred to her. "I suppose I should ask. Is there a Mrs. Kavanagh?"

He nodded, sending her heart to her knees. "Yes. My mother. But she goes to bed early, so I doubt she'd want to join us."

"So you *do* have a sense of humor," she taunted, refusing to admit—even to herself—that she was elated by the confirmation that he was single. Not all married men wore wedding rings, so she hadn't been sure. "I was beginning to think they removed your funny bone at birth."

His lips twitched. "I'm guessing you weren't spanked enough as a kid."

"And there you'd be wrong," she said, her stomach twisting involuntarily. "Let me shower and I'll join you in the lobby in half an hour. Does that work for you?"

He nodded slowly, regarding her with watchful eyes that were a brilliant, intense blue. Combined with his thick, coal-black hair, she began to see the Irish ancestry his name suggested.

She'd provoked him, and now he regarded her with a narrow-eyed gaze. "I'll be there, Ms. Chamberlain. And I'll have the kitchen deliver some special hors d'oeuvres to the bar."

"I've already had dinner," she felt compelled to point out.

"You'll enjoy these," he promised. "Nothing too heavy."

"Does every guest get this personal treatment?"

Now, there was no mistaking his interest. "Only the ones who ask," he said, the words calm and crisp. "I'll see you shortly."

Zoe decided not to shower in the dressing room. She hadn't brought clean clothes with her, so it was easier to dart back up to her room and use the sumptuous facilities that made her feel decadent and a bit naughty. The clothes she'd had on earlier were somewhat travel-weary, so she reached in the armoire for a slinky black knit dress that packed like a dream. It showed every curve of her body, but she had worn it enough times to feel at ease in the sexy garment. Most of a woman's appearance was dictated by confidence. Since she had learned stage presence long ago, it was easy to project an image, even if she didn't feel her best inside.

Timidity and nerves could be disguised. In some of her darker moments—when faced with a bully or an amorous drunk who didn't want to back off—she'd learned that the only way to prevail was to act like she didn't give a damn. How many times over the years had she done exactly that? Liam was no doubt a perfectly lovely man, but the ability to appear comfortable when she was uncertain of an outcome would stand her in good stead.

Shaking off the dark memories, she inserted small gold studs in her earlobes and slipped her feet into black patent high-heeled sandals. The sleeveless dress was fairly modest except for the fact that it hugged her body. She glanced in the mirror and sighed. How long had it been since she shared an elegant meal with a man?

Most of the time, she was the music in the background of someone else's life. She had planned it that way…enjoyed it mostly. But tonight, she looked forward to enjoying Liam

Kavanagh's courtly manners. And perhaps slipping past his facade of propriety.

She spritzed perfume at her ears and wrists and slipped a delicate gold chain around her neck. It hung between her breasts and caught the light. Somewhere, in a safety-deposit box far away, she had a large collection of expensive jewelry…pearls, diamonds, semiprecious stones. But as long as she played the role of gypsy, her baubles would go unclaimed. She didn't care. Not really. But tonight it would have been nice to gild the lily with a bit of sparkly, feminine bling.

Taking a deep breath, she tucked her room key and phone into a small bag and headed for the door. Liam Kavanagh was downstairs, and she didn't intend to keep him waiting.

Two

Liam bobbled his glass of wine—splashing a few drops on his hand—when Zoe walked into the bar. All heads swung in her direction, though she appeared oblivious to the interest she drew. Finally, he pinpointed part of her allure. It was the way she moved…graceful, energetic, as if she were always off on a delightful adventure.

Liam had been standing by the bar talking to the female bartender. With a lift of his hand, he caught Zoe's attention, hoping his smile appeared more natural than it felt. His limbs tingled and his chest tightened. The physical manifestations of his arousal were disconcerting. He'd had a number of lovers in his adult life. He understood sexual hunger. But the intensity of his response to Zoe rattled him.

The dress she wore should have been outlawed. Even the harshest of critics would have to concede that it was modest in cut. A shallow scooped neck front and back, plus a hemline that covered her ankles, might have added up to a demure appearance. But the soft, pliable fabric slid over Zoe's phenomenal body like a second skin.

He spent a good thirty seconds searching for any evidence that she wore underwear.

"Hello, Liam," she said, her voice smooth as cream. "May I call you that?"

He took her hand and lifted it to his lips. "I think you just did."

Chuckling softly, she allowed him to seat her at a table for two tucked away in a shadowy corner. The bar was crowded tonight. He was glad. The public setting gave him time to get to know her and to decide if she was any kind of threat. Kissing her later seemed a foregone conclusion, but he would at least pretend to himself that he had a choice.

She glanced around the room. "Nice place. You and your family have good taste."

"Thank you. I'm assuming you won't be offended if I use your first name as well?"

"Of course not."

"We've only just met. Some people prefer a bit of formality."

"Not me. Social conventions get in the way."

"In the way of what?"

She shrugged. "I don't know. Becoming friends, I suppose."

He took a sip of his wine, trying to read the subtext, if there was any. Before he could reply, a waiter appeared and set a plate of appetizers in front of them. Small wedges of melon and scallops wrapped in prosciutto had been skewered with toothpicks. He selected one and held it out. "Our chef is spectacular. Try a bite."

He'd anticipated an argument. Instead, her lips parted and she leaned forward, allowing him to slide the delicacy between her lush, glossy, pale-pink lips. "Wonderful," she said, after she chewed and swallowed. "Thank you."

The sensuality and simple enjoyment in her response made him shift restlessly in his chair. As she sat back and smiled at him, her wavy golden hair swung around her shoulders. He couldn't decide if she was trying to be provocative, or if he was overly sensitive to her allure.

At that moment, his mother appeared at his shoulder. "Hope I'm not interrupting. Please introduce me to this lovely girl," she said.

A waiter scurried over with a third chair, and Liam stood until his mother was seated. Maeve Kavanagh had never been able to resist poking her nose into Liam's affairs, either literal or metaphorical ones. Because he loved her dearly, he tolerated her interference, particularly since he hoped to get her impressions of the mysterious blonde. "Zoe Chamberlain, meet Maeve Kavanagh, my mother."

The two women shook hands. Zoe grinned wryly. "I'm happy to meet you. But you're far too young to be Liam's mother. I think he gave me the wrong impression when he described you." She crossed her legs beneath the table, the toe of her shoe brushing the crease in his trouser leg. Was she doing that on purpose?

Maeve shot him a glance that made the tops of his ears heat. "My firstborn has an odd sense of humor at times. We make allowances for him." She helped herself to an appetizer. "What brings you to Silver Glen, Ms. Chamberlain? Business or vacation?"

"Call me Zoe, please. And actually, it's neither. I had a nasty bout of pneumonia back in March. Spent a few days in the hospital. Since then I've been taking things easy. Your beautiful hotel seemed like the perfect place to rest and regain my stamina."

"You've come to the right spot. We'll pamper you so well you won't want to go home."

Serious illness explained her fragile appearance. Which led Liam to more questions. He inserted himself into the conversation. "And on that note, where *is* home, Zoe?"

For the first time, he saw her good humor waver. A shadow crossed her expressive face. But she recovered quickly. "I was born in Connecticut, but I haven't lived there in years."

"That's not really an answer."

Her jaw tightened. "Am I being interrogated?"

Maeve Kavanagh's phone buzzed, signaling the arrival of a text. She glanced at it and grimaced. "Duty calls." She stood and patted Liam's shoulder. "Try not to alienate our newest guest, son. I'd like her to stay for a while."

In the silence that followed his mother's departure, Liam stared moodily at his tablemate. "Since when is polite conversation categorized as interrogation?"

She shrugged. "So far, the conversation has been pretty one-sided. I'm picking up weird vibes from you. Is there a problem you want to talk about?"

"No." *Yes.* "Feel free to cross-examine me if it will make you feel better. My family is an open book. Ask anyone in town. They'll tell you."

"There's no such thing as a clan without skeletons in the closet. But I'll take you at your word. Do you have siblings?"

"More than I care to count. It's the Irish Catholic thing. My mother deserves sainthood."

"And your father?"

He couldn't help the wave of anger that made his entire body go rigid. "He died when I was sixteen."

"I'm sorry." Her response was quiet. In her steady gaze he saw recognition of his turmoil. But he didn't want anyone psychoanalyzing him. He ate another appetizer, his gaze drifting over the noisy but genteel crowd. "It was a long time ago," he muttered, and was relieved when she allowed the subject to drop.

"Did you always know you wanted to run the hotel?"

"No. In fact, I had dreams of becoming a major-league football player."

Her jaw dropped and she laughed out loud.

He scowled. "What's so funny?"

You don't really seem the type."

"I can assure you, Zoe, I've played more than my share of high school and college sports."

"I wasn't impugning your athletic ability or your masculinity. It's just that you seem rather sophisticated for the rough-and-tumble world of professional sports."

"Sophistication is nothing more than clothes and demeanor. After my father's death, it became clear that my studies were headed in a new direction. As soon as I finished an MBA, I returned home to assist my mother."

"Did you really have no choice?" It sounded like more than a rhetorical question.

"No one dragged me back in chains, if that's what you mean. But I felt the obligation of being the oldest. The others were still growing up. It was me or no one."

"I see."

His explanation seemed to bother her, though he couldn't fathom why. "At the risk of sounding nosy, what did *you* study in college?"

"I spent four semesters at Vassar. Decided I had no clue what I wanted to do with my life, so I dropped out and joined the Peace Corps."

"Are you serious?" More and more he got the impression that she was a throwback to the 1960s.

"It was wonderful," she said simply. "And eye-opening. I was young and naive and had no clue that extreme third-world poverty existed."

"Your parents were okay with you leaving school?"

"I didn't really ask them."

The more she revealed, the more he wanted to know. But she had accused him of interrogating her, and he had to respect her boundaries...not only because she was a guest in the hotel, but because it was the right thing to do.

"Would you like another drink?" he asked.

"A peach daiquiri would be nice." Zoe cocked her head. "Why are you entertaining me?"

He summoned a waiter and gave their order. When the young man disappeared, Liam met her gaze squarely. "Has it occurred to you that *you* may be entertaining me?"

For the first time since they met in the lobby, he saw her flustered. Her cheeks flushed a rosy pink and she looked away for a moment. He used the opportunity to study her profile. The only thing marring a classically beautiful face was the thrust of a stubborn chin and the smallest of crooks in her nose.

His scrutiny did not go unnoticed. Her hands fiddled with a fork as she faced him again. "Do I have food on my face?" she asked, the words acerbic.

"Sorry. I was just wondering if you had ever broken your nose."

"That bad, huh?"

"Not at all. But you have the features of a Greek goddess except for that tiny crooked place in your nose and the way you lead with your chin."

"I'm not sure that counts as a compliment."

"Merely trying to avoid social conventions."

Finally, he coaxed a smile from her. "Touché."

Their drinks arrived. Zoe sipped hers delicately, like a small child savoring an unaccustomed treat. He wanted to ask her flat out if she could afford a six-week stay at Silver Beeches, but of course, he couldn't. Attending Vassar indicated a certain level of financial ease. Then again, she could have gone on a scholarship. The fact that he was so obsessed with her background gave him pause. Was his interest related to the hotel, or something more?

A man could want a woman without knowing anything at all about her other than the way she walked and the scent of her perfume. Simple lust he understood. But this fixation on ferreting out Zoe's secrets alarmed him. Whether she was an eccentric heiress or a working girl with only months to live or European royalty hiding out from the press, her story was hers to tell.

Perhaps if he were patient, Zoe would open up to him. Two decades ago he had allowed infatuation to blind him to the truth about a woman. It had been a salutary lesson, and one he wouldn't repeat. The fact that he was already so intrigued by Zoe meant he had to be very careful not to let his hormones overrule his common sense.

Zoe was having the most marvelous time. Dressed up for a change. Chatting with a suave, worldly, handsome man. Feeling like a desirable woman. All in all, quite an exceptional evening.

Liam was fascinating. On the outside, the epitome of a sophisticated gentleman. But in his conversation and in his eyes, she caught glimpses of another man, another less polished persona.

What did it say about her that she wanted to see more of the second?

She savored the last bit of her drink, feeling the pleasant buzz in her limbs as the alcohol worked its way through her bloodstream. She was not much of a drinker and had little tolerance for strong spirits. The daiquiri had just enough of a punch to leave her relaxed and happy.

Liam seemed in no hurry to end their encounter, so she lingered as well, even as the bar emptied slowly. It was fun to pick out the honeymooners, the anniversary couples. A few duos exhibited the marks of enjoying a clandestine affair.

Watching people was a hobby of Zoe's. She knew how to fade into the background, especially with her guitar around her neck.

Over the years, her people skills had carried her far and had kept her out of harm's way. A single woman on the road had to be smart and well prepared. Despite her current slenderness, she knew how to fell an assailant and how to disable an aggressor.

Tonight, however, such skills would not be needed. Liam was not the kind of man who had to force himself on a woman. The intensity of his eyes made her shiver. They were technically the same color as hers. But in Liam's case, the blue was the searing shade found in the heart of a flame.

He had unbuttoned the top button of his shirt and loosened his tie. At the end of a long day, his jaw was shadowed. She imagined for a moment what he would look like in bed, ready for sleep after making love to a woman.

Her thighs tightened and her belly quivered. Perhaps Bessie had been wrong. Perhaps Silver Glen, North Carolina, presented danger rather than a safe haven. Zoe rarely had difficulty guarding her heart. Her transient lifestyle kept relationships at bay.

But then again, she had never met a man like Liam who appealed to her so immediately and so viscerally. Contentment ruled her days for the most part, even if loneliness had to be acknowledged and embraced.

For Liam Kavanagh she was willing to change all that. She knew it in an instant. Perhaps she was even willing to blindly follow the demands of her body and give in to the sweet rush of arousal. Throwing herself into an impulsive affair was completely out of character. But her illness during the late winter had shaken her.

Lying in a strange hospital in Albuquerque, New Mexico, near death at one point, she had hit rock bottom. No one knew where she was. There were no friends nearby to bring flowers and pop in for a visit. If she had slipped away into the great beyond, her passing would have sparked little more interest than a search for next of kin.

Shame and distress made her tremble. She had been on the run for so long that she no longer knew how to relax and enjoy life. She told herself that her needs were few. That traveling light was a virtue. But at the end of the day, what did she have to show for her twenty-seven years on this earth?

Contemplating change was difficult. And terrifying.

Liam reached across the table and took one of her hands in his. "Are you okay, Zoe? You've gone pale as milk. And you're shaking. It's late. If you've been ill, perhaps you need to be in bed."

Was it her imagination, or did his fingers tighten on hers involuntarily when he said the word *bed*?

She managed a smile. "I'm fine. Maybe a ghost walked over my grave."

"Are you superstitious?"

"No more than the next person, I suppose. But the Irish are, I'm told. Though you don't strike me as the type of man who leans toward whimsy or flights of fancy."

He released her. The color of his eyes darkened to midnight. His jaw set. "I've seen firsthand the pain caused by people who can't hold on to reality. So, no. I'm not superstitious."

The turn in the conversation had upset him. But she couldn't let it drop. "And I've seen the damage done by soulless individuals who can't see the magic in everyday life. So maybe the truth lies somewhere in between."

They stared at each other. A pleasant evening of flirtation had segued into something far more serious.

He shook his head, his expression rueful. "I think we've strayed into territory best left unexplored for the moment. I was supposed to be telling you about things to see and do while you're here."

"True." She glanced at his watch. "But it's late. We can finish this tomorrow. I need to get some sleep."

He stood when she did. "I'll walk you to your room."

"It's not necessary."

His gaze was teasing. "Merely one of our amenities."

They exited the bar and headed for the duo of elevators in the lobby. Someone had lowered the lights. A sleepy desk clerk sketched a halfhearted wave as they passed by. The intimacy of the hour shrouded everything in a hushed silence.

In the elevator, Zoe leaned against one mirrored wall, Liam the other. His gaze was trained on the carpet at his feet, as though he were lost in thought. The ride was short. A quiet ding, and suddenly they were at Zoe's floor.

"Good night," she said, thinking he would remain in the elevator.

Instead, he accompanied her down the hallway. "Perhaps I should check for monsters under your bed," he whispered, obviously not wanting to disturb his other guests.

She shot him a look, wondering if he expected to come in. "I'm sure a hotel like the Silver Beeches Lodge has a ghostbuster on retainer. But thanks for the offer."

At her door, she reached in her small bag and withdrew her key card. "I enjoyed our visit," she said primly. "Thanks for your time."

They were not touching. Liam stood a good three feet away. But the look in his eyes scorched her. Beneath the thin fabric of her dress, her nipples beaded.

Liam noticed, and took a step backward. "It was my pleasure," he said. The words were prosaic, but the intonation was not.

Desire shimmered between them, invisible but real. She didn't really imagine that her vehicle talked to her. That was a game she played. But if she believed in fate, and perhaps she did, then this moment in time was preordained. Something had brought her to a small, private getaway in the mountains where the man of her dreams awaited her.

It was entirely possible she was being naive. Perhaps Liam entertained a number of female guests who walked into his hotel.

Even so, she chose to keep the fiction alive.

She looked at him wistfully, wishing she had the guts to kiss him. "Good night, Liam."

He nodded tersely, his beautiful eyes turbulent. "Good night, Zoe."

Three

Liam didn't sleep worth a damn. His sex was stiff and aching off and on for most of the night. The few hours he did manage to close his eyes and doze, he dreamed of Zoe. When the alarm went off at seven, he groaned and slapped the snooze button. Normally a morning person, today he knew it was going to take more than a cup of coffee—or two or four—to keep him on track.

The dreams he'd experienced had been explicit and erotic. In his extremely vivid nocturnal imagination, Zoe was continually naked and smiling. And happy to see him. He could actually feel the warmth of her body draped across his. A pleasant notion that played well in his subconscious, but not so much in the harsh light of day.

The alarm shrilled a second time, and he gave in.

An hour later, showered, dressed and mostly awake, he headed down to the lobby. It was a weekday, so their check-ins would be light. Marjorie stopped him with a question about a multiroom booking. Pierre wanted to show him a website that might be of interest to their guests. By the time Liam finally made it to his office, it was almost ten.

He sat down at his desk and opened his laptop, gazing absently out his window that overlooked the side of the property. The groundskeeper had outdone himself this past year. Dogwoods bloomed in profusion amidst carefully sculpted banks of forsythia. Narrow paths dotted with ornamental benches invited guests to stop and enjoy the rainbow of irises, tulips and English wildflowers planted in traditional beds.

The tranquil view soothed Liam as a rule. But today it made things worse. Because he could imagine himself and Zoe walking in the moonlight out there. A glance at the calendar on the wall confirmed the fact that the lunar phase was full tonight.

Sucking in a disgusted breath, he forced himself to focus on work. He was a grown man too old to be ruled by his male anatomy. Last night was exhilarating and stimulating in more ways than one. But he had to slow down. He was the head of the Kavanagh family. He had responsibilities. Big ones. He didn't have the luxury of following every sexual whim.

The landline phone rang, startling him. He picked it up automatically. "Silver Beeches Lodge. Liam Kavanagh speaking."

The voice on the other end was familiar. "Hey, buddy. Do you have a minute to come down to the shop?"

"What's up, Gary?" He and the owner of the Silver Chassis had gone to public school together for years and remained friends to this day, despite the differences in their financial situations. Maeve had taught her children from the cradle that they were no better than anyone else. *Money is not the measure of a man.* Liam had heard those words from her a hundred times.

Silver Glen's most talented mechanic lowered his voice. "I don't want to say anything over the phone. But I think you'll want to see this."

Liam snagged a bagel and a banana from the hotel kitchen and ate them on the way down the mountain. The scenic drive was so familiar, he could have done it in his sleep, but the view affected him every time. This town would not exist without Kavanagh ancestors. Every part of the community had Kavanagh blood running through its veins.

For Liam it was both a blessing and a curse. He was proud to be a part of something so special, but he was ruefully aware that his heritage chained him here as certainly as any prison bars.

He'd taken up the yoke after his father's disappearance. He had stood beside his grieving mother and sworn to keep their family together and afloat. But in the process, he'd given up any autonomy over his future. The road ahead was never going to change. He had trained himself to ignore the bleak disappointment that knowledge occasionally evoked.

He parked on the street behind Gary's shop and went in search of the owner. Gary was in the pit, examining the undercarriage of a vintage VW bus. When he noticed Liam's presence, he called out. "Hold on." Moments later, he climbed up and joined Liam. "This is what I wanted to show you."

Liam frowned. "I don't understand."

Gary was balding prematurely and had a bit of a beer gut, but he knew cars better than anyone Liam had ever met. "It was towed here this morning by an automobile service. The owner contacted me and gave me carte blanche to replace the engine and anything else that needed attention."

"So?"

"So," Gary said with a grimace, "the owner has checked into your hotel."

Liam shook his head in disbelief as the light dawned. "Zoe Chamberlain," he said.

"How did you know?"

"A lucky guess. When she walked through the front door I pegged her as the reincarnation of a 1960s love child. But despite her eccentricities, I don't get your concern."

Gary rubbed his chin, smearing grease below his lip. "Take a look." He opened the back of the van. "Ms. Chamberlain has been sleeping in the back of her vehicle. On a regular basis. The mattress is well-worn, and she has a stash of personal toiletries in that small cabinet. Call me crazy, but how can a woman like that afford the Silver Beeches? She gave me a platinum card number with no limit. I'm a little spooked though. I can't afford to get ripped off on a job this big."

"Meaning you think the card might be stolen?"

"Well, what's your explanation?"

"I don't have one." Liam's stomach curled with frustration. Had he been taken in by a scam artist?

"How long is she staying?"

"She made a reservation for six weeks."

"Hell, man. You know your rates better than I do. Something doesn't add up."

Liam took one last look inside the van and closed the door. "Go ahead and start ordering parts. I'll cover it all if there's a problem. In the meantime, tell her it's going to be a week or more. I'll offer her a hotel vehicle to drive. That will buy us some time to make sure the credit card is legit." His own motives were muddled, but if he did Zoe a favor, perhaps she would be inclined to drop her guard around him and he could figure out what the hell was going on.

Gary slapped him on the shoulder. "Thanks, Liam. Sorry for interrupting your day, but I thought you'd want to know."

Liam grimaced. "I appreciate the heads-up. I'll keep you posted."

Zoe slept late and enjoyed a wonderfully lazy morning in bed. Breakfast was delivered via room service—a selection of handmade miniature pastries, generous servings of bacon and eggs, and a fancy silver pot full of coffee. By the time she finished, her tummy was uncomfortably full, but she didn't regret a bite of the overindulgence.

Setting the tray outside her door, she made sure the do-not-disturb sign was in place on the doorknob and then climbed back into bed. Because her room was on the top floor, she had the luxury of leaving the drapes open without worrying about anyone looking in on her.

The sunshine boosted her spirits. Pulling the covers up to her chin, she curled into the spot that was still warm and let her mind wander.

She felt safe in this room in a way she hadn't in a long time.

The only shadow over her current happiness was Bessie. The garage owner had called moments before and said the repairs would take a number of days because of the difficulty of getting parts. Which meant Zoe was stranded. The nearest car rental place was at the airport in Asheville. She didn't really want to go back there.

Maybe she could hitch a ride with someone going into town. She liked exploring new places, and Silver Glen, at least from a distance, appeared delightfully appealing.

The severity of her illness had scared her. It was difficult to maintain a healthy lifestyle on the road. Too much fast food and not enough rest and exercise. During the weeks she had booked at the Silver Beeches, she needed to take advantage of the hotel chef's expertise and eat well.

By one in the afternoon, she had reached her limit for *taking it easy.* After showering and changing into black slacks and a silky top with a geometric pattern of taupe and cinnamon, she went in search of the dining room. White linen tablecloths and crystal chandeliers set a standard for elegance, though she saw a wide variety of clothing choices in the diners. Everything from jeans to suits and ties.

Asking the hostess for a table for one did not bother Zoe.

She had lived much of her adult life on her own. Choosing what to order was far more difficult. The menu was amazing. At long last, she settled on chicken marsala with spinach salad and sautéed squash. The meal included hot yeast rolls that were to die for.

As she ate, she studied her companions surreptitiously. Everyone in the room seemed at ease with the upscale setting. No one pretending to be something they were not. But everyone had secrets of one sort or another, no matter their station in life.

She was drinking coffee with her sorbet when Liam strode into the room. He worked the crowd effortlessly, stopping to speak to one table and then another. His confidence and charm drew smiles from patrons who were clearly pleased to receive his attention. Today he wore a navy sport coat over khaki trousers with another crisp white shirt. His tie was a tasteful paisley pattern of blues and greens.

Despite his conservative clothing, his physique was impressive. Broad shoulders, narrow waist and hips, and long legs. If she had to guess, she'd say he was about six-two to her five foot nine.

Zoe smiled at him wryly when he finally made it to where she sat, her pulse skittering in a disconcerting fashion. "You should have been a politician. I can see you kissing babies and shaking hands all over the state."

Without asking, he pulled out a chair and sat down beside her. His quick grin took years off his age. "I hate lying and sucking up to fat cats. So I don't think so. I'm happy right where I am."

"Are you really?"

The grin disappeared, replaced by what she was coming to recognize as his familiar brooding intensity. "What does that mean?"

She shrugged. "Don't you ever have the urge to drive out of town and not look back? Hit the road for places unknown?"

"Is that how you live your life?"

The sharp retort with its hint of disapproval put her back up. "There's a lot to be said for travel. It broadens the mind."

"I've noticed you're good at dodging questions you don't like. Maybe *you* should have been a politician."

She stared at him, nonplussed. Not many people had the sharp wit and the perspicacity to silence her. "Are we having our first fight?"

He shook his head, clearly amused by her question. "I'm in too good a mood today for that. The sun is shining. The stock market is up. The hotel is full. I've got no complaints." He lifted a hand, and the server brought him a cup of black coffee. "I had a phone call from the garage in town," Liam said. "Gary tells me that your vehicle is in the shop. So I've brought you these." He tossed a set of keys on the table.

Eyeing him suspiciously, Zoe ignored the offering. "I've heard of full-service hotels, but this is ridiculous."

Liam leaned back in his chair. "Don't get your hopes up. It isn't a flashy sports car. Just an old Sentra that we keep for the occasional emergency."

"I can't imagine you're this attentive to every guest."

"You'd be surprised. And besides, I have a hidden agenda with you."

Her heartbeat quickened. "How so?"

"My mother accused me of trying to run you off. I need to prove to her that I'm a gentleman. And who knows? You might coax me into playing hooky from work a time or two while you're here."

"You seem like the least likely person I've ever known to be led astray."

"Then you'd be wrong. It's springtime in the mountains. Even a workaholic like me can see the attraction."

When he smiled, ever so gently, Zoe felt something inside her loosen and flower. Despite her tendency to hold people at a distance, something about Liam Kavanagh slipped past her defenses. He wasn't a warm, fuzzy person. In fact, he was rather intimidating. But nevertheless, she felt a strong pull of attraction.

Despite that unsettling truth, she wasn't yet ready to jump headlong into a flirtation that might make her time at the Silver Beeches uncomfortable. She picked up the keys and tucked them in her purse. "Thank you for the vehicle. I'll be careful with it."

He watched her like a cat watches a mouse. "I'm sure you will." After a momentary silence, he continued. "So do you have any specific plans for your stay with us, or are you more the type to be spontaneous?"

"You said that last word as if it put a bad taste in your mouth. Do you have a problem with spontaneity?"

"Not really. Though it isn't an attribute that fits my life-style very well."

"Because Liam is all work and no play?"

His eyes narrowed. "You must think me dreadfully dull."

"Not at all. I admire your work ethic."

"Hogwash," he said forcefully, startling her. "You probably don't even own a day planner, do you?" She had the odd notion that he was attracted to her and critical of her at the same time.

She'd been judged and found wanting too many times in her life to let Liam do the same. For the moment, her indignation overrode her appreciation of his masculine appeal. "I believe it's safe to say that our personalities clash, Mr. Kavanagh. Perhaps it might be best if we avoid one another while I'm here. Good day."

With clenched teeth, Liam watched his beautiful guest walk away. The sway of her hips was no less mesmerizing in pants than it had been in a flowing skirt. He had come to the dining room earlier with every intention of getting to know Zoe a little better. Instead, he had lit the fuse of her temper in record time.

Was it the spark of attraction between them that made

things so touchy? Or was Zoe right? Were the two of them oil and water?

Grumbling beneath his breath, he finished his coffee and stood up, ruefully aware that some of the luncheon guests had watched his encounter with interest. Schooling his face to a calm expression, he made his way across the room and exited to the hallway.

Pierre caught up with him en route to the lobby. The long-time employee's face was creased with worry. "There was a man here, Mr. Kavanagh. Asking about Ms. Chamberlain. I got a bad feeling about the guy. Looked like he might be law enforcement or a P.I."

Liam's senses went on high alert. "But he didn't identify himself as such?"

"No, sir. Didn't say much of anything at all except that he was inquiring as to Ms. Chamberlain's whereabouts. At least I think that's what he wanted. He called her Zoe Henshaw, though."

"What did you tell him?"

The concierge's expression was awash with guilt. "I told him we had no guest by that name. He left, but I wondered if I should let Mrs. Kavanagh know."

"I'll handle it," Liam said. "You did the right thing. Our guests expect and deserve their privacy. Keep an eye out for him and let me know if he shows up again."

Liam returned to his office, his gut clenched with worry. Who was Zoe Chamberlain? And why did he feel the need to protect her? Hadn't he learned his lesson long ago? Women were resilient creatures. His need to play Galahad was misplaced at best.

His jaw set, he picked up the phone and dialed the credit card company. After twenty minutes on hold listening to a watered-down version of Frank Sinatra tunes, he was finally connected to a customer service representative who was polite but not at all forthcoming. The woman cited pri-

vacy laws, but assured him that the card was not stolen and
that the line of credit was unlimited.

Liam hung up and drummed the fingers of one hand on
the blotter, no less agitated than he had been before. There
was no reason to suppose that Zoe was anything other than
an extremely wealthy woman who wanted to spend some
time in the mountains.

But somehow, that explanation didn't satisfy him.

Forcing himself to slog through a backlog of work, he
made it an hour and a half before he conceded defeat and
admitted that the Zoe situation was occupying his attention
to the exclusion of all else. Though he would like to think
he could let things play out in due time, he knew himself
well enough to realize that he wasn't going to be able to
let it drop. He had to know more about Zoe. Both for personal and professional reasons. Where was she from? Did
she have a job of any kind? Who was the man looking for
her? Why did she drive an ancient van, and why was there
evidence that at least some of the time, she wasn't sleeping
in four-star hotels?

Telling himself that he might be imagining trouble where
none existed, he typed the name *Zoe Chamberlain* into
Google's search box, hit a key, and waited. To his conster-
nation, the only match from this region of the country was an
African-American woman in south Georgia who produced
some kind of folk art out of old silverware.

Trying *Zoe Henshaw* produced little else of note. The
entries he found contained mostly generic information that
could have pertained to any one of a number of people.

Of the Zoe Chamberlain with the golden hair, blue eyes
and sunny disposition, there was no mention. Which meant
that his oh-so-beautiful hotel guest was probably lying to
him. Anger, disappointment, and an amorphous anxiety
threatened to choke him.

The Silver Beeches was his turf. Everything that happened beneath this roof was under his domain. Even so, did

he have the right to dig into the puzzle that was Zoe? Was he out of line in wanting to find answers?

Six weeks was a long time to wonder.

Four

Zoe loved the little Sentra. It was silver, of course. Although it sported a few dings and bruises, along with 150,000 miles on the odometer, the car had character, much like Bessie. It was also very easy to drive. Its age and appearance erased any concerns she might have had about borrowing someone else's vehicle.

Armed with a map of the town, courtesy of Pierre, she thanked the parking valet who brought the car to the door of the hotel for her. Seating herself behind the steering wheel, she checked the location of all the various knobs and switches and adjusted the mirrors.

If Pierre had thought it odd she was wearing a baseball cap and sunglasses and had her hair tucked back in a ponytail, he gave no sign. The disguise was necessary to calm her nerves.

Driving down the steep, winding highway was an adventure. Like the town itself, the mountain road conjured up images of the Swiss Alps. But the guardrail was sturdy, and the two lanes were plenty wide, so she had no real worries.

The hamlet of Silver Glen was laid out in a well-planned grid tucked between the two steep mountains that constrained its growth. Long and narrow, the peaceful community centered itself along a two-mile stretch of meandering road that wound in a lazy S from one town limit to the other. Cute shops and restaurants vied for space between quaint B and Bs and private homes.

The side streets were equally interesting. Zoe found a dry cleaner's whose sign proclaimed it to be the Silver Press, a movie theater called the Silver Screen, and finally, the place she had circled on her map…Silver Bells, a music shop that sold everything from handmade dulcimers to electronic keyboards.

She spent a happy hour prowling the sheet-music section and debating the merits of a new strap for her guitar. In the end, her only purchase was three sets of replacement strings.

Music softened the rough edges of her life. It was usually easy to strike up a relationship with someone in a new town and offer to play a couple of gigs for free. After that, she was often booked here and there for casual events. She loved being surrounded by the trappings of music. Today she felt a sense of kinship with the little business operated by a man who looked suspiciously like Willie Nelson's twin.

After leaving Silver Bells, she roamed on foot. A shallow river bisected the center of town at right angles to the road. Some long-ago citizens had constructed a covered bridge that was accessible to both cars and foot traffic. Zoe took out her phone and snapped a picture of the postcard scene.

There would be plenty here to keep her busy. Outdoor gear was available in stores everywhere, and the thought of hiking intrigued her. Perhaps she would invest in a good pair of boots.

When the dinner hour approached, she debated returning to the hotel, but she was leery of running into Liam again. She sensed he didn't trust her, and his suspicions stung. Though he was correct to think she was hiding something, it was nothing that would bring harm to his precious hotel. A woman had a right to her secrets, didn't she?

Feeling a bit down in the dumps, she spotted a business that promised to have a decent hamburger on the menu. Making up her mind in an instant, she opened the door and went inside. The Silver Dollar Saloon was dark but smoke-free, a fact that surprised, but pleased her.

Since it was far too early for the locals to really heat up the joint, she was able to grab the booth of her choice. Sitting so that she could look through the front window and study the activity on the street, she perused the limited menu. When the young waitress stopped by, Zoe ordered an Angus burger and sweet-potato fries with a root-beer float.

She took her time soaking in the ambience of the bar. The walls were decorated with black-and-white movie stills, some of them signed. North Carolina was a popular location shoot for producers, and apparently, a number of well-known faces had stopped in at the Silver Dollar to have a cold one at the end of a long day.

The booths that lined both sides of the room looked old. High-backed and made of dark wood, they bore the marks of time. The tables scattered down the center were constructed of the same wood. She almost expected an outlaw or two to come sauntering in.

As she was finishing up her meal, a man appeared from the back, startling her when he stopped at her elbow.

"Welcome to the Silver Dollar," he said. "Haven't seen you in town, so you must be a new visitor."

She looked up, way up, and was surprised to see familiar blue eyes. But the black hair was longer and shaggier. "I'm guessing you might be a Kavanagh," she said.

The man grinned. "Dylan. At your service. I own and operate this place, or perhaps it owns me, if you want to know the truth."

"I'm Zoe Chamberlain."

"So how are you enjoying Silver Glen?"

"I haven't been here long, but your brother is treating me well up at the Lodge."

Dylan raised an eyebrow. "Lucky you. Can't go wrong there." The waitress said something to him, and he started to walk away. "Nice to meet you, Ms. Zoe."

"Wait." The word came out impulsively and with some urgency.

Dylan paused. "You need another root beer?"

"No. I was wondering if you could use a musician one evening. I sing and play guitar. I enjoy doing it, and you wouldn't have to pay me. What do you think?"

His frown didn't say much for her chances. "Aren't you on vacation?"

"Not exactly. I've been ill and I needed a place to rest and recoup. Finding the Silver Beeches Lodge was serendipitous." No need to tell him about Bessie. "I'm going to be here for over a month, and I'm not accustomed to doing nothing all day. It would mean a lot to me. And I'm good, I swear."

Dylan's grin flashed again. Zoe was surprised to realize that, unlike his brother's, Dylan's sexy smile didn't cause her heart to stutter even a little. Apparently she had a thing for irritable, bossy guys in suits. Or at least one in particular.

The bar owner put his hands on his hips and stared at her. It suddenly occurred to Zoe that she wasn't looking her best. Hair tucked back in a ponytail. Well-worn Red Sox cap. He probably thought she was either eccentric or lying about staying up at the Lodge.

Dylan Kavanagh sighed, for the first time sounding much like his brother. "Let me look at the schedule. I have a few bookings coming up. When I know something, I'll call you at the hotel."

She had to be satisfied with that. Even if her hands were already itchy to be playing music. Dylan's bar was exactly the kind of place where she felt most comfortable. "I understand," she said with a smile. "I'll look forward to hearing from you."

* * *

Liam was more than a little surprised when Dylan showed up for a late dinner at the hotel. Maeve and Liam were sitting at a table by the window when his brother appeared. Dylan, wearing a dark sport coat over a pale blue dress shirt open at the throat and neatly pressed jeans, turned female heads as he crossed the room.

Maeve put her hand over her heart. "Dear Lord. It must be a sign of the apocalypse. My second-born son voluntarily dressing for dinner and climbing the mountain without a parental guilt trip."

Dylan bent and kissed his mother's cheek before being seated. "I heard there was prime rib on the menu tonight. You know that's my favorite."

Liam snorted. "You never leave that bar unattended without a good reason. 'Fess up, little brother. Tell us what's important enough to merit such a sacrifice."

"Last time I checked, I had you beat in height by an inch and a half. I haven't been your *little* brother since we both hit puberty, so don't try putting me in my place."

The sibling rivalry was good-natured and familiar. Liam didn't see enough of his brothers, though he loved them all fiercely. Conor and Aidan, and Patrick, Gavin, and James all lived nearby, but the seven brothers led busy lives. For Liam, the hotel was a demanding mistress. Not that it had to be. He employed good people whom he trusted. But perhaps he was too much of a control freak to let them take over.

Maeve beamed at both of them. "Well, whatever the reason, I'm delighted. How did you know when we were eating?"

"I called Pierre and told him I wanted to surprise you."

Liam nodded. "The man can keep a secret. I'll give him that."

The server came to take their order, and the next few minutes were taken up with food choices and wine selection. When the three of them were alone again, Liam sat back in his chair and folded his arms across his chest. "Spill it, Dylan. What brings you up to the rarefied air of the Lodge?"

Dylan's wavy hair was still damp from his shower. He pushed a hank of it off his forehead, pulled his chair closer to the table, and lowered his voice. "I ran into a guest of yours today."

The back of Liam's neck tingled. "Oh?"

"Zoe Chamberlain."

Liam kept his expression neutral, but inside, every Neanderthal impulse he possessed urged him to tell his brother to back off. The lady was taken. That his knee-jerk reflex was ridiculous, he freely admitted. "Where did you see her?"

"She came into the Silver Dollar for an early supper. We chatted for a moment, because the place was mostly deserted."

The salad course arrived, and Liam was forced to hold his tongue for long, frustrating moments while the waiter fussed about with fresh-ground pepper and grated Romano cheese. At last the man departed.

Liam picked up his fork and set it down again. "What did she have to say?" It galled him that his brother had seen as much or more of Zoe today than Liam had. He suspected that she was avoiding him. Without making it obvious, he had looked for her on and off all afternoon. There were a lot of places in the hotel where she could be hiding. The salon, the spa, the workout room, the library. Not to mention the grounds. But he had neither seen her nor heard from her since lunch. Clearly she had made use of the loaner car and decided to go into town.

Dylan chewed and swallowed a bite of his perfectly cooked prime rib, his expression beatific. "I'd forgotten how good this is," he groaned, taking a swallow of his 1972 burgundy. "I love my place, but I'll admit that a guy can get tired of burgers and chicken wings."

Maeve tapped his hand lightly. "I know you pride yourself on being a regular guy, but I happen to know that your bank account could handle a few luxuries. Besides, it wouldn't hurt you to make a standing date with your mother. It's not as if you have any romance in your life at the moment."

"Hey," Dylan said, aggrieved. "That's not fair. I can't help if my girlfriend thought Hollywood was more exciting than a small town in the middle of nowhere."

Liam frowned. Sometimes he thought that Dylan worked too hard at being *one of the guys*. Being a Kavanagh set a man apart in this town. Dylan could fight it all he wanted, but he was a rich man, and people knew it. "Your love life or lack thereof doesn't interest me, no offense. Tell me about your conversation with Zoe."

Dylan kept on eating, apparently intent on clearing his plate in time for dessert. In between bites, he paused to give his brother an assessing glance. "Why so interested? And since when did you get chummy enough with her to use first names?"

Maeve looked from one to the other of her offspring, shaking her head. "I swear you two needle each other every chance you get. I thought you'd grow out of it, but I suppose that was wishful thinking."

Dylan lifted an eyebrow, his smile innocent. "I don't know what you mean, Mom. But you might want to keep an eye on your eldest son. If he starts hitting on sexy hotel guests, we might have problems with jealous husbands."

"Zoe's not married." Liam ground his teeth together, incredulous that his brother's taunts were getting to him. It was an old game they played. But Liam was on a short fuse tonight. "Tell me what you know about her. Please."

Dylan wiped his mouth with his napkin and shrugged. "Not much. But she caught me off guard this afternoon."

"How so?"

"She asked if I would let her play and sing down at the bar."

The table fell silent. Even Maeve seemed perplexed. "Why?"

Dylan shrugged. "Who knows? She claimed it was because she was going to be here for a while and she wasn't used to twiddling her thumbs."

"Did she talk about payment?"

"Offered to play for free."

"What did you tell her?"

"I made an excuse. Said I had to look at the calendar. You know I wouldn't do anything like that without running it by you. Don't want to create a sticky situation. It occurred to me that she might be awful. And that could be damned awkward if she's dropped several grand to stay at the Lodge."

Maeve pursed her lips. "I don't see what it could hurt. She's an unusual woman. Call it my Irish ancestral intuition, but I think she's had a hard life."

Liam and Dylan stared at her in sync. Dylan pointed out the obvious. "She's booked a multiweek stay here at the Lodge. It's not like the woman has lived on the streets and played music so people would toss coins in a tin cup."

Maeve was a levelheaded female, but when she lost her temper, her sons blamed it on the auburn hair that now had touches of gray. "Dylan Matthew Kavanagh. Don't you ever say such a thing again. I thought I'd brought you up better than that. Having money is no guarantee against hardship. The poor girl is all alone on a trip that should be shared by a loved one. We must give her the benefit of the doubt. As our guest, she deserves no less."

Liam winced. "Sorry, Mother. You're right, of course. And as for you, Dylan…" He shot his brother a warning glance. "Let me know what you decide. I want to hear her play."

Dylan nodded, his face sober. "You can tell a lot about a musician through her songs. If Zoe Chamberlain has secrets, they'll be hard to hide when she's onstage."

Liam excused himself shortly afterward. Dylan hadn't been around in a while, so he and Maeve would enjoy catching up. Liam's intent was to go to his office and sift through a pile of paperwork before he headed to bed, but his feet led him in another direction.

The flagstone patio that fanned out from French side doors on the ground floor of the hotel was bathed in moonlight when Liam stepped into the night. Despite the warm day they had enjoyed, here at five thousand feet the temperatures dropped rapidly this time of year after dark.

Almost without realizing it, he turned and began counting windows on the top floor of the hotel until he could locate Zoe's. The drapes were closed. No light emanated from the cracks. Surely she wasn't already in bed. It was not quite ten o'clock.

What had she been up to in the hours since she'd visited Dylan's bar? Lost in thought, Liam wandered the narrow pathways that wove through the gardens like silvery spider webs. His hands linked behind his back, he walked slowly, the pale gravel crunching beneath his shoes. The fragrance of unseen flowers made him think of Zoe.

If he'd been a fanciful man, he would have said that she was very much like a flower—bright and graceful. He wanted to know more about her. In fact, the wanting was more like a gut-level need. It would be hard to sleep knowing that she was at the opposite end of the hallway. He had a suite on the top floor. Maeve went home each night to a modern condo in town.

For the first time that day, he was honest with himself. He wanted to take Zoe Chamberlain to bed. The silent admission sent a rush of arousal coursing through his body. His breathing harshened, and his fists clenched at his sides. Even as he acknowledged his physical need, his brain screamed out a warning. He knew little or nothing about Zoe. It was one thing to be sixteen and infatuated with a woman who turned out to be his father's secret mistress. It was another thing entirely for a mature man to abdicate his responsibilities and throw caution to the wind for the chance to bed a virtual stranger.

What did she look like nude? Her skin would be pale and fine. That much he knew. But what about her breasts? Did the nipples pucker like pink rosebuds when she was excited?

He dropped down onto an ornate concrete bench, his elbows resting on his knees, his head in his hands. Normally, the hotel occupied much of his time and attention. He didn't have hobbies. Occasionally he sought out longtime female friends in other cities for a weekend that satisfied them both. When he did have free time, he loved to be outdoors. But a hotel like the Silver Beeches had to run with precision. Vacationers in this price range expected perfection, or close to it.

Invariably, some crisis erupted once or twice a week. A drunken guest. A falling-out among the staff. A delayed shipment of food. Now that his mother was getting older, Liam tried to spare her the stress and distress of putting out fires. The Kavanagh brothers had lost their father far too soon. Liam wanted his mother to be around for a long, long time.

So he bore most of the burden of being in charge.

Occasionally he resented the yoke of command, but his turbulent feelings were directed at a man who was little more than a ghost in his past. If Reggie Kavanagh had lived, Liam's life would be entirely different. He might be living on the other side of the country, in another part of the world… or possibly even have a family of his own.

Speculation about what might have been was futile. He'd chosen his path. No one had forced him. But sometimes, like tonight for instance, he wished he had the luxury of selfishness at least once in a while.

If he had been a different kind of man, he would run away and join the circus. Sail the seven seas. Learn to speak Swahili. Find out who Liam Kavanagh really was.

But such wild excess was not in his DNA. As a sober, conscientious first child, he was his mother's right-hand man. The rock on which the Kavanagh family anchored its fortunes.

Disgruntled with himself for his maudlin self-pity, he stood abruptly and nearly ran smack into the woman who appeared without warning around a bend in the path. Automatically, his hands came out to steady her. "Zoe. Is that you?"

Five

Zoe gasped, startled and even frightened until she recognized the man who held her lightly. Liam…his face shadowed in the semidarkness. Although the moon was almost full, they were standing amidst large crepe myrtles that cast patterns on the path.

"You scared me to death," she said, feeling her heart thundering away in her chest. "I thought you were a ghost or a rapist or an ax murderer."

"We have so many of those in Silver Glen."

"You're mocking me."

"Maybe. A little." He released her and backed up a step. "Do you mind if I join you?"

She inhaled sharply. Sexual desire. So common and yet so powerful. She shook her head. "Of course not. I only wanted to get some fresh air. I suppose you should lead the way since I don't know where I'm going."

He looked down at her feet. "How are your shoes? Can they handle a bit of rough ground?"

Zoe was wearing the same clothes she'd had on during her excursion into town. The only difference now was that she had omitted the ball cap, and her hair swung free. "I'm good."

"Excellent."

For several minutes they walked side by side, close, but not touching. Eventually, the carefully manicured gardens gave way to forested terrain. Here—the moonlight held at bay by the foliage of large maples—the shadows grew deeper. At one spot where roots humped up in the middle of the trail, Liam took her elbow as they climbed up and over.

He was wearing dress clothes. And presumably his shoes were not meant for such circumstances, but he strode along in the dark easily, his gait comfortable. In this setting, she recognized his athleticism, his grace and power. Alone, she would never have dared go this far in unfamiliar territory. But she knew Liam would not allow her to come to any harm.

Gradually she began hearing the muted roar of water. "Where are we going?" she asked, intrigued and curious.

Even in the dark she saw his grin flash. "To the waterfall."

After that, talking became impractical, because the closer they got to the source, the louder the crash of the torrent.

Finally, Liam took her arm and leaned toward her, his lips brushing her ear. "We won't go any farther. The ledge drops off abruptly."

The silvery moonlight caught the spume and turned it into magic. Shoulder to shoulder, they observed the power of nature. When the wind changed direction, the spray floated toward them, misting their exposed skin and sending a chill down Zoe's bare arms. Liam took off his jacket. Without asking, he tucked it around her shoulders.

The fabric was warm from his body and carried the faint tang of his aftershave. She pulled the lapels closer, wrapped in the majesty of the tumbling water and the simple pleasure of sharing the mystical experience with a man whose company she enjoyed.

At last, when the damp became uncomfortable, Liam took her elbow once again and guided her back into the forest. She tried to return his coat, but he resisted. "Keep it," he said. "Don't want you catching a cold."

When they returned to the more refined landscape of the garden proper, Liam paused, touching her hand briefly. "Would you like to come up to my suite for a drink?"

"And to see your etchings?" she teased.

"Did that line ever work with women, even decades ago? And besides, I would never attempt to seduce a guest with such a corny come-on."

"And if she were willing to be seduced?" The question tumbled out uncensored. Perhaps she'd meant it to be voiced only in her head. But her subconscious was more direct.

They were standing so close, she felt him go rigid. "That's not funny, Zoe."

She leaned into him. "I'm not laughing."

He moved, or maybe she did. Their mouths met clumsily, the shadows making it hard to gauge what was where. Liam's lips were a wonder…firm and warm and confident. Zoe melted, letting him take her weight, straining on her tiptoes to accommodate the insanity.

At last she pulled away. "Coffee would be nice," she said, her breathing ragged. "I'm not much of a drinker."

He stared down at her, the blue of his eyes invisible. But she fancied she could see the turbulence in his azure irises. "Is that a yes?"

"I believe that it is." She tucked her arm in the crook of his elbow. "Will we raise eyebrows sneaking in at this hour?"

"It's hardly late," he said with a chuckle. "And no…we'll take the service elevator." Opening an unmarked side door, he led her down a dimly lit hallway.

She removed his jacket and handed it back to him. "I like the sound of that. Very *crime-drama-ish*."

Liam punched the up button and leaned against the wall

as they waited for the doors to open. "What is this obsession you have with death and dismemberment?"

"The curse of an overactive imagination," she muttered. Now, in the light, she felt a fillip of embarrassment that he was dressed like a man of sophistication, while she was definitely disheveled. She wished she had changed into something sexy and alluring before walking in the garden. Her dark slacks and lightweight blouse were respectable, but hardly the clothing to inspire mad passion.

With a quiet *ding* their clandestine transportation arrived.

The trip was short. But the tension filling the small enclosure multiplied with every second. Unfortunately, this boxy space was not the kind of fancy mirrored affair where a woman could check her reflection.

When they reached Zoe's floor, and what was also apparently his, Liam guided her away from the direction of her room toward his own quarters. Instead of a magnetized card, he had an actual key. Inserting it in the lock, he opened the door and stood back for her to enter.

If she had grown up in less elite surroundings, she would have been awed by the tasteful display of wealth and comfort. Modern, masculine furnishings were softened by warm textiles and the deep pile of moss-green carpeting underfoot. Her toes curled with the urge to kick off her shoes, but she resisted.

Liam loosened his tie and tossed his keys on a narrow table in the foyer. "Have a seat. Make yourself at home. I'll put the coffee on."

"Decaf?"

"If you insist. I'm a night owl, so it doesn't bother me."

She followed him into the kitchen, intrigued.

When he saw her on his heels, he shook his head. "You don't take direction very well, do you?"

"I told you I'm always curious."

While he busied himself with the coffeepot, she examined the amenities. Granite countertops in amber and chocolate tones graced every surface. Over the central island, copper-bottomed pots and pans hung artfully. The stove and refrigerator were a homemaker's dream.

Zoe hopped up on one of the stools that flanked the island and rested her chin on her hands. Liam had rolled up his shirtsleeves, and when he bent over to search the fridge for creamer, his expensive pants molded to a very nice bum.

"This is a fabulous kitchen," she said, seeing herself here, bustling around, making a meal. "Do you like to cook?"

He glanced over his shoulder, grimacing, with his hand on the door of the open fridge. "Actually, I do. But to be honest, it's quicker and easier to eat downstairs. A bad habit, I know."

"I could cook for you one night," she said impulsively. "If you want."

He set the creamer on the island and leaned against the opposite counter, his hands in his pockets. An expensive gold watch gleamed on his left wrist. His hands were big, the fingers long and masculine. Looking at him gave her a funny feeling in the pit of her stomach.

"That would be nice," he said, the inflection neutral.

She flushed, realizing that she was making assumptions. A man like Liam Kavanagh could have any one of a number of women. Standing like that, with a sensual gleam in his eye and the shadow of late-day stubble on his chin, he could have stepped right out of a magazine ad for fast cars or diamonds or gambling in Monte Carlo.

He was beautiful. A beautiful, masculine, physically mouthwatering man.

"Never mind," she said. "You have a five-star chef. I couldn't compete with that."

He lifted one wicked eyebrow. "Oh, I think you could."

Now there was no mistaking his meaning. Liam wanted her.

She swallowed, her voice trapped in her throat. "Is it ready?" she asked, the words squeaky.

"Ready?" He looked blank.

"The coffee."

"Oh…yes."

As he fumbled with mugs and accoutrements, she gathered her composure. "No wonder you never take time off if you *live* here in the hotel. That's a terrible arrangement."

He shrugged, bringing a tray to the island and setting it in front of her. Pulling a stool to the adjoining side, he sat to her right. "The staff is fairly considerate. They try not to disturb me."

"*Try* being the operative word. Don't you ever get the urge to cut loose and be irresponsible?" She stirred a dollop of real cream into her coffee, added a tiny bit of sugar and took a sip. This was no discount-store java. Someone must have ground the beans fresh. It was a luxury she shouldn't get too used to. Her usual M.O. was the drive-through window at McDonald's.

He drained his cup in short order and went back for seconds. "It *is* my hotel," he pointed out as he sat back down. "The buck stops here."

Suddenly, a wave of empathy swamped her. In his own way, Liam was as much of a loner as she was. Both of them surrounded by people much of the time, and yet still lonely. The difference was, Liam had his family nearby. Perhaps they didn't live in each other's pockets, but they were a unit.

Even so, she could see him in her imagination, rattling around in this big, fancy apartment at night with no one to talk to or sleep with. Perhaps he was a workaholic because he had never known anything different.

She had been lost in her thoughts for a long time, because when she finally surfaced, Liam was eyeing her quizzically. "Am I boring you?" he asked, a hint of *something* in his voice that said her checkout had either unnerved or irritated him.

"Sorry."

"What were you thinking about?"

She hadn't expected a direct confrontation, but she should

be learning by now that Liam was nothing if not direct. "Oh, this and that," she said.

Her evasion displeased him. His eyes flashed with irritation. "May I ask you a question, Zoe?"

It wasn't much of a request. More like a command. "I suppose so."

"What do you do for a living?"

Her ankles tightened on the rungs of the stool. "I sing," she said simply. "In nightclubs and bars and coffeehouses. Nursing homes, too, sometimes, but those are freebies."

The intensity of his stare made her want to escape, but she held her ground. She knew what he really wanted to know. His actual question was, how could she afford a six-week stay at the Silver Beeches Lodge if she was an itinerant musician?

But he wasn't rude enough to ask it that way, and she didn't volunteer the information. That was a subject she wasn't prepared to broach. At least not yet.

"I should go," she said, anxiety rising like a dark cloud in her chest. She liked being an anonymous stranger. Perhaps that was why Liam Kavanagh both attracted and threatened her. She sensed that he could break through her inviolable secrets. Walls and barriers and protective shields. She had them all.

"I'm sorry," he said stiffly, his cheeks ruddy with color. "I promised myself I wouldn't pump you for information. It was rude of me."

"Anyone would ask the same question over drinks or on a blind date. Don't beat yourself up because I'm an odd duck."

"Odd, but beautiful."

His honest compliment warmed her. And judging by the look on his face, he had decided he could live with her eccentricities. "I'm harmless, I swear," she whispered.

"That remains to be seen." He smiled to soften the blunt response.

She hopped down from the stool and rubbed her damp palms on her pants. "Thank you for the coffee."

Liam stood as well. "What's your rush? You haven't even seen my etchings yet."

She cocked her head. "I'm assuming you're talking about sex and not real pen-and-ink drawings—right?"

His lips twitched. "A woman who speaks without censoring her words. How interesting."

"Are you calling me a social disaster?"

"On the contrary." He moved closer. "I believe your species might be as rare as the unicorn."

"Don't malign the female sex. Men play games, too."

"How so?"

"Pretending they feel something for a woman when all they want is a quick hookup in exchange for buying her dinner."

He looked at her gravely, his expression guarded. "Unless I'm mistaken, I believe you bought your own dinner. And I haven't been all that interested in quick hookups since I left my grad school days behind."

She bit her lip, feeling outclassed and outplayed. Or perhaps that was a result of her insecurities kicking in. "What do you want from me, Liam?"

His fingers slid beneath her hair as he curled a hand behind her neck. "What do *you* want, Zoe?"

Though the room was plenty warm, gooseflesh broke out on her arms. "Answering a question with a question is classic avoidance behavior."

"But I'm not avoiding you," he said with perfect truth as he pulled her closer still. "You're a guest in my hotel and in my home. I want to please you...to gratify your slightest whim."

It was getting very hard to breathe. The heat from his body melted her synapses, making it impossible to think logically. "I think I read that line from a brochure in my room. Don't oversell the hospitality thing. Zagat won't revoke one of your stars."

He sifted his fingers through her hair. The sensation as his fingertips brushed the skin at her nape was pure pleasure.

"You're a bit of a smart-ass, aren't you?"

He didn't appear to mind. If anything her puny resistance had stiffened his resolve. The terrible double entendre, though thank God she didn't say it out loud, sent hysterical laughter bubbling up in her throat. She couldn't quite say when he had managed to pin her body between his big, masculine frame and the refrigerator. Her resistance was crumbling like day-old bread.

"I booked a six-week reservation," she pointed out, panting as he nipped the side of her neck with sharp teeth. "Perhaps we should weigh our options."

Now, his tongue teased the corner of her lips. His breath was warm on her cheek. "How many of our options include my taking you to bed?"

Her knees wobbled. She had started this madness with her flirty question in the garden. *And if she were willing to be seduced?* Liam couldn't be blamed for thinking she was willing and eager to get naked. And she was…sort of….

But in the moonlit dark, with fragrance all around and romance in the air, a woman could understandably rush a few fences. Now she was having second thoughts. And third and fourth.

Caution and common sense came uninvited to the party. If she let this go any farther, Liam would eventually expect to know things about her. Things she wasn't prepared to share. She sighed, arching her neck to give him access to the erogenous zone behind her ear. "Will you think me horribly gauche if I tell you I've changed my mind?" The man had not even kissed her yet, and her stomach was cavorting like a carnival goer on the Tilt-a-Whirl.

She both heard and felt his incredulous groan.

"Not gauche," he grumbled. "Merely frustrating."

Cupping his cheeks in her hands, she petted him like a baby. "Don't be mad, Liam. You should take it as a compliment that you made me lose my senses. I'm rarely so susceptible to blatant romance."

He released her and backed up twelve inches. Bits of his hair stood on end where she had raked his scalp with her fingers. His cheeks were flushed and his pupils dilated. She wasn't even going to acknowledge the way his trousers tented.

Pressing the heels of his hands against his temples, he squeezed his eyes shut. "No sex. I get it."

"No sex, *now,*" she clarified pedantically, not wanting to block the way for future opportunity.

His lashes flew open, his expression fierce as he jammed his hands in his pockets, no doubt to keep from throttling her. "Is kissing on the table? Really long, hot, make-us-both-so-crazy-we'll-never-sleep kisses?"

Licking her lips, she tucked her hands behind her back, her fingertips resting against the cool flat surface of the appliance that was currently holding her upright. What could it hurt? "Of course," she said, as if his question was the most ordinary thing in the world. "Shall I go first?"

Six

Liam knew in that instant that he was either a masochist or the luckiest bastard in the world. And for the moment, he didn't give a damn if Zoe had more secrets than the Sphinx. He cleared his throat. "I'd be delighted for you to go first, Zoe. Be my guest."

She regarded him with big blue eyes, as solemn as a child being offered a treat for good behavior. "I haven't kissed a man in over a year."

"Is that a euphemism for something?"

She shook her head. "No. That other thing you're thinking of is more like a *four*-year dry spell."

"I see." Was she playing him? Could anyone who looked like Zoe and who approached life with such reckless abandon avoid the kind of men who took advantage?

"You don't believe me."

The hurt in her eyes made him feel guilty, particularly since her quiet accusation was well-founded. "I *want* to believe you," he said. "But have you looked in a mirror? Men notice people like you."

"You'd be surprised how well I fly under the radar when I want to. But I understand. You don't know me. And even though you want me, in your gut you think it might be a mistake. You're torn, because you want to kiss me, and that might lead to something else, but you have a family and a hotel to protect. Have I summed it up?"

"I'd like to point out that *you* were the one who changed her mind about sex. Not me."

"Only because I share some of your reservations. Will you take me at my word if I say I have plenty of money to pay my bill? That I'm not a scam artist? Or a criminal of any kind?"

He shifted from one foot to the other, unhappy with the direction the conversation was taking, but reluctant to miss this chance for clarification. "You sleep in the back of your van."

She flushed from her throat to her hairline. Anger? Guilt? He didn't know. A maelstrom of emotions flowed across her expressive features. "Wow. Does everybody in town report to you? Are you some kind of king on the hill?" The sarcasm would have been far more cutting if not for the wobble in her voice.

Weighing his words, he spoke carefully. "My buddy, Gary, is a single dad who struggles to make ends meet. He asked my opinion about whether or not I thought you would stiff him for the repair charges."

Now the color in her cheeks faded, replaced by an aura of despondence. "And what did you tell him?"

Liam shrugged. "I said I'd cover the bill if there was a problem." He was pretty sure he had killed any chance he had of *ever* getting Zoe Chamberlain into bed. At the moment she was looking at him like some wretched creature who had crawled out from under a rock.

She straightened her spine. Moments before, she had been leaning against his fridge, temptation personified. Now her posture defied reproach. "I'll check out in the morning," she said softly, her expression bleak. "Good night, Liam."

Before he could blink, she was out of the kitchen and halfway to his front door. "Wait, damn it," he said, striding after her, his heart pounding. "Don't be ridiculous. Be mad at Gary, but don't be mad at me. I would like to point out, however, that he's a mechanic, not a shrink. It's not like he divulged personal information."

Now her eyes shot blue fire. "Where I sleep *is* personal information. He had no right to tell you that."

Oh, hell. "He didn't exactly *tell* me. He showed me, Zoe. And you certainly don't have to explain if you don't want to. I'm guessing that a handful of the world's richest people do far stranger things. I know personally at least a couple who clip coupons and keep their money in mattresses."

"So now you're calling me crazy, too. Unbelievable."

"You promised to kiss me," he said, desperation making him reckless. Zoe was wearing a sky-blue blouse that deepened the color of her eyes. Her hair was a cloud of sunshine that warmed his dull apartment. Though she was so angry with him she quivered with it, he had never wanted anyone more. "Give me another chance," he pleaded, even knowing in his heart that it was for the best if she walked out. "I didn't set out to violate your privacy, I swear." Reason and sense had left the building.

His passionate entreaty at least slowed her down. "You're not the kind of man to beg," she said. "It doesn't sit well on you."

"Then I won't beg," he muttered. "I'll just do this." Dragging her into his arms, he found her mouth with a shudder that quaked through him like a powerful rift in the earth's core.

If she had fought him, he would have been honor bound to release her. From early adolescence, Maeve Kavanagh had drilled into her boys the proper ways to treat women with respect. She would have Liam's hide for a handbag if she thought he had coerced any female, much less a guest at the Silver Beeches.

Fortunately for Liam, Zoe was not the kind to hold a grudge. She sighed and kissed him back.

Her acquiescence fired his hunger. He gripped her more tightly until she struggled. "Easy, big guy," she said. "I'm not going anywhere. You pled your case persuasively. If this hotel thing doesn't pan out, you ought to think about becoming a lawyer."

"Shut up and kiss me," he cajoled.

Her lips were as soft as the fog that rolled up over the mountain on winter mornings. And she tasted like the best wine in the cellars below. He ran his hands over her back, daring to slide one beneath her shirt. The delineation of her spine was more pronounced than it should have been. Thinking of her so ill bothered him in ways he couldn't explain.

Though her personality was tough, in his arms she seemed fragile, heartbreakingly vulnerable. "I'm sorry," he said again, urging her to believe in his sincerity.

Her waist was narrow, and without a belt, her pants rode low on her hips. Raw need blinded him as he imagined unzipping her clothing, dragging her beneath him and entering her hard and fast in hope of slaking the formidable hunger that gripped him.

Zoe's silence began to worry him. "Say something, damn it."

She tipped back her head and looked him straight in the eye, her expression rueful. "You don't know much about sweet-talking a woman, do you?"

"I've always preferred action to talk. Words can run in circles." Nuzzling her nose with his, he kept his hips pressed to hers, letting her feel what she did to him.

Her arms were wrapped around his neck, gratifyingly

tight. He grasped her chin with one hand, keeping her lips in kissing distance. His other hand fisted in a hank of her hair. Caught thus, she had no choice but to open to him as he gave in to the urge to claim her mouth again.

"Oh, Liam," she sighed. "You do this so very well."

Since he felt like a rank teenager in the grip of angst-laden crush, her words of praise affected him more than they should. "*We* do this well," he corrected. "I'm as surprised as you are." Sliding a hand between their straining bodies, he found a pert nipple and stroked it.

Zoe twined a leg around his thigh. "Don't stop."

"I don't plan to." Scooping her into his arms, he strode toward the sofa, collapsing onto the butter-soft black leather with Zoe in his lap.

She laid her head on his shoulder. "This is the best hotel ever."

"Brat." A wave of tenderness swamped him, for the moment taking the edge off his arousal and allowing his conscience to lobby for maturity and restraint. "You know we probably shouldn't do this, right?"

She sighed. "I know. We've only just been introduced."

"It's not that I don't want to. You are the sexiest, most appealing woman I've ever had the good fortune to meet."

Pulling back to look up at him, she raised her eyebrows. "Ever?"

He grinned, kissing her nose. "Well, I did get introduced to Gwyneth Paltrow once when she was filming a movie here. But movie stars don't count. And besides, she's a little too old for me."

Zoe chuckled, playing with a button on his shirt. "You're telling me you wouldn't have carnal relations with Gwyneth Paltrow if you had the chance?"

"Chris Martin might not like it."

"He's a musician. You're a wannabe football player. I think you could take him."

Fighting his baser instincts, he stood up, setting her on

her feet and moving himself out of temptation's reach. "If you stay here any longer, we both know what's going to happen. As much as it pains me to point it out, I think the timing is wrong. You said so yourself."

Folding her arms across her chest, she regarded him with stormy eyes. "If you think I do this with everyone I fancy, you'd be wrong. I was serious about the four-year thing."

"Then why me?" It was a legitimate question, not false modesty.

Her shoulders lifted and fell. "I don't really know. Your brother looks a lot like you, but I didn't get the urge to drag him into bed."

Liam was torn between relief and irritation. "Dylan says you want to play at his bar."

"Yes."

"And again, why?"

"I enjoy music. Is that so hard to understand?"

He knew she was hiding things about herself. And wasn't trying very hard to pretend otherwise. A sense of foreboding overtook him. Though he claimed to be pragmatic, he did, after all, have several hundred years of Irish blood flowing in his veins. There was no denying the occasional frisson of gut feeling that guided his actions.

"A man was here today," he said quietly. "Looking for *you*. Or rather, *Zoe Henshaw*. Since *Zoe* is a fairly uncommon name, Pierre and I assumed he meant you."

She dropped abruptly onto the sofa…as if her legs had simply folded beneath her. Every ounce of color leached from her face. "Who?"

"I don't know. Pierre dealt with him. The man didn't identify himself."

"What did Pierre tell him?" She looked as if the answer might be a knife to her chest.

"That we had no guest by that name. Then the guy left. We take privacy very seriously here, Zoe. You're safe. For however long you choose to stay at Silver Beeches." He would have written the vow in blood if it could have removed the look of panic and despair on her face. "Talk to me," he said softly. "I won't betray your trust."

Zoe read the sincerity in his face, the masculine urge to help. But she dared not let down her guard. "Thank you," she said quietly, wondering if she was capable of standing up. "But I'm fine."

Her answer visibly displeased him. "Do you know who it was?"

"No." God, it horrified her to realize how easy it was to lie. But keeping her own counsel had been her only protection in the last year and a half. "Thank you for telling me."

She forced herself to rise and move toward the door. It was foolish to think she could afford a relationship with Liam Kavanagh, no matter how tempting he was. The only person she could trust, in the end, was herself. "I enjoyed the waterfall," she said quietly, her hand on the doorknob.

Liam remained where he was. Clearly, this time he had no plans to stop her. The inscrutable expression on his face probably meant he was relieved to have dodged a bullet. Zoe came with baggage. Most men wanted easy sex with no consequences.

His nod was jerky. "My pleasure."

"Good night." Out in the hall, she leaned her head against the wall, her heart beating wildly. The urge to flee was strong. But she had no vehicle. Taking the little Sentra was not really an option. Even if she left behind the money to pay for it, she would not have the title. Through the years she had done a couple of things she was not proud of, but she drew the line at stealing a man's car. Even if it *was* a clunker.

Being alone in the world had its drawbacks. She envied Liam his close-knit family. She'd never had that kind of support growing up, and as long as she forced herself to keep running, she would never have a shot at the kind of roots and permanence she saw in Liam.

Wiping her damp eyes with the back of her hand, she sought out her peaceful room. With the door locked behind her, she took a deep breath. Tomorrow she would make a plan.

Liam paced his roomy apartment for an hour after Zoe left. Not only was he experiencing the aftereffects of their aborted intimacy, he was also worried. Deeply worried. Zoe was in trouble of some kind. Big trouble.

It wasn't Liam's problem. He kept telling himself that, even as his brain wrestled with the question of how to get her to trust him. On the surface, her personality was open and sunny. But dig a little deeper and you found a woman who resembled a house of mirrors. Just when he thought he had a clear idea of who she was, he ran into a dead end.

Glancing at the clock, he decided it would be okay to call his night-owl brother.

Dylan answered on the second ring. His voice was louder than usual, obviously struggling to be heard above the noise in the bar. "What's up? Didn't I just have dinner with you a few hours ago?"

"I've changed my mind."

"About what?"

"I wasn't sure before, but now I want you to invite Zoe Chamberlain to sing at the Silver Dollar. The sooner the better."

"What's the emergency?"

Liam laughed roughly, digging the heel of his free hand into his eyes one at a time. "I wish I knew. Our beautiful guest is in some kind of trouble. I don't know more than that. But I want to hear her sing. Is that a problem?"

"Of course not. I'll call in the morning and tell her we'll put together a set for tomorrow night. Will that do?"

"Yeah. Thanks, Dylan."

His brother's voice was wry. "You picked up the pieces when I was a mess. The least I can do is lend a hand with your new girlfriend."

"She's not my girlfriend," Liam said automatically. He wasn't sure how to categorize what he felt for Zoe, but he was pretty damned sure their situation was nothing as simple as that.

"Well, whatever she is, I hope she can sing. My regulars have been known to harass the few duds I've had."

"If she says she can sing, I believe her. I plan to bring her down to the saloon and stay with her. What time are you going to tell her to be there?"

"We'll need a few minutes to talk about songs. Do you want to grab a burger while you're here, or is that too plebeian for your refined palate?"

"You're such an ass. And yes. A burger sounds great."

"Seven o'clock, then. After we eat, I'll take her in the back for a few minutes and work on the set list."

Liam cleared his throat. "I think dinner will be just Zoe and me. No offense."

A second of silence stretched to two and then three. Dylan's response, when it finally came, was hushed. "Holee shee…it. Has my mighty brother fallen for a tourist?"

"Mind your own damn business. And just for the record, I'll be joining you *in the back*."

"Message received. But you don't really think I'd poach on your territory, do you bro?"

"Do you remember Pamela Fletcher back in middle school?"

Dylan chuckled. "Point taken. But I've matured since then."

"Says who?"

"Ask anybody. I'm an upstanding businessman."

"An upstanding businessman with an eye for the ladies."

"I've reformed, I swear."

"In all seriousness, Dylan, help me keep an eye on Zoe. Some guy was here at the hotel today asking about her. Pierre told him flat out that no such person had checked in."

"Go, Pierre. He takes his job seriously."

"We all do. And apparently this unwanted visitor gave off enough of a bad vibe for Pierre to be suspicious."

"Does Zoe know about the visitor?"

"Yes."

"Be careful, Liam. You can't always save the world."

Liam winced, feeling something a lot like hurt. "Am I really such an insufferable prig?"

Dylan's voice lowered to a more normal level. Presumably he had stepped into his office, because the background noise disappeared. "That's not what I said, or what I meant. You've sacrificed for all of us, and we're damned grateful. But sometimes you take on too much responsibility. You need to lighten up and live a little. If this Zoe gal is too complicated, find somebody else. But get laid and quit worrying."

"I can't believe I'm taking relationship advice from my baby brother."

"You could do worse. I've survived the pitfalls. I'm a cautionary tale."

"I don't think anything is going to happen with Zoe."

"But you want it to."

"Maybe." That was as honest as Liam was willing to be.

"I'll help you watch out for your little chick, I promise. But Liam…"

"Yeah?"

"Be careful. Just because she looks like an angel doesn't mean she is one."

Dylan had been deceived once upon a time by a woman with a pretty face and a cold heart. The experience hit him hard, and at no point since had he allowed any woman to get close to him. He was understandably cynical when it came to the opposite sex.

"I don't want to believe Zoe is a threat. I'm more concerned about a potential threat to her."

"Then we'll both be on the lookout. I'll see you tomorrow night."

"Thanks. I owe you one."

Seven

Zoe's stomach fluttered with nerves. Which was disconcerting, because she was rarely unsettled before a show. It usually took her father's goons a few weeks to find her latest bolt-hole. The fact that someone had come looking for her so quickly was alarming. But Pierre had sent the stranger away. Convincingly. So she was safe…for now. Perhaps her unusual restlessness could also be attributed to the fact that a polite bellman had delivered a note to her room an hour ago….

Dear Zoe—
I'd like to accompany you to the Silver Dollar Saloon
tonight, if I may. Meet you in the lobby at 6:30? Call
the front desk and leave me a message. Liam.

She had tucked the note in a drawer of the bedside table. Now she took it out and studied it again. Liam's bold scrawl was neat, though masculine. She could almost see him writing the words, in a hurry to get on to the next thing, but still concerned with making sure she had a ride into town tonight.

She had danced around her suite when Dylan called earlier. Given the bar owner's reaction yesterday, it seemed safe to assume she'd never hear from him. But not only had he called, he wanted her to perform tonight. With him. For the crowd at the Silver Dollar.

The whole thing had her jazzed and excited until Liam's note arrived. Was it possible to experience stage fright in front of only one person? She was confident about her talent, but what if she had an off night? What if she hit a couple of sour notes? Or sang in the wrong key? The prospect of appearing amateurish with Liam watching made her stomach curl with dread.

Unfortunately, she was unable to think of a polite way to tell him she would prefer he stayed home. Thus at 6:25, she made her way downstairs. As she stepped off the elevator, she spotted Liam immediately. He stood on the far side of the lobby conversing with Pierre.

Though he wasn't wearing jeans, he had clearly dressed for an occasion less upscale than dinner at Silver Beeches. A pale blue button-up shirt with the sleeves rolled to his elbows exposed his tanned forearms and strained across his broad shoulders. Light khaki pants and leather deck shoes completed his ensemble. Even dressed casually as he was, he still looked wealthy and powerful. His impact was in the set of his jaw and the aura of command he wore so comfortably.

When Liam saw her approach, he said something to Pierre and crossed the marble floor. "Zoe. You look amazing."

Liam struggled to keep his tongue from dragging the floor. It had been almost a full day since he had seen her, and his imagination had not exaggerated her appeal. Silky sunlit hair framed a face that was both girl-next-door and sex goddess. He wasn't sure how the combination worked, but it made him hotter than hell.

He didn't know what he had expected in terms of her performance attire. But she had surprised him. Dark-wash jeans fit her long, toned legs as if they had been sewn onto her. A narrow brown leather belt cinched her small waist. The silver and turquoise buckle was delicate and intricate.

Her blouse was the ultimate feminine weapon…a collarless, sleeveless red silk affair that clung to her breasts and tucked neatly into her jeans. He didn't count how many buttons had been left undone, but the rounded slopes of her cleavage were tastefully displayed.

The simple gold chain that encircled her neck nestled in the valley between her breasts. On narrow, high-arched feet she wore red stilettos that brought her almost up to his height.

He knew that he had never seen a sexier, more sensual woman.

His voice was embarrassingly gruff when he spoke a second time. "Are you ready to go?"

She nodded, her smile small, but genuine. "I am."

He took her elbow as they stepped outside. His classic silver Jag convertible, circa 1962, waited for them, engine running. After helping Zoe into the passenger seat, he put her guitar case in the back, ran around the car, and slid behind the wheel. "I decided to keep the top up since you're performing tonight. But one afternoon soon I'll take you for a drive in the mountains."

"Sounds lovely."

It was difficult to believe they had almost made love last night. Though Zoe had pulled away, he knew she wanted him. Perhaps a slow wooing was in order. For a skittish woman with defensive walls, a man needed tact and patience. Liam had both. And he was willing to do almost anything to lure Zoe into his bed. Wise or not, he had no choice. The wanting and the waiting were eating him alive.

The atmosphere today was definitely strained. He decided it was better to say nothing at all as they descended the mountain. Zoe was probably getting in the groove for her performance. And besides, he couldn't verbalize what he was really thinking. She would no doubt run away if she had a clue what he wanted from her.

He nearly clipped a guardrail when she crossed her legs and one of her call-girl shoes fell to the floor of the car. Her toenails were painted to match the vibrant color of her outfit. Though he had never once entertained a foot fetish, he had a sudden vision of lying naked in bed with Zoe, sucking each of those small perfect toes one at a time.

In his peripheral vision he saw her grimace as she replaced her shoe. "It's very kind of your brother to let me perform tonight. He's taking me at my word that I can sing."

"Were you exaggerating when you described your performance experience?"

"No."

He patted her knee, removing his hand quickly when the contact threatened to singe his fingertips. "Then you have nothing to worry about. Dylan knows how to loosen up a crowd, and even if you were the worst singer on the planet, I guarantee you that the clientele at the Silver Dollar will cut you some slack when they get a look at those jeans."

She turned toward him, her bottom lip caught between her teeth. "Are they too tight? I forgot how much I've eaten since I've been here. I guess I've already put on a pound or two."

"The jeans are perfect." End of story. A few moments later, he swung into the back parking lot of the saloon and rolled to a stop beside his brother's vehicle in the space that was always saved for family. "You want to go in, or do you need a minute?"

Clasping her hands in her lap, Zoe inhaled sharply. "I feel like I might throw up. But I think that's because I don't usually know anyone in the audience."

He ran the back of his hand down her cheek, feeling his gut tighten from that simple contact. "Are you saying that I make you nervous, Zoe?" The prospect delighted him, because it meant she was as attuned to him as he was to her.

"No comment." Her expression was rueful.

"You're the one who asked to sing here," he pointed out.

"And now I want to get it over with."

"Then let's find my brother."

The Silver Dollar was already packed. The hostess greeted them warmly and gave Liam a smack on the lips. "Where you been keeping yourself, gorgeous? I've missed you."

Delilah was twenty years his senior and thirty pounds overweight. But her exuberant personality drew men like bees to honey. He squeezed her arm. "Behave, Dee. Meet my friend, Zoe. She's going to sing with Dylan tonight."

Delilah stepped back and examined Zoe from head to toe. To Zoe's credit, she withstood the other woman's scrutiny without flinching. Delilah shook her head. "Where'd you get this exotic creature, Liam?" Then she smiled at Zoe. "You're a knockout, honey. Call me Dee."

Dylan showed up at that moment and took over the task of ushering them to a table. He had reserved one for them in the back. The cramped space was the closest the Silver Dollar came to privacy. A scraggly artificial tree served as a partial barrier between Liam and Zoe and the other diners.

Despite Liam's warning stare, Dylan seated himself at Zoe's elbow. He handed her a slip of paper. "Do you know any of these?"

She examined the list with a dawning smile. "Only all of them."

Dylan beamed. "Have your dinner, then, and afterward we'll do a quick run-through and take the stage around 8:30. Sound okay to you?"

Zoe nodded, her blue eyes sparkling. "Perfect."

Thankfully, Dylan took himself away and Liam was left

to entertain Zoe. "I can recommend the hot wings and the jalapeño poppers," he said, wondering how many hours it would be before he could take another shot at convincing her to be alone with him. And naked.

Zoe studied the menu with suspect concentration. She was jumpy as a cat with a mangled tail. Whether it was from being with him or the result of stage fright, he couldn't tell.

After they ordered, they watched the crowd. Zoe pointed to a large man wearing nothing but red suspenders and threadbare painter's pants. "Who is that guy?"

Liam took a swallow of his imported ale and grinned. "Big Tom. For most of the year he runs a sawmill outside of town. But from Thanksgiving to Christmas, he works at a mall in Asheville every year as Santa Claus."

"I can see why."

Big Tom's gut was hard to miss. Daring to change the subject to a more personal note, Liam stroked the back of her hand lightly where it lay on the table. "I'm sorry we argued yesterday."

Zoe's makeup was more dramatic tonight, which made sense, because she planned to be onstage. But her thickly mascaraed lashes, lowered to half-mast, shielded her eyes. She withdrew her hand. "It's okay."

"It's *not* okay. You're entitled to your secrets. But if I'm being completely honest, I hope that you'll eventually figure out that you can trust me."

"Trust is a two-way street."

"Indeed. But you make it difficult. *Chamberlain* isn't your real name, is it?"

She shot him a mutinous glance. "Yes it is. But it's my middle name. I use it for everything. That's not a crime the last time I checked."

"Zoe, I'm not attacking you. I want to help. Who is the man who's looking for you?"

"I don't know." Shoulders hunched, her body language screamed at him to back off.

She was lying. He knew it in his gut. But he wasn't willing to make a scene in Dylan's bar. Especially when Zoe was about to be in the spotlight...literally.

It went against his every instinct, but he swallowed his frustration and conceded that now was not the time for a confrontation. Their food arrived, and the moment was lost.

When Dylan came to get Zoe for their mini run-through, Liam gave his brother a pointed stare. "Your office is small. I'll stay here and check a few emails."

Dylan nodded, for once, his expression not teasing at all. "We won't be gone long. Tell the server if you want anything else."

Scanning the room for anyone who might resemble the man Pierre saw, Liam sat back in his chair and relaxed a bit. No one could harm Zoe in the middle of a crowd like this. He ate a few French fries as he scrolled through messages on his phone.

When someone sat down beside him, he looked up with a smile. Until he saw that it was Gary. And Gary looked far too serious.

The mechanic spoke in a low voice. "Is she here?"

Liam nodded. "In the back with Dylan. The two of them are performing together tonight. What's up?"

"I sure the hell don't know."

"Tell me, man. She'll be back soon."

Gary pulled his chair closer and lowered his voice. "She called this morning and asked if I would paint her entire vehicle brown. When I finished the other repairs."

"So?"

"Her current paint job is almost brand-new. Nary a ding or a scratch. The only reason I can come up with for covering over her daisies and all the rest is that she doesn't want to be spotted."

Liam's stomach churned. He didn't want to believe that his friend had a valid point. "Isn't that jumping to conclusions?"

Gary shook his head. "There's more. I decided to prep the vehicle since I'm waiting on parts. I found a small area of rust around one door hinge, so I removed the door. The inside panel seemed loose. I was going to fix it, when I found…"

He paused as the waitress refreshed their drinks.

Liam's neck was tight. "What, damn it? What did you find?"

"Money." Gary grimaced. "Lots of money. Cash. Bills."

"How much?" God in heaven.

"I don't know. I didn't touch it. Didn't want my fingerprints to show up anywhere. But I'd say at least forty or fifty thousand given the denominations and the size of the stacks." He paused, his expression torn. "Do you think I should call the police?"

Liam ran a hand over his face, his brain assessing and discarding a dozen possible explanations. "No. We have no proof that it's not hers." Hope curdled in his stomach and died. He'd tried so hard to tell himself that Zoe was trustworthy, and now this.

"Who carries that much cash hidden in a vehicle?"

"I don't know," Liam said grimly. "But I plan to find out."

Zoe strummed a chord as Dylan tuned his guitar. His instrument was beautiful. Highly polished wood inlaid with silver in random designs. "Did you have that made?" she asked.

He nodded, still fooling with one of his strings. "Yeah."

"Does the silver design have some special significance?"

"It reminds me that I'm a Kavanagh for good or for ill. Once upon a time our ancestors operated a silver mine in these mountains, hence the name of the town. We have a few large remnants, good-size nuggets, but the mine was lost years ago. Our father disappeared while looking for it when Liam was in high school. Not only did Dad never find the mine, he never returned."

"That's dreadful." Zoe could hardly imagine a tragedy of that magnitude, though her own family life hadn't been a picnic.

"A dark time in the Kavanagh clan, for sure. As the eldest, Liam bore the brunt of helping Mom cope. He was always mature for his age, but he had to grow up overnight."

"How did she manage when he was away at university?"

"We hired an assistant manager. Mom was in charge, but there was someone to help with the big decisions. And Liam would come home from school if he was needed."

"So he never got to go backpacking through Europe or take a graduation trip or anything like that?"

"No. And by the time our collective grief eased and things were finally on an even keel, both personally and professionally, Mom had come to depend on Liam. In case you hadn't noticed, my brother is the kind of man people turn to for support. In one way or another, he's been the cornerstone of our family for twenty years now."

"How old were you when it happened?"

"Fourteen. I'm the next in line. But there's a lot of difference between fourteen and sixteen. I was going through a rebellious phase, and Dad's death only made things worse."

Zoe fell silent, digesting the implications of what Dylan had shared. No wonder Liam had such a serious side. He hadn't had the luxury of being a goofy adolescent. Her admiration for him grew, along with the conviction that she was not the woman to get involved with him. If he knew the extent of her problems, she would become one more millstone of responsibility hanging around his neck.

Dylan finished tuning. "You feel okay with what we've sketched out?" he asked with a smile.

"Yes. I hope I don't disappoint you." It still amazed her that his sexy masculinity didn't affect her libido the way Liam's did. Some woman would be lucky enough to fall for Dylan Kavanagh one day in the future. But apparently Zoe had already cast her lot with the straight-laced older brother.

Dylan straightened his guitar strap around his neck, resting his arm on the instrument. "Now that I've heard your voice, I'm wondering how I can convince you to be a regular."

"That's very kind of you. But I won't be hanging around more than a few weeks."

"Why not?"

His simple question caught her off guard. Why not, indeed? Her gypsy lifestyle was her own choice. No one was making her crisscross the country and live out of a single suitcase. Only her cowardice and fear pushed her onward. "I suppose I've never liked being tied down."

Her answer didn't satisfy him. His unspoken empathy made her squirm. "Nobody can run forever," he said. "Trust me. I know."

"Who says I'm running?"

"Aren't you?" In his steady gaze she saw a kindred spirit. Her throat tightened unexpectedly, leaving her to blink back emotion. "I'm not sure I would know how to put down roots after all this time. I don't make friends very easily."

"And yet you're around people all the time when you're playing and singing."

"That's different. I can blend into the background."

"I think you're kidding yourself." His measured look was not insulting, but her cheeks heated. She glanced at her watch. "Is it time?"

He nodded. "You feelin' butterflies?"

"A million of them," she confessed.

Dylan stood and patted her shoulder. "I know my regulars. They're going to love you. Come on, Ms. Zoe Chamberlain. Let's go make some music."

She stood as well and wiped her damp palms on the legs of her jeans. "I'm ready. Let's do this."

Eight

The stage at the Silver Dollar was tiny, but Liam's brother had invested in a top-notch sound system and professional lighting. The house lights had already been lowered, so when Zoe stepped out onto the stage, a few steps ahead of Dylan, the audience made an audible sound of appreciation.

Even though Liam knew what she looked like tonight, he caught his breath along with the rest. She was radiant. Her smile, intimate and happy, encompassed the crowd, telling them that they were part of her inner circle and that she would be singing just for them.

Two stools sat side by side on the stage. Though Dylan sat down beside Zoe, Liam scarcely gave his brother a glance. It was safe to say that all the men in the room reacted similarly.

Zoe perched comfortably, her hair swinging softly around flushed cheeks. Her eyes sparkled, and her slender body practically vibrated with excitement. She wrapped her ankles around the rungs of the stool. In that one movement, Liam flashed back to sitting with her in his kitchen.

Dylan leaned toward his mike. "Welcome, regulars and first-time visitors to the Silver Dollar Saloon. Glad you're all here. We have a treat in store tonight. My friend, Zoe, is going to sing and play with me. She's just passing through Silver Glen, but I was able to persuade her to entertain us this evening. Please give it up for Zoe's first performance at the Silver Dollar."

After the raucous whoops and hollers quieted, Dylan began to pick out a melody, and Zoe joined in. In no more than a few seconds, the room fell silent, all rustling and coughing and other noises obliterated.

Liam had heard his brother sing and play a million times. Dylan was talented, and touched his guitar like he would a woman, with tenderness and reverence. He had the Irish gift of storytelling in song.

But with Zoe on stage as well, Dylan became the background to her luminance. They started out with the poignant lyrics to an old sixties tune about difficult goodbyes. With a jolt of distress, Liam saw Zoe standing at his bedroom door, her bags packed, not wanting to wake him up to say goodbye. The image was so vivid, for a moment he couldn't breathe.

The first time he met her, she had struck him as the reincarnation of a sixties love child, guitar in hand. Now, singing words that had resonated for decades, he felt as if all the grief of parting washed over him, though she hadn't even thought about leaving yet.

And somehow, Liam's father swam into the mix. Reggie Kavanagh had left, never to return. If Liam hadn't been sitting so far from the door, he might have cut and run. He wanted to howl with the knowledge that he was halfway in love with Zoe already and already bracing for the pain of a broken heart.

Fortunately for him, after one or two more ballads about being sad and lonely, Dylan launched into a crowd pleaser, and soon everyone was clapping hands and singing along. Several modern country songs followed.

Liam wasn't sure how long Dylan and Zoe played. No one left the bar. Waitresses worked the crowd, pausing now and again to watch and listen. The upward curve of Dylan's lips told Liam his brother was in his element. But it was the sheer joy on Zoe's face that kept the crowd in their seats. She sang from the heart, as if every emotion she had ever experienced could be communicated in song.

At last, Dylan announced the last number. "Zoe's going to sing and play for us an original composition. We're pleased you were here tonight, and we hope you'll return. Good night and God bless."

The spotlight trained on Dylan's stool went out. He was still there to play, but all attention focused on Zoe. At this moment, she no longer seemed aware of the audience. With her head bent over her instrument, she strummed the opening bars of a haunting tune. When she opened her mouth to sing, she captured each listener in the palm of her hand.

With a voice that was husky and pure, she sang of love and loss and the universal pain of a broken heart….:

"I never meant to hurt you…loving is a fearful game…
Few can win and most go home
Facing winters of the same…

"I thought we might be different…or at least we'd have a chance…
But life is not a promise
And I scarcely know the dance.

"Don't grieve long for might-have-beens…remember me with wonder
Like new roses crushed by rain
Our future's torn asunder…

"Goodbye, my love, so perfect…please forgive my gift of pain…

If I could stay, I would have
Always will my love remain...."

The final note of the final verse lingered on a hushed silence. Liam heard sniffles and saw women wiping their eyes.

Though he knew, intellectually, that Zoe was blinded by the spotlight shining in her eyes, it seemed to him as if she looked straight at him, sending him a message. *Don't care about me. Don't fall for me.*

What she didn't know was that it was too late. He wanted her with a desperate urgency that left no room to contemplate any ending other than a happy one. If Zoe was in trouble, he would help her. Even if she turned out to be a thief. He had to believe there were reasons for whatever she had done to get that money. He would stand by her. And when the danger had passed, he would bind her to him and shred the music to that dreadful song.

He might be making a mistake. In fact, he was *probably* making a mistake. But he was ready to suffer the consequences. He was prepared to do almost anything as long as it meant he could have Zoe.

While his emotions swirled from pride in her talent to frustration at her secrecy, the crowd rose as one to its feet, clapping and whistling and demanding an encore. At Dylan's signal, the house lights came back up and Dylan and Zoe launched into a rowdy, energetic rendition of an old Billy Ray Cyrus tune.

Afterward, Dylan gave Zoe a hug and insisted she take a bow. Her face was flushed and damp, and for the first time, she looked tired. Suddenly, Liam remembered that she had been ill. Working his way to the front of the stage, he handed her a bottle of water.

"Drink something," he said quietly. "You may have overdone it tonight."

When she had emptied the bottle, he held up his arms and lifted her down from the stage onto the plank flooring.

"Thank you," she said, not meeting his eyes.

When Zoe would have moved away, he stopped her by the mere expedient of keeping his arms looped around her waist. "Take a breath, sunshine. You were a big hit."

She rested her head on his shoulder. "Great audience."

He heard fatigue in her voice alongside the satisfaction of a job well done. "You ready to go home?" The words slipped out before he had a chance to censor them. The Silver Beeches was *his* home, not Zoe's.

She didn't call him out on his faux pas. "More than ready. But it was a great night."

Dylan walked them out to the car. "You were a hit, Zoe. I hope you'll plan to do this again. But I only accept a freebie once. I'd have to pay you from now on."

"You couldn't afford me," she said, laughing. Liam couldn't see the mischief in her eyes, because it was dark now. The only illumination came from the multicolored lights strung along the roofline of the Silver Dollar.

Liam helped Zoe into the car and turned to his brother, lowering his voice. "Call me in the morning. I need your advice about something."

Dylan snickered. "I say go for it."

Liam slugged his arm and slid into the driver's seat. "Good night, Dylan."

Zoe leaned across his lap to add her goodbyes. Her breasts brushed his chest, and her hair tickled his chin. "Thanks for letting me sing."

Dylan leaned on the window. "My pleasure. You kids get on home now. It's late."

"You're so full of it." Liam hit the up button on the window, causing his smart-ass brother to jump back with a curse.

Zoe giggled, straightening and returning to her own seat as Liam exited the parking lot with a flurry of gravel. "That was mean. But funny."

"My brother is a merciless tease. Be glad he likes you."

"He likes everybody, it seems. The bar was packed tonight. And I think he knew everyone there."

"That's Dylan."

Conversation lagged abruptly. Liam drove with an occasional surreptitious glance at the slightly rumpled and definitely weary angel occupying the passenger seat of his car. Near the top of the mountain there was a pull-off where the teenagers liked to park and make out. The idea had definite appeal. But what he wanted to do with and to Zoe required far more privacy.

He still hadn't decided what to do about Gary's latest revelation. There could be a hundred reasons why Zoe was hiding large amounts of cash in the panel door of her van. Unfortunately, a lot of them were worrisome.

Back at the hotel, Liam handed his keys to the valet and helped Zoe out of the car. It occurred to him that they could take a walk as they had the night before. But she had expended a lot of energy onstage, and she probably intended to have an early night.

He wanted to talk to her, to convince her they belonged together, even if for only this moment in time. And if she agreed to make love to him, he had to seek answers that would make him feel better about having her in his hotel and in his bed. Every time he had tried before, she shut him out. Bracing himself for the disappointment of a quick goodnight as a prelude to her disappearance, he walked beside her into the lobby, carrying her guitar case.

Making an excuse to go to his office would save him the awkwardness of riding up on the elevator with her, but he couldn't bring himself to walk away. On the top floor, the door opened, and they both stepped into the quiet hallway.

Zoe held out her hand for the instrument. "Thanks for going with me tonight."

To hell with this. He set the case on the floor and reached for her. "You mesmerized me with your singing. One kiss. That's all I need."

It was a lie. He knew it and she knew it. What he wanted would take all night. Given their semi-public location, he held her loosely, not wanting to embarrass her if another guest decided to walk by. He slid both hands beneath her hair, inhaling her scent as he bent his head and found her mouth. "You were amazing," he muttered, moving his lips over hers with light, teasing motions.

Zoe went up on tiptoe, her arms twined around his neck as she kissed him back. "That's sweet of you to say."

"I'm not a sweet man." He caught her tongue between his teeth and nipped it to prove his point. Zoe's soft moan hit him hard, stealing the breath from his lungs and weakening his knees, even as another part of him went hard as stone. He shook with the need to take her up against the wall.

"Come to my room," she whispered.

He froze, sensing some kind of test, or perhaps a trap. "I can't," he said hoarsely. "Not now. Not tonight. I'm past talking." He cupped her butt in those body-hugging jeans and squeezed it. "If I get you alone, there's only one thing that's going to happen. Fair warning."

She tilted her head to look up at him, her guileless blue eyes impossible to read. "I don't have a problem with that, Mr. Kavanagh."

The time for rational thought was long past. He had been imagining this moment since the first instant she stepped through the door of his hotel. What did it matter if her presence was only temporary? Why did he care if she was frustrating and secretive and slept in her van and had loads of hidden cash and people looking for her?

He wanted her. He needed her. And by God, he was going to have her.

Taking her by the hand, he grabbed the guitar case and strode down the hall, dragging Zoe in his wake. It took her several seconds to rummage in a small bag for her key. He didn't bother to tell her he had a master key that gained him access to every room in the hotel. This way was better.

Inside her room, he set her instrument in front of the closet and leaned against the door, doing his best not to pounce on her. Her red blouse was rumpled, her hair mussed. "I suppose you want a shower," he said, trying to be the gentleman his mother had taught him to be.

Zoe grimaced. "I need one. But there's room for two."

His vision hazed. Hands trembling, he stared at her. "You have to be sure, Zoe. No backing out at the last minute. It's okay to say no, but I want to hear it now."

She frowned, the movement creating two small lines in her forehead. "I believe I invited you to my room. That's a pretty clear signal in my book."

"We're practically strangers."

"I don't care."

"You're not sure you can trust me."

"And vice versa. But this is about sex."

"And if either of us wants more?"

"Do we have to worry about that now?"

The warning bells clanged in his head, but he closed his ears. "I suppose not."

She unbuttoned her blouse and let it fall to the floor. Her breasts were barely concealed by a lacy crimson bra. Against her pale skin, the color glowed like fire. "Last one in is a rotten egg," she said, smiling as she uttered the childhood taunt.

Something kicked in at that moment, some primeval urge to hunt and conquer. "Zoe," he warned. But it was too late. She had already disappeared into the bathroom. By the time he came to his senses and followed, she was completely naked, standing beneath the pelting water in the open shower. Droplets of water clung to her pert, pink nipples.

Though her actions indicated confidence, in her wary gaze he saw a diffident insecurity, as though even now she wasn't sure of his motives. Never taking his eyes off her, he stripped clumsily, stumbling against the counter when one leg of his pants caught on his shoe.

He stopped short of removing his boxers, because he was

far too close to an impatient climax. His hands fisted at his hips. He took deep, cleansing breaths, searching for control.

Zoe watched him intently, her golden hair darker now, the color of pale molasses. "You planning to stand there all night?" Again she taunted him. "I could use some help with the spots I can't reach."

To hell with control. He ripped his underwear down his legs and kicked it aside. Zoe's wide-eyed gaze settled on his penis and stayed there. He saw her swallow and lick her lips. "I'll wash spots you didn't even know you had," he threatened.

When he joined her in the shower, she backed against the far wall. Without asking, he took the soap from her lax grip and slid the sandalwood-scented bar from her throat to her navel.

Zoe's eyelids fluttered shut. Her lips parted and her respiration grew shallow. Now that he was in reach of what he wanted, he was able to gain a measure of delayed gratification. "Does that feel good?" he asked, pretending he was cool and calm. Inside his chest, his heart raced madly.

She stirred restlessly, one of her bare thighs brushing his. "Yes." The single syllable was slurred.

When he managed to move his gaze from her face to her breasts and onto the real estate below, he noticed the small fluff of feminine curls that had been trimmed in a tiny heart. He touched the shape with a single fingertip. "I like this, sweet Zoe. As far as I can tell, you collect hearts everywhere you go."

"Don't tease," she muttered, opening her eyes and gazing at him with such a beseeching look that for a single breathless second he would have given her anything she asked for.

He rotated his hand in the air. "Turn around. I'm not done."

Complying with just the right amount of sulky obedience, she flattened her hands against the wall of the shower and bowed her head. As he tucked her hair forward over her shoulder, Liam's heart bounced once and lodged uncomfortably in the vicinity of his throat. This was supposed to be a game. But looking at her like this swamped him with feelings that went beyond simple lust.

The nape of her neck struck him as painfully defenseless. Her shoulder blades were a tad too pronounced, but the line of her spine led to an ass that curved like a perfect, ripe peach.

Reaching for a washcloth, he lathered it and began to wash her back. If Zoe's little sighs and murmurs were any indication, she enjoyed his attention. Shortly, he abandoned the rag and used his bare hands to soap up her slick, creamy skin. His fingertips learned the dips and valleys of her body.

Unable to resist, he rested his erection in the cleft of her bottom, and pressed his lips to the top of her spine. "I don't know what I've done right in my life to deserve this moment, but I would walk through fire to have you again and again."

She lifted her head and glanced over her shoulder with a sultry smile that shot his blood pressure into the danger zone. "You haven't *had me* yet," she pointed out.

"Are you complaining? I thought women loved foreplay."

"I'm merely pointing out that you don't have to work so hard. I'm all yours, Liam."

Four simple words. Four teasing, erotic, knee-weakening syllables. *I'm all yours, Liam.* Did she really mean it? Did she have a clue how starved he was for her and only her, no matter the consequences?

His libido snapped the chains of his intellect. "Turn around, woman. Put your hands over your head."

Nine

When Zoe faced Liam, she realized in an instant that they had segued fast and hard from teasing flirtation to gut-deep lust. His pupils were dilated…. Only a tiny rim of royal blue remained. The dark flush on his cheekbones gave him the look of a warrior.

Shoulders that seemed impossibly wide bracketed a chest that was a miracle of nature. Muscle and sinew and a faint smattering of dark hair. The man who appeared so sophisticated and debonair in a tailored suit was a dominant male in his prime.

Oxygen evaporated, leaving her breathless and woozy. She could have blamed it on the hot water and the steamy air, but she had a clue it was more to do with the searing blue of Liam's eyes and the way he raked her from head to toe with a claiming stare.

Slowly, she lifted her arms until the backs of her hands rested against the ivory-colored marble wall veined in gold. "Take what you want," she said, wondering if she could push him beyond a civilized edge. Why it mattered so much to her, she couldn't say. Perhaps it hearkened back her earlier desire to know the Liam who existed behind the veil of courtly manners.

He vibrated with a hunger that was almost tangible. Deliberately, he caught each of her nipples between his thumbs and forefingers and tugged firmly. Fire shot from the sensitive flesh he tormented to the aching juncture of her thighs. Moisture bloomed in hidden places, moisture that had nothing to with the force of the shower and everything to do with Liam's touch.

Meeting his gaze at such close range became impossible. Her eyes downcast, she witnessed the fascinating swirl of his navel and the way his narrow hips gave way to powerful thighs. His erect shaft reared against his taut abdomen.

When he cupped her breasts with soapy hands, she jumped and moaned.

His forehead rested against hers. "You enchant me, lovely Zoe."

"I don't think I can stand much more of this," she said, with absolute sincerity. "I'm a heartbeat away from a world-class orgasm."

"Should I be flattered?" His husky voice teased her ear as he leaned into her and ran his hands up her arms so slowly she wanted to scream. When he reached her wrists, he gripped them tightly. Now his erection probed the soft flesh of her belly.

Her knees weakened to the point of collapse. She closed her eyes and whimpered.

Liam's response was instant. He kissed her hard. "Where did you go, Zoe? I want you here. With me."

Opening one eye, she managed a small grin. "Do you really want to know?"

His gaze sharpened as he absorbed her meaning. "God, yes. Tell me, wicked girl."

She dropped her head to the side, giving him better access to the sensitive spot beneath her ear. "I was imagining that you were a Viking marauder and I was your plunder."

Liam went perfectly still. Except for his thick shaft that twitched wildly. "Did you resist me, Zoe?"

She curled a leg around his hairy thigh, rubbing herself against him without shame. "I tried. But you smelled so good and you tasted like wine and decadence. I decided I had no choice but to cooperate."

The noise he made then was somewhere between a laugh and a curse. "I thought I was the one with Irish storytelling genes."

She flexed her fingers, testing the strength of the hands that manacled her wrists. "You inspire my imagination, Liam Kavanagh."

"Keep going. I'm intrigued." He kissed her temple and each of her eyelids. The delicate caresses were in direct opposition to the way his hips pinned her to the wall.

With her lower lip caught between her teeth, she pretended to ponder. "I suppose you could lift me and take me here and now, but it seems a mite dangerous with all this wet marble."

He bit her earlobe, sending a hot rush of blood to her core. "What other choice do we have?"

It was hard to form a coherent thought. But Liam appeared to be caught up in her little fiction, so she struggled for the image that would entertain him. "Your servants have prepared a bed for you. With velvet covers and silken sheets."

"Sounds comfy."

His wry comment forced her to stifle a giggle. Trying to stay in character was a challenge. "You are determined that I will obey you, so you stretch out on your back and force me to service you."

Liam scooped her into his arms with a rash intensity that threatened to dump them both on the shower floor. He grabbed for a towel and ran it carelessly over her breasts.

"Doesn't matter if we're wet," he said, his expression agitated. "Define *service*."

She linked her arms around his neck. "I have to taste your manly desire."

One dark eyebrow shot to his hairline. "Manly desire? Seriously?"

He deposited her on the bed and came down on top of her. "What happens next?"

"You're deviating from the plot." She shoved at his unyielding chest. "I'm supposed to be on top."

Rolling over onto his back, he wrapped a hand around his shaft. "I doubt that Vikings ever let women get on top."

"Not for actual sex, maybe. But surely if they wanted to get comfortable while the woman—"

"Tasted their manly desire?" His smile made her toes curl. "I'll do my best to cooperate."

Now that she had him where she wanted him, she almost lost her nerve. What did she know about satisfying a man like Liam? Her two sexual partners, both nice men, but not in Liam's league, had been quick off the mark and notably selfish.

Which was why she had decided to take a moratorium from physical interactions with the opposite sex.

But that high and mighty vow had evaporated when Bessie brought her to the Silver Beeches.

Shoving Liam's hand aside, she stretched out beside him on one elbow and stroked him from base to tip. "I'm pretty sure you promised to have me whipped if I don't give you pleasure."

A tiny drop of fluid leaked from the head of his erection. His voice sounded like gravel when he spoke. "I would never whip anyone as lovely as you. It would be a crime to mark that skin."

"Then maybe you threaten me with being chained in your dungeons."

"Vikings didn't have dungeons. They were always sailing on the high seas."

She sat up and glared at him. "Whose story is this, anyway?"

He waved a hand. His eyelids closed, and a smug smile lifted his lips. "Sorry, Scheherazade. Please continue."

She pinched his bicep, hard enough to bruise him if his muscles hadn't been so damned impressive. "No more talk from you." Though he pretended acquiescence, she knew that he could turn the tables at any moment. Deciding to take advantage of his momentary passivity, she bent over him and took him in her mouth.

"Sweet mother of God." Apparently her admonition about silence hadn't been taken seriously.

She licked him lazily, loving the way his hands clenched convulsively against the sheets when she let him feel the edge of her teeth. A feeling of feminine power mixed curiously with the yearning to bind him to her forever. Why did she have to be so tempted by something she could never have? She knew nothing of what it meant to build a home and a community, to be part of a tight-knit circle of love.

Most of her adult life had been spent in search of some elusive goal, an ephemeral vision of happiness. Now she could almost see the prize, but she had too many hurdles to cross before grasping it was possible.

Forcing back the negative emotions, she concentrated on giving Liam pleasure. His male body was so different from hers; lean and powerful and beautiful in a way that had inspired sculptors in ages past.

When she sensed she had pushed him too close to the edge, she drew back. "Did I please you, my Viking?"

Liam's chest heaved with the force of his labored breaths. If Zoe the chanteuse had brought him to his knees, then Zoe the Siren had finished him. He felt drugged, almost insensate with the exact pleasure she had described in her provocative tale.

It occurred to him that begging might not be his most manly option at this point, so he ground his teeth and sat up to stare at her. "Any more stories you want to tell?"

Her eyes rounded as if she sensed his imminent takeover. "No. Not really."

It appeared that she had forgotten her nudity. Earlier, in the shower, he had sensed her mild embarrassment at the way his eyes ate her up. But now, she was oblivious to the fact that her beautiful nakedness made him ache.

Without saying a word, he eased her onto her back. "Prepared to be ravaged, little captive." At the last moment, he remembered protection. Groaning at his complete lack of savoir faire, he dropped his head forward and put his hands on his thighs. "Condoms?" he muttered.

Zoe pointed. "In the vanity case. I hope they're not out of date."

He stumbled to the bathroom, took care of business and returned in record time.

Zoe lay exactly where he had left her, her arms outstretched above her head. Her hair had begun to dry in places. It was wavier now, giving her the look of a woman who had spent the last twenty-four hours in bed. She had one knee bent, with her foot planted against the mattress.

When she heard his footsteps on the carpet, she opened her eyes and smiled. "I've been waiting forever, Liam."

He stood beside the bed, his hand braced on the bedpost. Looking down at her fresh, pale-skinned body was almost enough. If he had been a poet, the sight of her would surely have inspired a sonnet. "The time for waiting is over." She had seduced him with song and then with her inventive imagination. "Tell me you want me, Zoe."

She arched her back, stretching from head to toe. "I do. I swear I do."

"Then we're both on the same page."

He eased down beside her and took his time with a tactile exploration. Her personality was so big, but her body was delicate of frame, more so since she had been ill. Laying his cheek on her belly, he played idly with the tuft of curls. Zoe inhaled sharply when his fingertip skated over a little bundle of nerves.

When he glanced up at her face, her eyes were squeezed shut and she had sunk her teeth into her bottom lip. Experimentally, he entered her with two fingers. The tight clasp of her body made him tremble. Soon, he was going to possess her. Completely.

Gently he used those same two fingers to simulate the act of lovemaking. With his thumb he brushed her clitoris repeatedly. Zoe quivered at his touch and came with a quiet sigh that indicated her satisfaction. At least he hoped so.

"There's more," he promised. Moving between her thighs, he fit the head of his erection at her entrance and pushed. Her passage gripped him in tight, moist heat as he slid all the way in. "Zoe," he groaned. "What have you done to me?"

She lifted her hips in invitation. "I might be able to go for round two. Just letting you know."

He chuckled hoarsely. "Always nice to get feedback." Humor in bed was a new one for him. But with Zoe, all the good things in life seemed to be rolled up in one beautiful package. Tenderness. Creativity. Laughter. Desire.

He moved in her deliberately, refusing to pick up the pace even when she wriggled beneath him and begged. The vision she made, lying beneath him with her face flushed in arousal, was a picture seared into his brain. He wanted to take her like this for hours. Every cell in his body was alive and humming with pleasure. He was hyperaware of his surroundings, all his senses on red alert.

The scent of their warm skin mingled with the fragrance of the freshly washed sheets. Zoe's limbs were sleek and strong as she curled her legs around his waist and clung to his shoulders.

The sounds she made as she came, not once but twice while he thrust repeatedly between her soft, firm thighs, were earthy, ragged…exhausted at the end.

The powerful surge of his impending climax left him breathless. He couldn't hold on, couldn't stretch the pleasure out one second longer. With a choked groan, his entire body shook in helpless release as he emptied himself until there was nothing left.

Zoe blinked as she tried to focus her reeling emotions. In a less ritzy hotel she might have found a water spot on the ceiling…something to latch onto while the universe cartwheeled around her.

Three orgasms in an hour? Sometimes she'd been lucky to have one. Liam Kavanagh possessed an impressive amount of knowledge about the female anatomy.

At the moment, he lay slumped on top of her, his body a heavy weight. That final go-round had short-circuited most of her synapses and left her feeling drunk and loopy with happiness.

She poked him in the back. "Are you still breathing?"

One male shoulder flinched as if to ward off a pesky fly. "No."

Since he couldn't see her face at the moment, she gave in to the urge to smile like a lovesick teenager. All her life she had searched for a place to belong, and turned out, it wasn't a place at all. It was a person.

The way Liam looked at her, even when they weren't in bed, made little bubbles fizz in her veins. She was pretty sure he saw her for who she really was. Not as an academic failure or an aimless wanderer, but a woman with worth and appeal. A woman who could make him laugh.

They might have skipped some steps in their budding *whatever-it-was,* but that could be remedied. She owed him a few explanations. After all, a relationship couldn't be built on evasions and half-truths.

Finally, Liam rolled onto his back, his chest still rising and falling more rapidly than normal. He sighed and stretched. "I think I entered another dimension."

Running her fingers along the nicely delineated muscles of his upper arm, she grimaced. "Don't lay it on too thick. I'm not *that* good."

He scooted onto his side and faced her, reclining on his elbow, head on his hand. "You're not good," he said. "You're incredible." With his hair rumpled and his chin covered in stubble, he looked like an invitation to sin.

Her face heated. Compliments were nice, but she didn't need flowery speeches. "I'm out of practice and underexperienced."

Liam tucked a stray lock of hair behind her ear, lingering to trace her bottom lip with his thumb. "I don't think that last one is a real word."

"You're awfully picky for a man who just—"

He put a hand over her mouth. "You mean for a Viking who enjoyed his barbaric spoils?"

"You make me sound like bad meat."

Liam laughed out loud, his expression far younger and more carefree than she had ever seen it. "I never know where your brain is going to go next."

She shoved him off balance and climbed on top, straddling his waist. "How's your recovery time? I know you're a lot older than me."

"Hey!" He scowled, but she could see the twitch of his lips. "Watch your step, little captive. I might consider spanking you after all."

She rested her hands on his chest. "Oooh, I'm so scared."

Something long and firm bumped up against her butt. Liam grinned. "Is that quick enough for you?"

Trying not to let him see that she was both impressed *and* aroused, she feigned indifference. "I suppose." She yawned theatrically. "As long as the main event isn't too quick."

He curled a hand behind her neck and dragged her down

to his chest until her mouth hovered over his. "This is the only way I know to shut you up."

The kiss was hard and warm and tender and insistent and passionate. It changed like a kaleidoscope, wooing her and winning her with every new variation. His tongue was slightly rough…and his apology gruff when his chin scraped hers.

At last she broke the connection and sat up, panting. "Is this where I'm supposed to take charge?"

Big hands clasped her waist and lifted her several inches, muscular arms flexing with impressive strength. "I'll get you started," he promised.

They both sighed when Liam lowered her onto his erection. The angle was new and tantalizing. Zoe rested her hands on his abdomen, her knees braced comfortably against the mattress. The sensation of being possessed, though she was in the dominant position, was inescapable.

Though Liam appeared to be relaxed, a flush of color had returned to his cheekbones. Inside her, his firm flesh moved impatiently with the slightest of motions.

Already, fresh ripples of sensation fluttered in Zoe's sex. Hoping her leg muscles had the endurance to please them both, she licked her lips and tucked her hair behind her ears. "Here we go."

Ten

Liam lost all track of time. When a woman like Zoe decided to take a man into her bed, the chosen male had no choice but to get down on his knees and thank the Almighty for the gift of such a fascinating, seductive woman. Only a fool would bypass this opportunity. Liam liked to think he was smarter than most men.

It wasn't just the sex. Though that was off-the-charts phenomenal. It was the fact that Zoe threw herself into lovemaking with an abandon and a giving nature that made her incredibly vulnerable.

How did she know that Liam wasn't only using her? Or maybe she didn't care. Maybe she was using him.

She was asleep now, her relaxed body draped over his like an exquisite throw. Her skin was hot and soft against his harder frame. As he winnowed his fingers through her hair, separating the silky strands, he inhaled the faint scent of her shampoo. In the aftermath of a physical cataclysm, his questions returned. Who was Zoe Chamberlain?

He told himself she had a right to her secrets, but now that he had tasted her essence and had learned the manner in which her body responded to his, he was obsessed with finding out more about her. Was he being taken in by a beautiful and accomplished con artist?

A few moments later when she stirred, he wasn't prepared for the way she looked at him. He'd expected a sleepy feminine smile, or a teasing suggestion that they start all over again. Instead, her expression was guarded…as if she expected him to do or say something that required armor on her part.

It struck him that she was right. His first impulse had been to ask his pointed questions while her defenses were down. Her startling ability to anticipate his responses so accurately both annoyed and shamed him. Was he *that* predictable? Disgruntled with himself and with her, he slid out of bed feigning a deliberately bland mood that hopefully disguised his turbulent emotions.

He picked up his boxers and pants. "I have an early conference call in the morning. I'll let you get your rest."

She sat up in bed, sheet tucked under her arms, and stared at him as he dressed. "Was it something I said?"

"What do you mean?" It irked him that her big-eyed solemnity made him feel guilty when he had nothing for which to apologize.

She nibbled her bottom lip, perhaps unconsciously. "I thought you might spend the night."

Pausing for a moment as he pretended to locate a renegade sock, he shook his head. "I have responsibilities. If no one can find me, they'll be worried."

"Well, heavens," she said, unmistakable hurt warring with indignation in her gaze. "What a tragedy that would be."

She was making fun of him. Again. As if dependability and steadfastness were traits to be mocked. Coming on the heels of what had been an incredible evening, her words stung more than they should have.

He shrugged into his shirt and fastened the buttons. "Not all of us have the luxury of flitting around the country wherever the wind takes us."

As soon as the words left his lips, he regretted them. "I'm sorry, Zoe," he said quickly. "That was low."

Sitting there like a courtesan dismissing an unwanted suitor, she shook her head, her smile bleak. "You're entitled to your opinion. I'm flighty and unfocused and selfish. God forbid that you should ever get out and have some fun. Is that what this is about? You took an evening off to go somewhere as bourgeois as a bar? You slept with me without analyzing the ramifications? Surely I must be leading you down the rosy path of destruction."

"Don't get carried away. I apologized."

"Yes, you did. But only for saying the words. Not for thinking them. I'd like you to leave now, please."

He took a step toward the bed, wondering why the hell he was dressed when all he wanted to do was crawl back beneath the covers with her.

Zoe stopped him with an upraised hand. "Go. Before I call the hotel owner and have you evicted. Oh, wait. That's you."

Crossing his arms over his chest, he glared at her. "Are you sure you aren't a natural redhead? That temper of yours is nasty."

"At least I *have* feelings," she said, her eyes shiny with what he hoped to God were not tears. "You stalk around your domain dressed to the nines and expecting everyone to dance to your tune. What a boring life that must be. I feel sorry for you."

A vein throbbed in his neck. The impulse to drag her to her feet and kiss her senseless was strong. But someone had to be a grown-up. "You've made your opinion very clear. Perhaps my brother is more your speed."

"Perhaps he is."

They were shouting at each other. Probably in danger of awakening everyone on the floor.

With a curse that came nowhere near expressing his mental state, he turned on his heel, dragged open the door, and despite his instincts to fling it shut with a crash, closed it carefully as he stepped into the hall.

Zoe cried herself to sleep. The next morning, puffy eyes and a splitting headache added to her general state of misery. Trapped by the breakdown of her automotive companion, she indulged in a much-deserved pity party.

Not that there was anyone around to offer sympathy. By midmorning she had run out of tears and patience. It was a beautiful day, and she was not going to let an uptight, play-by-the-rules jerk make her feel bad about herself. What he had going for him, though, was her memories of the way he had touched her so tenderly and yet with such hunger. As if he'd been starving for her and only her.

Well, that was that. She couldn't in all good conscience sleep with a man who thought so little of her. Her self-respect was important. If Liam didn't know how delightful it was to stop and smell the roses, then he didn't deserve her. Life was short. It deserved full participation or nothing at all.

In her travels she had seen the most magnificent natural scenery and the most bleak and disgusting of human situations. She had mingled with the elite of society and at other times shared soup with the down-and-outs who had little strength left to cling to the end of their ropes.

Though she had battled loneliness and fear from time to time, she had never lost her conviction that life was worth living and that the only way to grow and evolve as a human was to stretch your wings. She'd had some rough spots in her life. Everyone had. But she couldn't complain. Because she had never gone hungry, and she had never known true despair, though she had come close a time or two.

Liam had experienced rough spots as well. And like Zoe, he had adapted without complaining. But while Zoe was content to accept the world as it was, Liam's personality was more controlling. He was the kind of man who felt it necessary to take care of everyone and everything. He felt it was his duty to make sure the world turned on its axis as it should. Zoe was only interested in seeing the next sunrise. Perhaps she and Liam were simply too different to relate to each other.

When self-reflection and introspection palled, she rolled her eyes at her reflection in the mirror and showered rapidly, closing her mind and heart to images and memories of the last time she'd stood beneath the spray. Such self-indulgent reflections were counterproductive to her resolution to make the most of today.

Dressing in another version of the disguise she had worn into town previously, she made her way surreptitiously to the front of the hotel. Her heart beat rapidly, and her palms were sweaty. She wasn't sure which would be worse…seeing Liam or not seeing him.

By the time she had requested the loaner car and slid behind the wheel, it was clear that her host was engaged elsewhere in the hotel. Which was, of course, of no consequence to her.

Once again, she enjoyed the drive down the mountain. Springtime in western North Carolina was achingly beautiful. Mighty evergreens poked at the blue sky. Flowers blossomed everywhere. Birds flitted and sang their songs. Even without Liam, Bessie's choice of stopping places would get an A+ in Zoe's book. Despite the rocky start to her day, she appreciated the opportunity to continue roaming around the shops and spots of interest that comprised the heart of Silver Glen.

First off, she stopped by the Silver Chassis, only to be informed by an overly flirtatious teenager that the owner of the repair shop had driven to Asheville to pick up some parts, and that there was no progress to report about Bessie. The news didn't surprise her, but she had to fight an urge to sneak past the kid and take a look for herself.

After wandering for half an hour, she grabbed a soda and a hot dog from a fast food place disguised as a miniature chalet, and sat on a bench in the sun to eat it. The nature of her meal, compared to what she could have enjoyed had she not left the hotel, was amusing.

Food was not that big a deal to her. Which was why she could travel anywhere and everywhere with relatively little trouble. Deliberately choosing to live week to week with little in the way of material possessions was her own personal rebellion. The fact that her truculence might have had its day was an ever-growing source of concern and dismay.

She'd told herself for several years that she enjoyed her transient lifestyle, her gypsy itinerary. But the truth of the matter was, she was afraid to go home. She dreaded going back to the house where she had grown up. To start over again would mean facing her demons. A course of action that seemed not only depressing, but well nigh impossible.

Crumpling the paper sack that held the remains of her meal, she tossed it in a trash receptacle and stood to stretch. Once she returned to the hotel later this afternoon, perhaps she could make sure Liam was nowhere near the workout room, and she would be able to exercise in peace.

As she walked back toward her car, she glanced across the street at the Silver Dollar, its neon signs extinguished midday. The doors wouldn't open until four, but perhaps Dylan was around. She had a sudden urge to talk to the only other Kavanagh male she knew.

There was no doorbell, so she simply knocked and knocked until a rumpled Dylan answered, covering a yawn with his hand. He scrubbed a hand across his face. "I may have forgotten to mention that I'm not a morning person. If you want to sing here again, you might want to remember that."

She eased past him without an invitation. "Wow. Another grumpy Kavanagh man. Is it something genetic?"

Dylan wandered over to the bar and waved a hand. "You may as well have a seat since you're here." He grabbed a filter, put on a pot of coffee, and yawned again.

Zoe scooted up onto a stool and propped her elbows on the bar. "Rough night after Liam and I left?"

He poured himself a glass of water and downed a couple of aspirin. "Some of the guys stayed after I closed to play poker. It was close to three before they left, so I crashed on the sofa upstairs instead of driving home."

"Did you win?"

His wicked grin was much like his brother's. "I always win." He lifted a container of lemonade. "Want a drink?"

She nodded. "Might as well." It occurred to her that she might need an ally if she ever hoped to secure Liam's affections. Not that she was sure such a goal was admirable or even possible. But after last night, she'd probably be willing to give it a shot if the eldest Kavanagh weren't such a pain in the ass.

"Tell me," she said as she sipped her drink and studied the rather large painting of a nude reclining woman that hung over the bar. "Is it just me, or is your big brother an opinionated, judgmental, arrogant, overbearing pig?"

Dylan winced as he rubbed the spot between his eyebrows. "You should cut him some slack, Zoe."

"Why? I really want to know."

"Well, for one thing, he's a damned nice guy."

"Couldn't prove it by me."

"I guess he didn't take my advice."

"What advice?"

"Never mind," Dylan said quickly. "Let's get back to Liam. It's not really his fault he's so serious. When most sixteen-year-old kids were playing video games and going out for sports, my brother was taking a crash course in becoming the head of a big, loud, complicated family and running the business with Mom. All the rest of us had the luxury of doing whatever we wanted to with our lives. But Liam got stuck with the hotel."

"He claims he enjoys it."

"And he does, I'm sure. To a point. But he gave up a lot for us. So, if he occasionally has the annoying habit of thinking he's always right, it's probably because he is."

"I might have known you'd take his side. All you men stick together."

Dylan drained his first cup of black coffee and poured a second. Standing behind the bar, he looked as natural in his element as Liam did in his. "It might not be a bad idea, though, for you to coax him out of his office while you're here. Tell him you want to hike."

"Do I?"

"There are dozens of trails up and down and over the mountain. Several waterfalls, too."

Zoe felt her face flame and couldn't do a thing to stop it.

Dylan lifted an eyebrow. "I'm guessing he's already led you down the garden path?"

"Is that a euphemism?"

He gave her an innocent smile. "Not at all. The Silver Beeches gardens are legendary."

"I'll just bet they are," she muttered. Glancing at her watch, she grimaced. "I'd better get back. I want to work out in the gym before I eat another one of those calorie-laden dinners."

Dylan rinsed his cup and set it in the sink. Raking both hands through his hair, he shook his head. "You know that no one holds a gun to your head and makes you eat that crème brûlée."

Her stomach growled, no longer appeased by the hot dog. "I'm well aware of that. But I wouldn't want to hurt the chef's feelings."

"Whatever helps you sleep at night." He came out from behind the bar and paused to kiss her cheek before grabbing a broom. "You were a hit last night. Several of the guys were none too happy to see you going home with Liam."

"You're being kind."

He made her lift her feet, sweeping peanut shells into a pile. "Not at all. Anytime you want to do an encore performance, just ask. But in the meantime, try to forgive my brother for whatever dumb-ass thing he did. We men are clueless sometimes."

"I've noticed."

"And take my suggestion to heart. I'll bet you a hundred dollars that all you have to do is invite him to take you exploring and he'll shed that suit."

The image made her smile. "Is that what he is to you? Superman?"

"Damn straight. But I'll deny it to my grave if you tell him I said that. We like to keep him humble."

She hopped down from the stool and avoided the peanuts. "Thanks for the advice. What do I owe you for that and the lemonade?"

Dylan shook his head and yawned again, leaning against his broom. "It's on the house."

Returning to the Silver Beeches, Zoe was torn about whether or not she wanted to seek out her host or to avoid him entirely. As she swung around the final curve and slowed down to ease onto the flagstone apron in front of the hotel, the matter was settled for her. Liam stood on the top step, decked out in what looked to be an expensive hand-tailored suit and a crisp white shirt. It never failed to impress her that he managed to look so impeccably groomed every damn minute of the day.

Of course, there *had* been a few moments last night when she'd managed to rumple his sartorial perfection. The memories made her neck heat. For one second, she contemplated making a U-turn and beating a hasty retreat back down the mountain. But the venue was much too public for such a humiliating escape.

Instead, she put the car in Park, took a deep breath, and reminded herself that she was a woman of the world. Liam Kavanagh could not rattle her if she kept her cool. She wouldn't allow it.

His eyes narrowed as he watched her step out of the car. "I didn't see you in the dining room at lunch."

She handed the keys to the valet, shouldered her purse, and picked up the package she'd purchased after her talk with Dylan. "I've been out," she said airily.

As she climbed the shallow steps, Liam stared at her, his gaze intense. "Where?"

She stopped in front of him, one step down. He towered over her like a judge as he awaited her answer. "Does it matter?" she asked, trying not to notice how wonderful he smelled.

Guests milled around them, and the valet was still in earshot. "Of course not," Liam said, his voice stiff. "I was merely wondering if your day had been pleasant."

"Aren't you concerned about my nights, as well?"

Shock flared briefly in his eyes before his lids lowered and his jaw clenched. "Your nights are not my affair."

She brushed past him, running her free hand along his forearm as she walked by. "I'm hurt that you've abandoned me so easily," she whispered in his ear. "If you'd like to chat about it and regroup, I'll be in the parlor for high tea at four. Why don't you join me?"

Eleven

Liam didn't particularly like tea. Even so, he found his way to the parlor at 4:10 determined to let Zoe see that she wasn't calling the shots. To his dismay, once he finally entered the room, he saw her surrounded by a bevy of admirers. He decided not to fight the crowd, and instead, worked the room, conversing with guests and generally making sure his presence was known and appreciated.

In upscale hospitality, as in most things, the personal touch was what made a business stand out from the competition. Many of the people in this room were repeat bookings. Liam kept tabs on every aspect of the hotel's services, from the most mundane detail to the most outrageously expensive special request.

Though he had come to his mother's aid originally out of necessity, in the intervening years, he had discovered that he enjoyed making people feel at home in Silver Glen and welcome at the Silver Beeches Lodge. He wasn't the kind of man who would enjoy idle time spent on yachts or in casinos. This life at the Lodge had perhaps chosen him and not the other way around, but it was a good match for his set of skills, and it was different every day. He enjoyed the challenges.

Zoe met his gaze across the room at least twice before she finally dismissed her contingent and crooked a finger. It was a small matter of pride and control that Liam lingered a couple more minutes in another conversation before crossing the expensive carpet and stopping in front of the woman who was rapidly driving him out of his wits.

She patted the seat beside her. The particular item of furniture upon which she sat was an antique love seat with a carved wooden frame and plump, red-velvet upholstered cushions. Zoe reclined against the arm comfortably, one foot tucked beneath her. Her short and sassy madras skirt would have been more suited to the tropics, but on Zoe, it worked. The short-sleeved jersey knit T-shirt in a shade of teal that matched one of the stripes in the skirt was modest. But it clung to her breasts in a way that made it impossible for him to ignore her sexuality.

Sitting down beside her, he leaned back with a sigh. "I suppose you want to talk about last night."

She shook her head vehemently. "Not at all. I've never enjoyed rehashing my mistakes."

He winced. "Is that what it was? A mistake?" They were situated in a small island of intimacy, far enough away from the other occupants of the large room that they couldn't be overheard, but still on public display. The venue was guaranteed to keep his more reckless impulses under control. Probably.

Zoe picked at a loose thread on her skirt. "If it hadn't been a mistake, you would have stayed the night. It was pretty clear that you were having second thoughts. It's okay. I get it."

"I'm fairly certain you don't *get it*," he said, "because I'm pretty sure I don't even *get it*." He had regretted leaving her the moment he walked out her door last night. But there was enough confusion churning in his gut to stop him from going back and taking her over and over until morning…the way he wanted to. Wild abandon was not his M.O. Being around Zoe showed him facets of his personality he'd either deliberately buried or had never acknowledged at all.

She shot him a sideways glance from beneath thick, sooty lashes. Her blue eyes were one of her most beautiful features. Luminous and lovely, they by rights should have been windows into her soul. But Zoe was a pro at dissimulation. Though her bubbly personality appeared open and guileless, the truth was, she was secretive and kept her own counsel.

"I'm sorry I make you angry," she said quietly.

He ground his teeth. "I'm afraid for you."

"You don't have to be. I've been taking care of myself for a long time."

Both of her feet were now planted on the floor, her black ballet flats side by side. He wondered if the change in physical position meant she was prepared to run.

"You can trust me, Zoe."

"Is trust a prerequisite for crazy sex?"

"Most people would say so."

"I'm not most people," she pointed out with perfect truth.

"No, you're not. But I think you're in some kind of trouble, and if you and I are going to spend some time together, I'd prefer not to be blindsided. Especially if I might need to protect you."

At last a faint smile lifted the corner of her kissable lips. "Ah, the caveman thing. I love it. Though it's quite ridiculous, you know. I've been on my own for a long time."

"Okay, then. What if I just *want* to protect you? Would you agree to that? As long as I freely and fully admit that you don't have to have a man to look out for you?"

She patted his knee. Briefly. Decorously. "I can live with that. As long as you promise you won't protest or resist me if and when I try to get you to lighten up."

"Does that mean what I think it means?"

"In your dreams."

He loved sparring with her. The quick banter with its sexual overtones stimulated him both physically and mentally. No other woman of his acquaintance spoke to him the way Zoe did. Except for his mother—who had the ability to take him down a notch or two when the occasion warranted—most people, both male and female, either kowtowed to him, or at the very least treated him with deference.

Not that he expected or demanded such a thing. In fact, it often irritated him that his money and position caused people to treat him as some kind of exalted being. No danger of that with Zoe. Perhaps that was what drew him so strongly into her orbit. The childlike innocence of her outlook on life and the way she related to him simply as a man was refreshing and deeply appealing.

"Is this what you call regrouping?" he asked, hearkening back to her invitation to tea.

She leaned forward and picked up a china cup, lifting it to her lips. As she sipped delicately, she eyed him over the rim. "I bought hiking boots today."

The odd segue caught him off guard. "You did?"

"For a man who is disgustingly wealthy, you work too hard."

"Is there a question in there somewhere? And besides, working hard is not a crime."

"Most people with your bank balance would be traveling the world."

He shrugged. "Plenty of time for that."

She carefully returned the cup to its saucer and snagged a small cookie. "You can't bear the thought that all this could toddle along just fine without you."

Her comment was uncomfortably close to the mark. If the hotel and his mother no longer needed him, he would be adrift in a sea of uncertainty. "No one is indispensable. But I like to think that what I do is important."

"Of course it is. But you need balance, my friend."

"That's not the first time you've alluded to our being friends. I'm honored...I think." He grinned at her. The residue of powdered sugar on her bottom lip made him desperate to lick it away, but he and Zoe were surrounded by interested eyes.

Her exuberant smile dimmed. "I don't have close friends. Tons of acquaintances on at least three continents, but not the kind of people I can call at three in the morning. That's the downside of always being on the move, I suppose."

Again, he glimpsed a deep vein of vulnerability. A woman like Zoe was alone only by choice. What in her past had prompted the vagabond lifestyle? The only way he was going to get answers was to spend time with her. That would be no hardship. And in doing so, he could prove to her that he knew how to kick back and have fun.

"You mentioned boots," he said.

"*Hiking* boots. You'll be impressed."

"I'm guessing this is where I'm supposed to offer my services as a guide?"

Her smile was innocent. The expression in her eyes was not. "That would be lovely...if you're not too busy."

He recognized the challenge for what it was. "I think I can make time for you." The prospect was damned appealing. Spring in the mountains was his favorite time of year. "How about tomorrow morning? Nine o'clock. Meet me in the lobby...I'll ask the chef to pack us a picnic."

Her delighted smile bathed him in sunshine and warmth. "I can't wait."

Zoe felt a definite pang moments later as she watched him walk away. This game she played, pushing him to see if he would go along with her mischief, was dizzyingly fun. As she dabbed her lips with a crisp damask napkin and prepared to rise, a woman appeared at her elbow. "Ms. Chamberlain. Lovely to see you. Do you mind if we chat for a moment?"

Liam's mother wore a navy dress that complemented her coloring and suited her air of dignity.

The sinking feeling in the pit of Zoe's stomach felt much like the time she had been summoned to the principal's office for cutting her best friend's hair without permission. "Of course," she said, waving a hand. "Please join me."

Maeve summoned a waiter for a fresh pot of tea and waited as he poured each of them a cup. Zoe had drunk so much by this time that she could have floated away. But she wasn't about to refuse an overture from the Kavanagh matriarch.

When the formalities were complete, Maeve sat back and eyed Zoe with a faint smile. "I notice that my son is spending a fair amount of his time with you."

"He's an attentive host," Zoe replied, the words matter-of-fact. Surely Maeve couldn't know what had happened in Zoe's room. "And your son, Dylan, has been kind enough to let me sing at the Silver Dollar." She was hoping to steer the subject into less volatile territory. Discussing one's lover with the lover's mother was more than a little awkward.

Maeve set her cup on the low table in front of them. "I am a firm believer in innocent until proven guilty."

Zoe gulped inwardly. "I don't follow."

"It's simple." Maeve shrugged. "You are an unconventional woman. And some of the details of your life have raised questions with my son, as you know. But you are a guest in my hotel, and as such will be afforded the utmost courtesy. I do, however, have one gentle warning."

"Yes, ma'am?"

The respectful address did nothing to alleviate Maeve's somber expression. Her gaze pinned Zoe's without apology. "Don't screw with my son's emotions, or I'll have to intervene." The words were crisp and unequivocal. "He's a grown man. But men can be blinded by their physical needs. If you are what you seem to be…a nice girl with a penchant for traveling lightly and often, then so be it. But if you have any notion of manipulating my son for your own personal or financial gain, I *will* send you packing."

It was possible Zoe's mouth gaped. She wasn't accustomed to such blunt speaking, nor such evidence of a parent's love and determination. Some women would be highly offended by Maeve's speech. Zoe, however, couldn't help but think how lucky Liam was to have such a force of nature guarding his back.

She swallowed the rush of envy and yearning. Maeve would be an awesome mother-in-law. The thought brought her up short. Where had that come from? "I swear you have nothing to fear from me, Mrs. Kavanagh. I'm only passing through. Your son is a wonderful man, but we have little in common."

"Because you see Liam as staid and serious?'

"I wouldn't have said *staid.*" More like sexy as hell.

"It might help if I tell you a bit of the Kavanagh story," Maeve said. "Do you have a few moments?"

"Of course."

Maeve poured herself another cup of tea and selected a macaroon from the plate of delicacies. Taking a bite, she put it on the saucer with her teacup and grimaced. "Living in a hotel with a world-renowned chef is a terrible strain on my willpower."

"You're an attractive woman. I can't see any extra pounds."

"Dear girl." Now Maeve had a twinkle in her eye. "No wonder my son is smitten with you."

That didn't seem to require an answer. Zoe pretended to sip her zillionth cup of tea, beginning to feel like a character in a period drama, minus the cool clothes.

Dylan's mother sighed, her expression reflective. "The original Kavanaghs came to this country in the 1920s. Times were hard, and this rocky, mountainous land was all they could afford. Our Kavanagh story and indeed our whole family might have died out long ago except for the fact that at the height of the Great Depression, an ancestor discovered a thick vein of silver hidden deep in a cave somewhere here on the mountain."

"Sounds like a fairy tale."

"It does, doesn't it? That one event swung the tide, and from then on, the family fortunes prospered. Though a landslide eventually obscured the mine, there was enough money and sufficient sound investments to keep marching forward."

"Had the mine been tapped out?"

"No one really remembers. But my late husband, Reggie, was convinced that he had to locate it. Unfortunately, he was egged on by a woman who came over from Ireland claiming to be a distant cousin. She said she was writing the Kavanagh family history, and we had no reason to believe otherwise." Maeve's expression for a moment reflected pain. "The woman was quite lovely, and I'm sorry to say that my husband was very weak. They began an affair."

Zoe's heart broke for Liam's mother. "I'm so sorry."

Maeve shrugged, her lips twisting. "Even Liam was infatuated with her. Until he realized what was going on. Then he hated her. Once she and Reggie were sleeping together, she became even more insistent that it was possible to find the mine. Reggie believed her because her certainty fed his own fantasies of reopening the mine. It became an ugly obsession. One winter day when Liam was in high school, Reggie took off on one of his jaunts and never returned."

"And the woman?"

"She went back to Ireland. I had her investigated eventually. She lives in a low-rent flat in Dublin and works as a bank teller. I'm sure she was hoping that the American Kavanaghs would be her ticket out of a boring life."

"That's terrible."

"It was a long time ago. But a disappearance is not a clean break like a death. There are always questions. And of course, there was no possibility of my finding anyone else to love. By the time the requisite years had passed for Reggie to be declared legally dead, my children and the hotel had become my life."

"I can tell from what Liam says that you're a close-knit family."

"Yes. Liam and I even more so, because we work so closely together. He grew from a scared, angry teenager into a capable, caring man. But losing his father like that marked him. Though I never encouraged it, Liam was convinced he had no choice but to step up and be the head of the family. He was determined to be the antithesis of his father."

"How so?"

"Reggie was a wonderful, outgoing, loving man. But he was unable to see that his obsession with finding the mine was terribly selfish. The tragedy of his presumed death took something from my sons that I could never give back to them. I did my best to play the role of both parents, but a boy of any age needs his father. Because of Reggie's blindness, he robbed his children and did them a grave disservice. He had a responsibility as a dad, but he abdicated that obligation in favor of pursuing a fantasy."

"And now Liam is the exact opposite."

"In many ways, yes. I appreciate his dedication, and in fact, as a young man, he sacrificed much for me and for his family as a whole. I've prayed that he won't grow to resent me, but still sometimes I worry."

"Liam loves what he does. And he loves you." Zoe said the words with absolute conviction. And was rewarded by the look of gratitude in Maeve's damp eyes.

"Thank you for that," the older woman said. "I'm so close to the situation, it's difficult to be impartial."

"I think you're worried about nothing. I've seen men who resent their lot in life, and Liam isn't one of them."

"Tell me about your family, Zoe."

The sudden question, commonplace though it was, took Zoe completely off guard. She stuttered and buried her face in her teacup, taking a long gulp as she tried to regain her composure. It was one thing to analyze the Kavanagh family. Another again to delve into Zoe's past and present. Her kin were neither as charming nor as caring as Liam's. And Zoe had no real desire to reveal the skeletons in her closet.

When she thought she could speak without sounding defensive, she smiled. "My parents live in the northeast. Sadly, we're not very close."

"You're an only child?"

"Yes, ma'am."

Maeve shook her head, her expression exasperated. "Quit *ma'am-ing* me, if you please. It's unnecessary. Call me Maeve."

"I'd be honored."

"You know, Zoe…" She paused, her shoulders lifting and falling. "I don't have any daughters, only sons. But I think you are an extraordinary young woman, and I'd like to know you better."

Danger, danger, danger. If Zoe became too entwined in the life of the Kavanagh family, she might find it even harder to leave. And she always left eventually. Always.

Nevertheless, Maeve was waiting for an answer. "I'd like that, too," Zoe said, feeling the truth of the words in her heart. "And you don't have to worry. I'm not a threat to your son."

Twelve

The following morning when Liam watched Zoe step out of the elevator, his heart jolted. As she sauntered across the lobby to meet him, he realized he was in danger of doing something—or maybe even a few somethings—that was either irrational or stupid or wildly impetuous. The urge and the recognition of that urge alarmed him. He was not that kind of man.

Every set of male eyes in the vicinity tracked Zoe's progress. She wore her brand-new boots with the scrunched tops of big socks visible. But it was the miles of long, slim legs and the abbreviated khaki shorts that walloped him with a punch of lust and longing.

Every teenage boy in America had seen legs like those in naughty magazines hidden beneath mattresses.

When Liam finally dragged his gaze upward, the view was equally stunning. Zoe wore a plaid button-down shirt with the sleeves rolled to her elbows and the tails tied in a jaunty knot at her waist, exposing a shallow, sexy belly button.

Her golden hair was caught back in a ponytail. She lifted her hand and donned a pair of large tortoiseshell sunglasses, effectively shielding her gaze. "Good morning, Liam. Are we ready to go?"

It was a good thing he was standing behind the front desk. He needed a moment to capture his equilibrium. His throat dry as dust, he managed a smile. "I am. Did you use sunscreen?"

She nodded. "Top to bottom and everywhere in between."

Now there was an image. One he couldn't dwell on at the moment. "Good." His conversational expertise had been reduced to single syllables. Without further ado, he ushered her outside where one of his employees had brought around Liam's Jag.

Zoe patted the hood ornament as she walked around to the passenger side. "Promise not to bite me."

He wasn't sure if she was talking to the chrome cat or to him. If it was the latter, she was out of luck. Once the picnic basket was safely stowed in the backseat, he glanced at his companion. "All set?"

She nodded, her smile cheeky. "Bring it on."

The next half hour was the most fun he'd had in a long time…if you didn't count that night in Zoe's bed. He sent the Jag whizzing around curvy mountain roads, hanging just above the speed limit, but plenty fast enough to make Zoe shriek and laugh out loud.

Her enthusiasm and joy were contagious. The cloud-dotted sky was as perfectly blue as a brand-new crayon, full of pictures and dreams waiting to be summoned. The day was warm, but not miserably hot, the breeze a soothing balance for the sun's intensity.

Liam drove with one hand on the wheel, his left arm resting on the door. "I thought I'd take you to Rooster's Rest."

"How quaint. Sounds high."

He glanced deliberately at her bare legs. "You can make it."

For a moment, she took off her sunglasses and stared at

him. Though he dared not take his gaze off the serpentine road for longer than a split second, one look in her direction registered the awareness that hovered between them. His sex tightened uncomfortably, and his breathing quickened. Today's outing was all well and good, but he planned on persuading her to join him in a far more private, much more luxurious rendezvous. Very soon.

When they reached the pull-off that accessed the trail he had in mind, Zoe hopped out of the car and stretched. East of them and far below, the town of Silver Glen seemed to slumber in the sunshine. Zoe practically bounced on her toes. "Come on, slowpoke," she said.

Liam removed their lunch and raised the top of the car. The small picnic basket was fitted with two straps that slipped over the shoulders like a backpack. He donned it, adjusted the fit, and pointed. "Okay, Miss Impatience. Let's see what you've got."

In truth, Zoe had serious doubts about her ability to keep up with Liam. When wearing a dress suit he cut a formidable figure. But today, in professional-looking gear that had probably cost a fortune, he looked like a cover model for *Backpacker Magazine*. Broad shoulders...muscular calves and thighs. Boots that had the wear on them of a serious hiker.

His vented dark-green shirt hung loose over khaki shorts. In this environment, he was the ultimate male. Capable of conquering the wilderness and killing a bear with his two hands.

Okay, so maybe that last part was one part Daniel Boone legend and one part prehistoric female admiration, but wow...Liam Kavanagh was one hunky guy.

Though she suspected he was attempting to shorten his stride, she was breathless in half a mile. "Stop," she said, bending at the waist and trying to inhale oxygen. "Your legs are longer than mine."

"Sorry."

He didn't look sorry at all. In fact, he looked distinctly *something*. She couldn't quite put her finger on it. "What's wrong with you?"

His jaw tightened. "Nothing."

"Liar."

His sudden move startled her. Without warning he had her up against a tree, his hips wedged against hers. *"This* is what's wrong with me," he said. His breath was hot on her cheek, the glaze of passion in his eyes unmistakable.

Rough bark pressed uncomfortably into her back, but she wouldn't have moved for anything. "Did you leave your polished manners back at the hotel along with your Italian-made suit?"

Finally, his monumental self-control snapped. "Damn you," he groaned. Like a man desperate for a lifeline, he took her mouth in a possessive kiss.

Her legs weakened as his voracious hunger devoured her. This was the reaction she'd been seeking, but the reality was far more intense than she had expected. Pulling away from her only long enough to dump the picnic basket on the ground, he was back in a half second, capturing her head in two big hands and tilting her mouth to his so he could slide his tongue between her lips and stroke the inside of her mouth.

Breathing was not all that important, she decided hazily. Her fingers clenched in his hair. "Please tell me you have condoms."

His answer was a muffled grunt that could have meant anything or nothing. She flinched when one of his hands slid beneath her shirt and shoved her bra aside to play with a taut nipple.

"Seriously, Liam," she said. "Do you?" They were rapidly reaching a point of no return. Her body was so primed, she would probably be embarrassingly quick off the mark the moment he entered her.

Rearing back to look at her, he inhaled sharply. "You

drive me insane," he said, his brow creased as if in confusion. "We're supposed to be exploring the great outdoors."

At that very moment, laughter and conversation reached them only seconds ahead of a large group of college-aged kids striding up the trail. There was barely time enough for Zoe to adjust her blouse and for Liam to take two quick steps backward.

The group was boisterous, calling out greetings and joking comments and jostling for position. In a few moments, the cluster of hikers disappeared around a bend up ahead.

Liam squeezed the bridge of his nose between his eyes. "Good Lord."

"Do you think they caught on?"

He lifted an eyebrow. "Oh, yeah."

"What do we do now? I don't want to run into them again. It would be too embarrassing."

"I hate to waste those new boots."

"They'll keep for another day."

"In that case, let's go someplace quiet and private for our picnic."

Zoe straightened from the tree, assuming her legs could now hold her up. "What a lovely idea, Mr. Kavanagh. I'm in your hands."

"Not yet, but we're getting there."

Liam drove with purpose, eager to reach their destination. The spot was farther away than he had planned to go, but minus the hike, they had plenty of time. He glanced sideways at his passenger who was being unusually quiet. "You okay?"

She nodded, her expression pensive. "Yes. Just enjoying the day."

He wished he knew what she was thinking, but women were complicated creatures, and Zoe more so than most. It wasn't conceit to say he could have taken her up against the tree back there. Zoe had been every bit as into the moment as he had been. Now, however, she seemed a million miles away.

At last, he spotted the sign he was looking for.

She perked up when he turned off the highway. "What's this?" she asked.

"A good friend of mine owns a series of rustic cabins that he rents out only in the summer months. I have a standing invitation to use them off-season, complete with a key. There's no electricity, but on a day like today, we won't need it."

A few hundred yards up a gravel road he had to unlock a gate. After driving the Jag past the metal swing bar, he relocked the barrier. The cabins came into view around the next bend.

Zoe got out of the car and examined the buildings. "These are cute," she exclaimed. Her shirt had rucked up, exposing a smooth pale abdomen.

Liam's fingers clenched around his keys, hard enough to leave marks in his palm. He had to get ahold of himself. But Zoe's innocent sexuality hit him hard, making him ache to have her. Pointing to the closest of the one-room structures as he put up the convertible top, he said, "The porch is covered. How about we sit over there to eat?"

She nodded. "Perfect."

There was no outdoor furniture, but between them they managed to spread a square damask cloth on the floor of the porch. The chef had done himself proud. Fresh salmon drizzled with a light sauce, a broccoli salad, sourdough bread, and apple-caramel cake for dessert.

Liam had added a bottle of expensive champagne. He popped the cork, filled two flutes, and handed one to Zoe.

They sat on the edge of the porch, their legs dangling, and consumed an impressive amount of food in short order. He was glad to see that Zoe had a good appetite. She needed a few extra pounds to satisfy him that she was truly recovered.

Though he knew the risk he was taking, he counted on the meal and the champagne to mellow her. "Will you tell me about your parents?" he asked quietly. "I would never betray your confidence." But if he went any farther with this relationship, there couldn't be secrets between them.

She didn't look at him, but he saw the way her jaw tightened. Resting one arm on an upraised knee, she sipped from a crystal flute, as comfortable as any princess at court.

When she finally spoke, her gaze was trained somewhere off in the distance. "I know I can trust you. I wouldn't have slept with you otherwise, but there's not much to tell. My mother is a wraith of a woman who has no opinions or interests other than the ones my father approves."

"Is he abusive?" It was a legitimate question and one he needed answered.

"It depends on how you define that word. Emotionally? Yes. He's very controlling."

"So you butted heads when he realized you weren't likely to let yourself *be* controlled."

"Very good. Go to the head of the class. When I left college, he was furious, but I was halfway around the world, so there wasn't much he could do about it. After my stint in the Peace Corps, I continued to travel. I've waitressed in Rome, taught English in South America and done laundry in Thailand. Whatever it took to fund my adventures."

"You're very resourceful." He couldn't help wondering how the platinum credit card and the money in her van fit into her explanation. "What was it like when you came home?"

"My father thought the ball was finally in his court. I made the mistake of moving back into the house, because I had really missed my mother, and I felt guilty about leaving her under my father's thumb unprotected."

"Then what happened?"

"He began to pressure me into going to work for him. Having a child like me instead of the son he wanted was always a great disappointment in his eyes, but I suppose it finally dawned on him that his only offspring was better than nothing."

"It must have been nice to know your father wanted you."

She looked straight at him for the first time, and he was appalled by the bleak sorrow in her gaze. For one brief second he caught a glimpse of another Zoe. The woman who carried secrets and hurts hidden from the world. "No." The negative was flat, no intonation. A statement of fact.

"What is his business?"

"Corporate greed. Crush the competition. Even without the specter of being under my father's domination, it was not a world I ever wanted."

"And he didn't take that well."

"Oh, no. Not at all. Things became unbearable in the house. My mother was caught in the middle, and the tension made her physically ill. I used to resent her for not standing up to him, but as I grew up, I finally understood that she is incapable of that. She had a wretched childhood. My father was her ticket out of a dreadful home environment. And he's been her security ever since."

"So what did you do?"

"I left. Again. That's when I started my music career, if you can call it that. There were still plenty of places in the good ole U.S.A. that I hadn't seen, so I went where the wind and the work took me."

"Is it lonely?" He genuinely wanted to know.

She shrugged. "Being human is to be lonely. It's a rare gift in life to find the person who completes you. Let's just say that the good outweighed the bad. My mother and I still communicate. I bought her an iPhone she keeps hidden from my dad. We call and text when he's out of town."

"I'm sorry, Zoe."

"I tried once more. I don't want you to think I'm as stubborn as my father. This past Christmas, my mom begged me to come home for the holidays. I was feeling blue and orphaned, so I did."

"And?" Her story riveted him.

"At first I thought we were mending fences. My father was on his best behavior. My mother actually glowed. There were parties and dinners, most of them business related, but still. On Christmas Eve, Dad called me into his office. I was expecting maybe a hug or a word of thanks for making my mother happy."

Liam saw the muscles in her throat work as she swallowed. A great ball of dread gathered in his chest, but he had asked the questions and now he had no recourse but to hear the tale to the end.

"That wasn't it?"

Her lips twisted in a cynical grimace so unlike the Zoe he knew that it gave him a pain in his chest. "He backhanded me across the face. Hard. I was so shocked I didn't know what to do. But he did all the talking. He told me he was sick to death of my immaturity and selfishness. That it was time to grow up and quit hiding behind my suitcase."

Liam's chest heaved. He wanted to say something, but the wrong words could hurt her, and he would slice his own wrists before he would do that. "Go on," he said softly.

"He told me that he had a friend on the police force. If I didn't cooperate with my father, I would be accused of stealing money from the safe in Dad's office. I would be arrested and taken to jail."

"Goddammit." Fury mixed with incredulity choked Liam and made it hard to breathe. Hard on the heels of that reaction was the sick realization that Zoe's van was stashed with money. Lots of money.

She had disappeared into some bad place, barely seeming to know he was there. "It was Christmas Eve," she said dully, as if he might have forgotten that fact. "I slipped upstairs and tried to explain to Mama why I couldn't stay. But I didn't tell her about his threat. I couldn't. She cried so hard it ripped my heart in two. While my father was on the phone, I packed a small bag and slipped out the back of the house."

"He didn't try to stop you or come after you?"

"No. Not at first. But sometime in early March I began to get the feeling I was being followed. I would see someone in the audience watching me, someone who looked out of place. I'd have to slip away under cover of darkness. Again. And again."

"It could have been your imagination." He was trying to convince himself that her story wasn't as awful as it sounded. But then he remembered the mysterious man Pierre had intercepted. The man looking for Zoe.

She shook her head. "Last week in Asheville I saw the same man. Twice. On the street. Following me on foot. That's when I hit the road again and ended up in Silver Glen."

"So the man who showed up here and talked to Pierre was probably the same fellow?"

"That would be my guess. And he'll come back again. So I won't be able to stay the whole six weeks. I can't go back home and be arrested. And I can't put your family through an ugly situation or a confrontation."

"That's why you asked Gary to paint your van. Even though it didn't need a paint job."

Shock lifted her eyebrows. "You and this Gary fellow must be bosom buddies. Remind me to pick another mechanic the next time."

There was a bite in her words, one he deserved. "I'm sorry."

"It doesn't really matter now, does it?" She drained her champagne, her expression for once so inscrutable he had no clue what she was thinking.

She curled her knees to her chest in a defensive posture, her arms linked around them. "If you brought me here to fool around, we've definitely killed the mood now, haven't we?"

Thirteen

Zoe felt like a punctured balloon. Again, like the hospital experience weeks ago, she experienced the notion that life was using her for a punching bag. This day had begun with such effervescence and simple joy that it was particularly painful to be dragged to a place she'd tried so hard to escape.

She understood Liam's questions. He was trying to understand her. The trouble was, she barely understood herself. But she cared about Liam, and for the first time in a long time, she wanted to let someone in.

Rising to her feet with one fluid motion, she brushed crumbs off her hands. "I'm going to wander into those trees over there for a private moment."

"Watch out for snakes."

Her nose wrinkled. His admonition wasn't a joke. That's all she needed. A snakebite on her lady parts.

After relieving herself and straightening her clothing, she wandered through the little grove of hardwood trees, enjoying the beauty of the somnolent afternoon. Perhaps she could stay here forever, hiding out from her father like a paranoid survivalist. The Unabomber had managed it for a long time. But Montana and North Carolina weren't exactly the same.

Despite having no concrete proof, she was very afraid that she was still being followed. Even though Pierre had done his best to hide her existence in the hotel, and even though she had told herself the danger was past, in her gut she knew it would never be over. Not until she put a stop to it once and for all. It would only be a matter of time before the mysterious man understood that he had been duped. He would come back, because the man paying him would never give up.

When would her father learn that she would not accept being under his domination the way her mother was? If Zoe could have rescued her mother, she would have. But she knew in her heart that her mom would never leave.

As she walked back over to the cabin, her heart began to splinter into a million little pieces. Liam waited for her. He stood with one hand braced on a support timber, his stance casual, but his gaze watchful.

She had to leave Silver Glen. It had been stupid and naive to think she could actually stay six weeks. She knew better than to let anyone get close to her, but Liam had slipped beneath her defenses. There was no future for them. But dear God, she loved being here in North Carolina with him. She loved the town and the hotel and sense of community and singing at the Silver Dollar, but most of all, she knew she could love Liam. If she allowed herself. But she wouldn't. She couldn't.

The only way she had been able to survive her nomadic lifestyle was to enjoy the people she met along the way, but never to fall into the trap of thinking they were family. She had a mother she loved very much, but her father had separated them. Imagining a dream in which Liam's family *became* her family was pathetic.

He liked her. And he desired her. That much was clear.

But Zoe lived on the road and Liam was rooted in Silver Glen. Permanently.

She didn't climb the stone steps to the porch. Instead, she shaded her eyes and stared up at him. Her sunglasses were in the car. "Do you mind if we go back now?" she asked.

Liam was torn. And deeply concerned about his own judgment. Was he allowing his sexual attraction to Zoe to blind him to the truth? In the minutes when she had left him briefly, he had pondered the existence of the money. Hidden in a panel of her van. An enormous amount of money. Enough for a man to hire an investigator to retrieve it. Did she plan to use it to pay her credit card bill?

Forcing himself to take a mental step backward, he asked a silent, hard-edged question. Could Zoe possibly be a manipulative con? Had she spun Liam this story in order to cover her tracks so that when her father caught up with her, Liam would take her side?

His mind shut down, refusing to deal with such an ugly supposition. The notion was repugnant in every way. Despite the growing mountain of evidence that said Zoe had secrets galore, and despite the experience in his youth that told him women could be devious, he trusted Zoe. Was he making the same mistake twice?

She stood, waiting for his answer. "Sure," he said. "But if you're up for it, we could climb to the top of this hill. There's a beautiful lake on the other side."

He watched her visibly hesitate and wished he could appease whatever demons she was battling. "I suppose it couldn't hurt."

Liam jumped off the porch and touched her arm. "I have an idea." He indicated for her to follow him, and they began walking around the cabin and up the grassy hillside behind. He matched his pace to hers and then gave voice to what was becoming an irresistible notion. "I have to go to New York tomorrow," he said. "I'm speaking to a consortium of high-end hotel owners about hospitality in the twenty-first century. I'd like you to go with me."

Zoe trudged beside him, head down. "Why?"

He sighed. "Nothing is ever easy with you, is it? Can't it be enough that I want to spend time with you?"

"How long would we be gone?"

"Three days."

"And what about my room at the hotel?"

"Which hotel?"

She stopped and struggled to catch her breath. The hill wasn't all that high, but it was steep. "I meant the Silver Beeches, but I suppose the question stands for both."

"We'll simply put your room at my hotel on hold. And in New York, it's up to you. One room or two."

"I don't want to fall in love with you, Liam."

The shock of her words knocked him back half a step. He ran a hand across the back of his neck. "I don't know how to answer that. And besides, I don't think you're in much danger. According to someone I know, I'm bossy and uptight and judgmental and I have a king complex."

"Don't forget arrogant."

He held out his hands. "See? You have nothing to worry about."

They continued walking, but his mind was not on the magnificent scenery. Had Zoe been expecting some sort of reciprocal response on his part after she made her veiled statement about having feelings for him? Had he hurt her by remaining silent? And did he want her to love him? Did he want to love her?

The questions threatened to drive him mad. That and the memory of thousands of dollars hidden away in her van. As a teenager he had watched his father be seduced by a woman with secrets. Liam had been infatuated with her as well. When her true colors were revealed, his entire family had been crushed, and his father was dead.

Liam was no longer an impressionable youth. But love could make a man blind.

At the crest, they stopped, joined in mutual accord by their admiration of the view. A small lake in the distance glittered, its surface silvered by the sun. "Have you ever sailed?" he asked her, searching for topics that weren't booby-trapped.

"Some. While I was in France. I made friends with sisters whose father was Comte something or another. They would take me home with them on the weekends and we would do all sorts of crazy things."

"Do you still hear from them?"

"No. We lost touch." She left it at that, so he didn't push.

A rumble of thunder sounded in the distance. The fluffy white "sheep" clouds that dotted the sky earlier in the day had morphed into angry, gray, roiling masses. "Better head back," he said. "We don't want to be trapped up here when it hits."

Their luck ran out halfway back to the cabin. The sky let loose with a deluge as if someone had opened a huge zipper overhead. In seconds, they were both drenched. Lightning danced around them and thunder roared. Liam cursed himself for not paying closer attention to the change in weather. Running now, they hurtled down the last incline.

A few hundred feet from the cabin, Zoe's heel skidded on wet grass, and she went down hard, tumbling twice before he could get to her. In other circumstances, her appearance might have been amusing, covered as she was in mud and grass, but he was too worried to pay much attention.

He scooped her into his arms, and with a stride that was long but steady, carried her the last few yards to the cabin. The only entrance was through the front door. He kicked it open. Musty air met them, the inside of the place cheerless and dark. Tiny rodents ran for the cover of darkness.

Zoe clung to his neck. "I'm not touching anything."

"Only for a second." He eased her down onto one foot

while he reached for a straight-backed chair that appeared to be fairly clean. Sitting down, he settled her in his lap. "How badly are you hurt?"

"Mostly just my pride. Though my ankle may be sprained and I think my hand is bleeding where I landed. Can't we go back to the hotel? I could sit on a jacket or towel or something so I don't mess up your car."

A thunderous boom made them both jump in sync. "Screw the car," he said forcefully. "We need to get you to a doctor. But it's too dangerous to move until this passes."

Her skin was covered in gooseflesh. If they took off her wet clothes, he had nothing to cover her with. Some Boy Scout he had turned out to be.

Zoe burrowed into his embrace, her teeth chattering audibly. "I don't need a doctor, but I'd kill for a hot shower."

"May I join you?" The words tumbled out. He hadn't meant to say them. But suddenly, despite the wretched conditions, he felt the return of the sexual bond that had taken them both by surprise.

She stroked his collarbone through his shirt. "Why not?" she drawled after a moment. "It's only a fantasy at this point."

"Since you checked into the hotel, I've had lots of fantasies," he confessed. "I believe you must be an Irish fairy in disguise come to grant me three wishes."

He felt her laugh, the sound almost a caress against his chest. "I think one wish is enough. Don't be greedy."

"So will you go with me to New York?"

"I won't be in the way?"

"No."

"Have you ever taken a date to something like this?"

"No."

"Why now? Why me?"

The storm was moving away, the sound of the thunder fading to a muted boom. "I hear the ticking clock," he said, being as honest as he knew how to be. "You won't be in Silver Glen for long. I want a chance to get to know you better."

She sat crossways on his lap, her legs dangling. When his hand brushed her bare thigh, her skin was cold and damp. "I do love New York," she sighed. "I suppose I'll go."

"You don't have to sound so happy about it."

"I'm wet and cold. What do you expect?"

"Now who's the grumpy one?" he asked, grinning though she couldn't see his face.

She pinched his arm. Hard. "You should be nicer to the woman you bumped and made fall down the hill."

"Hey," he said, indignant. "I had nothing to do with it. I can't help it if those new boots tripped you up."

"I'll get more sympathy with the other story."

"Try it and I'll spank you."

"Oooh," she said. "Macho threats. Don't expect me to believe you've read *Fifty Shades of Grey*."

"God, no. I'm more of a John Grisham fan." But should he admit that the idea of turning Zoe's bottom pink turned him on? "We can go now," he said gruffly, desperate to get out of the small, semidark cabin. The only thing keeping his hunger in check at the moment was the lack of a clean flat surface. That and the fact that Zoe might need medical attention.

It wasn't easy for a man to hold a scantily dressed woman in his arms and not think about sex. Particularly if that woman was Zoe Chamberlain. He stood abruptly, lifting her into his arms. "Hang on."

Fortunately for his peace of mind, she was quiet and docile during the trip to the car. The ground was littered with storm debris. Hard-packed dirt had turned rapidly into a mud pit.

After he deposited her in the passenger seat, he ran around to his side, wincing when he realized he had no choice but to put his dirty boots on the mat. If he'd been smart, he'd have brought his Jeep. But he had wanted to pamper Zoe.

He turned on the engine, the heat and the defroster. Zoe had already flipped on her seat warmer. Reaching behind them, he snagged an old sweatshirt. "Here. Put this over your legs. And let me see your hand."

She did as he asked but not without her usual sass. "Bossy, bossy, bossy."

With her small palm turned upward, he examined the series of gouges caused by rocks and whatever else she'd landed on. "I don't think it's going to need stitches, but it's probably going to hurt like hell for a few days. We're lucky you didn't break your arm."

"I'm well aware of that, trust me."

Now that he could see better, he noticed she also had a scrape on the side of her cheek. And there would no doubt be bruises to follow. He glanced down at her leg. "Do you want to try and get that boot off so I can examine your ankle?" How she would do that in the confines of the car, he wasn't sure.

"No, thank you. Let's just get back."

It was a silent drive, each of them lost in thought. A couple of times they ran through rain again. "That ankle needs to be examined." He tried to persuade Zoe to see a doctor, but she flatly refused.

"I'm tired and I want to go to my room. If it's still hurting in the morning, I'll get an X-ray."

"You promise?"

"I do."

When they pulled up at the hotel, Liam handed off the keys to the valet. Zoe insisted on walking up the shallow steps on her own, though she did lean on his arm for support. He escorted her all the way upstairs to the door of her room and halted. "Will you have dinner with me this evening? After you've cleaned up?" He wanted to mention the offer of a shared shower, but he could tell she was drooping.

"I think I'll get room service after a hot soak in the tub. But thank you."

Well, hell. "I understand. Tonight I'll buy a second ticket for New York. The flight is midafternoon. We'll have to leave here at noon in order to drive to the airport in Asheville."

"I'll be ready."

Her body language was screaming at him to back off, but her odd mood disturbed him. What if she chose to bolt? To run away? He brushed the back of his hand down her cheek. "May I come in for a moment?"

Zoe nodded slowly as she inserted her key card. "If you want."

He followed her and shut the door behind him. "I'm sorry our day didn't turn out as planned."

"Life is usually like that," she said.

He looked for irony in her expression, but found none. Zoe had a slant on the world that not many people attained. He wouldn't call it fatalism. That was too negative. What she had was the ability to enjoy the twists and turns, both good and bad, with equanimity. As if everything that happened to her had purpose and value.

Pulling her close, he nuzzled the side of her neck. "I won't keep you. I know you need to get out of those wet clothes."

"I'm fine," she said, but the words were unconvincing.

He kissed her gently, trying to convey feelings that were unformed but strong. She felt good in his arms, as if she had been created to exact specifications that matched needs in his own life he hadn't even known existed.

Holding her like this had a predictable effect on his anatomy. But he wasn't going to push it. Zoe was wet and cold and tired. He forced himself to release her and back step back. "A good day?" He made the words a question.

She nodded. "Of course. I had fun. Despite the weather."

"And the rowdy hikers?"

Her cheeks reddened. In her eyes he saw the memory of almost making love up against a tree. "Their timing could have been better," she agreed, the words wry. Then she shifted gears. "I don't have clothes for New York."

Damn. He should have thought of that. The woman spent part of her nights living in a van, and she had checked into the Silver Beeches with a single suitcase. "Well," he said slowly. "I invited you. So the wardrobe will be my treat. There are several designer boutiques a block from the hotel. We'll go there as soon as we land."

"You won't be buying me clothes. That's ridiculous. I have money. But yes, if I could shop first, that would be helpful."

"Do you?" he said, not pausing to censor the words.

"Do I what?"

"Do you have the money to pay for new clothes?"

He saw her go still, like a wild animal trapped in the headlights of an oncoming car. "I'm staying here, aren't I?"

It wasn't really an answer to his question. "Talk to me, Zoe. If you're strapped for cash, don't rack up a credit card bill for new clothes. It's nothing to be ashamed of."

He was baiting her deliberately. The knowledge made him feel sick, but he was desperate to know the truth. She had given him bits and pieces of her story, but there was more. Something she was withholding. And it involved the cash in the van.

She stared at him, nonplussed. "My finances are in good shape," she said evenly. "But thank you for your concern." The flat words struck him with a force he deserved. Why couldn't he trust her unequivocally?

He was no closer to unraveling the mystery that was Zoe, and yet he had pissed her off. "I'm sorry. I didn't mean to insult you. I only wanted to help."

"You could help by trusting me to manage my own life." The retort was sharp, but he saw humor in her eyes.

"I get the message. Am I forgiven?"

She leaned in and kissed him softly on the cheek. "Of course. Now go before I get hypothermia. I'll talk to you later."

Fourteen

When Zoe awoke the following morning, she practically bounced out of bed. It seemed like days since she had seen Liam, instead of a few hours. He surely had matters to attend to before he could leave town, so she hadn't been surprised not to hear from him.

Her evening had been pleasant enough…and actually cozy. After a hot shower and a change of clothes that finally chased the chills away, she ordered a double serving of mac and cheese along with a big glass of chocolate milk. Wearing her most comfy pajamas as she curled up in the middle of her decadent king-size bed, she had watched half a dozen episodes of her favorite sitcom.

This morning, though, she was ready for adventure. Fortunately, her ankle was almost as good as new. Dressing rapidly in a skirt and top and her favorite gold-and-bronze sandals, she took the time to tidy her belongings and pack everything back into her suitcase. It felt odd leaving this hotel room. In a short amount of time she had made it her own. The only item she would be leaving behind was her precious guitar.

Though she was excited about traveling with Liam, she felt guilty that she was still keeping secrets from him. Last night had been her opportunity to come clean and tell him she was going to leave sooner rather than later. But keeping her own counsel had ensured her safety thus far, and it was a habit hard to break.

Since she skipped breakfast, she went down to the dining room at eleven. Liam hadn't mentioned lunch in their itinerary, and she was starving. As she was enjoying her last cup of coffee, he showed up at her table looking distinctly harried.

"Have you eaten?" she asked.

He didn't sit down. "I'll have to grab something on the plane. It's been a hell of a morning. Somehow we booked an Arabian sheikh and a presidential hopeful in the same suite for the upcoming weekend."

"Oh, good grief."

"I think it happened when we switched over to a new computer system. We've managed to juggle some bookings and comp a few guests for the inconvenience, but the whole fracas ate up my morning."

"Are we still going to make it?"

He leaned down and kissed her cheek. "You can bet on it. Meet me out front in fifteen minutes."

Liam was as good as his word. When Zoe stepped outside, he was standing beside the open door of a limo. She raised an eyebrow. "Is this for us?"

He leaned close and whispered in her ear. "Pierre loves driving it, and it makes him feel good, so who am I to complain?"

Zoe slid into the roomy backseat and sighed. Bessie would be jealous, but Zoe planned to enjoy herself anyway. "Maybe my van will be finished by the time we get back," she said.

"Are you in that much of a hurry?" Liam loosened his tie and reached in the mini fridge for two bottles of water, handing her one.

"I don't like using someone else's car all the time."

"It's a piece of junk."

"Says the man who drives a Jag. The silver Sentra is fine, but I'm not used to accepting favors."

"It's not always a virtue to do everything yourself."

"I'm pretty sure that's a case of the pot calling the kettle black. You don't even trust your mother to run the hotel without you."

His jaw dropped. "That's not true."

"Of course it is. You never travel. You live on the premises. The Silver Beeches Lodge is your baby."

Liam reeled mentally. Could what Zoe accused him of possibly be true? "My mother was grieving when my father died," he said automatically. "It was hard for her to shoulder the responsibility of the hotel without help."

"I'm sure that was true once upon a time. But she's still a young woman. And from what I can tell, she's smart and energetic and capable. Maybe she doesn't want to hurt your feelings by telling you she can carry on without you."

He leaned back in his corner and toyed with the cap of his water bottle. It was okay for him to psychoanalyze Zoe, but when she turned the tables, he didn't much like it.

Perhaps sensing his mood, Zoe ignored him, doing something on her phone. The uneasy silence lasted all the way to Asheville, through security at the airport and onto the jet. Liam took the window seat in first class, leaving Zoe to chat cheerfully with the male flight attendant. The man was under her spell in five minutes.

Disgruntled and inexplicably irritable, Liam closed his eyes and pretended to sleep.

* * *

Zoe loved to fly. The sensation of speed at takeoff, the beauty of sailing above the clouds, the anticipation of an exciting destination at journey's end…all of it gave her a buzz unlike most anything else.

It was disappointing that Liam had chosen to sleep. She had hoped to chat with him about what they might do when his meeting was over. But she had to be content with reading the in-flight magazine cover to cover and sipping a Diet Coke.

The trip north was smooth, despite a hurried connection in Atlanta. The landing at LaGuardia was textbook. Neither she nor Liam had any carry-on bags other than Zoe's purse. After they retrieved their luggage, they met a private car near the taxi stand. Liam gave an address on the Upper East Side. In moments they were speeding toward the city.

And still Liam hadn't said a word. Finally, his silence began to make her mad. "You don't have to sulk merely because I pointed out the obvious."

He glared at her. "I am *not* sulking. I have a lot on my mind."

"Whatever." She turned her attention out the window, noting the frantic traffic and congested roadways that were so unlike western North Carolina. Perhaps she should try living in New York for a while. There were thousands of venues here for aspiring musicians who were willing to play for little or nothing. Maybe a change of scenery would do her good.

She was taken totally off guard when a big hand grasped her wrist and tugged. "Come closer," Liam said.

Now almost in his lap, she glared. "What are you doing?"

His smile was lopsided. "Apologizing. And kissing you."

"But I—"

Two fingers touched her lips. "Shhh," he crooned. "Let me grovel."

When his mouth settled over hers, she could have sworn that the chauffeur began driving erratically. Her stomach flipped in dizzying loops and her heart raced. The setting was not exactly private. Liam didn't seem to mind. He was barely touching her, but she began to melt.

That a man could convey so much in a kiss was eye opening. He kissed her sweetly but desperately, as if trying to convince himself or her that what they had was going to last. She clung to his waist, attempting to maintain some semblance of dignity. "I think the driver is watching us in the mirror," she whispered.

"No, he's not." Liam's sharp teeth nipped her lower lip. "Close your eyes, Zoe."

She obeyed his command, not because she wanted to, but because she had no choice. His taste seduced her, as did his touch. And the sound of his harsh breathing told her she wasn't alone in the midst of this sensual exploration. The wine-dark river of pleasure that Liam conjured made her move restlessly, her knees bumping his.

"Are we almost there?" she asked, wanting to unbutton his shirt and stroke his warm, hard chest. His suave facade seemed nothing more than a thin veneer at the moment. In every way he was a male predator, and he had fixed his sights on her.

Liam nodded, his teeth raking a sensitive spot on her neck. Pulling away suddenly, he sighed, his chest heaving. "You'd better do something to your hair."

She took a mirrored compact from her purse and felt her face go hot when she saw her reflection. Her lips were swollen, her eyes hazy. While she managed some quick repair work, Liam gently smoothed her skirt where he had shifted it to caress her bare thighs. His hands were warm against her skin.

Moments later, the car pulled up in front of a small, elegant hotel tucked beneath the shadow of two larger buildings. Colorful flags hung from a parapet over the main entrance. Enormous planters shaped like lions flanked the

glass doorway, only partially constraining masses of bego-
nias, tulips and hyacinths.

Liam took care of the fare and gave Zoe a hand as she
climbed out. A smiling doorman welcomed them while a
bellman hurried forward to take their luggage.

At the front desk, Liam handed over a platinum card. His
hold on Zoe's hand was firm enough to make her wince.
When the clerk apologized profusely because their room
would not be ready for an hour, Zoe had to bite her lip to
keep from laughing at the look on Liam's face.

She patted his arm. "It's okay. We'll shop first."

There was a certain look a man got when he was fixated
on carnal matters. Liam had it. "Fine," he grumbled, not
quite managing a smile for the poor hotel employee.

Outside on the sidewalk, Zoe dared to tease him. "We'll
have all night for what you have in mind."

Liam's expression went from thundercloud to mildly irritated. "Is that a promise?"

She rested her cheek on his shoulder for a brief moment.
"I think that it is."

Liam relaxed in an armchair and sipped the champagne
supplied by an obsequious woman whose eyeglasses were
an unlikely shade of neon-green. If that was the big color
on the runway this year, he had to hope Zoe wasn't a slave
to fashion.

His little flower child wandered around the shop, her lips
pursed, as she examined one thing after another. This was
the third boutique they had visited. The first one had been
big on rivets and studs. Zoe had turned up her nose. The
next one had had a definite Jackie Kennedy vibe, which as
Zoe pointed out, was beautiful, but not her style.

This particular establishment seemed more her speed.
"So what do I need?" she asked, her attention focused on a
rack of gowns.

"Two nice dresses for daywear, and two fancy ones for

the evenings." He was looking forward to showing her off. Zoe's fresh charm would be a hit among his colleagues. The group was mixed, about half female and half male. That all of them would be enchanted by his date, he had no doubt.

With the saleslady's help, Zoe collected an armful of clothing and headed for the fitting rooms. "I'm going to start with these."

"Make sure you come show them to me," he said. If he were being forced to shop instead of make love to Zoe, he might as well get something out of the experience.

She started with the regular outfits, the first one a traditional *little black dress* that fit her beautifully. The hem stopped just above the knees. "What do you think?" she asked.

He cocked his head and studied her. The more sophisticated attire made her seem older, but didn't detract from her appeal. "Perfect for the meeting."

Next was a more casual striped frock in yellow and cinnamon and orange that hearkened back to the days of Grace Kelly. Spaghetti straps held up a fitted bodice that flared out in a short, flirty skirt underlain with multicolored petticoats. Forget Grace Kelly. Zoe's smile made him think of Audrey Hepburn, all innocent delight.

Though she went through several more choices, they both decided that the first two were the best. For a moment, he debated asking her if she wanted to try on lingerie, but doubtless that would embarrass her. When Zoe switched to evening gowns, Liam knew he was in trouble. She looked amazing in everything she put on.

Even so, some were easily discarded. The ones with too many beads and sequins tended to overpower her delicate frame. Gradually she gravitated toward choices that were exceedingly plain on the hanger, but transformed when Zoe modeled them.

She came out in a fire-engine-red number that dried his throat. The collar fastened high on her neck, but the arms and shoulders had been cut away, barely leaving enough fabric to mold to her firm breasts and to cover her shoulder blades. The skirt was fluid and slit to midthigh. "How about this one?" she asked.

"Do *you* like it?"

Glancing in the three-way mirror, she looked over her shoulder and studied the image of her backside. "This is definitely a grown-up dress."

He smiled at the doubt in her voice. "I have every confidence you can pull it off, sweet Zoe. Now pick one more and we'll be done."

The clerk, already sniffing a fat commission, refilled his glass. "Your young lady is lovely, Mr. Kavanagh."

"Yes, she is," he said softly.

In moments, Zoe changed and tiptoed out one last time, stopping to look at her reflection. Their eyes met in the mirror, his hot and hungry, hers filled with a dawning awareness of the sexual power she wielded.

The final gown was a brilliant aquamarine that complemented her blond hair beautifully. It was made almost like a wedding dress, strapless, cinched at the waist, and with a skirt that billowed in layers of tulle on top of silk and taffeta.

Zoe twirled, an involuntary motion that brought a smile to his face. He wondered if he handed the saleswoman a wad of bills if she would agree to close the store and disappear for an hour. Liam was imagining everything he could do *to* and *with* Zoe in view of those three mirrors.

He cleared his throat. "I don't think there's any question," he said gruffly. "That dress was meant for you."

Zoe's starry-eyed gaze tangled with his. She wet her lips. "I feel like a princess." Smoothing the skirt with both hands, she lifted her shoulders and let them fall. "This dress costs more than my van."

"I told you it was my treat."

She shook her head vehemently. "No. If I'm going to live outrageously, it will be on my dime." She turned the saleslady. "All four of these, please. I'll be out in a moment to pay."

The older woman hurried to zip the couture gowns and dresses into clear garment bags. Zoe handed out the last one and appeared moments later, back in her own clothes.

"I'd forgotten how lovely it is to dress up. Makes a woman feel special."

He stood and put his hands on her shoulders, moving behind her as they faced the mirror. "You *are* special," he murmured. "Very special."

Nothing about their current situation was conducive to intimacy, but he was not going to be able to wait much longer. Zoe made him hunger in a way he couldn't quite fathom. Sexual desire was a common thing for a man, an ingrained component of the Y chromosome. Men could look at a stranger crossing the street, a girl in a magazine ad, an actress in a movie…and get aroused. It was predictable and inevitable.

But with Zoe, something else happened. Something he didn't quite understand. All he knew was that she made him tremble with lust. How could he be rigid with passion and yet incredibly weak at the same time? In her presence he experienced the full measure of his masculinity and a simultaneous and inescapably humbling recognition of his vulnerability where she was concerned.

Before he could do something foolish like drag Zoe back into one of those little dressing rooms with the fancy gold doors, the store employee returned, taking Zoe's card and running it through a nearby register. "Would you like me to have these delivered?" she asked, finishing the transaction and producing Zoe's receipt.

Liam nodded. "In the morning will be fine." He gave the hotel's address, and finally, they were back out on the street. He looked down at Zoe. "Would you like to have dinner somewhere nice? See a play? My evenings are all yours, even if I do have to pay attention to business during the day."

All around them, crowds of people passed by. Not the manic movement of Times Square. Just a steady stream of men and women returning home from a busy day. He and Zoe created an island of calm. She took one of his hands and lifted it to her lips. "At the risk of sounding incredibly gauche and boring, I was thinking we might order room service and then have an early night."

Fifteen

Zoe knew she had made the right choice when Liam's eyes darkened to navy and his strong cheekbones went ruddy with color. "I brought you here to have a good time," he said, clearly trying to be a gentleman.

She went up on tiptoe and pressed a kiss to his firm, wonderful lips. "I've been to New York City before. And there are a lot of ways to have a good time."

Liam held her at arms' length, staring at her intently as if he could read some secret in her eyes. "You amaze me. Everything is more fun with you. How do you do that?"

"I don't know. But I think it's both of us together. When I first met you, I thought we were too different, but maybe that's what makes it work."

"C'mon," he said, slinging an arm around her shoulders. "If our room is not ready now, we're going somewhere else."

Zoe decided to let Liam take the lead in what happened next. Not that she thought a woman couldn't initiate sex. But he seemed to be on a short fuse, and it might be fun to

be wooed. Fortunately for her companion's peace of mind,
one of the two penthouse suites awaited them. Their French
doors opened out onto a lovely rooftop garden. Though the
view was blocked by other structures, the spot was intimate
and appealing.

After Liam gave a terse nod of approval to the terrace,
he tipped the bellman generously and ushered him out the
door. Zoe watched from a distance as her would-be lover
investigated the spacious accommodations. His one glimpse
into the sybaritic bedroom was short. She gauged his mood
pretty well. Perhaps room service could come afterward.

Stepping back inside and locking the double glass doors,
she leaned against them. Her earlier burst of confidence had
winnowed away. Liam's brooding intensity churned all sorts
of feelings in her belly. She wanted him desperately, and yet
some primitive female reaction to the male's arousal abashed
her and kept her from making a move.

He ripped off his tie and tossed it on an antique escri-
toire. Next followed his conservative jacket. It landed short
of an ottoman. Liam made no move to retrieve it. His manner was agitated. "What do you want to order for dinner?"
he asked gruffly, not looking at her.

"Um…"

The air in the room was charged with something fierce,
something erotic. She didn't know how to respond. Or perhaps she knew but was afraid. And with every second that
passed, Liam shed another layer of civility. He prowled like
a fierce animal.

Whirling to face her suddenly, he lifted a dark eyebrow.
"What did you say?"

"Well, I…"

"You pick," he said impatiently. "I don't care what we eat.
I'm going to take a shower while you order."

Before she could say a word, he disappeared.

The air whooshed from her lungs audibly. She hadn't even
realized she was holding her breath. Never had she felt less

like eating dinner. So that was that. She refused to pick up the phone. Because she was fairly certain that Liam had no interest in food either.

But without a meal to ease the way with social convention, what was her next move? Stealthily, she hung out a do-not-disturb sign and locked the door firmly, bolting it for good measure. She did use the phone after all, but only to call the front desk and ask not to be disturbed. With the sun still shining brightly, though low in the sky, the request seemed extremely wicked and daring.

Any moment now, Liam would reappear, so she had to decide her course. Gazing at her reflection in the large ornate mirror that hung over the sofa in the outer salon, she began to take off her clothes.

Liam remained beneath the icy cold spray for longer than necessary, trying to tame the raging beast of lust and desire that made him tremble. He wanted Zoe so badly, he feared overwhelming her.

Taking his sex in his hands, he thought about relieving some of his agitation in the shower. His erection was full and heavy, the skin taut and sensitive. But when he moved his fingers restlessly up the shaft, he realized that he wanted Zoe's hands on his body more than he wanted momentary release.

Shivering beneath the frigid water, he soaped himself and washed his hair. By rights, this punishment should have helped. But when he got out and dried off, his need was not diminished in any way.

The hotel had provided plush robes in male and female sizes. He put on the larger of the two and scraped his hands through his hair. Planning to dress quickly and meet Zoe back out in the salon, he opened the bathroom door and padded barefoot into the bedroom.

Stopping dead in his tracks, he felt his mouth go dry and his throat tighten. "Zoe," he said hoarsely.

"I was hoping for more of a reaction than that," she said, her smile cheeky. But in her eyes he saw the same vulnerability that had attracted him in the beginning and made him want to protect her at all costs.

Her pose was designed to seduce. Propped up in a nest of pillows against the headboard, her naked beauty caught him off guard. He rested one hand against the armoire, more for support than anything else. Her bare breasts were as perfect as any classical statue, but warm and pink, the visage mouth-watering.

Leaving his robe on for the moment was a tactical choice. He moved toward the bed, wondering if he could keep her here for a week, a month, forever. "I thought you wanted dinner," he said, realizing as he uttered the words that they were ridiculous and unnecessary. Zoe had made her wishes more than clear.

She patted the mattress beside her. "All I want is you, Liam Kavanagh. Come woo me with that famous Irish charm."

"I'm feeling more like a Viking marauder." The flat statement was entirely true. And should have warned her that she was in danger. But his reference to their fantasy play the first time they made love made her laugh softly.

"Then perhaps you should tie me up. So I don't try to murder you with a poison dagger." She held out her hand, and he saw for the first time that she had a couple of ties, obviously filched from his suitcase. They were silk. Ridiculously expensive.

"Why didn't I think of that?" The words came out hoarse and ragged. Breathing was difficult. Resting one knee on the bed, he took the ties and examined his options. The headboard was solid, but each corner was adorned with an ornamental spindle. If the mattress had been a king, this little game wouldn't have worked.

Their suite, however, was decorated in antiques, and the

ornate bed was a queen. Which meant that if he spread Zoe's arms wide, he could restrain her easily enough.

Fastening the strips of cloth around her wrists and securing them to the wooden anchors gave him an entirely Neanderthal rush of exhilaration. She looked up at him the entire time, her sky-blue irises almost obscured by the dilation of her dark pupils. The only sign that she might be at all alarmed was the way her small white teeth worried her lower lip.

Sitting back on his haunches when the deed was done, he stared at her. It was like giving a starving man access to a smorgasbord. He didn't know where to start first.

Zoe was silent, her chest rising and falling rapidly. "Are you cold?" she asked politely.

He lifted an eyebrow. "Not even a little." In fact, he felt like he was burning up from the inside out.

"Then why don't you ditch that robe?"

Without leaving the bed, he shrugged out of the heavy terry garment and tossed it aside. Zoe's eyes widened a fraction more as her gaze landed on his erection. It grew beneath her appreciative regard. Her legs moved restlessly against the soft sheets.

The air was redolent with the scent of desire and the fragrance of lilacs in the arrangement of fresh flowers tucked in a crystal vase across the room. Nature's perfume would mark his sensory memory forever.

He was not sure how long he hovered on the edge of reason. The room was silent but for the tick of a mantel clock. Outside, traffic rushed madly, but the cacophony of blaring horns and squealing brakes was muted and distant, barely impinging on his consciousness.

He ran a hand down her hip to her thigh to her ankle. "Are you comfortable?" he asked, not quite able to make the full leap to realistic barbarian.

"Does it matter?"

The taunt snapped what little control he had left. "I suppose not." Sliding down in the bed, he positioned his body between her legs and maneuvered until he could taste her intimately. With the first pass of his tongue, she cried out.

He stopped and lifted his head. "Perhaps I should have gagged you," he said, injecting silky menace into the words.

Her whole body quivered. "No. Please. I'll be quiet."

The begging added a nice touch. Without responding, he returned to his enjoyable task, trying to make her lose her senses. Her sex was moist and swollen, clear evidence of her arousal. The taste went to his head like strong liquor. When he bit gently at the one spot that begged for his attention, Zoe's back arched as she groaned and thrust helplessly against his mouth while he coaxed the last ounce of response from her quivering body.

In the aftermath, he rested his head on her hot, damp thigh, listening to the beat of his own heart. The frantic thuds raged like the waterfalls that crashed down the mountains as the snow melted. No longer able to defer his own need for release, he moved away only a moment to don a condom. Then he came down on top of her, supporting most of his weight on his elbows. Her body was a welcoming foil to his.

They were nose to nose. So close he could see the blond tips of her darker eyelashes.

Zoe moistened her lips with her tongue. "If you need a reference next time you go out marauding, I'll be happy to testify on your behalf." Her words were husky and low.

He pressed his mouth to hers softly. Tenderness mingled with impatient arousal, tempering his urgency. "I may retire," he said. "I've heard the life span of a Viking is pretty short and I don't want to miss a minute of this." Raining butterfly kisses across her nose, her cheeks, her forehead, he tried to convey what he couldn't put into words.

But soon, the feel of her soft belly pressing against his erection derailed his efforts to be gentle. With one hand, he opened her passage and pressed inward.

Zoe gasped.

Everything about the first time they made love faded away, and he moved in her as if this was brand-new. An unminted experience. A story waiting to be told. The pleasure was intense, each moment layering upon the next with hushed anticipation.

The muscles in Zoe's arms quivered visibly as she pulled at her restraints. The evidence of her wild impatience shored up his desire to make the intimacy last. "I can do anything I want to you," he said, pausing to wet one pert nipple with a swirl of his tongue. "You're completely helpless. Totally at my mercy. Every inch of you belongs to me."

"Barbarian," she hissed. But it was a weak protest at best. The rosy tint to her cheeks told him she was enjoying the pretense.

"All men are barbarians beneath the skin," he said. You can dress us up and tame us like lap dogs, but at the first opportunity, we'll grab for what we want." He withdrew almost completely and slid back in to torment them both. "And I want you." The squeeze of her inner passage around his rigid flesh was intense. He wanted to come more than he wanted his next breath, but he couldn't bear to end it. Not yet.

"Untie me," she pleaded. "I want to touch you."

"You should have thought of that when you devised this little game." Leaning to one side, he ran one of his hands from her shoulder up her arm to her wrist. Twining her fingers with his, he thrust lazily. "I'll make you come again," he promised.

Her eyelids fluttered shut on a sigh. "I can't." The pout of her lips was petulant.

"Why not?" If the involuntary clasp of her body on his was any indication, she was well on her way.

"I won't let myself receive pleasure from a barbarian."

He chuckled, returning to his earlier position and picking up the pace. "Wanna bet?"

Humor fled in the face of dark, urgent hunger. His control snapped, and he slammed into her repeatedly. Heat rose in his belly, spread to his loins and sent flash fire to his sex. Dimly he realized that Zoe's inner muscles gripped him tightly as she climaxed, but he was lost in a physical bliss so pure it seemed impossible.

When he finally regained his senses, remorse swamped him. Her arms must be aching like hell. "I need to untie you," he muttered, his words slurred with exhaustion. He felt bone-less, as if she had sapped every bit of stamina he possessed.

When he thought he could stand, he rose to his feet and disposed of the condom. As he came back to deal with his prisoner, he saw that his neckwear had been rendered unus-able for anything other than erotic fun and games.

Because of the way Zoe had writhed and struggled, the knots were tight. He picked at them impatiently, already wanting her again.

She pursed her lips, a frown marking a tiny crease be-tween her brows. "Shouldn't you have a knife to cut me free?"

"I'm pretty sure TSA wouldn't have approved that in my carry-on. Be still, will you? I'm never going to get these loose at this rate."

Zoe stared at him wide-eyed. "Are you in a hurry?"

Her innocence was not convincing. "Yes, damn it. I'd advise not testing my patience."

"Duly noted." The snappy response was designed to ir-ritate him. And it worked.

When he finally got the first knot undone and unwrapped the tie from Zoe's arm, he was chagrined to see the deep red marks on her wrist. Were barbarians capable of feeling remorse? Probably not.

He smoothed his thumb over the damage. "Is it sore?" Even knowing he had given her two satisfying orgasms, the visible result of their love play distressed him.

Twisting her wrist to get the blood flowing, Zoe curled a hand behind his neck and pulled him down for a kiss. He went willingly, ignoring the fact that he still had one knot to go.

"It's fine," she said. "I'm fine." At that very moment, her stomach rumbled loudly.

Obviously, he needed to feed his captive. There were rules about that kind of thing. Liam reluctantly released her and struggled with her other hand, this one taking him even longer. "If we do this again," he grumbled, "we're going to use professional equipment."

Zoe raised an eyebrow. "Someone makes professional *barbarian* equipment?"

"I haven't actually seen such a thing, but I'm betting that on the internet you can find just about anything."

At last, he freed her. Zoe crossed her arms across her chest. As if he hadn't seen everything there was to see already. For a split second he debated initiating an immediate round three. But then he thought better of it. If they were going to keep this up all night, they needed calories.

He climbed out of bed despite the fact that every instinct told him to stay. "I'll leave the bathroom to you for now. Do you trust me to order dinner for us?"

She nodded, now with the sheet pulled all the way to her shoulders. "I'll eat pretty much anything except for lima beans and tofu. But make sure there's lots of whatever you order. And chocolate. And wine."

Bending to pick up the robe he had tossed on the floor, he shrugged into it, belting the waist. "Anything else?"

"Some strawberries wouldn't hurt. And maybe some whipped cream. You never know when that might come in handy."

He stared at her. "Are we talking about dinner or sex?"

"Dinner first. Then more sex. But we might save the fruit for later."

Hands on his hips, he regarded her, shaking his head. "I don't know where I ever got the idea you were a sweet, innocent woman. But I like the way you think. How do you feel about bananas?"

"I put a condom on one once in health class."

"Was it good for you?"

She burst out laughing. "I don't know where I ever got the idea you were a serious-minded stuffed shirt."

"Turns out, we were both wrong."

Although they weren't touching, he experienced the oddest feeling of connection. For this one moment, they were in perfect accord. His ancestors would have called it fate. Or a gift from the fairies. Liam preferred to think of it as destiny. Fate was a whimsical, occasionally coldhearted bitch. But a man could control his own destiny.

"There's a robe for you in the bathroom," he said. "But don't get too attached to it. My plans for later include you being naked."

Sixteen

Zoe freshened up and donned the soft, comfy robe, flipping her hair over the collar. One look in the mirror told her she looked exactly like what she was…a woman who had spent several hours in bed with her lover.

She was sore in more places than her wrists, but it was a good kind of sore…the sort of feeling that curved her mouth in a smug smile.

After splashing her face with water and brushing her hair, she spritzed her wrists with perfume and used a bit of gloss on her puffy lips. Now, her reflection was more like the usual Zoe.

When she entered the living room area of their suite, Liam was clearing a spot by the window for their meal. He looked over his shoulder as she entered. "Should be here soon."

She perched on the arm of the sofa, enjoying the view. Liam in that robe was only slightly less yummy than naked Liam. But before she could go too far with that particular fantasy, a knock sounded at the door.

The young man who rolled a serving cart into their room and uncovered the dishes never batted an eye at their dishabille. Presumably he was used to the eccentricities of hotel guests. But Zoe couldn't help feeling a bit embarrassed. With the do-not-disturb sign on the door and the robes she and Liam were wearing, the guy had to know they'd been having sex.

Even a more seasoned employee would have goggled at the tip Liam handed over. The kid's effusive thanks were still bubbling when Liam eased him out the door and shut it behind him.

"How much *was* that?" Zoe asked.

Liam shrugged, his grin wide. "A couple hundred. I'm in a good mood. Come sit down before everything gets cold."

The meal was a hodgepodge of delights. Thinly shaved prime rib on homemade rolls, fresh asparagus and cinnamon apples were Zoe's favorites. "You've been paying attention to what I order at the Silver Beeches," she accused, suddenly realizing that such appealing choices couldn't have been entirely random.

Liam nodded, entirely unrepentant. "Of course. It's my job to make you happy."

"I like the sound of that."

With tousled hair and the shadow of a late-day beard darkening his chin, Liam was the epitome of a lazy, satisfied predator. A lion maybe, relaxing in his domain before his next hunting mission. He ate with gusto, devouring twice as much as she did, and draining a bottle of wine with a little help from her.

Over dessert, chocolate cake filled with dark-chocolate ganache, they chatted lazily of this and that. Silver Glen. Dylan's bar. Politics. The books they had read and liked.

When she was feeling completely mellow and utterly content with life, Liam dropped an unexpected bomb. "May I ask you a personal question?" he said.

She stiffened automatically. Though she knew intellectually that he had no wish to harm her, her shields went up. "I suppose."

"You're an only child...right?"

"Yes."

"So when your father dies, his company will go to you and your mother...or only you if she is gone."

"Yes. What's your point?" She was not happy that he had decided to introduce this topic in the midst of their romantic idyll.

Liam sipped his coffee, his eyes meeting hers over the rim of his cup. "Has it ever occurred to you that if you cooperate with him now, you might be able to shape the company and help steer it in the direction you want it to go?"

A knot of hurt formed in her stomach. Clearly Liam hadn't understood the full measure of her father's ruthless determination. "I don't want the company," she said flatly. "And no. I have no wish to cooperate with him. I tried plenty of times when I was younger, believe me."

"I know it's hard, but he's your family, no matter how much you dislike his methods. Are you sure you want to permanently sever that tie?"

Her fists were clenched in her lap where he couldn't see. And though his perspective was understandable, she wished that just once in her life someone would take her side.

"You don't understand," she said quietly. "You come from a family where support is freely given, where you all love each other despite your differences. My father is not like that. My mother and I are little more than chattels to him, incidental pawns in his game."

"That's a pretty cynical view."

"And you're being presumptuous. You know nothing at all about my life. So I'd appreciate it if you would resist the urge to pass judgment."

"For God's sake, I'm not judging you."

"You *are,*" she cried passionately. "Your father was a disappointment to you, but instead of writing off the Kavanagh empire, you sacrificed your dreams on the altar of filial responsibility. That was *your* choice. But it's not mine. I've seen the world and had some amazing experiences. I haven't allowed my father to dictate who I am or what I make of my life. I've been free."

"You call roving from town to town, always looking over your shoulder being free?"

Zoe's face went white, and Liam knew he had gone too far. Her family situation was not his business. He understood that. But she wore loneliness like a hair shirt, and it hurt him to see her that way. "I'm sorry," he said.

She stood up, her eyes bleak. "Me, too. I'm going to pack and catch a late flight back. You can call and cancel the dress order."

"Now wait a damn minute."

Though she had been halfway to the bedroom, she stopped. "There's nothing more to say."

"So we disagree about something and our relationship is over? Is that it?"

"There's no relationship, Liam. You're in charge of your realm and I'm passing through. It was never going to be anything else."

He approached her slowly, knowing it was going to take a miracle to make her to stay. "Then give me this interlude to remember you by...two more days. I swear I won't say another word about your father."

"Why? What's the point?"

"Because I won't let you go. Not now. Not tonight." Scooping her up in his arms, he carried her to their bedroom. Something eased inside him when he felt her arms loop around his neck. "I can make you happy, Zoe. I promise."

For the next forty-eight hours he did exactly that. With a mutual unspoken agreement between them not to delve into sensitive topics, they set out to enjoy one of the greatest cities in the world.

First on the agenda the following day was his luncheon keynote. Zoe sat in the audience looking prim and perfect in her new black dress while Liam struggled to keep his mind on what he had to say. People seemed to like the speech. There were cordial handshakes and a few hugs, and plenty of hearty congratulations. At least half of the group lingered to be introduced to a blushing Zoe.

She was charming and funny and perfectly at home in this world of movers and shakers. After everything she had told him, he knew his initial assessment of her background had been comically off the mark. Zoe might have spent some time living in her van, but it wasn't because she came from impoverished beginnings.

During the afternoon they returned to the hotel for another round of sweaty, wonderful sex followed by a shower and a nap. He lay with her in his arms, trying to wrap his head around the sea change in his life. In a dramatically short time, Zoe had shattered the notion that his life was complete.

She had danced into his world like the brightest of butterflies, the most brilliant of flowers, showing him by sheer virtue of contrast what he had been missing. His brain whirled with possibilities, but he knew in his heart that until Zoe settled things with her father, either a reconciliation or a total break, she would never be able to settle down.

And what about her mother? The questions went on and on.

The following day was much like the day before, except that instead of the luncheon, he dropped Zoe at the Met while he pursued a very important errand. Once he returned, he spent another hour with Zoe wandering the museum before they finally went in search of food.

The day was sunny and bright, so they bought hot dogs from a vendor in the Central Park and watched dads and kids sail model boats on the lake. Zoe's face was wistful. "They look so happy."

He wanted to ask what her childhood had been like, but he had promised not to talk about her father anymore. It was hard to imagine any parent not being delighted with the child Zoe must have been.

"Come on," he said, linking his hand with hers. "You look sleepy." They had been out late the night before, taking in a Broadway show and dinner afterward.

They caught a cab and were back at their hotel in no time. As soon as the door to their suite closed, Zoe threw herself into his arms. "I want to make love to you," she said, her expression cajoling.

Didn't she know that no persuasion was necessary? Intimacy with Zoe was never far from his mind.

Allowing her to take him by the hand and lead him to the bedroom, he hid a smile when she began unbuttoning his shirt with sweet concentration. The touch of her hands made him inhale sharply. Would it always be like this? She had woven some kind of magic, invisible chains around him, and he was a willing victim.

When they were both naked, he lifted her in his arms and carried her to the bed. "You are the most beautiful thing I've ever seen," he said, resting his forehead on hers.

As he bent to deposit her on the mattress, she scooted over to make room for him. They came together in mutual accord, silently, slowly, the moment filled with yearning and poignancy. Somehow he had to get through to her. But that could wait.

Her slim legs tightened around his waist as he canted her hips, deepening the penetration. Her golden hair fanned out across the pillow. This room had become their haven, their escape from the realities of a world that was not always kind to hopes and dreams.

The end this time was more of a gently rolling wave, sweeping them onto a distant shore of contentment. Zoe curled into his embrace. They dozed for half an hour. Liam slipped in and out of sleep. He didn't want to miss a moment of what might be his last time with her.

When she roused, he brushed the hair from her face. "I want to ask you something."

Yawning, she ran her toes down his shin. "Okay."

"I want you to stay at the hotel for longer than six weeks. My treat. Better yet, in my apartment. And if you like, we can move your mother to Silver Beeches as well. Perhaps a change of scenery could help her see that she needs to leave your father."

Zoe played with the hair on his chest. "I don't know if she would come."

"And you?"

The silence was long. Scary. But finally, she nodded. "I could do that."

"Good. I'm glad." He left it at that. He was afraid if he made too big a deal of her consent it would spook her.

By the time they returned to Silver Glen, he and Zoe were comfortable with each other in a way he wouldn't have been able to manage with her as a guest in his hotel. They had created a special kind of intimacy in New York. When she wore the blue dress the final night, he had taken her to a gala fund-raiser for a charitable foundation. They had danced until 2:00 a.m. and had gone back to their hotel to sleep and make love and sleep again.

Now, on the plane back to North Carolina, he began to feel a sense of dread. He couldn't quite say why. Zoe sat in the seat beside him sleeping peacefully, her head resting on his shoulder. Nothing had changed. Perhaps it was a taste of regret for having to leave the city where they had forged a tenuous accord. That and the realization that he still had unanswered questions about Zoe's father and how she intended to handle him.

Because their flight had been delayed indefinitely in

Charlotte, Liam had called Pierre and told him not to bother meeting them. After they deplaned and claimed their luggage, Liam rented a car and soon they were on their way home.

Zoe was awake now, but quiet, her gaze trained out the window, though it was dark. It irked him that he never knew what she was thinking. Just when he began to think he knew her well, she threw him off balance in one way or another.

Back at the Silver Beeches, the facade of the hotel was lit up. Liam felt the sensation of homecoming and yet had no real urge to stop by the front desk and check on things as would have been his usual habit. All he could think about was taking Zoe upstairs to bed. His or hers. It didn't matter.

While he was passing off his keys to the valet, Pierre came rushing out of the hotel. The dignified man never hurried anywhere, so Liam's radar went up. The concierge lowered his voice as he came closer. "A man who appears to be Ms. Chamberlain's father is here. He's in the lobby refusing to leave until he sees her. And he's threatening to call the police and accuse you of kidnapping."

"What a load of crap." Liam debated rapidly. "We'll go in the side door and head to my office. That will give Zoe a few minutes to collect her thoughts. Is that okay with you, Zoe?"

She was standing on the opposite side of the car, her hand resting on the hood. "Oh, so I get a vote?"

The acerbic words reminded him that she didn't like to be coddled. "Sorry. What do *you* want to do?"

"I don't want to see my father, but I knew this showdown was coming sooner or later. It's probably for the best, anyway. I'm not going to be afraid of him anymore. I'm an adult woman. It's time he knows that he can't use me as a pawn in his games."

Liam looked at Pierre. "Stall him a little longer. Tell him Zoe just got in and she's freshening up."

"Yes, sir."

Pierre disappeared as Liam took Zoe by the arm and led

her into the relative safety of the shadowy side courtyard. Before they went inside, he stopped short, having just had an epiphany that shocked him. "Zoe," he said urgently. "Is it true that you've been living off the grid for the last eighteen months?"

He felt her nod. "More or less. Why?"

"When you came to Silver Beeches, you used a credit card…a traceable credit card."

"I'm sure you wouldn't have let me check in without it."

"That's not my point. Were you somehow subconsciously setting up a confrontation with your father? You had to know that if he hired someone to trace your whereabouts from place to place that he would have no compunction about investigating you in other ways."

"So?"

"So I'm asking if my theory is true."

"If it is, I didn't do it deliberately. Can we please go inside now? I'm getting chilly."

Zoe felt as if she were walking in a nightmare. But there would be no waking up from this. The last thing she wanted was for Liam and her father to meet. It embarrassed her that the Kavanaghs were such a wonderful family, and her own father was a bully and a mean-spirited dictator.

In Liam's office she sat in a chair, her knees wobbly and her hands icy cold. Dealing with her father was never pleasant, but coming on the heels of the wonderful hours spent with Liam in New York, this encounter was going to be particularly bleak.

Liam knelt in front of her, his eyes watchful, but kind. "How can I help?"

She shrugged, not quite able to meet his gaze. "I don't know. I guess it depends on whether he still plans to arrest me."

Liam flinched. She saw it and felt it.

"Look at me, Zoe." He stood and pulled her to her feet.

"Before anything else happens, I want you to know that I love you."

Shock rendered her boneless. Her legs threatened to collapse beneath her. "Your timing sucks," she said, staring at him, her voice hoarse with tears. Of all the times she had daydreamed about hearing him say those words, the scenario had never been this. "Why are you telling me now?"

His smile was lopsided. "Well, for one, it's true. But before you go in to see your father, I want you to know that whatever happens, I'll be there for you."

She shook her head, confused and anxious. "I don't understand. What do you think is going to happen?"

Easing her back into the chair, he pulled another chair up beside her so he could hold her hands, warming them between his. "I know about the money, Zoe."

She stared at him blankly. "What money?"

Now he looked grim. "You said your father accused you of taking money from him."

"But I didn't." He wasn't making sense.

"Zoe." He stopped, looked down at their hands, and shook his head slowly. "It's okay, sweetheart. You aren't in this alone. You don't have to pretend with me. I love you."

Truly bewildered, she searched his face. "I don't have a clue what you're talking about."

For the first time, he let his frustration and disappointment show through his mask of caring. "I *know* about the money, Zoe. I know you have it. Gary found it when he was getting ready to paint the van."

"And he told you?"

"Yes. He was worried about it. But it's okay. We'll tell your father you didn't spend it. That you took it because you were angry. We'll give it back. And if necessary, I'll hire you the best lawyer we can find. I won't let your father hurt you."

Zoe stared at him aghast, all her dreams disintegrating around her like hundreds of falling stars. "You think I stole from my father. Even though I told you I didn't."

His jaw was granite, his eyes pools of something…regret, maybe. "People do crazy things when they get pushed into a corner. I don't blame you. Really."

"How generous of you." She stood up, no longer aware of any emotion at all. She was encased in ice. "I will see my father now."

"Wait," Liam said, lurching to his feet and grabbing her by the shoulders. "I told you I love you. Doesn't that warrant a response of some sort?"

She smiled at him politely, as she would a stranger. "Of course, it does…. Go to hell, Liam."

Seventeen

He chased her down the hallway to the lobby, his emotions reeling. What in the devil was going on?

Before he could stop her, Zoe walked right up to a distinguished gray-haired man and greeted him evenly. "Hello, Father. I hear you've been looking for me."

The elder Henshaw seemed taken aback. Zoe was wearing one of the dresses she had picked out in New York, and she looked both poised and confident.

"How dare you run from me?" the man said. It was bluster, but it sounded oddly weak.

Zoe eyed him with disdain. "There was no running involved, Father. I am a grown woman. My whereabouts are my own business."

"You've worried your mother sick."

Zoe didn't rise to the bait. She had told Liam about the phone calls between mother and daughter, and he knew she would never say anything to get her mother in trouble.

Zoe tucked her hands in the pockets of her skirt, perhaps so her father wouldn't see them shake. Liam knew her pretty well by now. Beneath her pretense of calm, she was very upset. "Why are you here, Father?"

"I want you to come home. I want you to join me in the business."

"You know that's not going to happen."

"So you're going to throw your life away? Is that what you want? To spend all your time flitting from one town to the next?"

Liam winced inwardly. Had Zoe seen Liam's opinions as mirrors of her father's disapproval?

She shook her head. "I enjoy my music and it makes people happy. What you do makes people want to kill themselves."

"Now you're being ridiculous."

"I don't think so. The last covert takeover you staged caused a very nice man to commit suicide."

"You don't understand the ins and outs of business." His voice was haughty and patronizing.

Liam stepped forward. "I think Zoe would like you to leave."

"And who the hell are you?"

"My name is Liam Kavanagh. I own the Silver Beeches. I won't let one of our guests be harassed."

"I'm taking my daughter home with me."

"No, you're not." Liam took a deep breath. "Even the worst of fathers wouldn't send his daughter to jail. She has the money, and she'll give it back, won't you Zoe?"

To his eternal astonishment, Zoe took a step closer to her father, as if to say clearly that Liam was not speaking for her.

Mr. Henshaw frowned. "What money?"

Zoe turned to Pierre who had been hovering nearby. "Would you please send someone to my room to retrieve my guitar? Everything else is still packed in my suitcase." She faced her father. "I *will* go home with you because my vehicle is in the repair shop. I want to see Mother and let her know I'm okay. But you must understand that if you want me to have any kind of relationship with you at all, you're going to have to find someone else to join you in the business. Is that clear?"

Liam watched as her father seemed to deflate. "You'll change your mind."

"No, Daddy. I won't. And if you ever lay a hand on me again, or Mother for that matter, I'll have *you* arrested."

Liam realized that he had just witnessed a tiny kitten grow into a lioness. Zoe had found the courage somewhere to face down her father, and like most bullies, her autocratic parent caved when confronted by real confidence.

"What's gotten into you?" Mr. Henshaw muttered. But it was a rhetorical question.

Liam took Zoe's arm. "I need to speak with you…privately." When she resisted, he was shocked. The irrepressible light of joy and happiness that lit her blue eyes from within was gone. "I won't let him involve the police, Zoe. You don't have to go with him."

She jerked free of his grasp. "I have no reason to stay here." Seven words. Seven flat, icy words.

"I don't understand. Doesn't your father want his money back?"

For a brief moment, a flame of anger and hurt broke through her mask of calm. Her lips trembled. "The money is mine, Liam. I inherited three million dollars from my grandmother when I turned eighteen."

Before he could come up with a response, a bellman returned with Zoe's luggage, and in minutes, she and her father were gone.

For his entire adult life up until this point, Liam had known exactly where to plot his course. He had a purpose and a mission. His job was to steer the Kavanagh fortunes and support his mother in the way his father never had.

In the wake of Zoe's departure, he was lost. He spent days floundering in a sea of confusion and guilt. When the pain of losing her became too much, he hiked the mountains, trying to outrun the knowledge that he had let her down. He had called her a thief and a liar. All in the guise of being supportive. No wonder she had left.

As the days passed, several things became clear. He was as fallible as the next human being. And his father had not been an evil man. Liam's dad had chased a dream with mortal consequences. He had betrayed his marriage vows. He had deserted his family. But his death was an accident. An awful, tragic accident.

One month to the day after Zoe walked out of his life, Liam stood in front of the Silver Beeches, keys in hand, ready to return Zoe's at-long-last-repaired van to her. It would be a lengthy road trip, but he had a feeling that he needed the time alone behind the wheel to prepare for what would most likely be a chilly reception.

His mother, who had urged him to take an extended leave of absence, came outside to bid him goodbye. She ran her hand along the side of the vintage VW van painted aqua and white with yellow daisies. "Take all the time you need, Liam. I want you to be happy. Your brothers are nearby if I need them. You're free, my dearest boy. God bless."

He hugged her, feeling a trace of guilt for leaving, but more importantly, exhilaration and hope for the road ahead. "Thank you, Mom. I love you."

"I love *you,* son. And if it's any comfort, I'd stake my life on the fact that Zoe loves you, too."

"I treated her badly." His lack of faith in the woman he claimed to love still scored him with guilt.

"We all make mistakes, Liam. She understands that. Sometimes a simple, sincere apology means the world."

"I hope you're right." The alternative didn't bear thinking about. "I'll keep you posted. Don't work too hard."

Maeve grinned, taking years off her age. "Work keeps me young. Now go. Get out of here. And don't come back until I have at least some hope of having grandchildren one day."

Zoe felt the sun warming her back as she knelt to pluck weeds from among the seedlings in her mother's well-tended flower bed. The Henshaws employed a full-time gardener, but this monotonous task was one Zoe enjoyed. She let her mind wander, hearing the birds sing around her and smelling the piquant odor of freshly turned earth.

She realized that she was more centered, more at peace than the young woman who had slipped away on Christmas Eve so many weeks ago. Loving Liam had taught her to look inside herself for the truth of her emotions.

She didn't hate her father, but they would likely never see eye to eye. Finally finding her backbone and dealing with him these last few weeks had not been easy, but Zoe's reward was the way her mother had blossomed. The older woman smiled now.

Beneath the familial triumphs, though, was the ever-present ache of losing Liam. She missed him terribly. Without even realizing it, she had come to regard Silver Glen as home, and the head of the Kavanagh clan as her heart's desire.

No matter how much she grieved, she knew she had been right to let him go. He still had doubts about her, perhaps because they were too different. In all fairness, some of the rift was her fault. She had kept too many secrets. She hadn't trusted him quickly enough, nor deeply enough. She was tempted to go back to North Carolina and apologize for that, if nothing else.

But she didn't want Liam to take her back for the wrong reasons. Though he'd said he loved her, she suspected that his declaration was the result of an overdeveloped sense of responsibility. She knew he *wanted* her. And perhaps he had convinced himself that what he felt was the real thing. The truth was, however, Liam took care of people. His mother, his family, the hotel… Zoe would be just another millstone around his neck.

She was in the zone, as they say, intent on her task, when two male feet appeared in her peripheral vision.

"Need a hand?"

The all-too-familiar voice sent a chill down her spine. She stood up slowly, wiping her fingers on the legs of her ancient, faded jeans. "Liam." It wasn't much of a response, but it was the only one she could come up with. Her heart leapt in joyful surprise, but her brain beat the girly response into submission. "What are you doing here?"

He looked so good it made her chest hurt. The only time she had seen him dressed so casually was the night she sang in Dylan's bar. Today he wore a dark blue knit shirt that matched his eyes. His hair was a trifle longer than usual, and he looked tired.

With hands in his pockets, he regarded her intently. "I brought your van back to you. It's parked out front."

"Ah. Well, thank you."

"I left Silver Glen a week ago and took my time getting up here. Toured Monticello. Caught a couple of museums in D.C. Saw the world's largest Coke can in a little town in Jersey. Slept in your van almost every night."

"I see." But she didn't. Not at all. Was he trying to tell her something? "How are you getting home?"

"I'm not going home. At least not yet."

"Okay." Still she was baffled.

His lips twisted. "I'm sorry I didn't believe you about the money."

She saw genuine regret on his face. "I overreacted, Liam. And I was partly to blame for your assumptions. It's hard for me to trust people. If I had told you the truth sooner, you never would have thought I was a criminal."

His theatrical wince made her smile.

"*Criminal* is a strong word. But tell me something, Zoe. Why *did* you carry all that cash?"

"That part is easy to explain. When my father and I first had our falling-out, not this past December, but earlier, I hit the road not wanting to be found. I knew if I used credit cards, he could trace me."

"But you used one to check in at Silver Beeches."

"True. So I guess a shrink would say I was tired of running."

"No comment." His smile was rueful. "Sorry I interrupted. Please continue."

"Anyway, the first time I left, I withdrew a large sum of money from my own account and hid it inside Bessie."

"Bessie?"

"That's what I call my van. I've traveled the world enough to know that a single woman needs to have a backup plan for emergencies."

"I hope you never have an emergency that big. Aren't you wondering if your money is intact?"

"Is it?"

"Of course." He ran both hands through his hair. "Gary thought I was insane when I asked him to paint the van. Again. To its original color."

"That was sweet of you."

"It seemed the least I could do."

Zoe shifted from one foot to the other. Perhaps she should ask him in for tea, but she wasn't at all sure why he had come, other than to return her vehicle. "Well, thanks again," she said brightly.

His gaze grew stormy. "I told you I loved you."

Like she needed reminding. "I know you did. But you're a fixer, Liam. A caretaker. You see people in trouble and you want to help. I seemed like a desperate case, so you convinced yourself that you loved me and needed to save me from myself. It was a heat-of-the-moment kind of thing. Very noble, but not legally binding."

"Do you care about me at all?"

His steady question set her feet in quicksand. The more she struggled, the faster she would sink. "Of course. I had a lot of fun with you."

"Fun." He said it like a curse.

"You seem to be getting upset. Perhaps you should go."

"Damn it, Zoe." Without warning, he yanked her close, his strong arms binding her to him as he kissed her senseless.

She might have gotten too much sun already. Her mother always warned her to wear a hat. When she could finally catch a breath, she pushed her hands against his chest. But it was like trying to move Mt. Rushmore. "You don't have to do this. I'm fine."

He glared at her. "Well, I'm not. You waltzed into my life and painted it all the colors of the rainbow. After you left, everything was gray again."

"You have a great life. Everything a man could want."

"No." He said it simply. "I don't have you, Zoe."

"You think I'm unfocused and lack ambition."

He nuzzled her nose with his as his hands stroked up and down her arms. "I think you're amazing, and just the person to plan our road trip."

"Our road trip?" His kisses must have fired a few synapses.

"I've taken a sixty-day sabbatical from the hotel. My mother sends her regards."

Zoe gaped. "But you love that hotel."

He shook his head, his eyes filled with happy tenderness. "I love *you*. And at the risk of sounding egocentric, I'd like to know how you feel about me. Am I too much of a stuffed shirt for a pretty gypsy with sunshine hair and a voice like an angel?"

Tears welled in her eyes. "I couldn't bear it if things didn't work out." She didn't want to get her hopes up. Walking away from him once had nearly destroyed her. And their relationship had been so complicated, it was hard to believe he loved who she really was.

"Then we'll take a trial run. In Bessie. On the open road. Wherever you like."

"Really?" It felt like Christmas and her birthday all rolled into one.

"Really. But I do have one condition."

"That sounds ominous." She patted his chest and rested her cheek over his heart.

"Look at me, sweetheart." He backed away and fished in his pocket, extracting a small, elegant box. "That day in New York when you were studying French impressionists at the museum, I sneaked away and bought this. I know you need time to think about marrying me, but I want you to wear it."

The ring was a flawless square-cut solitaire, at least two carats or more, surrounded by tiny sparkling stones. She barely breathed as he slid it onto the ring finger of her left hand. "Oh, Liam…"

He lifted her fingers to his lips and kissed them. "Please, Zoe."

"Please what?"

"You know what."

She stared down at her hand, tilting and twisting it so that the sun caught the facets of the diamonds and sent prisms of color in every direction. When she looked back at Liam, he had his arms crossed over his chest. His gaze was watchful.

Flinging herself into his arms, forcing him to catch her, she kissed him with every bit of the longing she had bottled up for the last few weeks. "Of *course* I love you, you big doofus. And if you ever get around to proposing, I'll say yes."

His eyebrows went up. "I thought I already did."

"You alluded to it. That's different."

He was breathing hard, his face flushed. "Marry me, Zoe. Create babies with me. Sing to our children. Make love with me in our bed. You've taught me how to stop and smell the roses. Let me share my big, boisterous family with you."

"Oh, Liam…"

"You already said that," he teased.

"My parents will probably want a big society wedding. I *am* their only child, you know."

"I can live with that. I just can't live without you."

He scooped her up in his arms and strode toward the front yard.

Zoe linked her arms around his neck. "Where are we going?"

"Bessie should be the first to know, don't you think?"

"Well, she *was* responsible for bringing me to Silver Glen."

"We're never getting rid of this van," he said fervently.

"Whatever you say, dear."

He dropped her on her feet and backed her up against the

door that concealed a huge chunk of cash. "Thank you," he said, his lips brushing the tender skin below her ear.

"For what?"

"For being you, Zoe. For being you...."

* * * * *

A sneaky peek at next month...

Desire™

PASSIONATE AND DRAMATIC LOVE STORIES

My wish list for next month's titles...

In stores from 18th April 2014:

- ❏ The Sarantos Baby Bargain – Olivia Gates
- & The Last Cowboy Standing – Barbara Dunlop
- ❏ From Single Mum to Secret Heiress
  – Kristi Gold
- & Your Ranch...Or Mine? – Kathie DeNosky
- ❏ A Merger by Marriage – Cat Schield
- & Caroselli's Accidental Heir – Michelle Celmer

2 stories in each book - only £5.49!

Available at WHSmith, Tesco, Asda, Eason, Amazon and Apple

Just can't wait?

Visit us Online

You can buy our books online a month before they hit the shops!

When five o'clock hits, what happens after hours...?

Feel the sizzle and anticipation of falling in love across the boardroom table with these seductive workplace romances!

Now available at
www.millsandboon.co.uk

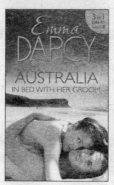

MILLS & BOON® *Book Club*

Join the Mills & Boon Book Club

Want to read more **Desire™** books?
We're offering you **2 more** absolutely **FREE!**

We'll also treat you to these fabulous extras:

- **Exclusive offers and much more!**

- **FREE home delivery**

- **FREE books and gifts with our special rewards scheme**

Get your free books now!

visit www.millsandboon.co.uk/bookclub
or call Customer Relations on 020 8288 2888

Discover more romance at

www.millsandboon.co.uk

The World of Mills & Boon®

There's a Mills & Boon® series that's perfect for you. We publish ten series and, with new titles every month, you never have to wait long for your favourite to come along.

By Request

Relive the romance with the best of the best
12 stories every month

Cherish™

Experience the ultimate rush of falling in love
12 new stories every month

Desire™

Passionate and dramatic love stories
6 new stories every month

nocturne™

An exhilarating underworld of dark desires
Up to 3 new stories every month